Michael Wood is a freelance jou
Newcastle. As a journalist he
throughout Sheffield, gaining
procedure. He also reviews bo
dedicated to crime fiction.

        𝕏 x.com/MichaelHWood
        f facebook.com/MichaelWoodBooks

# Also by Michael Wood

### **DCI Matilda Darke Thriller Series**
*For Reasons Unknown*

*Outside Looking In*

*A Room Full of Killers*

*The Hangman's Hold*

*The Murder House*

*Stolen Children*

*Time Is Running Out*

*Survivor's Guilt*

*The Lost Children*

*Silent Victim*

*Below Ground*

### **DCI Matilda Darke Short Stories**
*The Fallen*

*Victim of Innocence*

*Making of a Murderer*

### **Dr Olivia Winter Thriller Series**
*The Mind of a Murderer*

### **Standalone Thrillers**
*The Seventh Victim*

*Vengeance is Mine*

# LAST ONE LEFT ALIVE

## MICHAEL WOOD

One More Chapter
a division of HarperCollins*Publishers*
1 London Bridge Street
London SE1 9GF
www.harpercollins.co.uk
HarperCollins*Publishers*
Macken House, 39/40 Mayor Street Upper,
Dublin 1, D01 C9W8
This paperback edition 2024
1
First published in ebook by HarperCollins*Publishers* 2024

Copyright © Michael Wood 2024
Michael Wood asserts the moral right to
be identified as the author of this work

A catalogue record of this book
is available from the British Library

ISBN: 978-0-00-861878-0

This novel is entirely a work of fiction.
The names, characters and incidents portrayed in it are
the work of the author's imagination. Any resemblance to
actual persons, living or dead, events or localities is
entirely coincidental.

Printed and bound in the UK using 100% Renewable Electricity
by CPI Group (UK) Ltd

All rights reserved. No part of this publication may be
reproduced, stored in a retrieval system, or transmitted,
in any form or by any means, electronic, mechanical,
photocopying, recording or otherwise, without the prior
permission of the publishers.

*For Jennie Rothwell*
*Writing is scary. A good editor makes it less so. Thank you.*

# Part I

DAY ONE

# Prologue

I have been surrounded by murder for years – so much so that it has become part of me. It has absorbed me, infected me, and it's found its way to my brain. There is no stopping it. Murder is in my life and all the signs are telling me to kill, to take the lives of others. I know what to do to get started. I know how not to get caught.

On the second of January 1981, Peter Sutcliffe was stopped by police with twenty-four-year-old sex worker Olivia Reivers on Melbourne Avenue right here in Sheffield. A routine police check found the car had false number plates. He was arrested and transferred to Dewsbury police station in West Yorkshire. Whilst there, he was questioned about the crimes of the Yorkshire Ripper, in which thirteen sex workers were killed, because his likeness matched the known physical description of the killer given by witnesses.

The next day, Sergeant Robert Ring had a hunch, and he returned to Melbourne Avenue in Broomhill where Sutcliffe was arrested. During his arrest, Sutcliffe had told the police he needed a pee and went behind an oil storage tank. There, Sergeant Ring found a knife, a hammer and rope that Sutcliffe was most likely intending to use on his next victim, Olivia Reivers. It wasn't long before Sutcliffe was identified as the Yorkshire Ripper and charged with thirteen murders.

*Had Sutcliffe become complacent? I think so. He'd successfully killed thirteen women. He must have thought he was untouchable.*

*Dennis Nilsen dissected his victims and flushed them down the toilet. Eventually, the drains became blocked, and a plumber was called who found skin and bones clogging up the pipes. That really was foolish.*

*David Berkowitz received a parking ticket for parking illegally in front of a fire hydrant and Joel Ritkin was caught driving without any licence plates with a body in the boot of his car.*

*They were all caught unnecessarily. A little more brain power, a touch more attention to detail, and they could have continued killing for as long as they wanted to.*

*The secret to a successful killing is to never let your guard down. Ever. By all means, taunt the police with your crimes, that's what I intend to do, but the key is to remain calm, in control, and always keep one eye on the investigation.*

*The first step is to know the mettle of the detective who is going to be hunting for you. I know everything there is to know about Detective Chief Inspector Matilda Darke. She has an exemplary record in catching murderers and the odds of catching me are greatly in her favour. The question here is: can she find me before I physically and mentally destroy her?*

*Deep breath. Let the games begin.*

From: <5ew4h5tu9@hotmail.com>
Date: **Monday, 1 January 1900 at 00:00**
To: Darke, Matilda
<matilda.darke@southyorkshire.police.co.uk>
Subject: **1 of 5.**

Hello Matilda,

I've committed the perfect murder.

How's that for an opening line? Let me see if I can guess what you're thinking. You're probably thinking I'm some kind of crank who's a few sandwiches short of a picnic, as my mum likes to say. Maybe I'm a fantasist who wants to confess to a murder he hasn't committed just to get a bit of attention. Or maybe I'm being truthful.

Now you're thinking that there's no such thing as the perfect murder. Nobody can get away with killing someone, especially in this day and age with advances in technology, forensics, and DNA profiling. Well, I'm sorry to break this to you Matilda, but the perfect murder does exist. I know. I've committed five of them.

You're an expert in murder, aren't you? You and your team. You've worked on some challenging cases over the years, and you've always found your killer. How does it feel to know that I've unravelled your entire life's work in two paragraphs?

So, here's the paradox. If I want to be known as a great serial killer who's managed to get away with my crimes, then I need to keep my mouth shut so I don't appear on the police's radar. Unfortunately, nobody will know who I am, or that I am a great serial killer. However, if I reveal who I am, then I'll achieve the notoriety, yet I'll increase my chances of being arrested. The question here is: what is more important to me?

Firstly, what's important is that I need you to believe me. So, I'm going to tell you about my victims. My first victim was back in September. Liam Walsh. His death was ruled to be a suicide. He jumped from the roof of the Arts Tower. He even left a note for his mum. But he didn't jump. I pushed him. Figure out how I did it and you'll know you have the perfect serial killer in your neighbourhood.

I want to teach you all about murder, Matilda. I want to tell you what it's all really about. You see, in your line of work, you investigate the crime, you catch the criminal, you send them to prison, and you move onto the next case, leaving the debris behind you. But murder is much more than that. It should be savoured, understood, explored, and enjoyed. We're going to have so much fun together.

I'll be emailing you again, Matilda.

Bye for now

## Chapter One

Monday, 14 March 2021

DCI Matilda Darke read the email for a second time. She moved the cursor over the delete button using the track pad on her laptop. She was about to press it, but something stopped her from doing so. Matilda had been a detective for more than twenty years and had worked on many high-profile investigations. She had received more than her fair share of crank phone calls and emails in that time. But something about this one stopped her from deleting it and consigning it to the bin. She hit print instead.

She looked up. She couldn't get used to no longer looking through the glass and seeing her team in the Homicide and Major Crime Unit going about their work. She always expected to see Scott stealing a bar of chocolate from Sian's snack drawer, Finn with a concentrated frown on his face as he read something from his tablet, or Tom and Zofia sharing flirtatious glances over the tops of their computer screens. Life had changed for Matilda, and she didn't like it.

In January, Matilda had been kidnapped. There was no ransom

demand because the kidnapper had no intention of her ever leaving the windowless basement she had been confined to. Her kidnapper blamed Matilda for the way her life had turned out and wanted Matilda to reach desperation point and hang herself. The plan would have worked, too. Matilda was seconds away from death when her colleagues – her friends – Christian, Scott, and Finn broke into the basement and saved her life. She would be eternally grateful to them all. The fact she was no longer working with them upset her greatly. Though she refused to show it.

After a short period of convalescence, Matilda was back at work. Unfortunately, the Covid pandemic, Brexit, and governmental idiocy had ensured massive cuts needed to be made and the police force was no exception. Matilda's role had changed. She was no longer in charge of the Homicide and Major Crime Unit. She was the overseer of the HMCU and CID. She was out of the offices she shared with Christian, Sian, Scott, and the others, and in a small, cramped room on the next floor up. Her duties were primarily desk-bound. Her time of getting out onto the streets and investigating crimes was over. And she hated it. This was not the reason she became a police officer. This was only the beginning of the second week of her new role but she was already feeling the effects of working on her own, ostracised from her team.

Matilda inhaled and released a heavy sigh. The room she was confined to was small, impersonal, depressing, and tired. She needed light, space, and conversation around her. Her kidnapping had led her to be fearful of enclosed spaces. At home, she no longer slept with her door closed and a sleep mask; her door was wide open, and the landing light left on. At work, her office door was kept ajar, and the window open a crack, despite the smell from the bins wafting up from below. She hadn't seen the outside of this room for ages, as she struggled with operational budgets, overtime sheets, staff appraisals, crime rate clear-up figures, cold case reviews, and the dreaded weekly morale-boosting Zoom meetings. She had a meeting later this morning with the chief constable. She had been told she couldn't cancel or rearrange. She had a feeling more budget cuts were coming. If it wasn't for the fact that it would hurt, Matilda would smash her head through the plate-glass window.

'Fuck it,' she said to herself. She jumped up from her chair, grabbed the printed email, and left her office.

She entered the HMCU suite to see DI Christian Brady at the end of the room leading the morning briefing. It was a reduced attendance. Of the main players, DC Tom Simpson and DS Sian Robinson were absent. She knew Sian had taken a few days' annual leave and would be back tomorrow, but she had no idea where Tom was.

'Matilda, hello. Come to see how the hoi polloi are getting on?' Christian asked with a smile.

She went over to Sian's desk, pulled open the bottom drawer, and removed a packet of Maltesers.

'Sian isn't going to be happy tomorrow morning when she comes back to find this practically empty.'

'No. We've got a plan in place,' Scott said with a sly wink.

'Can I borrow Finn?' Matilda asked.

'Now?'

'Please.'

'We're a bit low on staff at the moment,' Christian said. 'Tom's acting as FLO for Natasha Klein's family and we're missing Sian.'

'Any news on Natasha?' Matilda asked, nodding at the photograph of the smiling blonde nineteen-year-old on the white board behind Christian.

'Nope. A mobile phone was handed in on Saturday morning, found by our good friend the dog walker. It's been confirmed to be Natasha's. The thing is, it was wiped of all prints. Not even Natasha's were on it.'

'Where was it found?'

'At the side of East Bank Road. The opposite direction from where she should have been heading for home.'

'Anything on it?'

'Everything.' Christian rolled his eyes.

'Scott, are you making a cuppa?' Matilda asked Scott quietly, and with a sly smile.

'No.'

'Would you like to?'

'Not really.'

'Thanks.'

Scott gave an exaggerated tut, before pushing his chair back and walking over to the drinks station.

'The contents of Natasha's phone have been downloaded and sent to me,' DC Zofia Nowak began. She was the team's technology expert. What she didn't know about what you could do with a computer wasn't worth knowing. 'It looks like she lived by her phone. She's got text conversations going back years, literally thousands of photographs, the majority of which are selfies, and she's on every social media app you can think of.'

'Alibis from the family?' Matilda asked.

'Ongoing,' Christian replied. 'We know where the mother was. The father said he was at a meeting in Attercliffe, but we've just had that torn apart. Tom's at the family home now so we'll ask him to question him about it. The only thing is, the parents are due to come in later to do a televised appeal. If Derek can't give us an alibi, do we really want to put a potential suspect on TV?'

'No, we don't, but if he has done something to Natasha, the weight of doing an appeal might break him.'

'True.'

'Right. So, can I borrow Finn or not?'

Christian looked exasperated. He was now in sole charge of an elite unit with more responsibilities, no more money, and a reduced staff. He ran his hand over his buzz cut.

'Can it wait until after the briefing?' he asked, pleadingly.

Scott handed her the mug of tea. She thanked him and he returned to his desk without a word.

'Sure,' she said. 'Finn, if you could come up when you've got a minute.'

'Will do.'

'Thanks. I'll… I'll leave you to it then,' she said, reluctant to leave, desperate to pull up a chair and join them in the hunt for the missing teenager.

'We'll be needing that mug back,' Scott called after her.

'Of course. After all, I don't belong here anymore, do I?' She cheekily stuck her tongue out at them all, before leaving the room.

---

It was another half an hour before the tap on her office door came, half an hour in which Matilda had familiarised herself with the Natasha Klein case.

On Thursday afternoon at 3:30, Natasha left the Olive Grove campus of The Sheffield College and was heading straight home to Park Lane, Broomhill. She never made it. Her mother, Cara, arrived home at six, expecting to find her daughter making a start on tea for the family. She wasn't there. An hour later, she began ringing Natasha's phone, which went straight to voicemail. She tried all the friends she had the contact details for, before, at ten o'clock, she finally made the call to the police to report her daughter as a missing person.

The following day, students on Natasha's media studies and psychology courses were questioned and they all said the same thing, more or less: Natasha was her usual self on Thursday: happy, confident, smiling, funny, and normal. She didn't plan on meeting anyone after college and was heading home to create some content for her Instagram page. The wannabe influencer didn't have a care in the world. But something had happened to stop her from going home, and now her mobile had been found, it wasn't looking good. Time was also of the essence. Natasha had type 1 diabetes and had to inject herself with insulin several times a day. According to her mother, she carried an insulin delivery pen with her wherever she went, but had she become separated from her bag? Matilda blew out her cheeks. The worst didn't bear thinking about.

She moved on to Liam Walsh and read a little about him before she noticed Finn standing in the open doorway.

'Finn, come on in.' She laughed to herself. 'That rhymes. I'm a poet and I didn't know it. Have a seat, can I get you something to eat? Wow, look at me, I'm on a roll.'

'I'd love to come back at you with something, but I can't think of anything that rhymes with Matilda off the top of my head,' he said, sitting down.

Newly promoted DS Finn Cotton had recently completed an Open University degree in criminology, and it was this new-found knowledge that Matilda wanted to make use of. She told him about her anonymous email and handed it over.

Finn read the email. Matilda watched as his eyes ran back and forth, his lips moving slightly as he read. With each line, his brow grew heavier as he took in the enormity of the content. When he'd finished, he read it a second time.

'Well?' Matilda asked.

'I think we need to look up Liam Walsh, see what we've got.'

'From what I've read so far, it's looking very open-and-shut. You think this is genuine?'

'He says Liam's death was ruled as a suicide. That means a coroner was involved and there was an inquest which found that Liam took his own life. Case closed. Why send this email unless there was something more to his death?'

'If it was a murder made to look like a suicide, wouldn't we have noticed in the investigation and post mortem?'

'It depends how clever he's been. The fact we haven't shows

he's very clever. I don't recall us dealing with a Liam Walsh in September. Do you?'

'No.'

'Which means the case didn't come to us because there was nothing suspect about it. I tell you something, though, I don't like this subject line, "one of five".'

'Neither do I. What does your psychologist brain tell you?'

'Criminologist,' he corrected her.

'It's an ologist, it's good enough for me.'

'Well, it's very conversational in tone. He's asking you a question even though you can't answer him.' He cast his eye over the email again. 'He calls you Matilda four times; that's quite personal. He's talking to you like he's a friend.'

'Anything else?'

'He's intelligent. Let's say, for the sake of argument, that this is real, that he has killed five people and managed to get away with it, he knows that by emailing you he increases his chances of being caught. He knows about the paradox of being an infamous killer. I think...' Finn thought for a moment. 'I think he's showing off. This email is screaming of a man with confidence.'

'A confident killer is never a good thing. What do you make of the signature symbol? Does that mean anything?' Matilda asked.

'Don't you recognise it?'

'Should I?'

'It's the symbol the Zodiac Killer used when he wrote his letters to the police and journalists.'

'The Zodiac Killer? When was he active, the seventies?'

'Late sixties. If memory serves me correctly, he killed five people but there are some who believe he could have killed as many as twenty. He was never caught. However, he taunted the police and journalists by writing to them and signing the letters with that symbol. Did you see the film with Jake Gyllenhaal? It's chilling.'

'I did. Good film. Why is he using his symbol? Surely this guy doesn't think he's the new Zodiac?'

Finn thought for a moment. 'I don't get the impression he's wanting to pick up his mantle or copycat an infamous killer. I think… hmm… I think he's using the symbol to show that he's getting away with his crimes just like the Zodiac killer did. I mean, he's claiming to have killed five people. Surely we'd know about it if he had. He's either a fantasist or a very dangerous man.'

Matilda shivered. 'I'm not sure which is the safer option.'

'Leave it with me. I'll do some digging. I'll look up Liam Walsh and I'll get Zofia to check out the email address. I might be a while, though, what with us being short-staffed. Can I keep this email?'

Matilda nodded.

Finn stood up and left the office. He made to close the door until Matilda called out and stopped him.

'It's like an oven in here with the door closed,' she lied, hiding her sudden-onset claustrophobia.

Matilda waited until Finn had gone before looking back at the open email on her desk.

'If you think you can play games with people's lives, you've picked the wrong opponent, you bastard.'

## Chapter Two

DC Tom Simpson was standing in the kitchen of the stone-built semi-detached house in Park Lane, Broomhill where Natasha Klein lived with her family. When he qualified as a Family Liaison Officer late last year, he thought it would be an extra string to his bow, something interesting to add to his CV. All he seemed to have done this weekend was listen to Cara crying and make endless mugs of tea.

His phone vibrated in his pocket. He took it out and saw a text from Zofia asking him to quiz Derek about his alibi, seeing as the one he'd given was full of holes. He sent her a quick reply, with a couple of kisses added on the end, then finished making the round of teas he was currently occupied with, and took the tray into the living room.

Cara was sitting on the edge of the sofa, rocking slightly, a screwed-up tissue in each hand. Her sobs were the main background noise throughout the house. Tom could understand how upset she was, but she really needed to compose herself. She would make herself ill if she didn't. He placed a mug of tea on the table in front of her. She looked up at him with wet eyes and nodded her thanks. She was wearing a black oversized cardigan, navy trousers, and a navy sweater. Tom hadn't seen her in anything else since Friday morning.

Derek came into the room. He'd gone upstairs to shower and had come down in fresh clothes, bringing with him an air of a fragranced shower gel. He was clean-shaven, his thinning hair neat, and wore a red sweater which seemed too tight for his straining build.

'Ooh, tea,' he said, picking up the mug Tom set down for him. 'I could get used to having you around.' He turned to his wife. 'Cara, sweetheart, why don't you go and have a shower? You'll feel better.'

She shook her head.

'Or a bath? A relaxing bath might help.'

'A relaxing bath?' she asked in a dark tone, looking daggers at him. 'Oh, yes, why don't I take a glass of wine up, maybe light a few candles and listen to a bit of music as well. You don't understand, do you?' She gave into her sobs again. 'How can I relax? How can any of us relax?'

Derek looked at Tom and raised an eyebrow.

'Derek,' Tom began, swallowing hard. 'I've had a message from one of my colleagues. We're going through a timeline of events from Thursday, trying to work out where Natasha was, who she was with, the usual. And, for elimination purposes, we need to know where everyone who knew her was, too. Can you tell me where you were on Thursday around half-past three?'

'I've already told you all this,' he said, sitting in an armchair and crossing his legs at the knee. 'I had a meeting at Brotherton's at three down Attercliffe. I was seeing Richard Sharp, he's their head finance chap.'

'We've called Brotherton's, and they said the meeting never took place.'

'Well … no,' he said. Cara looked up, her stare burning into him. 'It turned out he'd forgotten all about me and had gone to their site in Barnsley for the afternoon.'

'So, you didn't have the meeting?'

'No. Still, never mind. It got me out of the office,' he said with a smile.

'Did you go back to the office?'

His smile started to droop. 'Erm, no, actually, I didn't.'

'Where did you go?' Tom asked.

'I decided to call it a day. I'd been at work since before eight, and I'd not had lunch, so I thought I'd come straight home.'

'What time did you arrive home?'

'I'm not sure. I didn't look at the time. Possibly half-past three, maybe twenty to four.'

'Was anyone here when you came back?'

'No. The house was empty. Cara got in about ... what was it, about six-ish?'

'Yes,' she nodded. Her steely gaze never once left her husband.

'Did you make any phone calls?' Tom asked.

'No. I... I came home, made myself a sandwich and just relaxed.'

'That's not like you,' Cara said.

'Sorry?'

'You never just relax. You're always doing something.'

'I know. That's why I decided to relax. It's good to sit down and do nothing from time to time.'

Cara looked at Tom, back at her husband, back at Tom, then blew her nose into an already disintegrating tissue.

'What time should Natasha have come home?' Tom asked.

'If she was coming straight home, she'd have been here about four o'clock,' Cara said.

'Did you call her when she didn't come home?' Tom turned to Derek.

'No. I mean, she doesn't always come straight home. I ... she could have gone somewhere with friends. She wouldn't have thanked me for calling and checking up on her, you know what teenagers are. I think I'll go and get some breakfast,' Derek said, standing up and leaving the room.

Tom looked at Cara. She looked back at him with a blank stare.

'Is Natasha close to her father?' Tom asked Cara once the door was closed. He lowered his voice so Derek would be unable to overhear.

Cara seemed to be struggling to find the right words. She opened and closed her mouth a few times. 'I… It's… I wouldn't say close. No.'

'Why not?'

'They're … they're very different people. You know what teenagers are like when they're finding their feet in the world, they clash with their parents, don't they? I'm sure you did when you were Natasha's age.'

Tom didn't say anything. The less said about his teen years the better. 'But you and Natasha are close?'

'I like to think so,' she said, trying to smile, but it just screwed her face up more. 'You know, I think I will go and have that shower. Do you mind?' she asked, standing up and practically running for the door.

'No. Take all the time you need.'

Once the door was closed, he took his phone out of his back pocket and fired off a text to Zofia:

*There's something really off about Natasha's mum and dad.*

## Chapter Three

Matilda Darke knocked on the door of Chief Constable Ridley's office and waited to be called in. It was 9:30. She was bang on time for her appointment.

It was always easy to tell what time of day it was by Benjamin Ridley's appearance. When he arrived at work every morning he was straight-backed, his head high, his uniform fitted and pristine, clean-shaven, his hair neat and tidy. As the day wore on, the jacket was discarded, the sleeves rolled up, the tie loosened, and the top button of his shirt undone. The stress of the day-to-day job and the wrangling with politicians took its toll and by the time he was ready to go home, he would drag his body out of the station, jacket slung over one shoulder, tie in his pocket, thick five o'clock shadow on his face and in urgent need of a double whiskey. It was a shame he didn't drink.

Matilda entered his office and found him sitting at his desk looking as if he had the weight of the world on his broad shoulders.

'Matilda, come on in, sit down.'

Tentatively, she pulled out the chair on the other side of the desk and sat down, placing her hands between her legs.

*Why do I feel like I'm about to be told off for being caught smoking?*

'Coffee?' he asked, standing up and going over to the small filing cabinet where a Nespresso machine was plugged in.

'Please.'

'I never used to drink coffee until I became chief constable. I never used to eat processed foods, either. I'm thinking of taking up smoking and recreational drugs next.'

'Feeling stressed?'

He let out a heavy sigh and glanced at his reflection in the mirror over the filing cabinet.

'Do you know, I didn't have a single grey hair when I took this job,' he said, handing Matilda a black coffee. 'I also had low blood pressure and a trim waistline. Now look at me.'

Matilda didn't know what to say so decided to keep her mouth shut.

Ridley sat back down at his desk. 'My wife tells me I look like Barack Obama.'

'That's a compliment, surely. He's a very attractive man.'

'He's also twelve years older than me.'

'Ah. Would it help if I say you resemble Lil Nas X?'

'I have absolutely no idea who that is. Something tells me you shouldn't know who he is either. However, if he's under forty, I'll take it as a compliment.'

'I'm pretty sure he's under thirty.'

'It's been a long time since I've been able to pass for under thirty, but I appreciate the ego boost. Now, I'm afraid I don't have very good news for you, Matilda.'

'I didn't think you would have.'

'We're over budget in every department and I need to make some major cuts.'

'You're getting rid of the HMCU?'

'No,' he replied firmly. 'At least, I'm hoping not to. It would be a very last resort. However, we are closing the canteen and we're going to be employing more civilian staff for the administrative roles uniformed officers are currently doing.'

Matilda shook her head. Policing shouldn't be about budgets. You shouldn't put a price tag on attending a house being burgled or persistent shoplifting, but nowadays everything was about doing things the cheapest way around. The politicians and the decision-makers were blaming Covid, but the people on the ground, the uniformed officers and the detectives, had been told what to investigate based on priorities for years. If a house had been broken into yet nothing was taken, victims were given a crime number and told to contact their insurance companies. Nobody was sent out to take statements, knock on the doors of the neighbours or collect fingerprints. It just wasn't financially viable.

'The two DCs I promised HMCU have been reduced to one, but it won't be happening this financial year, and we may just have to transfer someone over from CID rather than recruit from outside. That way we won't be adding another wage.'

Matilda rolled her eyes. She could feel a headache coming on.

'Also'—he swallowed hard and gave Matilda a quick glance from his tablet, before looking back down at it—'there are three detective sergeants in the HMCU when they only require two.'

Matilda wanted to say something but waited for more bombshells from Ridley.

'You need to make a choice, Matilda. You need to lose either DS Sian Robinson, Scott Andrews or Finn Cotton. They won't be going to another department either. They'll be getting made redundant.'

'What?' she fumed.

'We cannot afford for the HMCU to have three sergeants.'

'So, you're just getting rid of one of them? It's supposed to be an elite team, which means the best officers.'

'I know it's not ideal.'

'No shit.'

'I'm guessing none of them would volunteer for redundancy.'

'Of course they won't,' she said. She could feel her blood boiling. 'Sian's just bought a new house. Scott's getting married this year and Finn's just completed a course in criminology. They're all working hard. They're all valuable members of my team. *The* team,' she corrected herself.

'I know they are, and I'm really sorry. But you need to lose one of them.'

'How can I...?' She stopped herself. She had no idea how she could choose between them.

'Let me know your decision by May bank holiday. We'll be issuing redundancy notices in mid-June.'

'This is wrong,' she said. 'This is not why I joined the police force. And I know it's not why you joined either. You cannot solve crimes on a fucking budget.'

'I'm aware. My hands are tied. I'm hating this, Matilda, I really am.'

'Less than a year ago, you asked me to come back to work after my unit was disbanded. You practically begged me. You promised me everything.'

'A lot has happened in this last year. The fallout from Covid...'

'Bullshit,' she said, standing up. 'The politicians are using Covid as an excuse. First it was Brexit, now it's a pandemic. If we had more competent people in central government who actually knew what real life was like in twenty-first-century Britain, we'd be a thriving country. Unfortunately, we've got public-school dickheads who've never stepped foot further north than the Home Counties.'

'Matilda...'

'No,' she interrupted. 'I'm not doing it. Scott and Finn saved my life in January. Sian almost died at the hands of Simon Browes. I'm not choosing between them. If you want one of them to go, you choose.'

'It's your department.'

'If it was my department, I wouldn't be doing this. You want one of them gone, you do it.'

'Matilda, when you're in a position of responsibility like you are, you have to make difficult decisions.'

'Not this one.' She went to the door, opened it, and slammed it hard on her way out.

## Chapter Four

For the first time in as long as he could remember, Danny Hanson had nothing to do today. Last week he filed a feature he'd been working on for the *Guardian*, and a reshuffle at BBC News had seen him phased out as one of their freelance presenters. They contacted him sporadically whenever anything was happening in the North of England, but he seemed to be out of favour with them at the moment. Last week, Danny had received a boxful of paperback proof copies of his delayed non-fiction book about the sexual abuse scandal at Magnolia House. He'd sent a few out to fellow journalists for them to provide a quote for the finished hardback, but still had plenty left. Seeing his name on a book gave him a feeling like no other. He couldn't wait until it hit the shops in the autumn.

On Thursday, a book had been published that he wished he'd written. He'd been involved in the original investigation, sort of, and had even drafted a proposal to a publisher, but he'd been beaten to it. He'd kept an eye on this book and as soon as the hardback hit the shelves, he was straight into Waterstones and bought a copy. Over the weekend, he read *The Perfect Killer* by Sebastian Lister. He wanted to hate it. He wanted to scoff at the stereotypical sensationalist prose, but he couldn't. The truth was it was brilliant. Sebastian had done his homework; he'd researched the crimes and conducted interviews meticulously. There was no way Danny could have done a better job. There was, however, one aspect missing from Sebastian's book and that was where Danny held the trump card.

*The Perfect Killer* told the story of Stuart Mills and his reign of terror as he killed eight sex workers and one key witness over a number of years. The crimes had gone unsolved until an undercover operation by South Yorkshire Police saw rookie detective Zofia Nowak play the part of a sex worker on the streets of Sheffield. Stuart had picked her up, and she would have been his next victim, had Detective Chief Inspector Matilda Darke not arrived at the eleventh hour. Stuart's arrest didn't quite go to plan and Zofia put herself in the way as he tried to make his escape. She ended up being crushed between Stuart's car and a tree, leaving her paralysed from the waist down.

What made Stuart the perfect killer, what kept him from appearing on the police's radar for so long, was the fact that he was the husband of Detective Sergeant Sian Robinson, as she was now known, having reverted to her maiden name following her divorce from the convicted killer. Stuart and Sian had been married for over twenty-five years, and he had listened, attentively, as Sian came home from work every day and told him about her day and the cases she was investigating. He'd taken in all the advances in technology and criminal investigations, so when it came to committing his own murders, he knew exactly what to do so as not to arouse suspicion.

It was obvious from Sebastian's book that Sian hadn't consented to an interview. Danny had spoken to Sian many times and told her he knew a book was in the pipeline. She had said she wanted nothing to do with it. She was trying to put her ex-husband, and the past, behind her, and concentrate on protecting her four children. He had a great deal of respect for Sian, but at the end of the day, he was a journalist, and he knew there was a story here. The world was interested in true crime. Netflix was full of documentaries about serial killers, dramas were made about them, the public couldn't get enough. There had been a whole table dedicated to *The Perfect Killer* in Waterstones, though that may have been because of the local angle. Danny had kept a close eye on the publication of this book and had seen what Sebastian Lister was doing for publicity to make it a bestseller. It was being serialised in the *Daily Mail*, it had featured on Radio Four, Sebastian had been on *BBC Breakfast*, *Good Morning Britain*, and *This Morning* to talk about it. He'd given interviews to *ABC World News Tonight* and *NBC Nightly News*, and had had an extended slot on *60 Minutes*. That could have been him. He was jealous of Sebastian's coverage and bitter that he hadn't been able to write the book, but there was still more of the story to tell. Sian Robinson, aka Sian Mills, hadn't given her side of the story. He wanted her story more than anything.

Danny had taken extensive notes while he'd been reading *The Perfect Killer*. There were aspects of the investigation he hadn't known about that Sebastian had somehow managed to discover. He also made notes on what was missing, on what Sian could tell him, on what he could write about. There was a second book here, a book from the point of view of the wife of a serial killer, and he was going to be the man to write it.

Over the years, Danny had been a thorn in the side of South Yorkshire Police, Matilda Darke in particular. He first met her when he was a reporter on the local newspaper, *The Star*, and soon discovered that her cases almost guaranteed front-page leads. He took an interest in Matilda and her team, and followed them everywhere. Occasionally, even Danny had to admit, he overstepped the mark, and he apologised to Matilda for posing as a doctor and, when she was shot, sneaking into her room in the hospital while she was in a coma and taking her photograph.

However, recently he'd been able to furnish Matilda with

information. The investigation into historical child sexual abuse at Magnolia House Children's Home involved some very high-profile people, politicians and members of the police force. Between them, they'd cracked the case wide open, and even now, two years later, people were still coming forward to talk about the abuse they suffered while at the home. Danny was sure he'd be able to write a few updated chapters for the paperback version of the book, maybe even a second book, down the line, as more and more people were arrested and jailed. Matilda had warmed to him. She had even allowed him to interview her for the book and they'd shared a few light-hearted moments over a coffee. As much as he knew he could benefit from being in Matilda's inner circle, contacting Sian and trying to get her to reveal all to him about her marriage to Stuart could destroy all that. Matilda would protect her team at any cost, professionally and personally. To Danny, it was a sacrifice he was willing to take. He wanted Sian's story. He needed Sian's story. He was going to get Sian's story.

---

Over the years, Danny Hanson had created a huge following on social media. In the last week, he had passed the one hundred thousand followers mark on Twitter, and he wasn't far behind that on Instagram. It helped that he had a trademark. Whenever he was on TV, he always wore a dark checked shirt, and his ruffled, wavy dark hair was a hit with his female followers, and a large number of male ones, too. #DannyHanson and #DannyHansonsHair were often trending at the same time. Unfortunately, it took him longer than he would have liked to get his hair into the perfectly messy state that had gained him so much attention.

He reread the final chapter of *The Perfect Killer* while waiting for his hair to dry naturally. It ended with Stuart settling into a life behind bars. For the sake of his wife and children, he admitted his crimes so there wouldn't have to be a trial. In an interview with Sebastian, Stuart stated that he regretted what he did and blamed a snowball effect. He'd made a bad decision in using a street worker for sex, and tried to cover it up when he was almost caught. Then events soon spiralled out of his control, and he couldn't stop. He hoped that one day Sian would see how sorry he was for what he did. While he could never turn the clock back, he wanted to forge a relationship with his ex-wife such that she would visit him in prison and they could become friends.

To the reader, there was a hint of positivity, of sadness, of hope, but Danny knew the truth. Sian wanted nothing more to do with Stuart. She had reverted to her own name almost as soon as the divorce was finalised, and even the children had changed their surname. Either Stuart was deluding himself or Sebastian, using creative licence, was trying to show a serial killer in a sympathetic light.

Danny checked his reflection in the mirror before he left his flat. He put his satchel over his shoulder, weighed down with the hardback book, and headed for his car. He had saved Sian's life in January. Surely she would grant him an exclusive interview as a thank-you. Danny lived in hope. He was an optimist.

---

DS Sian Robinson had taken a few days off work. The closer the publication day of *The Perfect Killer* came, the more adverts she kept seeing for it in the media and online. It was even a recommended item when she opened the Amazon app last weekend. She hated the title. Stuart was not the perfect killer. He was a destroyer of lives. How could that be perfect? She had no intention of reading it. She'd lived through the whole nightmare – why would she want to return to those dark days when the man she loved told her he'd visited sex workers, strangled them, mutilated them, then come home and snuggled up in bed with her? When his arrest was imminent, he'd even held a knife to her throat. If it hadn't been for Matilda, he would have killed her and their children to stop them discovering the truth.

When Sebastian Lister first came calling, she slammed the door in his face. She assumed he was some tabloid hack trying to cash in on her misery. She looked him up online and saw that he was a trained forensic psychologist. He worked in London for the Behavioural Science Administration, interviewing serial killers to try to understand how their minds worked. He was braver than Sian would ever be. She didn't want to know how their minds worked. Sebastian called a few more times, he waited for her outside the police station, he turned up at her home unannounced. He phoned her, emailed her, and posted letters through her letterbox, all of which she ignored. It was only when he approached two of her children that she decided to take action and threatened him with an injunction if he came anywhere near her family again. Surprisingly, he acquiesced, and she hadn't heard from him since.

Sian's children were taking the publication of the book better than she expected, much better than she was. Her oldest, Anthony, had now left university and while trying to find an engineering job was busy running Donnie Barko, Sian's dog-walking service, which was thriving. He still lived at home but was either out working or at his girlfriend's flat in Rotherham. He recommended they had a book-burning party, where they each bought a copy of the hardback, set a bonfire, and took it in turns to throw a book on the pyre. Sian managed to talk him out of it.

Her second child and only daughter, Belinda, had left home. She was currently at the University of Southampton studying Law with Psychology. She phoned home once a week and filled her mother in on university life. She was studying hard, working part-time as a barista in Costa, and, despite saying she was concentrating on work, she kept slipping the name Rebecca into the conversation, so Sian guessed she had a new girlfriend to distract her. Belinda had sent Sian a text yesterday telling her she'd read the book and it was shit, but suggesting a couple of red-headed actors to play Sian in the inevitable TV adaptation. Belinda wanted Catherine Tate to play her mother, but Rebecca thought Katherine Parkinson would bring a more sympathetic tone to the character. This made Sian smile. Belinda was obviously taking it all in her stride.

Sian's two youngest sons, Daniel and Gregory, were a complete contrast. Daniel was taking a break following his disastrous delayed A-Level results. It was understandable given the circumstances he'd been living in at the time of taking his exams. He was currently trying to decide what he wanted to do with his life. His sulky teenage mode seemed to be extending into his twenties. Sian barely got a word out of him. He'd been incredibly close to his father and took Stuart's crimes hard. Gregory had been full of questions about what prison was like and could write a thesis on Wakefield Prison, considering the amount of reading up on it he'd done. Now he had developed an interest in Formula One. His new best friend's father was a former mechanic for Red Bull Racing and he and Sian spent many a Sunday on the sofa watching the cars go round and round and round. Gregory was loving it. Sian had no interest whatsoever and found it mind-numbingly boring, but it was mother-son bonding, so she was happy to watch it with him.

Sian had spoken to both of them about the book coming out last Thursday. Gregory had no interest in books at the best of times but was interested to know what it said about him. Daniel said he'd like to read it but wasn't ready yet.

Daniel was sitting at the table in the kitchen eating a bowl of Frosties. His head was down, spoon in one hand, mobile phone in the other, tapping away as he scrolled social media.

Sian came into the house from hanging some washing out and placed the empty laundry basket on the floor.

'I didn't hear you get up,' she said.

He didn't reply.

'Are you going out today?' she asked.

He didn't reply.

She pulled out the chair opposite him and sat down. 'I've got the day off today. Fancy doing something?'

He didn't reply.

'We could go to Meadowhall if you like. I'll treat you to those trainers you've had your eye on.'

He looked up from his phone, mid-chew. He swallowed.

'Seriously?'

'Yes.'

'Why?'

'Why what?'

'Why are you buying me trainers? It's not my birthday.'

'I just thought you deserved a treat. I... I saw that email you printed off. You're going back to college, I'm so pleased,' she said, smiling broadly.

Daniel shrugged. He chewed his cereal, swallowed, dropped his spoon in the bowl and leaned back in his chair. 'Why are you off today? You were off Thursday and Friday, too. It's not like you to just take time off work unless it's for a reason.'

'I just fancied a few days' rest. What with the house move and everything, I'm shattered.'

'Nothing to do with the book about Dad coming out?'

Sian sighed. 'Okay, cards on the table. Yes, I've been worried about the book coming out, about how you're all dealing with it. It's not easy having it dragged back up again. I want to make sure you're all all right,' she said, reaching across to him. He pulled his hand away. 'We haven't talked about your dad for a while.'

'What's there to talk about?' He shrugged.

'Daniel, at the end of the day, he's still your dad. People are talking about him in the news and it's not nice. I want to know how you're feeling.'

He shrugged again. 'I'm fine.'

'Really?'

'Yes.'

'You don't hate him?'

'Mum, it's obvious that neither of us knew him at all. He wasn't the man we thought he was. I can't hate someone I don't know.'

Sian thought about that. He was right. 'This book—'

'I do want to read it,' he interrupted. 'I'm quite keen to know what's been written about us. But I'll read it in my own time. I'm too busy trying to get my head around sodding Chaucer.' He broke into a smile.

'Bloody hell, I studied him at school, too. I'd have thought the syllabus would have been brought up to date. There are much better books to study.'

'Tell me about it.'

'Are you all right?'

'Fine.'

'You need to tell me if you're struggling.'

'I'm not.'

'Are you sure?'

'Positive.'

She smiled. 'Good. So, new trainers or not?'

'Of course, new trainers,' he said, pushing his chair back and standing up. 'I'll just go and change.'

He smiled a warm smile at his mother and left the room. Sian felt heartened. All four of her children were dealing with this better than she was. She was itching to scream and swear, and maybe a book-burning party would have been cathartic, but getting on with life was the best way to confront this.

The doorbell rang.

She went over to the front door and pulled it open. She was feeling buoyed and happy after the chat with Daniel. Her smile dropped as soon as she saw Danny Hanson on her doorstep.

'Hello,' she said.

'Sian, how are you?' the journalist asked, his tone shallowly sympathetic.

'Fine, thanks. I'm just about to pop out, so now isn't a good time.'

'I won't keep you. I was wondering if I could have a private word.'

'About?' she asked, expecting him to mention the book.

'It's about what happened in January with you and Adele and her boyfriend.'

'Ah. I see. I can give you five minutes.' She stepped to one side.

'Thanks,' he said, entering the house.

Sian closed the door behind him and led him into the living room. She sneezed as she inhaled whatever fragrance he'd bathed in this morning.

'I really like what you've done to the house, Sian. Are you settled in now?'

'Yes, thanks. Have a seat.'

He sat down, looking around him at the framed photographs of her children on the wall. He looked back at her and smiled.

'So, what do you want?' she asked when he didn't seem in a hurry to move the conversation forward.

'Well, you know, I was thinking about what happened earlier this year when Simon attacked you and Adele, and you both almost died. I turned up and managed to save you both.'

'You did,' Sian said, though it pained her to admit it.

'We've come a long way, haven't we?'

'Sorry?'

'You know, the police usually hate journalists, but we've sort of become, well, maybe not friends, but there's a professional courtesy.'

Sian frowned. She had no idea where this was going. 'I suppose.'

'I was thinking that since I helped you and Adele, maybe you could do something for me in return.'

'Are you asking for a favour?'

'A little one.'

She clenched her fists. She could feel the tension rising inside her as her blood boiled. 'Go on.'

'I know you had nothing to do with Sebastian Lister's book coming out last Thursday, and I applaud you for it. That kind of cheap sensationalism is uncalled for. I can understand why you wouldn't want to be interviewed by a forensic psychologist who would print the words you didn't say rather than the ones you would.'

'Danny—'

'Hear me out,' he interrupted. 'I know you. You know me. You've seen an advanced copy of the book I've written about Magnolia House. You've seen how sensitively I've written about the abuse. I'm not a hack. If you let me interview you, get your side of the story, I promise—'

'No.'

'I promise that I will let you see it before I get it published.'

'No,' she said, more firmly.

'One element that's missing from Sebastian's book is how Stuart's crimes impacted you and your children's lives.'

'Danny, no.'

'People are going to read that book and make up their own minds about how you feel.'

'I don't care.'

'Let me interview you and your children.'

'Out!' Sian stood up. The mention of her children was the last straw.

'Sian, I will write a book you will be proud of.'

Sian grabbed him by the collar of his blue checked shirt and hauled him to his feet.

'You think you're something special,' she seethed through gritted teeth as she dragged him into the hallway. 'You think you're an amazing writer, someone with a heart and compassion.

Well, you're not. You're a deceitful, lying, two-faced, sneaky, talentless bastard, and I want nothing to do with you.' She pulled open the front door. 'If I see you within a foot of my home or any of my children, I swear to God I will have you arrested. Talk to me again, and I will take great pleasure in throttling you with my bare hands. Do you understand me?' she shouted.

She didn't give him a chance to answer but slammed the door in his face. She turned, looked up the stairs and saw her son Daniel looking down at her.

'Are you all right?' he asked.

'Is it too early to get pissed?'

He laughed.

## Chapter Five

As Matilda's door wasn't closed, Finn didn't bother knocking. He walked straight in.

'William Edgar Walsh,' he said, reading from his tablet. 'Born on February the fifth, 2001, and died on September twenty-fifth last year. He jumped from the Arts Tower in town. According to his mother's statement he'd been suffering with depression for a number of years. This was backed up by his tutors at the university, where he was studying English literature. There's also a statement from the university's counsellor, confirming that. The coroner's inquest had letters from his GP which listed his medication for depression and anxiety. In the note left in his bedroom for his mother to find, he stated how he simply wasn't cut out to live in this world and his mum shouldn't be sad but thankful that he was no longer in pain. The coroner recorded a verdict of suicide.'

'The poor lad,' Matilda said, genuinely upset. 'Was there a toxicology screening?'

'Yes,' Finn said, looking back at his tablet. 'He had alcohol in his system, but he wasn't drunk. A couple of units.'

'No drugs?'

'Only his prescription medication. He hadn't overdosed either. It was the usual dose.'

'Is there anything about the death that stands out as suspicious?' Matilda asked.

'Nothing at all. Statements were given by his mother, a couple of friends, tutors, and the counsellor. They all said Liam was struggling with his mental health and incredibly depressed and disillusioned with life in general.'

'Bless him. It sounds like he was really going through it.' Matilda chewed the inside of her cheek as she thought. 'Finn, try and get hold of a copy of the suicide note.'

'You think it might have been forged?'

'It's possible.'

'In an Agatha Christie book, yes. Surely his mother knows her own son's handwriting.'

'Let's find out if it was written by hand first.'

'Do you not think this could just be a prank?' Finn asked, holding up the printed email.

'Why would anyone play this kind of prank?'

'I... I don't know. People get their kicks in strange ways these days. However, what kind of a person emails the police and confesses to a murder that so obviously isn't a murder?'

'Did Zofia get any joy with the email address?'

'It doesn't exist.'

'Isn't there some kind of an IP address attached to an email?'

'Yes. She did tell me, but it was too technical and went over my head. Basically, it's been doctored, and it was bouncing her signals all over the world.'

Matilda leaned back in her chair and folded her arms. She wore a thoughtful expression. She looked at Finn. He was a dedicated detective. He'd paid for an Open University degree with his own money and did the course work in his spare time, even when he was working unpaid overtime here. He was married to Stephanie. They had a lovely new house and were happy. With his new qualification, he was an asset to the team, to the whole station. There was no way she could choose Finn as the one to be made redundant. South Yorkshire Police needed more people like him.

'Hello?' Finn asked.

'Sorry?'

'I thought you'd wandered off. I asked you where you want to go with this next. I mean, do you want to wait to see if there's a second email, or continue digging with Liam Walsh?'

'Is there anything else you can get from his email, Finn?'

'I have made a few more notes,' he said, scrolling through his tablet. 'If he'd written us a letter, we could have had a graphologist come in and look at the handwriting and the stresses on each word. The fact he's sent an email removed the personal element. However, we can look at the words he uses and the style and tone.'

'And? Anything?'

Finn pursed his lips. 'I'm not sure.'

'I'd ask for my money back from the Open University if I were you,' she said, a glint of humour in her eye.

'Like I said before, it's chatty, it's conversational. It's friendly almost, but I think he's telling us a lot about himself, subconsciously, but until…' he trailed off.

'Until what?'

'Until we get a second email and we can compare, it might just be a throwaway comment.'

'I don't think I want a second email,' Matilda said.

'Well, no, but it would be useful if you did get one.'

'Tell me about this throwaway comment.'

'Okay,' Finn began. 'Put yourself in the killer's shoes for a moment. You've committed the perfect murder and you're wanting to show off to the police, yet you don't want to give anything away about yourself. You've done all that technological business so the email can't be traced, so it's highly likely you've written this email several times before pressing send, so it's spot-on, yes?'

'I suppose.'

'So, what's the reason for mentioning his mother?'

'I wasn't aware he did mention his mother,' Matilda said, turning back to her laptop and opening up the email again.

'In the first full paragraph he says that you're probably thinking he's "some kind of crank who's a few sandwiches short of a picnic, as my mum likes to say". What's the point of that?'

She didn't answer.

'I'm guessing it's a phrase his mother does use often, and it's stuck with him because his mother is very important to him.'

'I'm not following,' she said.

'This email is the opening of something big for him. If we're taking this as real. He's committed five murders and got away with them all so far. He wants to impress you by showing what he's capable of, but I think he wants to impress his mother, too. He's mentioned her straight away in a very important document.'

'Oh, great. A killer with a mother fixation. Why am I suddenly imagining Anthony Perkins in a dress?'

'Like I said, picture yourself as the killer,' Finn continued. 'This wouldn't have just been the first draft of the email. He wanted to get it spot-on. He'll have written it and rewritten it and rewritten it, taking out any little thing that isn't necessary or might be too revealing.'

'So why didn't he spot the thing about his mother?'

'Because he didn't notice it,' Finn said. 'Because to him, his mother is absolutely necessary.'

'Wow. You're good.'

'Not just a pretty face.' Finn smiled broadly. 'Now, please don't tell Christian, but when I was looking at the original investigation by uniformed police there was CCTV footage found of Liam Walsh walking to the Arts Tower. I've emailed it to Zofia for her to have a look at and do some more of the computer wizardry that she's good at. She said she'll get to it when she gets a moment, but Natasha Klein's social media obsession is giving her a headache.'

'That's more important right now. This is just … well, I'm not sure what this is at the moment.'

'I did have another idea.'

'Go on.'

'To all intents and purposes, Liam Walsh jumped from the roof of the Arts Tower. However, if he was murdered, we have to ask ourselves: how? It could be that he was pushed or thrown off the roof. He wasn't drunk or under the influence of drugs. If someone had tried to push him off the roof, it's likely he'd have resisted. There may have been bruising on his body.'

'Which would have been picked up at the post-mortem,' Matilda said.

'Not if they weren't looking for bruising. They've got a young man at the bottom of a building and a suicide note left in his bedroom. Conclusion: suicide. Straightforward PM, release the body, send it for burial. Simple.'

Matilda raised an eyebrow. He was right. 'Your brain is working much harder than mine, Finn.'

'Can I make a remark about being more than fifteen years younger than you?'

'Not if you want to keep your jo—' She stopped herself, suddenly remembering the redundancy hanging over his head. 'Just this once,' she said, standing up. 'Can you do me a favour?'

'Sure.'

'Pop along to the university and talk to the counsellor Liam Walsh saw. I know he gave a statement, but it would be useful to get the inside story on Liam's mental health issues. How severe were they and who did he confide in?'

'Okay. What are you thinking?'

'Let's say Liam was murdered. Isn't it just a little convenient that the killer murdered someone on the brink of taking their own life, so he could kill him and make it appear like it was suicide?

This killer had to be in Liam's life to know how depressed he was so he could take advantage of that and lead him to his death.'

'I hadn't thought of that.'

'Old brains do have their uses. I'm going to pop along and talk to the pathologist. Is there a replacement for Adele yet?'

'Yes. He started last week. I haven't met him yet.'

Matilda grabbed her jacket from the back of her chair. 'I need to get out of this sodding shoebox. It's doing my head in.'

'Should you be going out and investigating? I thought you were desk-based now.'

'Finn, take a look at my windowsill, what do you see?'

Finn turned to the window. There were two pathetic pot plants on the ledge. 'I see a couple of plants that seem to have been overwatered.'

'They're Clarissa and Clarence.'

'They have names?'

'I named them. Can you believe that? I actually named some plants. If I stay in here on my own much longer I will literally go mad. I'm going out and I don't give two shits about it.' She left the office and stormed down the corridor.

'What shall I say if someone asks where you are?' Finn called after her.

'Tell them I'm being measured for a straitjacket,' she said over her shoulder.

## Chapter Six

Danny Hanson sat behind the wheel of his second-hand Ford Focus. He was annoyed. If it hadn't been for him, Sian would have died in January. He had saved her from the hands of a killer. All he was asking for in return was a little interview. It would only take an hour or so for them to sit down, have a chat about what her life was like with Stuart before and during his killings, and that would be it. He'd never bring up the subject again. Discussion over. He was so sure Sian would have at least considered his suggestion. He needed something else to write about. While the buzz surrounding his book about Magnolia House was still high, he needed to give his editor at HarperCollins something amazing so they would see him as a major power in the future of non-fiction.

'Fuck!' he said out loud, punching the steering wheel.

He'd watched, sunk in his seat, as Sian had reversed out of the driveway with her son in the front passenger seat. They were smiling and chatting, not a care in the world now she'd moved to a leafy, affluent part of Sheffield – while he was still slumming it in a shitty flat in Hillsborough.

His mobile started to ring. He searched for it in the front pocket of his satchel and looked at the display.

'Oh, piss off, Mother,' he said, sending the call to voicemail. He wasn't in the mood to talk to her right now.

He slumped back in his seat and chewed his thumbnail. He thought long and hard. Then it came to him. He knew Sian. He'd known her for years. He knew who her friends and family were. Her colleagues wouldn't talk to him about her, they'd want to protect her, so people like Matilda, Christian and Scott weren't worth pursuing, but there were others he could approach. Sian's children, especially the eldest two, Anthony and Belinda; they were starting out in life and probably wouldn't have much disposable income. He was sure Belinda wouldn't mind a few twenty-pound notes in her back pocket for a little chat, and if she didn't, there was bound to be someone on her course who could be bribed. And Anthony was still doing the dog walking business. Danny doubted it paid much so maybe he could use a little extra.

He grabbed his phone, opened the Facebook app, and typed in 'Belinda Robinson'. Like the majority of people her age, her security was basic. The University of Southampton was a long way for him to travel just to have her slam the door in his face, but his mother now lived in London so he could kill two birds with one stone and pay her a much-delayed visit. He smiled to himself as he started the car. It would do him good to get out of Sheffield for a while. He was starting to hate this city. It was holding him back. There was very little happening here anymore. He needed to make something happen.

## Chapter Seven

Matilda parked in the visitor's space in the car park of the Medico-Legal Centre on Watery Street.

In 2019, Matilda had been shot twice in the line of duty. The first bullet entered her left shoulder, the second grazed the side of her skull. She spent several months in an induced coma and when she woke, she found she had to learn her motor skills all over again. She was back at work within a year, but she hadn't been cleared to drive until a fortnight ago.

Unfortunately, she no longer had a car. She was itching to get back behind the wheel of a Range Rover again, but the waiting time for a brand-new one was more than eighteen months. She couldn't wait that long. However, there was one car in her double garage, safely tucked away beneath a tarpaulin – Adele's Porsche 911. Who knew when it was going to be driven again, if ever?

Matilda had felt sad taking off the cover and slipping in behind the wheel. This had been Adele's pride and joy. Matilda had never been in it without her best friend beside her. It seemed strange, wrong, almost illegal, to be in it without Adele's say-so. The urge to drive, though, was too strong.

She was slightly rusty at first and drove along a few of the quieter streets while she familiarised herself with the controls, but it wasn't long before she hit Ringinglow Road, slammed her foot down on the accelerator, and headed for the Peak District National Park, where she put the car through its paces. Her grin spread from ear to ear. It had been a cold day, but she opened the window and let the stiff breeze clear away the cobwebs. She loved every minute of it.

When she arrived back home, she put in an order for a new Range Rover Autobiography. Driving a Porsche was a huge difference, but it would more than do for now.

Matilda looked at the building containing the mortuary suite. She had been here so many times over the course of her career that she could make the journey in her sleep. She was buzzed in and made her way along the many rabbit-warren-like corridors to get to the main post-mortem suite. Matilda said hello to the administrative staff she knew and, when she came to the double doors, paused, took a deep breath, and forced herself to relax and smile. It was never a joy to enter a morgue. She pushed the doors open and stepped in.

The first person she saw was Donal Youngblood. Since he and Scott announced their engagement, Scott had moved out of the flat above Matilda's garage, and into a beautiful, but small, two-bedroom house, thanks to a very generous early wedding present from Donal's grandmother, whose recent cancer diagnosis had prompted her to give away her assets while she was still alive. Donal was busy washing down a stainless-steel gurney, the water running from red to clear. He looked up, saw Matilda, and gave her a smile.

'You're going to tell me how many days there are until your wedding, aren't you?' she asked.

'No. Scott said I'm not allowed to do that anymore as I'm starting to annoy people.'

'Starting?'

'Scott said last night that he's asked you to be his best man, or best woman, I suppose.'

'Yes, he has.'

'It means a lot to him.'

'He's been through so much,' Matilda said. 'Listen, Donal, is the new pathologist in?'

'Yes.'

'Who is he? What's he like?'

'Dr Odell Zimmerman. He's really nice. I like him.'

'What's his name?' Matilda asked, frowning.

'Odell Zimmerman,' Donal repeated.

'Odell?'

'Yes.'

'What kind of a name is Odell?'

'It's of English origin,' a voice said behind her.

Matilda's eyes widened. Slowly, she turned around to face the man she supposed to be the new Home Office Pathologist for South Yorkshire, Odell Zimmerman. She felt her face blush with embarrassment.

He continued, 'It means "woad hill". Woad is a flowering plant that was once an important source of blue dye and a treatment for wounds. The name isn't widely used but can be found in England, America, and Canada.'

'Ah' was all Matilda was able to say.

'As for Zimmerman, I'm afraid I haven't a clue. You must be the notorious Detective Chief Inspector Matilda Darke I've heard so much about,' he said, stepping forward and holding out his hand for her to shake.

'I am.' She winced as he gripped her hand almost too hard. 'Sorry about that. I didn't see you there.'

'That's fine. I've been answering questions about my name for as long as I can remember. Darke is an unusual name. Where's that from?'

Matilda hadn't heard a word he'd said. She was struck dumb.

Odell was well over six feet tall with a mass of thick strawberry blond hair, with flecks of grey here and there. He had a firm jawline and was cleanly shaven and gave off a sweet fragrance. He was broad-shouldered and his clothes fitted like a glove, Matilda didn't fail to notice that the seams of his trousers were straining against his muscular legs.

'I'm sorry?' she asked when she realised they were all standing like statues in silence.

'I was enquiring about your name.'

'Oh, yes, you were. I… I've no idea where it comes from. It's not mine.'

'Sorry?'

'Well, I mean it is mine, obviously, but it's my married name. I'm married. Well, I'm not married now. I'm widowed. My husband died. Well, he would have done, wouldn't he, or I wouldn't be a widow,' she said, her words tripping over themselves as she continued to make a fool of herself in front of this impossibly handsome man. 'My birth name is Doyle. It's Irish. My family is from Ireland.'

'I see,' Odell said. He had a confused look on his face, possibly wondering if this jabbering woman in front of him really was a famous DCI. 'So, you wanted to see me?'

'Did I?'

'I don't know, did you?'

'Oh. Yes. Yes, I did. I… Sorry.' She paused, took a breath, and composed herself. 'I want to ask you about a death.'

'My specialist subject,' he said with a smile.

Matilda felt her heart skip a beat. 'It's a closed case. I was wondering if you could answer some questions.'

'Of course. Would you like to step into my office?'

'Sure.'

Odell turned and headed for his office.

'Did I just make a complete tit of myself?' Matilda asked Donal.

'I'm afraid you did.'
'Will you be telling Scott?'
'Of course.' He grinned.
'Shit.'

---

Matilda followed Odell into the office. She stopped dead in the doorway. This was the first time she had been here since Adele left. It felt strange to see someone else sitting on her chair and using her computer. Her calendar of hunky firefighters had gone, as had her mug, and the plush zebra she'd had on the top of her filing cabinet. It felt wrong being in here without her.

'Is everything all right?' Odell asked.

'Yes. Fine,' Matilda said, shaking her head.

'Ah.' The penny dropped. 'You were very close to Adele, weren't you?'

'Did you know her?'

'I did. We met at many a conference over the years. A brilliant woman,' he said with a smile. 'Donal has already told me I have massive shoes to fill. As if I didn't know that when I took the job. Apparently, she liked Marvel films, white wine, and hunky men.'

Matilda softened and, as she pulled out a chair and sat down, she remembered many a night when she and Adele would drunkenly put the world to rights while having an intense debate about who was hotter – Captain America or the Winter Soldier.

'She lived with you, didn't she?' Odell asked.

'She did.'

'It must be strange, being on your own again.'

Matilda didn't know how to answer. It was more than strange. It was … it was painful.

'I'm trying to work out your accent,' she said, rapidly changing the subject.

'I wouldn't. Even I don't know where I'm from.' His face lit up when he smiled, and the twinkle in his eyes danced. 'I'm the son of a British government diplomat and a general in the British Army, who divorced almost as soon as I was born. I spent a great deal of my childhood flying from one part of the world to another to spend time with each parent. When I reached school age, I spent most of the time with my mother and was schooled alongside other children of diplomats. My mum died when I was eight years old so I went to live with my father on an army base in Germany. Then we moved to Greece, then Somalia, then Oman, Gibraltar, back to Germany, on to England for a couple of years, before heading to Canada.'

'Quite the globetrotter.'

'Yes. Unfortunately, it's left me with itchy feet syndrome. I can't seem to settle in one place. The longest I've lived anywhere was Iraq, but that was mostly for work reasons.'

'I'm guessing you're not married with kids then?'

'No. That suggests a stable lifestyle. I don't even have a mortgage. How about you? I know you said you were widowed, but have you any children?'

Matilda swallowed hard. Even now, six years after the death of her husband, it was still difficult for her to talk about anything related to James.

'No. It's just me.'

'A free spirit,' he suggested.

'Hardly. My job takes up a great deal of my time.'

'Don't let work dictate your lifestyle, Matilda. We're not here for a long time, make sure you have a good time whilst you can.'

Matilda found herself smiling. If it wasn't his eyes she was lost in, it was his smooth accent and his confident way with words.

'I'll try to remember that.'

'Make sure you do. Now, about this work-related question.'

'Ah, yes,' she said, suddenly remembering the reason for her visit. 'In September last year, a young man committed suicide by jumping from the Arts Tower, not far from here. I know you weren't here then, but could you have a look at the post-mortem report and check that he did definitely kill himself?'

'Why the doubt?'

'I received an email this morning from someone claiming to have killed him.'

'How would he have killed him?'

'That's what I want you to tell me.'

'Okay.' Odell moved a few folders and books to one side and pulled the wireless keyboard towards him. 'Name?'

'Liam Walsh. William Edgar Walsh.'

Odell brought up the relevant file. He didn't flinch when he opened the photographs file, though Matilda quickly looked away.

'The injuries are consistent with a fall from a height. How tall is this Arts Tower?'

'Now you're asking,' she mused. 'Seventy, seventy-five metres.'

He nodded. 'As I'm sure you know, when a body falls from a height like that it builds up a great deal of speed, thanks to gravity, as it races to the ground. When it lands, it's a massive deceleration and the impact is going to be messy. Here, for example, the primary impact is usually the site of the most severe injury, but in this case, there are two areas that hit the ground at speed. The head and the shoulders. He bounced, or rather ricocheted, very quickly and that's why there are two areas of massive injury.'

'If he jumped, he would have been feet first, wouldn't he?'

'Not necessarily. He could have been sitting on the edge of the building and rolled off.'

Matilda hadn't thought of that. 'Is there a scenario where he might have landed on his feet?'

'Yes, if he was a cat,' he said with a smile. 'Seriously, though, there are many variables here. Did he jump off feet first? Did he roll off? Did he take a running jump? Was he pushed? Was he thrown off? How strongly was the wind blowing? Was he wearing anything that could potentially act as a windbreaker? Did he actually jump from the roof or was it from a floor lower down?'

'So you can't tell if he was pushed or jumped?'

'If he was pushed, there could be bruising on his body from whoever was pushing him. If this Liam Walsh had to be dragged kicking and screaming to the edge of the building and thrown off, whoever was doing it will have had to grab hold of him hard. There will have been evidence of that.'

'Is there?'

Odell looked back at the photographs. He scrolled through them. 'There are no photographs of his back. They're all taken from the front and are detailed close-ups of his head, or rather what's left of his head.'

'Can you see anything suspicious from the autopsy report?'

'No. Toxicology came back clear. He had a couple of units of alcohol in his system. The medication he was prescribed was in his blood, as was expected. There were no trace needle marks or anything untoward on him that suggests foul play.' He looked up at Matilda's blank face. 'I can't tell if I'm telling you what you want to hear.'

'The sender of this email says he killed Liam Walsh, yet everything is pointing to suicide. Do I ignore the email or keep digging into Liam's background?'

'Shouldn't you be asking your boss that question?'

'No.'

'Why not?'

'Because he'll tell me there's no case here and the email writer is cuckoo bananas.'

'And you think there is a case?'

'I'm just wondering why claim an obvious suicide as a murder. I'm sure whoever this guy is could have found other deaths that might have raised a question or two if he was just some random attention seeker.'

'So…' he said, allowing the start of a question to linger.

Matilda looked at him, saw the hopeful smile in his eyes. 'You want to see the email, don't you?'

'I am a tad curious.' The smile in his eyes transferred to his lips and turned into a sly grin.

She shook her head, dug into her inside jacket pocket, and brought out the folded sheet of A4.

He eagerly opened it and read it, his eyes out on stalks. By the time he'd finished, he was pale.

'What's wrong?'

It was a while before he answered. 'I don't know. I felt a chill.'

'Well, we are close to the fridges,' she said, glancing out of the window at the bank of stainless-steel refrigerators.

'No. It just came to me that these could be the words of a killer. I think I've seen every single true crime documentary on Netflix, but this, well, I've never been this close to a killer before. It's chilling.'

'Are you okay?' she asked.

He nodded, folding the sheet of paper and handing it back to her. 'If you and I went to a dinner party and complete strangers asked what we did for a living, they'd all recoil when I told them I was a pathologist. They'd all wonder how I could possibly cut open a person and handle their organs. But what I do is safe. What you're doing … it's something else entirely. This bloke could be a psychopath. And you've got to try and figure him out. To me, that's a hundred times worse than putting your hands into someone's chest cavity and taking out their heart.'

'And on that bright note, I'll be off,' she said, getting up and heading for the door.

'Sorry,' he called after her. 'I didn't mean to…' He stopped himself.

'It's fine,' she said, looking back. 'I can never understand why some people believe some jobs to be exciting. A great deal of my work is writing reports nobody will ever read. Especially at the moment,' she added as an aside. 'I'm sure airline pilots find their job boring from time to time.'

'Matilda.' Odell followed her out of the office. 'I'm relatively new to Sheffield and don't know my way around yet. I drove in this morning and passed the Showroom and saw they're having a season on the great directors. How do you feel about David Lynch?'

'Oh. Well, I enjoyed *Twin Peaks*.'

'They're showing *Blue Velvet* followed by *Mulholland Drive* this Saturday. I don't suppose you fancy accompanying me, do you?'

Matilda could feel herself blushing again.

*Am I being asked out on a date? Why do I feel like I'm fifteen all over again?*

'Erm…'

'You already have plans for Saturday?'

*I don't have any plans full stop.*

'No. Not that I'm aware of.' She was trying to sound coy but in her head she sounded ridiculous.

'Great. It starts at eight. We could have a bite to eat somewhere first. Do you know anywhere good?'

Matilda pulled a face. Sheffield was doing considerably worse than other major cities in the aftermath of the pandemic. Many shops and restaurants had closed down and the council was putting the city through a mass regeneration project. There were huge building works going on everywhere. Footfall had dropped; independent eateries and shops couldn't withstand the loss of trade and had closed. The whole of the city centre looked like the plug had been pulled long ago. Where was there anywhere good to eat in Sheffield that wasn't fast food? Matilda couldn't think of anywhere off the top of her head.

'We could grab some food in the Showroom, if you like?'

'Excellent. It's a date.'

'It certainly is.'

She turned away and headed for the doors. She wouldn't have

been able to erase the smile from her face with wire wool and a bottle of acid. Although seeing Donal giving her a knowing grin made her face fall.

'You heard all that, didn't you?'

'I may have done.'

'Were you earwigging?'

'Possibly. So, you're going on a date,' he teased.

'One word to anyone and your wedding in one hundred and fifty-nine days' time will be a funeral.'

'Ouch,' he said as he took a step back.

## Chapter Eight

The silence in the living room of the Klein household was deafening. The atmosphere was heavy and oppressive. Tom Simpson had tried to make conversation with Cara and Derek, but their monosyllabic answers soon caused him to run out of chatter, and the lack of news regarding the whereabouts of their daughter was frightening.

Cara was sitting on the sofa, squeezed up to the end, constantly sniffling and wiping her eyes. Her shoulders were hunched up around her ears, her entire body tense with worry and fear of the unknown. Derek, in contrast, was on the armchair, a whole world away from his wife. He was staring into the distance, his face blank, unreadable.

Derek leaned forward in his seat, took his iPhone out of his back pocket, and looked at the display.

'It's work. I'll take it in the kitchen,' he said, standing up and hurrying out of the room.

He had the phone on silent.

Derek went into the kitchen, closed the door behind him, and crossed the chessboard-tiled flooring to the far end of the room, close to the double doors leading to a long and narrow back garden. He swiped to answer.

'Is there any news?' The caller asked straightaway. No hello. No friendly greeting.

'No. Nothing,' Derek replied, his voice barely above a whisper.

'What's happening?'

'I can't talk. The police are here.'

'They've interviewed me. I had to give a statement.'

'What did you say?'

'They asked when was the last time I saw Natasha and how she was.'

'And?' Derek asked urgently when the caller didn't elaborate.

'I just said she was the same as she always was. Which she was. I didn't lie.'

'Did you mention anything else?'

'Of course I didn't. The police asked me about her home life.'

Derek turned and looked back at the kitchen door. It was still closed. 'Go on.'

'I didn't say anything. There was nothing I could say. I said how you and Cara are lovely people, good parents, you're very proud of her. I just... I did the right thing, didn't I?'

'Yes. Yes, you did.'

There was a long and awkward silence.

'They asked where I was when Natasha went missing,' the caller eventually said. 'Did they ask you?'

'Yes. Unfortunately, I can't tell them thanks to you bloody cancelling.'

'I told you why.'

'I know.'

'Did you see Natasha on Thursday?'

'No.'

'She said she was going straight home.'

'I didn't see her, all right?' He tried his best not to shout, but he was struggling to rein in his emotions.

'Did she speak to you? Did she mention anything about—'

'I've got to go,' Derek interrupted, ending the call before anything else could be said.

He turned around and saw Cara standing in the open doorway.

'Who was that?' she asked.

'Jason. From work. He wanted to know how we were doing.'

'Oh. That was nice of him.'

'Yes. He's a good bloke.'

'Derek, I'm scared,' Cara said, on the verge of more tears. 'Something's happened to her. I know it has. She's a beautiful girl. What if … what if she's been…?' She couldn't finish her sentence; her emotions wouldn't allow it.

Derek went towards her and placed his arms around her. He pressed her head against his chest. He couldn't remember the last time he'd held Cara so close. The smell of her shampoo was almost alien. He found himself relaxing with his wife needing him so much. Finally. Would this tragedy bring them closer together? Maybe. Maybe it was too late. Only time would tell.

'Are you both OK?' DC Tom Simpson asked, coming out of the living room.

Derek wrapped his arms tighter around Cara, pulling her closer into his body in a protective cocoon. He looked at the young detective over his wife's head and proffered a sympathetic smile.

'We'll be fine,' he said in his best soothing tone.

'We need to get to the station for the appeal.'

Derek looked away from Tom, burying his face in Cara's shoulder so the detective couldn't see his expression.

A statement had been prepared for Cara Klein to read out in front of a roomful of journalists. Cara kept asking in the car on the way over if Derek could read it, but Tom told her the public always preferred to hear from the mother. More weight was given to the appeal if an emotional, tearful woman made a plea for her daughter's safe return.

The media liaison officer was preparing Cara and Derek one final time while Christian took Tom to one side.

'Derek's alibi?' Christian asked. His voice was quiet, and he was looking over his shoulder at the father who didn't seem to be paying any attention to the media officer.

'He says he was at home on his own. He made no phone calls or anything. He just sat and relaxed.'

'Do you believe him?'

'No,' Tom answered firmly.

'Why not?'

'Because Cara doesn't believe him. And she should know.'

'Did she tell you she didn't believe him?'

'Not in as many words. You can tell by her look, and how she's acting towards him.'

'Cara's definitely reading the statement, isn't she?'

'Yes. She doesn't want to, though.'

'Who would? Look, you go out there with them and sit by Cara. She's going to find this very difficult and I'm struggling to believe Derek is going to offer any support. You need to jump in if he doesn't. Finn's at the back of the room. Hopefully he'll be able to see if Derek is behaving suspiciously. We've also got our own cameras rigged up so we can watch the whole thing back afterwards.'

Tom nodded, turned, and saw that the Kleins were ready to walk out onto the platform to tell the world to look for their daughter. He gave them a sympathetic smile. Cara returned one. Derek remained expressionless.

Christian pulled back the curtain and the media liaison officer led the way, followed by Derek and Cara with Tom bringing up the rear. The cameras from the sea of reporters immediately started flashing. On the large screen behind the table was a photograph of Natasha Klein. The teenager was smiling broadly, a picture of happiness. She was a beautiful young woman, very photogenic. The press would get a kick out of plastering her face on their front pages tomorrow.

The press liaison officer made the introductions and the room fell silent as all eyes turned to Cara Klein.

She didn't move.

Tom leaned to her and whispered that she was to begin.

She picked up the paper in front of her. The statement had been printed in a large font to make it easy to read. Her hands were shaking. Her entire body was shaking. She didn't look up at the expectant faces of the reporters glaring at her but concentrated on the text. She spoke, but her voice was low. Tom reached for the microphone and pulled it closer to her. He whispered for her to speak a little louder.

Cara cleared her throat and started again. 'My name is Cara Klein. My daughter, Natasha, is nineteen years old. On Thursday afternoon she left the Olive Grove campus of Sheffield College at three-thirty and hasn't been seen since. Natasha, like any other teenager, seems to be permanently attached to her mobile. As it was found by the side of the road by a member of the public on Saturday morning, we can only assume that Natasha has not gone anywhere of her own free will. Na—' Cara broke down. 'Sorry,' she said, putting a hand to her mouth.

'Take your time,' Tom said, leaning over to her.

Derek remained seated next to his wife, a chasm between them. He was sitting on his hands and staring straight into the distance.

'Natasha has type 1 diabetes. She carries an insulin pen with her and requires injections two, sometimes three times a day. If someone is watching this and you've taken her, please, please, make sure she receives her injections.' Cara paused. It was written on the statement for her to pause here. She looked at Tom, who nodded, telling her to continue. She wiped her eyes with the back of her hand. 'Natasha is a bright, happy, intelligent young woman. She's always smiling, always chatting, and making us laugh. The house isn't the same without her and we need her back home. If … if you've taken her, please…' Cara paused. 'Please…' She tried to speak again but her words were lost in her tears.

'Derek, perhaps you could finish the statement,' Tom said.

Derek looked at him. 'Me?'

Tom put his arm around Cara, something he felt Derek should be doing. Derek nodded towards his wife who was crumpled against the detective for comfort.

'Oh. Of course.' He reached for the paper and spent a while trying to find where Cara had finished. He cleared his throat. 'If you've taken her, please call the police and tell us what you want, tell us that she is safe. If you've seen her, or know where she is, please, call 999 and tell the police. We need Natasha found and brought home as soon as possible. She's our only child and we miss her.' He looked up at the room of reporters watching him. 'Thank you.'

---

At the side of the room, behind the curtain, Christian and Sian were looking on.

'My God, I've heard the shipping forecast read with more emotion,' Christian said.

Sian was looking out towards the journalists. 'They're going to tear Derek apart in the papers. They're not going to be focusing on Natasha at all.'

'Oh, bloody hell, look at this,' he said.

The appeal was over. Derek stood up from the table and made his way to the curtain, leaving Tom to practically carry Cara. The whole room lit up with the cameras' flashing lights as they captured a husband leaving his distraught wife to be comforted by a police officer.

'Goodness. That was something different, wasn't it? I think I felt every pair of eyes burning into me,' Derek said as he stepped through the curtain and unfastened the top button of his shirt. 'Is there any chance I can get a coffee?' he asked Sian.

## Chapter Nine

It wasn't easy for the administrative staff at Sheffield Hallam University to track down the student wellbeing adviser, Jamie Peterson. Finn had rushed from the press appeal to the university before Christian could collar him. He was kept waiting in the large reception area for more than twenty minutes until someone found the counsellor, and then he was with a student, so Finn had to wait even longer before he turned up. Still, it gave him time to jot down some notes about the appeal made by the Kleins.

Jamie Peterson was a tall man, painfully thin, with a receding hairline and an unruly tangle of mousy hair. He wore dark red corded trousers that looked as if they'd had an argument with his shoes as they were well above the ankle, revealing colourful Argyle socks. His white shirt was untucked from his trousers and his jacket seemed too big for him at the shoulders, yet the sleeves finished before they reached the wrists. He gave the impression of a clumsily put together human being. Finn hoped his mind was sharper than his appearance.

'I've been told you wish to see me,' he said to Finn in a hushed tone. His accent was local.

Finn stood up and showed his ID card.

'DS Finn Cotton, South Yorkshire Police. I understand you were acquainted with Liam Walsh while he was studying here.'

Jamie's face fell. He bowed his head. If it was possible, his pale skin took on an even lighter hue.

'Yes. I must confess I'm still coming to terms with his death. It was my first suicide.'

'Would it be possible to talk to you about Liam? Somewhere quiet?'

'Of course. Follow me.'

Jamie led Finn along a complicated maze of corridors to his office. It was small but cosy and presented a relaxed atmosphere. There was a bookcase with a few paperbacks, a couple of framed pictures of generic landscapes, a cheap vase of wax flowers, and a view from the window of the sprawling city; a sliver of countryside just visible through the throng of high-rise buildings.

Jamie sat in an armchair, his back to the window. Finn was instructed to sit on the three-seat sofa, pointing towards the window. He wondered how deliberately the room had been laid out to make students feel comfortable when talking through their issues. Gazing out of the window on a clear and sunny day like today might help them to open up, but what about when it was grey, cold and pissing it down with rain, which was the norm for a city in the north of England? He wondered if then the blind was lowered to reveal a sunny Hawaiian beach.

'Mr Peterson,' Finn began.

'Jamie. Please.' He smiled.

'Jamie. How often did you see Liam?'

'Many times. He had a regular appointment with me.'

'We know he suffered with depression and was taking medication. What was the cause of his depression?'

'He struggled with the world, and his place in it. He often commented that he was born a hundred years too late. Everything was moving too quickly for him. Everything was too loud and too much. He struggled to focus on things against the backdrop of twenty-first-century life.'

'That's incredibly sad,' Finn said.

'It is,' Jamie agreed. 'He was a deeply unhappy young man.'

'Did he have many friends?'

'I kept asking him to focus on the positives in his life, the things that he found joy in. Unfortunately, that wasn't people. He said he was only truly happy when he was alone with a good book and when he was surrounded by silence. He was content with silence.'

'Apart from you, was there anyone he could confide in?'

'He said not. His father died when he was a child. I asked if he was close to his mother, and he said he wasn't. He struggled to tell her about his depression.'

'But he did tell her?'

'Eventually. I told him that he needed to tell her. It would help to speak to someone close about it. I'm afraid it didn't have the effect I had hoped for.'

'What do you mean?'

'His mother, Helen, she wasn't receptive to Liam's illness. She struggled to understand why someone starting out in life, who spent their days reading books and examining literature, should be depressed.'

'Did you speak to her?' Finn asked.

'No. I offered to. Liam was adamant that he didn't want me to talk to her.'

'Did you attend his funeral?'

'I did. I gave my condolences to his mother. She thanked me for trying to help her son,' Jamie said, a catch in his throat. He turned his head away and looked out of the window.

Finn cleared his throat. 'Did Liam ever talk to you about taking his own life?'

It was a while before Jamie replied. His gaze was fixed on the view. Finn wondered if he'd even heard his question.

'It was me who first brought it up,' Jamie said. 'I needed to know if he'd ever thought of harming himself or ending his life. We have procedures in place if a student is considering it.'

'What did Liam say?'

Jamie swallowed hard. 'He said he wanted to kill himself, but he couldn't.'

'Why not?'

'He was terrified of dying alone. He said it was a paradox that as much as he disliked being around people he didn't actually want to be on his own at the end.'

'He used the word paradox?' Finn asked.

Jamie frowned, confused by the change in questioning. 'Erm… I… Yes, actually, I think he did. Is that significant?'

'No. Did Liam mention suicide often?'

'Yes. I'm afraid he did. He physically hated waking up in the morning and willed himself to die in his sleep. He was in constant torment twenty-four hours a day. He really did want to die.'

'When you first heard of his death, what did you think?'

Jamie took a deep breath. 'I was incredibly sad that I'd been unable to help him. I've never had someone kill themselves before. I'm afraid it shook me terribly. It was a couple of days before I was able to see it from Liam's point of view. I knew he was no longer in pain. He was very unhappy, and nothing was going to change that. I believe he felt he had no alternative.'

'Yet Liam told you he was afraid of dying alone.'

'Yes. I simply assumed he'd talked himself into it. You… Sorry, I've just realised. Why are you asking me all this about Liam? He died in September. The inquest is over with. Why are you bringing this up again now?'

'We've received information that Liam's death might not be as it appeared on the surface. We're simply looking into it before making a more formal decision,' Finn said, struggling to find the correct words without giving too much away. That last thing he wanted was to suggest that a psychopathic serial killer might be roaming the streets of Sheffield.

'You think someone killed Liam, that he didn't kill himself?'

There was a hint of hope in Jamie's eyes. He was clearly still beating himself up about his inability to save the young man's life. If Liam was murdered, Jamie would surely sleep better at night.

'I can't say any more at the moment. We're simply just checking the information we've received. Nothing may come of it.'

'Oh. I see.'

'Is there anything more you can tell me about Liam, Jamie?' Finn asked. 'Is there anyone he would have spoken to about ending his life?'

Jamie seemed to think for a long time. He turned back to the window as if the answer to Finn's question was written on the Sheffield skyline. Slowly, he turned back to the detective.

'No,' he said, firmly.

Finn didn't say anything. He had the dark feeling that Jamie might know more about Liam's death than he was letting on. They'd had many sessions together, many conversations in which Jamie was unable to help Liam with his deeply rooted mental illness. If he saw no way out of his depression, would he help him with ending it? Finn thought of this while he studied the student wellbeing officer. He couldn't tell from simply looking at him, though the fact that Jamie was unable to meet his gaze told him more than words could.

## Chapter Ten

Matilda sat in her car in the car park of the Medico-Legal Centre, unsure what she should do next. She knew what she *wanted* to do next but whether that was the right thing, or the moral thing, was anyone's guess. She could feel the folded copy of the email burning against her skin in her inside jacket pocket.

'Screw it!' she said to herself, as she started the engine and used voice control on her mobile to phone Zofia.

Zofia obviously answered the phone without checking the display first as Matilda heard, '…chuck us that Curly Wurly' followed by 'HMCU DC Nowak.'

'I hope you'll be replacing that Curly Wurly before Sian gets back,' Matilda said.

'Shit. I mean … oh God, did you hear that?'

'I certainly did. Your secret is safe with me on one proviso.'

'Go on,' she said, tentatively.

'Without telling anyone, can you find out the address for Liam Walsh's mother and text it to me?'

'I've already looked it up. I had a feeling you'd want to pay her a visit. I've got it on a Post-It here. I'll text it to you.'

'I'm all for efficiency, but there's something quite creepy about someone knowing my plans before I make them myself.'

'Call it female intuition.'

'That'll scare the men in the office.' Matilda looked at her phone. 'It's just come through, thanks.'

She ended the call and stole a quick look at the text as she pulled up at a red traffic light. Liam Walsh's mother Helen lived in Elsecar, in Barnsley. It would take a good half an hour to get there, giving her plenty of time to come up with something to say to Helen Walsh that wouldn't sound alarming or add to the pain she would still be coming to terms with.

Helen lived in a detached stone-built property on Armroyd Lane with a private front garden and driveway. Matilda parked a few doors up and walked back to the house. She still didn't have a clue how to approach the subject of her son's death and how to phrase the questions she wanted to ask. She wished Sian was with her. As a mother, she would know exactly the right words to use.

Matilda rang the doorbell, stood back, and looked up at the double-fronted house. It was a stunning building, and well maintained. The garden was looking a bit windswept, but it was still early spring and, after a harsh winter, everyone's gardens were just beginning to come to life again.

The door was opened by a woman Matilda estimated to be in her mid-forties. She wore a floor-length black skirt and a white roll-neck jumper. Her hair, dyed a deep red, was pulled back tightly into a painful-looking bun. She wasn't wearing any make-up and when she smiled at her visitor it was merely out of politeness. This woman had nothing to smile about. The grief was still raw.

'Mrs Walsh?' Matilda asked. 'My name is Detective Chief Inspector Matilda Darke,' she said, taking out her ID card and showing it to her. 'I'm with South Yorkshire Police. I was wondering if I could have a word with you.'

'What about?' she asked, firmly gripping the front door and

pulling it towards her slightly, barring Matilda's view of the rest of the house.

'It's about your son.'

'Liam?'

'Yes.'

'What about him?'

'Would it be possible for me to come inside?'

Helen seemed to think for a moment. She took a deep breath, nodded, then stood back, opening the door for Matilda to enter. She showed her into the living room, a huge expanse of space with two large and comfortable-looking sofas, a couple of matching armchairs, and coffee tables of various sizes. The room was tastefully decorated in muted pastel colours but there was an underlying fustiness about the place, a stale smell in the air. This room wasn't used much.

'Can I get you a tea or coffee?'

'I'd love a coffee, thanks,' Matilda said.

'I'll just go and make a pot,' she said, hesitantly. 'Take a seat. I won't be long.'

Matilda took the opportunity to have a look around the room. The rear window looked out onto a sprawling back garden. On a dresser in the corner of the room were several framed photographs, all of Liam at various stages in his life. As a child, playing in a field, or sitting precariously on a donkey on the beach, he was grinning from ear to ear, the embodiment of happiness. As he grew up, the smile seemed to shrink. Even the school portraits he posed for looked sad. She picked one up with both hands and looked deep into Liam's eyes. He couldn't have been more than fourteen or fifteen when it was taken. He was looking into the camera, smartly dressed in his uniform blazer, shirt and tie. His hair was neat, his skin clean and clear. His lips were smiling, but there was a deep sadness in his eyes.

'That's one of my favourite photographs of Liam,' Helen said.

Matilda jumped, turned, and saw Helen standing in the

doorway holding a tray with a full cafetière and two matching mugs.

'Sorry. I…'

'It's okay. There are photos of Liam all over the house.' She placed the tray on the coffee table between the two sofas and sat down. 'His presence is fading. I don't get his smell anymore. It's nice to have his pictures looking at me.'

Matilda turned. There was a framed newspaper article on the back wall. On closer inspection, she saw the main photo, taking up half the page, was of Liam chained to a tree. The look on his face was one of pure emotion. He wasn't posed. He wasn't struggling to smile in a supposed relaxed environment. He was genuine.

'I was so proud of Liam there,' Helen said.

Matilda stole a glance at her. There was the real warmth of a loving mother in her face as she looked at her son in print.

'He protested a lot when Sheffield council started cutting down all those healthy trees. He was arrested shortly after that photograph was taken.' Helen quickly turned away to hide her tears. Seeing her son, so passionate, so full of life, transformed due to a mental illness was difficult for her.

Matilda sat on the opposite sofa and watched as the grieving mother poured the coffee.

'My husband died in 2015,' Matilda found herself saying. 'We hadn't been married long. His illness was sudden and by the time I could get my head around it he was gone. He was an architect, and he built the house we lived in. I saw him in every room I went in. It was comforting, at first.'

'At first?' Helen asked, looking up at her.

Matilda decided not to tell her about her rival at work hating her so much he decided to hang himself in her hallway to destroy the home she loved so much.

'I wasn't moving on,' she said, which was partly true. 'I needed to say goodbye to him. I had to move.'

'I've no intention of moving.' Helen said, an iciness to her voice. 'Help yourself to cream and sugar.'

Matilda picked up the coffee mug. She drank it black. The aroma was strong.

'Why do you want to talk about Liam? Has something happened?'

Matilda took a deep breath. She decided not to lie to Helen. She deserved the truth. 'I really am sorry for having to say this to you, but I received an anonymous email this morning from someone claiming to have killed five people. One of them is your son.'

Helen looked bewildered. 'Liam killed himself.'

Matilda nodded. 'I've read the police report and the coroner's report and I've seen the post-mortem report, too. Everything points to Liam taking his own life. What I can't get my head around is why someone would claim such an obvious suicide to be murder.'

Helen frowned as she thought. 'I can understand that. Can I see the email?'

There was no reason why Matilda shouldn't show it to her. She took it out of her pocket and handed it over.

Helen's face was unreadable as she scanned it. She handed it back to Matilda without a word.

'Would you like to see Liam's note he left me?'

'Please.'

Helen left the room, returning barely a minute later with a cream envelope in her hands. She handed it to Matilda. The single word 'Mum' was written in faint, neat handwriting in the centre.

*Dear Mum,*

*This is the hardest thing I've ever had to write. I'm so sorry that I'm going to be putting you through so much pain, but I literally cannot go on living like this. Every morning I wake up and I hate the fact that I've survived through the night and have to face another day. Everywhere I look there's suffering, anguish, greed, anger, selfishness, and heartache. Societies are crumbling. Nobody cares about anything but themselves anymore. Politicians don't care for their constituents or their country. They're looking to line their own pockets and further their careers for when they're eventually caught out by their own ineptitude. There are too many people living on this planet. We've evolved too far, too fast. We're killing our home. Wildlife that has survived since the dinosaurs is suffering because we're raping the world of its natural elements. Over the next eighty years we are going to lose half the species on our planet through human behaviour. The last time there was an extinction level event on that scale was sixty-five million years ago when the dinosaurs were wiped out. That was a natural disaster. This is all man-made. I don't want to be part of a world that will see so much destruction just so we can have more choice of things we don't really need.*

*I'm sorry to do this to you, Mum. I've tried talking to so many people about how I'm feeling, but nobody seems to understand. Nobody gets it.*

*Don't blame yourself and don't be sad. You've been an amazing mum. You've brought me up on your own, been both parents to me. I couldn't have asked for a better childhood.*

*I love you. I'll always love you.*

*Liam xxx*

Matilda was crying. She could feel the torment leaching out of the page, the pain in every word written. She carefully folded the letter and placed it back in the envelope. She passed it back to Helen.

'I dismissed him,' Helen said, wiping away her own tears. 'A few months before he died, he sat me down and told me that he'd been diagnosed with depression, that he was on medication and having regular therapy sessions with a counsellor at the university. I told him he was just struggling to adjust to adult life. I said it wasn't depression, it was just growing up. Looking back

… looking back further than that conversation, I could see what it was. It's what everyone Liam's age is going through. They have too much information at their fingertips and too many opinions being thrown at them on social media. I don't know about Covid being a pandemic, but that's what's happening to the next generation. Mental health is a serious concern. It's a silent killer.'

Matilda swallowed her emotion. She could feel the sadness and guilt radiating from Helen. She obviously blamed herself and wished she could go back in time and reach out to her son.

'Helen, in light of the email I received, I have to ask, is this definitely Liam's handwriting?'

She nodded. 'Absolutely. I've saved all the birthday and Mother's Day cards he sent me. You can have them compared if you like, but there's no denying it's Liam's writing. I don't know who this individual is who sent you that email, but Liam definitely killed himself.'

Matilda nodded. She was more confused now than ever. She remained still on the sofa, cup of coffee in hand, confusion on her face.

'Liam was incredibly sensitive to everything that was wrong with the world,' Helen said after a long silence. 'Just going around the supermarket with him was a nightmare in itself. He had a huge bee in his bonnet about KitKats.'

'KitKats?'

'Did you know there are more than three hundred different flavours of KitKat around the world?'

'No.'

'I didn't either. Until Liam told me. KitKats were first launched in 1935. It wasn't until the 1990s that a second flavour was introduced, the orange KitKat. Within twenty years, more than three hundred flavours were created. Then you've got the two-fingered KitKat, the Chunky, KitKat Bites. I even saw a KitKat cereal in the Co-op the other day. H spoke, very determinedly, about how many ingredients and how much energy were used to make all these different varieties, and how much carbon from the factories was being put into the atmosphere, how much packaging was used then wasted. Then he went on to other products, shampoos and cereals and breads. Did you know there are more than fifteen varieties of Head and Shoulders shampoo alone?'

'No.'

'Me neither. All that choice. All that packaging. All those ingredients and the carbon emissions and the wastage. It was really killing Liam. He cared about everything too much. I kept telling him that he shouldn't allow it to eat away at him, but he couldn't. He said that if KitKat, for example, simply went back to just one variety of product, they would still sell successfully and might even increase profits by not needing such massive overheads to create all the varieties. He was consumed with trying to save the planet, but he saw corruption and profit and greed everywhere. He knew he was fighting a losing battle. He didn't want to be a part of it.'

Matilda couldn't think of anything to say.

'I think I always knew he would end up taking his own life. Every time I looked at him, I saw the unhappiness oozing out of him. He could never relax, not even on happy occasions like Christmas and birthdays.'

'Helen, has anyone contacted you since Liam's death, anyone you don't know?'

'A few people from the university came round. I spoke with the counsellor; can't recall his name. I had so many sympathy cards,' she said, a faint smile on her lips.

'Any from people you didn't know or any that stood out as being ... I don't know, strange in some way?'

'Not that I'm aware of. I've saved them all. You're welcome to look at them.'

'Please.'

Helen stood up and went over to the sideboard. She opened a

cupboard and took out a shoebox. She handed it to Matilda then went back to the sofa.

Matilda removed the lid. The box was full, all of the cards in muted pale colours showing flowers, doves, and butterflies, or cartoon bears hugging. Matilda had received a great many of these herself when James died. She hadn't saved them all in a shoebox to take out and look at. After the funeral, she'd thrown them all in the bin.

'I should have done more, shouldn't I?' Helen asked. Matilda looked up and saw tears streaming down her face. 'He was my only son. I should have been aware of what was going through his mind. I should have tried to do something.'

'I'm not sure what you could have done, Helen. Even if you'd moved away, left the country, the issues that were causing Liam so much angst would be there on the news, on social media. You can't blame yourself.'

Helen gave her a shaky smile. She placed her cup on the coffee table, said, 'Excuse me' and left the room. As Matilda returned to looking at the cards, she could hear Helen sobbing from the downstairs toilet.

Matilda lifted up one card that caught her eye. It looked handmade. A pencil drawing of a dinosaur looking sad, a tear falling from its eye as the asteroid came hurtling towards it. Beneath the picture it simply said, 'I'm so sorry.' Matilda opened it. The message, in the same hand, said, 'Thinking of you', and was signed by Dorothy Arnold. In the top corner of the card was written '1 of 5', the same as the subject line in the email she received.

'I'm sorry about that,' Helen said, coming back into the living room.

'Who's Dorothy Arnold?' Matilda asked, holding up the card.

Helen took it from her and read it. She looked at the picture, then back at the message. 'I've no idea. I assumed it was someone from the university.'

'In the top corner, it says "1 of 5". Does that mean anything to you?'

'I hadn't noticed that. No, I don't think so. Why?'

'Can I keep hold of this?'

'Why? What is it?' Helen asked, wrapping her arms around her, holding herself tight.

'I'm not sure. I'm hoping I'm just being paranoid.'

'But you think it might be something, don't you?'

'I'd rather not say right now,' Matilda said. She put the card into her bag and stood up. 'I'll be in touch.'

She made her way out of the living room and headed for the front door.

'You don't think Liam killed himself, do you?' Helen called out after her.

Matilda stopped, one hand on the door handle. She turned and looked back at the woman still grieving heavily for her son. There was nothing she could say to make her feel any better.

'You think he was murdered, don't you?' Helen asked, wiping the tears away.

Reluctantly, Matilda nodded.

## Chapter Eleven

As Matilda drove back to South Yorkshire Police HQ in Sheffield she went through the conversation with Helen Walsh in her mind. The facts seemed clear. Liam had written a suicide note to his mother, which she found on the morning after he'd taken his own life. The evidence was irrefutable that he'd died by his own hand. Yet the sympathy card containing a similar message to the one Matilda had received via email was also an indisputable fact, one she couldn't ignore. There seemed to be someone standing on the outside of all this who was creating a very dangerous game of playing with people's lives and emotions.

She pushed open the door to her office and found Finn and Zofia inside waiting for her.

'What are you doing here?' she asked. 'If Christian finds out you're skiving, he'll go ape.'

'We're having a late lunch,' Finn said.

'Very late lunch,' Zofia added under her breath.

'By the way, did you know the canteen is closing? We're starting up a petition.'

'Yes. I'm aware. I'll sign it, but I don't think it will do any good. How are you and Tom getting on now you're living together?' Matilda asked Zofia, eager to change the subject from budget cuts.

'We're getting on great. It's brilliant,' she said with a huge grin on her face.

'I'm glad. Oh, how did the press appeal for Natasha Klein go?' Matilda asked, suddenly remembering.

'You don't want to know,' Zofia said.

'Unfortunately, I have to. It's kind of my job,' Matilda replied mockingly.

'It's trending on social media for all the wrong reasons. The Twitterati have practically got Derek hung, drawn, and quartered,' she said.

'Why? What did he do?'

'What didn't he do, you mean,' Finn said. 'He had to take over the statement from Cara as she fell apart. He was so robotic. It was like listening to an appeal from C3PO.'

'And if you're not crying over your missing daughter, the public immediately assume you're guilty,' Matilda guessed.

'Got it in one.'

'Jesus. Anyway, I'm guessing you didn't just decide to use my office as a canteen alternative.'

'No. Zofia has been doing things on the computer I didn't think were possible,' Finn said.

'That sounds like a sentence that could lead to an arrest warrant. Do I really want to hear this?

'You really do. I've done some digging,' Zofia said. 'As part of the coroner's investigations, there was a full assessment of Liam's state of mind, especially in the days leading up to his death. Now, on the night in question, Liam is caught three times on CCTV footage heading towards the Arts Tower.' She turned her laptop around so it was facing Matilda at an angle and started the footage. 'As you can see, he is walking from a pub on West Street to the Arts Tower. Now, I've been onto the two pubs where Liam was picked up on their footage and it's since been wiped. They can't keep these things for ever, obviously. However, when Liam is picked up a third time out of the city centre, he's captured by a private house. I've called the owner, and his footage is saved in the cloud for a year before it's automatically erased. He's emailed it over and I've watched the footage. Now, I'm going to play you the video.'

They both watched as the black and white silent film played out. The angle was from above the front door of the house, aimed primarily at the pavement and road. Cars were briefly captured driving at speed, headlights shining in the camera lens. Eventually, Liam Walsh entered the screen from the right. He had his hands deep in his pockets. His head was slightly down, and he walked with a slow, heavy gait.

'Bless him,' Matilda said, almost to herself.

Liam disappeared from view, yet the footage continued.

'What are we waiting for?' Matilda asked.

'Just keep watching,' Zofia instructed.

A few minutes later, a second figure entered the shot. He was wearing skinny jeans and an oversized hoodie with the hood pulled up. He had his head down and was strolling at a similar pace to Liam. He disappeared in the same direction as Liam. Zofia stopped the film.

They both turned to look at Zofia to explain what they hadn't seen.

She split her screen and brought up one of the other photographs of Liam Walsh.

'If you look in the background of Liam leaving West Street, you can see a blurred image of a figure in a hooded sweater. It's the same figure following him on Bolsover Road.'

'How the hell can you tell that?' Matilda asked.

Zofia cleared her throat. 'Okay, this gets quite technical, but stay with me. I've got a program on my computer that can calculate the height and weight of a person by taking in the surrounding areas. It uses the height of buildings and width of roads and pavements and the angle of the camera to pinpoint where the figure would measure up. Also, using stride patterns and shoulder width, et cetera, I can tell you, with a high degree of accuracy, that this figure in the photo is the same one as in the footage on Bolsover Road.'

'Liam was being followed?' Matilda asked.

'Playing devil's advocate, they could simply be walking in the same direction,' Zofia said. 'However, given the email we've received, it's something that stands out.'

'Can we get a clearer image of him?' Matilda asked.

'No. The photo of him in the background is too blurred. All I'd get is clearer pixels. In the video, I've zoomed in as much as I can and all I can see is the top of his head. You can't make out any features at all. He's even got his hands in his pockets. I can't see skin colour.'

'Is there any way we can identify him?' Matilda asked.

Zofia shook her head. 'I'm sorry. All I can give you is a close estimate of his height and weight.'

Matilda took the sympathy card from her bag and placed it on the desk. 'Helen Walsh, Liam's mother, received this shortly after his death. Look in the corner. One of five.'

'Jesus,' Finn said. 'He sent a card to his victim's mother? That's dark.'

'Did the Zodiac killer ever do that?'

'I don't think so.'

'Who's Dorothy Arnold?' Zofia asked.

'I've no idea. Helen Walsh doesn't know anyone by that name either.'

Zofia turned her laptop back around to herself and began tapping in her usual frantic way, fingers a blur.

'This is real then, isn't it?' Finn asked Matilda, looking serious. 'He wormed his way into Liam's life, knowing he was depressed and on the verge of suicide, and used it to his advantage to kill him and get away with it.'

'It's beginning to look that way.'

'That really is sick,' he said, disgusted. 'So, who knew he was depressed apart from his mother and the counsellor at the university?'

'That's what we need to find out.'

'I've found a couple of Dorothy Arnolds,' Zofia said. 'There was an actress in the 1940s and 50s who was the first wife of Joe DiMaggio. She died in 1984 at the age of sixty-six. There's another who was a socialite and heiress who disappeared under mysterious circumstances in New York in 1910 at the age of twenty-five. She was declared dead in absentia.'

'I doubt it's either of them,' Finn said.

'The socialite who disappeared,' Matilda began. 'Any suspicions or theories?'

'A few actually. Hang on,' she said as she quickly read. 'Her father initially thought she'd been kidnapped and murdered, many of her friends thought she committed suicide due to a failed writing career, there was also a rumour that she'd died in a botched abortion, and five years after her disappearance a convicted felon claimed he had been paid to bury her body, though he later denied it.'

'Oh,' Matilda said.

'What?'

'I was just wondering if this Dorothy Arnold's case mirrored Liam's, but it doesn't.'

'The case is still unsolved more than one hundred years later,' Zofia said. 'Nobody knows what happened to her. There are just a bunch of theories and rumours.'

'Did you see Liam's suicide note? Was it handwritten?' Finn asked.

'Yes. And the writing was Liam's. Also, there was no way Liam could have been forced to have written that. It was incredibly heartfelt. It even had me crying,' Matilda said. 'I think we were right when we said this is someone who managed to get so close to Liam that they knew he was planning to kill himself and took advantage of that.'

'A fellow student?' Zofia offered.

'His counsellor?' Finn asked.

'You spoke to him, Finn, you tell me.' Matilda looked at her watch. The working day was almost over. 'First thing tomorrow, Finn, I want you to bring the counsellor here to question him formally. Zofia, trawl through Liam's social media accounts. See who he had contact with on a regular basis and who commented on his posts.'

'I've already made a start. He wasn't a prolific social media user and didn't have many followers. He used Instagram mostly. He posted photos he'd taken of landscapes around Sheffield. He was very good actually. He had a keen eye. I'll keep looking though.'

'Thank you. Both of you. You've done amazing work on this. Now, go on, back to the HMCU before Christian comes barging in and seriously kicks off.'

Once they'd left, Matilda returned to her seat and sat down. The email from the killer was still on her laptop screen.

'I can't make my mind up yet whether you're genuine or a complete fruit loop. But I'll find you, and one way or another, I'll make you wish you'd never heard my name.'

## Chapter Twelve

Chief Constable Ridley looked more than ready to be going home. His jacket was hanging over the back of his chair, his tie was missing and the top couple of buttons of his shirt were undone. His sleeves were rolled up and the bags beneath his eyes seemed to have grown bigger since Matilda saw him this morning.

'Can I have a word?' she asked as she approached his desk.

'As long as it's not about money. I've had enough of funding and budgets to last me a lifetime and I've still got two more Zoom meetings to do today.'

'Do you want me to come back?'

'No. It would be nice to have a conversation about what policing really is all about rather than charts and costings. Have a seat.'

Matilda sat down.

He glanced at his computer screen. 'Oh, piss off.'

'Problem?'

'Another email with the subject heading of Derek Klein. Does this man want his daughter found or not? He really fucked up in that appeal.'

'I'm dreading seeing tomorrow's papers.'

'You and me both. Now, I'd offer you a coffee but if I make you one I'll want one myself and I'm pretty sure I'll be able to see through time if I have any more caffeine today.'

'That's fine.'

'So, what's on your mind? Is it about what we discussed this morning?'

'No. I'm still trying to get my head around that bombshell.'

'Nobody said the position was easy.'

'True. Anyway, I think we might have an incredibly clever serial killer on our hands.'

Ridley was silent for a long moment. He didn't even blink. 'Can you say that sentence again but use completely different words? Maybe say something about cake and puppies,' he said.

Matilda didn't respond.

Ridley's body visibly drooped as if someone had just ripped out his spine. 'I sometimes wish I'd become a gardener. All I'd have to worry about is greenfly.'

'When I was a child, about nine or ten years old, we went to visit my grandparents in Bray in Ireland. They lived on the outskirts, close to the countryside. The man who lived next door was digging up his garden. I think he was building a conservatory or something. Anyway, he found two skeletons buried beneath his house.'

'Or maybe I could open a sweet shop. Unless you have a story about a killer who choked people by ramming humbugs down their throat.'

'I don't, actually. Though I could get Zofia to do some research. I'm sure she'll dig up something.'

'I could really go off you,' he said with a smirk.

Matilda snorted a smile.

'Go on then, upset me with your news. I know you're dying to.'

Matilda filled him in on the email, the sympathy card, the

CCTV footage, and the breadcrumbs of information they'd amassed. She handed him the email. His mouth dropped open as he read.

'This does not sound good. Look, first of all, I don't want this getting out to the media,' Ridley said.

'Obviously.'

'This could still be some kind of crank. Maybe he sent this card so you'd see a link to a murder that isn't there. We need more information than this.'

Matilda nodded. 'We're bringing in the counsellor tomorrow to have a more formal interview with him.'

'Is it Finn who studied criminology recently?'

'Yes.'

'Has he come up with anything regarding this email?'

'Yes. He's been very knowledgeable.'

'That's good. I was worried you'd want to bring in a psychologist from the university. They don't come cheap.'

'I'd be lost without Finn at times.'

'Is that a dig?'

'It is actually, yes.'

'Matilda, the situation we're in is not of my doing. Don't make me out to be the bad guy here.'

'Nobody said the position was easy,' she said, firing back his earlier comment.

'Touché.'

Matilda gathered the email and sympathy card.

'Why the dinosaurs being wiped out by an asteroid?' Ridley asked.

'I'm not sure. I'm sure there's some reasoning behind it. I can't think of it at the moment.'

'Keep me informed, Matilda. I need to be kept in the loop with this one.'

'Will do.'

Matilda left the office and headed for the stairs. She wanted to go home. She wanted to lock the door behind her, close the curtains, and cocoon herself in her comfort zone.

On the drive home, Matilda stopped off at a supermarket and picked up a few essentials; two bottles of white wine, a large bar of Whole Nut and a tube of Pringles. She turned off Ringinglow Road, down the narrow driveway, a sharp turn to the left, and up the incline to her home, a former farmhouse with large detachable garage.

It was dark and the sensor lights came on. Using a remote from the glovebox, she opened the garage doors and drove in. She was getting used to driving Adele's Porsche. She climbed out and carried her snacks in her arm to the house. She turned back and glanced at the garage over her shoulder. Usually, at this time, there would be two cars parked outside belonging to Scott and Donal, and lights on in every room of the flat above. It was strange to see it in darkness once again. She really was completely alone here.

Inside, she closed the front door behind her and locked it with the bolts at the top and bottom and the security chain. She carried her shopping into the kitchen, placed the items on the work top, then went into the living room, where she lit a fire.

It seemed strange to be living alone again. When she first moved following her husband's death, Matilda sought the solitude and quiet of the countryside. She loved the fact she had no neighbours, and the only sounds came from nature. However, after Scott and his boyfriend, Chris, moved into the flat above the garage, it was comforting to have someone close. Following Chris's death in the shooting, his mother, Adele, fell apart. Matilda took control and had her move in with her. She was surrounded by people once more and she enjoyed the company. Now, they were all gone. The silence had returned. This time, Matilda didn't like it.

She stalked through the house, floorboards creaking underfoot. The fridge in the kitchen seemed to hum loudly… Did clocks always have to tick so noisily? It wasn't only the silence Matilda noticed; it was the loneliness too.

Often, Matilda would spend her nights in the living room by the fire reading a book from her massive collection of crime novels. She had recently bought *The Perfect Killer* by Sebastian Lister for reasons of morbid curiosity. She had read the first four chapters and wasn't exactly enthusiastic about continuing to relive a case that still haunted her. When away from work, Matilda preferred her crime to be completely fictional. She was currently reading a David Jackson hardback and loving the story, but occasionally she looked up from the book and noticed she was alone. She lived in a sprawling four-bedroom house with a massive living room, dining room, conservatory, library, an unnecessarily large kitchen and utility room and a garden that stretched far into the countryside. It *was* bliss. Past tense.

She shivered in the cold, turned, and saw the fire was slowly dying. The clock on the sleeper told her it was almost midnight. It wasn't worth throwing another log on the fire. She closed her book, took the empty bottle of wine into the kitchen to add to the recycling, then went around the house making sure all the doors and windows were locked and she was secure in her home.

Since the kidnapping, she hadn't felt comfortable in her home anymore. She needed the locked doors for security, to make sure nobody could get in when she didn't want them to, but that also meant she couldn't get out quickly, if she needed to. She had turned her home into a prison. She had to feel safe in order to relax enough to go to sleep, yet she had to see a way out.

She padded up the stairs, taking the book and what was left of the chocolate with her, and climbed into bed, leaving the door ajar. She often fell asleep with a book open on her lap. Gone were the days of turning the light off at a sensible time, turning over and waiting for sleep to claim her.

Matilda's eyes closed and she fell into a deep sleep brought on by exhaustion and alcohol, a lethal combination. Her dreams were filled with flashes of memory from her past, serial killers, brutal murders, kidnappings, body parts, the sound of screaming, the look of pure horror on Adele's face when Matilda came home on that cold day in January and found her on the floor of her hallway with Simon Browes.

This was why Matilda hated falling asleep. She was petrified of the torment her mind would put her through, and hoped to God she wouldn't remember any of it when she woke the next morning.

## Chapter Thirteen

Derek Klein woke suddenly. He could hear a noise downstairs. He looked at the time on his phone. It was a little after midnight. He threw back the duvet and slid his feet into carpet slippers. He struggled with his dressing gown and stepped out onto the landing. He passed Cara's bedroom, the door slightly ajar, and pushed it further open. It hadn't been slept in yet.

Derek and Cara had had separate rooms for more than ten years now. He couldn't pinpoint a time in their relationship when they decided separate bedrooms were needed, but they'd both commented since on how their sleeping patterns had improved.

He went downstairs, not tiptoeing, fearing he might mistake a burglar, for he knew full well who would be pacing the ground floor at this time of night. He glanced into the darkened living room as he passed and headed straight for the kitchen. Cara was sitting on a stool at the island, a bottle of vodka and an empty glass in front of her.

'Cara, what are you doing? You don't drink,' Derek said from the doorway.

She turned to him slowly. Her eyelids were heavy with

exhaustion. Her face was pale with fear and stained with dry tear tracks.

'I was hoping it would make the pain go away,' she said. She was on the verge of her entire body collapsing in on itself. Nothing was holding her together. She could barely speak.

He went over to her and pushed the bottle and the glass out of her reach. 'How's that working out for you?'

She didn't answer.

'Cara, you need to go to bed. You need to get some sleep.'

'How can I? Natasha is out there. Someone could be doing God knows what to her and I'm upstairs in a comfy bed getting my eight hours. I don't think so.'

'You'll be in no fit state for Natasha when she comes home and finds you sozzled at the bottom of a vodka bottle.'

Cara looked up at Derek. 'She's dead, isn't she?' she asked, tears choking her.

'We don't know that,' he said with a heavy sigh in his voice.

'She's been gone five days. If she hasn't had her injections since Thursday, she'll be dead, even if someone hasn't taken her.'

'Cara…'

'I was looking at all the photos on my phone,' she said, pulling her mobile out of her pocket. She opened the photos app and began scrolling through. 'She's so beautiful, isn't she?'

'Yes. She is,' he said, nonplussed.

'Tall, shiny hair, always smiling, smooth skin. Men would look at her…'

'Don't do this to yourself, Cara,' Derek said. He didn't make a move to comfort her and stood well back, as if distancing himself from her grief.

'I don't know how you can be so calm about all this. Aren't you frightened that something might have happened to her? Aren't you scared? Aren't you worried?' she cried, looking at him.

'What will crying do?'

'Really? Is that it? Is that all you can say?' She jumped down from the stool and almost lost her balance as the effects of the alcohol kicked in. 'You've never liked her, have you? She's always been in the way.'

'Now you're being ridiculous.'

'Am I? Every holiday you tried to palm her off on my mother. You never wanted to take her anywhere.'

'I tried…'

'You shouldn't have had to try, Derek,' Cara shouted. 'You married me. You married me knowing I came with a daughter. You took her into your life, into your heart. How can you stand there and act like you've misplaced a pair of gloves? She's *our* daughter, Derek. You may not be her biological father, but you've brought her up as if you were. Where's your compassion? Where's your anger? For fuck's sake, Derek, get mad, for once in your life. Scream. Shout. Do something,' she said, her screams echoing around the vast kitchen.

She stared at her husband. Her eyes searched his face for something, anything.

'I've been looking on social media,' she said.

'Oh, God, Cara, why?'

'I wanted to see what people were saying about the appeal.' She looked at Derek. 'Don't you want to know?'

'Why should I care what a load of strangers have to say?' He shrugged.

'Are you even interested to know if anyone has seen or heard from her?'

'Surely they would have contacted the police if they had.'

Cara studied her husband. Her eyes widened as a dark realisation dawned. 'My God, you're glad she's gone, aren't you?'

'Don't be stupid, of course I'm not.'

'Have you done something?'

'What?'

'Where were you on Thursday afternoon?'

'I came home early.'

'You never come home early.'

'My appointment cancelled.'

'When that's happened in the past you've always gone back to the office.'

'I told you, I wanted some me time.'

'That's rubbish. She was here, wasn't she, Natasha, when you came home on Thursday. She was here and something happened and now she's not. Where is she, Derek? What the fuck have you done with my daughter?'

## Chapter Fourteen

Tuesday, 15 March 2021

Matilda made the conscious decision to go back into therapy while she was still in hospital recovering from the kidnapping. She needed someone to talk to, someone impartial who wasn't going to judge or gossip about it. She knew Sian and Scott would never do anything like that, but any advice they gave her wouldn't be entirely neutral. The last time Matilda saw a therapist, she couldn't relax with her. Diana Cooper-bloody-sodding-Smith was smug, and Matilda often felt she was being judged. She probably wasn't, but that was the aura she gave off with her Mont Blanc fountain pen and knitted cardigans. While recuperating, Matilda did a little research and found Doctor Who.

Within seconds of meeting him she stopped the session and asked, 'I'm sorry, but is your name really David Tennant?'

The therapist, who looked nothing like the *Doctor Who* actor, told her it was, and her question was the one he was asked the most. It also acted as an icebreaker among his more nervous clients.

David Tennant, the therapist, was tall with blonde hair and light hazel eyes. He was of medium build but looked fit. He wore tight shirts and there wasn't a hint of anything soft and squidgy around his middle. The framed photographs on the wall of mountain bikes and mountain ranges told Matilda he often spent his free time pedalling away in the countryside. The seams of his trousers straining against his muscular thighs backed up her theory. He had a soft Geordie accent, smiling eyes and a relaxed attitude about him that made Matilda want to open up and tell him everything. He was the polar opposite of Diana Cooper-bloody-sodding-Smith. He didn't sit with his legs crossed and an overpriced fountain pen poised over a leather-bound notebook waiting for Matilda to say something compromising. In fact, he didn't have a notebook at all.

'I prefer to write my notes after our sessions, when you've left, and base them on the memorable parts of the conversation, rather than jotting down the number of times you're blinking,' he'd told her when she questioned the absence of note-taking.

When Matilda left her sessions, she felt uplifted, energised, optimistic and ready for the week ahead. These sessions were helping, and she'd gladly visit David Tennant (and his thighs) for the rest of her life. It was no hardship.

One of the things she told David was how the intrusive thoughts she had developed since being kidnapped scared the living daylights out of her. She'd be driving along a dual carriageway and the thought would pop into her head: *just slam your foot down on the accelerator and take your hands off the wheel*. She came so close to doing it once. She didn't want to kill herself, but the thought came from nowhere and chilled her to the bone.

'As disturbing as the thought is,' David told her. 'It can't harm you.'

'But what if I act upon it? What if, one day, the thought is so powerful I just decide to throw myself out of my office window?'

'Isn't your office on the ground floor?'

'It used to be. Okay, bad example. But you know what I mean.'

'I do,' he said with an impish smile. 'What you need to do is take control of your thoughts. Don't allow them to control you. Let me give you an exercise. Now, sit back, close your eyes and just listen to my voice. Listen to the words.'

Matilda closed her eyes. 'I always imaging you're sticking two fingers up at me when I'm doing this.'

'Bloody hell, she's psychic,' he laughed.

Matilda smiled. She kept her eyes closed.

'Now, picture yourself on a platform at a train station.'

'Are you going to ask me to jump off?'

'I will do if you keep interrupting me.'

'Sorry.'

'Okay. No talking. Just listen. Now, you're on a platform at a train station. There's a train coming in from your right. You can hear it. Now, you're not planning to get on this train and anyway it's not stopping at this station – it's just going to go straight on through. This train is one of your intrusive thoughts. So, stand back, let it come into the station and let it sail straight on past and off to the left, into the tunnel and out of sight. It's gone. No interaction with the train, or the thought, whatsoever. You can open your eyes again now.'

Matilda opened her eyes. She didn't suddenly feel a hundred times better. There was no quick fix, but the fact that she had something to focus on whenever she had another intrusive thought gave her some hope. She wondered what other tricks Doctor Who had up his sleeve.

She smiled at him, and felt herself relax, slightly.

'Do you think you'll be able to do that?'

'I think so.'

'Just focus on that train and nothing else until it's disappeared from view. I promise, it will work.'

'Thank you.'

He looked at her and took in the pained expression on her face.

'I get the impression there's more you want to talk about today but you're holding back. I'm guessing it's work-related.'

'Now who's psychic?'

'Anything you say in this room is completely private. It's between me and whoever is watching the live feed as it's broadcast on YouTube.'

'Would you say that to your paranoid patients?'

'Only if they were coming to the end of their sessions with me and I wanted to draw out their therapy. Caribbean cruises don't come cheap these days.'

Matilda found herself relaxing. David Tennant was easy to get along with. She loved his playful sense of humour.

'There's a killer,' she began. 'He's claimed to have murdered five people. I don't know if he has or not. His first victim was ruled as a suicide. He's saying he killed him. Something in the back of my mind is telling me I'm not going to be able to catch this one.'

'Why is that?'

'It would appear that he's playing the long game. He's intelligent. He's knowledgeable. He knows exactly what to do to avoid capture.'

'But don't people usually give themselves away with their confidence?'

'I think he may have thought of that. I… I just don't think I'm the right person to lead this investigation.'

'Why?'

'Something's different. Something's changed. I don't have the energy for this anymore. I don't have the same thirst for catching criminals.'

'Is this since the kidnapping or did you notice this happening before?'

Matilda thought for a while before answering. 'I don't know. The kidnapping certainly didn't help. I've lost a great deal of confidence and I'm worried about making a mistake. One that could cost lives. I don't want more deaths on my conscience.'

'How many people are employed by South Yorkshire Police?'

'I... I've no idea. Why?'

'Because the way you're talking, it's as if you're the only employee. You are not responsible for the entire police force. If people die, you are not to blame.'

'I'm aware of that.'

'Are you? You're a DCI. Beneath you, you have several inspectors, sergeants and constables, all of whom are capable of working a murder investigation. You are not a one-woman police force.'

Matilda nodded.

'Put more faith in your team. You chose them. You obviously know they're capable of the job or they wouldn't be there. Allow them to grow, to make decisions, to have an input into what direction the investigation takes. Don't let them turn to you for answers, let them come up with the answers for themselves.'

'Maybe you're right,' Matilda said as she thought about it.

'For the amount of money you're paying me, you'd better hope I'm right.'

Matilda looked at him, saw the smile in his eyes, and laughed.

'Something tells me you don't laugh as much as you used to.'

'No.'

'You've lost the ability to see the good in things, in other people. You only see the darkness. You surround yourself with murder and criminals. You've worked on some high-profile and challenging cases, and it's bled into your soul. You need to put yourself first for a change and allow in a chink of jollity.'

'I've been asked out to a David Lynch double bill on Saturday.'

'I wouldn't call the works of David Lynch jolly, but whatever floats your boat.'

The sessions with Doctor Who seemed to pass by much faster than those with Diana Cooper-bloody-sodding-Smith. The reason for that, she surmised, was because she was actually getting somewhere with this one. She trusted him to give her the correct advice. She liked him, too.

As she walked back to the car, she felt light, having unburdened herself. There was a definite spring in her step as she tried to think of the positives in her life at the moment. Despite everything that was going on, she really did love her job. She'd been doing it for more than twenty years. If she didn't love it by now, she was doing something wrong. And … there was potentially a new man in her life. Odell was … Matilda found herself smiling as she tried to think of the right word to describe him. What was he? 'Lovely' was too twee a word. 'Nice' was a non-word. He was… She stopped herself. She had met him once and he was already taking up time in her head. Why was that? She knew why.

*Be honest with yourself, you fancy the pants off him.*

She paused and took a breath while she acknowledged her new feelings. She believed Odell was the kind of man who would take her out of herself, show her a different kind of life from the one she was currently (not) living, and, right now, that's exactly what she needed. She was looking forward to the cinema on Saturday night. It would be a good night out, and afterwards, well, she wouldn't push anything but if Odell wanted to escort her home, she'd let him.

## Chapter Fifteen

Matilda could hear Sian before she reached the double doors of the HMCU suite. Judging by the tone and volume of her voice, she was not a happy woman.

'You have a few days off work and the scavengers swoop in like vultures and pick the carcass clean.'

Matilda pushed open the door. 'Good morning, Sian. Welcome back. I see you're a beautiful ray of sunshine this morning.'

'I'm guessing you had a hand in this, too,' Sian said, turning to her.

'What's that?'

'Don't look so innocent. There isn't a single packet of Maltesers left in this drawer. I know they're your favourites.'

Matilda feigned shock. 'I don't even work in this office anymore. How can I be to blame?'

'The drawer is empty apart from a packet of Iced Gems. By the way, who put those in? Because they're bloody horrible.'

The bottom drawer of Sian's desk was infamous around the station. It was where all the treats were kept – bars of chocolate, packets of biscuits and crisps, everything unhealthy, bad for your teeth and utterly delicious. Anyone could help themselves to anything at any time of day. There was just one proviso – you had to replace what you took within twenty-four hours with something equally calorific. There were only two occasions when this rule went out of the window. The first was during a particularly disturbing investigation, when they were all affected by trauma, and a little pick-me-up in the form of a sugar rush was needed. The second occasion was when Sian was not here to police the pilfering.

Matilda looked at the assembled team who were struggling to hide their smiles.

'Come on then, let's give Sian what she wants,' Christian said.

He went back into his office while everyone else opened a drawer in their desk and pulled out a heavy, bulging carrier bag. In turn, they all went over to Sian's desk and emptied the contents into her snack drawer. It wasn't long before it was overflowing, yet still the chocolate and biscuits and crisps kept on coming. Zofia handed her bag to Tom, who made a second visit. He upended the bag and the whole lot fell onto the floor.

Sian stood stock still. Her face reddened in embarrassment at being taken for a fool. She was itching to smile and eventually burst out laughing as Matilda went up to her and placed an arm around her shoulder.

'You're so easy to manipulate, you know that?' Matilda kissed her on the cheek.

'You're a bunch of sods, the whole lot of you,' she said, looking down at the bars of chocolate and packets of biscuits around her ankles. 'What am I going to do with all this lot?'

'Well, if someone puts the kettle on and hands the teas round, I'm sure we'll find homes for a few Maltesers and Crunchies.'

Tom got up to make the tea and Scott took out his mobile and began taking photographs of Sian's embarrassment.

Matilda felt buoyed. It was important, according to Doctor Who, to look for the brightness in every day, especially so for people like Matilda and her team. They were doing difficult work.

The crimes they investigated were frequently dark and challenging. They saw murder and horror every day and came into contact with the most evil of people. They needed a touch of levity in order to avoid the encroaching darkness.

She looked through the window into her old office, now being used as a storage space. She hated the change. She hated being away from what she still thought of as her team. She turned back to see Scott with his arm around Sian, who was still flushed with embarrassment at being taken in so easily. He helped her pick up the spilled treats. Something else to add to Matilda's former office.

Matilda and Sian had been through so much together in the twenty-plus years they'd known each other. Matilda was even godmother to Sian's daughter Belinda. They'd investigated murders, serial murders, child abusers, rapists, had nights out together, laughed and cried together, been there for each other when they needed it the most. Matilda's recovery after being shot, Sian's recovery after her husband was unmasked as a serial killer. They were a constant support for each other. How could Matilda even consider Sian for redundancy? It was unfair. That left it between Scott and Finn. She couldn't even bring herself to look at them right now.

Christian approached Matilda as she was studying the whiteboard and Natasha Klein's smiling face.

'Sian's face was a picture, wasn't it? Scott took a couple of photos. Shall we have them made up as T-shirts?'

'That would be funny.'

'Have you seen the newspapers this morning?' he asked.

'I've been avoiding them.'

'They're actually not as bad as I expected.' Christian went over to the table at the end of the room where several newspapers lay in an untidy heap. 'They all focus on Natasha going missing and her face is on literally every front page.'

'That's good.'

'It's only when you look inside and read what the analysts say that you wonder if anyone is actually going to look for Natasha.'

'What do you mean?'

'Reading between the lines, they've all got it in for emotionless Derek, suggesting we should be questioning him to discover Natasha's whereabouts.'

'Maybe we should. He can't give us an alibi for Thursday afternoon.'

'No. But he has given us the same one several times. His story doesn't change. Maybe he simply was home alone.'

Matilda looked up and noticed DC Tom Simpson sitting at his desk, chatting with Zofia. 'Why is Tom here? Isn't he FLO for the Kleins?'

'Derek sent him away. He said they didn't need babysitting.'

'Or anyone earwigging.'

'My thoughts exactly.'

Matilda picked up the *Daily Mail* and looked at Natasha's smiling face. It was the same photo used on all the front pages. 'I'm guessing there's no further news on Natasha.'

'Not yet. We've put out a request for the public to check private CCTV, and for any drivers on East Bank Road around the time she went missing to check their dashcams.'

Matilda opened the paper and saw a double-page photo of Natasha's parents sitting so far apart at the table. Cara had fear and horror etched on her face. Derek might as well have been sitting on a train platform. He looked bored. 'Do either Derek or Cara have a motive for wanting to get rid of Natasha?'

'That's what we're looking into.'

'Is Natasha streetwise? Would she get into a car without knowing the driver?'

'I don't know. We're going through all of Natasha's social media to see if she's interacted with anyone who stands out, but it's going to take a lot of time. She practically lives her life by social media. She posts videos of herself eating a sandwich and just talking about random crap. It's all so...' he struggled to find the right word. 'I don't know. It's just dull. Who cares if she's eating a tuna sandwich or that she's got a crush on Henry Cavill or she's selling some clothes on Vinted. It's all shit.'

'To us, yes. To Natasha and her followers, it's not.'

'It's not important, though, is it? In the grand scheme of things.'

'You sound like Liam Walsh.'

'Who'd be a teenager these days?' Christian said. 'I'm dreading my kids getting to that age. I'm hoping the fuss around social media has died down by the time they're teenagers.'

'I can't see that happening.'

'Me neither.'

Matilda stole a glance at Christian and saw the look of worry on his face.

'Have you checked known sex offenders?' she asked.

'Yes. Tom handed me a report this morning. There's a Lloyd Tatlock who lives on Thornborough Road, just off East Bank Road where Natasha's mobile was found. He was convicted for raping two teenagers in 2010. He was released from prison in early 2020. His two victims were both teenagers and blonde.'

'Shit.'

'Indeed. We're bringing him in for a formal interview. Now, opposite Thornborough Road there is East Bank Road Open Space. Plenty of trees and quiet areas. There's a forensic team going out there this morning.'

'Send Tom along, too. Sorry,' she said, suddenly realising she was taking over. 'That's your decision to make, not mine. I keep forgetting. Jesus, I feel like I've been demoted.'

'Not enjoying a less operational role?'

'Not in the slightest. I was emailed a four-page report yesterday regarding the cost-effectiveness of streamlining. I'm still looking up half the words used. Why can't politicians use normal words?'

'Because they're worried we'll work out what they're really up to. Personally, I think politicians should keep their sodding noses out of policing. They haven't a clue.'

'Kettle's boiled.' Tom called out.

Matilda decided to stay for the morning briefing. She was looking for any hint of a reason to delay returning to her isolated office. She took the proffered coffee from Tom, grabbed a packet of Maltesers from Sian's overflowing snack drawer, and pulled up a chair next to her desk.

'Did you have a nice few days off?' she asked Sian quietly.

'Yes. It was good. Although, that reptile Danny Hanson turned up on my doorstep yesterday. He only asked if he could interview me and the kids about Stuart. He wants to write a book of his own.'

'Why? There's already one out.'

'He says it's missing the personal angle.'

Matilda thought about the book for a moment and the few chapters she'd read. 'Well... I can see that.'

Sian's eyes widened. 'You've read it?'

'I'm reading it. I'm on chapter four or five, I think.'

'I didn't think you were going to read it.'

'I'm interested in seeing what he says about us all.'

'Has he made me fat?' Sian asked.

'It's true crime, Sian, not fiction. And no, he doesn't say you're fat.'

'Thank God.'

'He does say you're fifty, though.'

'What?'

Matilda almost spat out her tea. 'I'm joking.'

'You'd better be. I'd bloody sue.'

Christian gave a loud and exaggerated cough. 'When you've both quite finished.'

They both looked up and saw everyone was watching them, waiting for them to be quiet so they could begin work.

'Sorry,' Matilda said. She mimed zipping her mouth shut.

'Thank you. Now, where are we on the Natasha Klein investigation? Have we had any response from the press appeal?'

'Yes,' Scott said. 'They're all saying to bring back hanging and start with Derek.'

'A lot of calls have come through from armchair psychologists,' Sian said.

'Anything from someone who saw her on Thursday specifically after she left college? Christian asked.

'No,' Scott said. 'It's literally like she walked through the gates and disappeared into thin air.'

'I can't believe nobody has seen her,' Christian said, looking back at Natasha's smiling face. 'It doesn't make any sense. How are you getting on with social media, Zofia?'

'The problem is that Natasha has got a lot of followers. Now, the majority comment saying things like *'great video'* or *'nice hair'* or *'love how you've done your eyes'*, but then you get a few who are slightly more ... how can I phrase it?'

'We're all adults here, Zofia. You can be crude if you need to be,' Matilda said.

'Okay. I'll read you a couple.' She turned to one of her screens. *'You can see your nips through that top. I'll give you a hundred quid to suck on them.'*

'Oh my God,' Sian said in disgust.

'They get worse,' Zofia said, a look of distaste on her face. 'Listen to this one: *You've got blowjob lips and I've got eight inches to ram down your throat.*'

'Jesus Christ! What makes people think they can say things like that?' Matilda asked.

'I've managed to find out who these people are and where they're from and I'm putting together a list to send to their nearest police station, asking them to go round and have a word. They may not have anything to do with Natasha's disappearance, but they need to know they can't get away with saying things like this online.'

'Good thinking. Thank you, Zofia,' Christian said.

'I'm sorry you're having to read through all this, Zofia, but you're doing a great job. I also think we should be reporting these people to the relevant social media sites, maybe trying to get them banned from posting,' Matilda added.

'I know a lot of them will be just saying these things because they're hiding behind a keyboard,' Sian said. 'But there are some who will take it further. They need sodding castrating.'

'Getting back to topic,' Christian said, clearing his throat. 'Let's turn to the parents. Tom? You've spent the most time with them.'

'Unfortunately. I'm so glad I'm out of that house,' Tom said. 'It's got a very strange atmosphere. Cara is the only one who seems to be reacting as you expect someone to react to their daughter missing. Derek doesn't seem bothered in the slightest. And not a single neighbour has called round. It's weird.'

'What have they said about Natasha?' Matilda said.

'Very little.'

'I think you should bring them in and separate them,' Matilda said to Christian.

'Okay.' Christian said. 'I'll book a couple of interview rooms and sort it out. Anything from the neighbours?'

'Door-to-door enquiries were very eye-opening,' Scott said as he swallowed a mouthful of Snickers. He picked up his tablet and scrolled through. 'Hardly anyone knows her. I mean, Broomhall is a lovely area, but it's not very neighbourly. There are a lot of self-important people living around there who spend most of their time in their own little bubble. Hardly anyone knew the Kleins by name and when they were told someone was missing, they nearly all asked if *they* should be worried rather than what's happened to the poor missing girl.'

'Welcome to twenty-first-century Britain, where nobody gives a tiny rat's arse about anyone but themselves,' Matilda said.

'Wow, that's jaded,' Sian said.

'True though.'

'Sadly, yes.'

'Right,' Christian clapped his hands together. 'Actions for this morning…'

'I'll leave you to it,' Matilda said, rising from her seat. 'I have a three-hundred-page report about acceptability in the police force to read and I'm so excited,' she said, rolling her eyes.

'Can I just say something while DCI Darke is here?' Finn asked. 'It's nothing to do with the Natasha Klein case, though.'

'Sure,' Christian said.

'It's about the email received yesterday about Liam Walsh,' he began as he bent down to his bag and pulled out a notebook. 'I was thinking about this all last night. I've written a thing about the psychology behind the email, but I've actually thought of a way to check to see if Liam was murdered. But I need to know if it's possible first from Zofia.'

'Why me?'

'Liam was suffering severely with depression. He mentioned a few times to his counsellor about wanting to die yet not wanting to die on his own. He could have gone online, accessed the dark web and entered a few suicide chat rooms.'

Zofia turned to her computers and began rapidly typing on the keyboard.

'I'm assuming Liam's computer, phone, tablet, whatever he had, weren't analysed when he died because it was taken to be a straightforward suicide. If we get access to his tech, I'm pretty sure Zofia would be able to find out if he accessed these kinds of sites and if he chatted to anyone. Maybe the killer is lurking in there.'

'Good idea,' Matilda said.

'The whole point of the dark web, obviously, is to access various sites without being seen. However, I'll happily have a dig around and see what comes up,' Zofia said.

'Excellent,' Matilda said. 'I'll go back to his mother and see about getting his computer or whatever brought in. Finn, what else did you want to say about the psychology behind the email?'

He pulled a face and suddenly looked unsure of what he'd come up with.

'Okay. So, the thing is, when we talk about the mind of a criminal, we look at the crime and work backwards to try to figure out what type of person we're looking for. When we look at a murder, we take in things like method, opportunity, access, victimology. Basically, I don't think this killer is as clever as he wants us to believe.'

'Why not?' Matilda asked.

'For a start, committing murder, although it's the worst crime we can think of, is also the easiest. Anyone can take another life. Any one of us in this room can do it. We have an argument, we lash out, someone falls, bangs their head and it's lights out. It might not have been premeditated, but you've taken a life. You've killed someone. Things like a bank robbery and a heist take planning and thought and intelligence. Killing doesn't.'

'That actually makes sense,' Zofia said.

Finn continued. 'However, on the flip side, he is a very calm and rational person. Liam died in September. It's now March. Six months pass until he decides to contact us. If we take his email as accurate then he's spent the last six months killing four other people, yet he's not appeared on our radar, so he's been able to calmly and carefully go about killing people, and not a single person in his life has noticed what he's doing. And we haven't either. That doesn't necessarily make him intelligent, but it could make him dangerous.'

Matilda was taking this all in. She'd retaken her seat and had her elbow on the arm of the chair, head on her hand, a perplexed look on her face. 'Anything else?' she asked.

When Finn didn't answer, she looked up and made eye contact with him.

'Finn?' she asked.

His eyes darted left and right and he licked his lips.

'Come on, Finn, say what you want to say.'

'Last night, Stephanie asked me if the killer had emailed you or the team. Obviously, he used your work email, so I started thinking, why you? I looked you up online. Now, I know you. We all know you, but I wanted to look at you through the eyes of a stranger. You're very well known. Or, rather, your work is very well known. You have no social media presence at all, and you've given very few interviews. That makes you incredibly desirable. The world knows you as Detective Chief Inspector Matilda Darke, a highly respected investigator and catcher of criminals. You despise injustice, and thanks to the feature by Danny Hanson following the Magnolia House case, you're painted as a no-nonsense, hardened career detective. You brought down Steve Harrison. You brought down Laurence Dodds. You brought down … erm, Stuart,' he said, catching a glimpse of Sian. 'You brought down all those connected with Magnolia House, and you haven't flinched. You're the perfect opponent to the perfect killer.'

'This is a game to him?'

'Yes. He'll have completely removed himself from his everyday life to do all this. When he's "killing",' he said, using air quotes, 'and when he's writing his emails to you, he's not being the person who can go to work or university every day and chat to his friends and colleagues. He's elevated himself, and the more he gets away with it, the more his elevated self will take over.'

'But won't that then make him easier to catch if he's changed in his behaviour?' Christian asked.

'Yes. But how long do we have to wait until he gets there? There's something else, too.' Finn shifted in his chair. 'In the past, serial killers have tended to target people who fit specific boxes. Sometimes they kill people who remind them of a domineering mother or wife or of someone who abused them or someone they're fixating on, like women who have blonde hair, for example. I don't think we're going to get anything from the victimology in this case.'

'Why not?' Matilda asked.

'Because, if his email is true and he's already killed five people, we'd know about five people dying who have something in common – whether it's gender, sexuality, hair colour, or they all work in the same office or whatever. I don't think the victim means anything to this man. It's the killing and getting away with it.'

'But don't serial killers like this usually like to get involved in the investigation?' Zofia asked. 'They like to get up close and see the drama and danger they're causing.'

'He already has done,' Finn said. 'He's written to Matilda. He's made himself known, and he will continue to do that as this goes on. He's sent you an email, and he'll send another. Soon, that won't be enough, and he'll find some other way of contacting you.' Finn cleared his throat. 'Someone new has recently come into your life. Or someone has been lying dormant in your life and they've been woken up. I strongly believe you know who the killer is, Matilda. If you want to find him before this escalates even further, you need to look into your past. Because I believe, hand on heart, you've met this man already.'

## Chapter Sixteen

Matilda stood at the window in her office. She had been given a lot to think about, and she needed to be alone to sort out her thoughts. Saying she knew who the killer was didn't sound as frightening or as threatening as she first thought. She was a detective who specialised in homicide and violent crime. It was safe to say she knew quite a few killers. This didn't necessarily have to be someone new. Steve Harrison had manipulated his own brother into continuing his work. It's just possible there was a killer in prison who was seeking revenge against Matilda for his imprisonment.

A knock on Matilda's door made her jump. She turned to find Christian in the doorway, mug of tea in one hand, packet of Maltesers in another.

'I thought you might need cheering up.'

'Thank you.'

'Quite a heavy discussion. Do you think Finn's right?' he asked, handing her the mug.

Matilda sat at her desk. She took a sip of the tea, opened the packet of Maltesers and threw a few into her mouth. She thought as she crunched. 'I'm not sure. It does make sense.'

'It does. But it doesn't mean it's the solution. Don't get me wrong, I like Finn, he's a great bloke and a brilliant detective, but he has only just qualified in criminology, and he isn't as experienced in the field as we are. A lot of his research is textbook. Not every killer fits into the textbook. We know that. Don't let this set up home in your head, Mat. And remember, you need to be open and talk about things.'

'I know. I will. I just never understand killers who feel a need to taunt others about their crimes.'

'No. It's bad enough they're committing them.'

'Exactly.'

'Anyway, Jamie Peterson has arrived. Do you want me to interview him?'

'No. You've got your hands full with Natasha Klein and her family. Me and Finn will do it. I promise I won't take up all his time.'

'No. It's fine. I think this needs looking into. Liam Walsh may have been suffering, mentally, but he should have been helped, not been taken advantage of.'

'Thank you for understanding, Christian. Look, before I go in, can I share something with you?'

'Of course.'

'I had a meeting with Ridley yesterday. More budget cuts are coming—'

'I've heard a rumour that we're losing the canteen. Is this true?' he interrupted.

'I'm afraid so.'

'Oh, no. Dolly was asking me about it when I went for my dinner yesterday. She's been here for thirty years. And she makes a mean moussaka.'

'There are cuts coming to every department, Christian. Including mine. Well, ours. Well, yours. You're only going to get one new DC, not two as promised, and it won't be happening this financial year.'

'I'll try and hide my shock,' he said with sarcasm.

'Also, you have one DS too many. One has to go, and they won't be getting transferred either. They'll be getting made redundant.'

'What?'

'*I* have to choose who to give the elbow – Sian, Scott or Finn.'

'Fucking hell!' he exclaimed.

'I said something similar.'

'How are you supposed to choose?'

'I've no idea.' She shrugged. 'Look, keep this to yourself for now. But will you help me decide?'

'Oh, Jesus, I don't know about that. I love those three.'

'So do I. I'm genuinely gutted.'

Christian thought for a while. Eventually, he nodded. 'I'll help. Two heads are better than one and all that shite.'

'Thanks, Christian.'

'Promise me one thing.'

'Go on.'

'If you ever have to make me redundant, soften the blow by buying me something nice. A Ferrari will do.'

---

After the briefing, Sian went to the toilets at the far side of the building. There was no point in them being there as they were out of the way, but they were perfect if you needed to make a private phone call and didn't want anyone overhearing.

Sian went into the furthest cubicle, closed the door behind her and sat on the toilet lid. She lifted her feet up off the floor so nobody would know she was there.

She took her iPhone out of her back pocket, scrolled through the contacts, and made a call. It was a while before it was answered. Sian almost gave up.

'Hi, Cliff. It's Sian Robinson from South Yorkshire Police.'

'I know who you are, Sian. I've got you saved in my phone. You always introduce yourself when you call.'

'Sorry. Force of habit.'

'How are you?'

'I'm okay, thanks.'

'Settled into the new house?'

'Yes. Very. How are things with you?'

'They're going well, thanks. Not long since back from Egypt. You ever been?'

'No.'

'You're not missing anything. Those pyramids are tiny. I was very disappointed. Anyway, what can I do for you?'

Sian took a breath. 'It's quite complicated.'

'It usually is. Go on. I'm all ears.

Cliff Lombard was a prison officer at Wakefield Prison in West Yorkshire. The same Wakefield Prison where Sian's ex-husband, Stuart, was currently serving a life sentence. When Finn mentioned that Matilda already knew the killer, Sian immediately thought of all the previous killers the team had put away in recent years. Serial killers, by design, were great manipulators, her own husband included, and while she didn't think he was behind this, she needed reassuring.

She told Cliff everything she felt able to reveal before asking him about Stuart.

'Does he get any visitors?' she asked.

'No. There was his sister, for a while, but even she's stopped now.'

'She's moved away,' Sian said. 'She runs a bed and breakfast up in Inverness.'

'Lovely part of the world.'

'Yes. So, Stuart doesn't get any visitors at all now?'

'None whatsoever.'

'Phone calls?'

'I haven't seen him make any for months. I can ask around for you.'

'Please.' Sian fell silent. She was conflicted. The man she had been married to for more than twenty-five years was a multiple murderer. Yet he was the father of their four children. She had spent a great deal of her life with him. Although she had said she felt nothing but revulsion for him, it saddened her to think of him locked in a prison cell for the rest of his life. 'How is he?' she asked, reluctantly. 'His health. In general.'

'He's fine. He's doing well, Sian. He's a model prisoner.'

'Right.'

'I can ask him to put you on his list of approved visitors if you want to come and talk to him.'

She thought about it for a long moment. 'No. No, I don't... I can't do that. Just ... will you keep an eye on him for me? If you notice a change or if he gets any visitors, will you let me know?'

'I will. Look after yourself, Sian.'

'Thanks, Cliff. You too.'

Sian ended the call. She looked at the wallpaper on her phone. All four of her children in ridiculously bright Christmas jumpers, mugging to the camera last Christmas morning. How could Stuart have destroyed them all as he had? And, more importantly, why couldn't she hate him as much as she wanted to?

## Chapter Seventeen

Matilda and Finn opened the door to Interview Room Number 1 where Jamie Peterson was waiting for them. He looked up, his face a map of worry, his eyes wide in anticipation of the unknown. He gave Finn a frightened smile of acknowledgement.

'Mr Peterson, thank you for coming in,' Finn began as he pulled out a chair and sat down. 'This is my boss, Detective Chief Inspector Matilda Darke.'

'Lovely to meet you,' Jamie said. He half-rose and held out his hand for Matilda to shake.

Matilda shook his hand, noticing that it was clammy, possibly due to nerves, and they all sat down.

'Am I being recorded?' Jamie asked.

'No,' Finn said. 'This is an informal discussion. You're not under arrest and this isn't an interview under caution. The video camera and voice recorder are both switched off.'

'Okay.' He gave a nervous chuckle. 'This is my first time in a police interview room. I wasn't sure what to expect.'

'You've nothing to worry about. We just wanted to have a follow-up discussion from yesterday.'

'Right, though I don't think I can tell you any more than I already have done.'

'You told us that Liam wanted to kill himself, but he didn't want to die alone. Yet that's what appears to have happened. When did you last see Liam before he died?'

'I saw him four days before his death. On the Monday.' Jamie spoke clearly and concisely, though there was a slight shake in his voice.

'Did he say anything to indicate he was going to kill himself?'

'No.'

'How did he seem?'

'Looking back, he seemed … I don't know. He was different. He was more talkative.'

'How so?' Matilda asked.

'He chatted. He was very open about his feelings and emotions, but he always took a while to warm up. Our sessions lasted an hour and sometimes we were twenty minutes in before he spoke. That final time, he spoke as soon as he sat down.'

'You mentioned that he seemed different?'

'I commented that he seemed lighter and that perhaps he might be having a better day than usual.'

'Was he?'

'He said that he'd got some things sorted out in his head.'

'What sort of things?'

'He didn't say.'

'Didn't you ask?'

'He didn't say,' Jamie repeated, more forcefully.

Finn cleared his throat. 'Jamie, we're currently treating Liam's death as unexplained because of new information received. Can you tell us, purely for elimination purposes, where you were on the night Liam died?'

Jamie looked at Matilda then back at Finn. He nodded. 'Yes. I was at home that night.'

'On your own?'

'No. Yes. Well.' He stopped to compose himself. 'I split up with my wife last year. My father is living with me, though. He moved in a few months ago. He suffers with dementia.'

'I'm sorry to hear that,' Finn said.

'There's no need. But thank you.'

'Were you working at the university on the Friday Liam died?' Matilda asked.

'No. I have a number of roles within mental health. On that day I was working at a couple of sites run by The Sheffield College.'

'Had Liam ever contacted you on days when he didn't have an appointment?' Finn asked.

'No. He always stuck to his appointments.'

'You said yesterday that Liam wouldn't change his mind; that he was unhappy and wanted to end his life. It must have been difficult to see him like that,' Finn said.

'It was.'

'Knowing that there was nothing you could do for him.'

'I tried my best. I really did,' Jamie said, looking pained.

'Did Liam ever ask you for help?'

'Help?'

'To die.'

Jamie didn't move. His gaze remained fixed on Finn. He didn't say anything. The temperature in the room seemed to drop several degrees.

'He did, didn't he?' Matilda said. 'Liam asked you for help.'

Jamie swallowed hard. His eyes filled up with tears, but they refused to fall. Eventually, he gave a single nod.

'How did that come about?' Matilda asked. 'What did Liam say?'

It was a while before Jamie answered. He seemed to be struggling to find the right words and also battling against releasing his emotions. A single tear rolled down his face. Finn took a tissue out of his pocket and handed it to him. Jamie wiped his eyes and blew his nose.

'I'm sorry,' he said through the tears. 'I'm so sorry.'

'For what?' Finn asked.

'Liam was desperate,' he said. 'He was in agony. He was tormenting himself. He wanted to die but was frightened of the pain, of being alone. I… I…' He choked. 'He asked me… He asked me to help him. I told him about…' He looked down at the table and began tearing the soggy tissue. 'I told him about the dark web.'

'What did you tell him about the dark web?' Finn asked.

'I said there were message boards. I've looked at them myself, purely for research purposes. There are suicide forums where people arrange to meet up with other people who want to die. It's not just people with depression but people with terminal illnesses who want to take control of their own death. They meet, and they … you know … they die … together.'

'You told Liam about this?'

'Yes.'

'Did he say if he was going to look into it?'

'He said he'd consider it.'

'Did he ever tell you if he'd looked on the dark web?'

'No. I knew what I was telling him was wrong. I made a point of never mentioning it again.'

'When you heard he'd died, did you think he'd found someone to die with?'

Jamie nodded.

'But then you heard he'd died alone.'

'Yes. I just assumed he'd decided he'd had enough. That he'd just killed himself. But, if he had gone on the forums and spoken to someone, someone who… Do you think someone was looking for a victim? Is that what you think? Did I hand Liam over to his killer?' Jamie asked, crying once again.

'We don't know,' Finn said. He sounded sympathetic. 'It's possible.'

'Will anything happen to me?' Jamie asked, wiping his eyes with the backs of his hands.

'That all depends on what we uncover,' Finn said.

'There are rules in place, aren't there, for when a student expresses an interest in harming themselves or others. You need to contact the police or a medical professional. You could have had Liam sectioned if you believed he was a danger to himself. Why didn't you?' Matilda asked.

Jamie shook his head. 'There are some people who you just know are beyond being helped. Liam was one of those people. Having him sectioned would have made his problems public. His mother, and the university, would have known about it. That's not what he wanted. And, when he was eventually released from hospital care, he wouldn't have been any different than when he went in. My first priority is to Liam. I did what was right for him.'

'But he died,' Finn said.

Jamie struggled again with his words, his tears. His bottom lip was wobbling but he managed to take hold of himself and trust himself to speak. 'It was what he wanted,' he said quietly.

'A more intensive course of therapy could have worked,' Matilda said. 'Maybe he needed different medication. Maybe he needed more than a counsellor. I'm aware there is still a stigma around mental health, but people would have understood Liam's struggles. You didn't even try to seek alternatives for him.'

'He didn't want an alternative,' Jamie pleaded, wiping his eyes again.

'You didn't offer them. Your job is to make sure the people in your care have someone to turn to when they need it. If they need further help, you give it to them, you put them in touch with specific organisations that can provide treatment. You led Liam Walsh straight to his death,' Matilda said. Her tone was calm and quiet, but there was a dark edge to it.

'It was what he wanted,' Jamie repeated, barely audibly.

'But his mind wasn't working correctly. He wasn't thinking clearly as he was so consumed with depression and anxiety. When a person is at their lowest point, like Liam was, you help them to get back up. You don't finish them off.'

'I didn't.'

Matilda stood up, pushing her chair back. 'You might as well have pushed him yourself.'

She stopped at the door of the Interview Room. Something came to her mind. She turned back, a thoughtful look on her face.

'Jamie, you mentioned that you don't only work at the university. Where else do you work?'

'I work at various sites within South Yorkshire. Schools, colleges. I give assemblies and talk about mental health, the issues surrounding addiction to online gaming and social media.'

'Last Thursday, where were you?'

He sniffed hard. 'I was at The Sheffield College all last week. Granville Road.'

'The Olive Grove campus?'

'Yes. Why?'

Matilda turned to Finn. 'Go and fetch Christian.'

Finn jumped up and left the room.

'A student there is missing. Natasha Klein.'

Jamie didn't respond. He looked down. Tears fell onto the table.

'You know her, don't you?' He didn't reply. 'She's one of your clients, isn't she?'

He nodded.

'She's been missing since Thursday. It's been on the local news and social media throughout the weekend. It's now Tuesday It's all over the bloody papers. Didn't you think to come to us?' Matilda raised her voice.

'I didn't want to get involved.'

'What? Jesus Christ! What kind of a counsellor are you?' She looked behind her and made sure the door was closed. She leaned on the table, hovering over Jamie Peterson, and whispered into his ear. 'When we've finished with you, providing you're not in prison, you're going to be looking for another job. You're an incredibly dangerous man.'

She left the room, slamming the door hard behind her.

## Chapter Eighteen

Matilda was fuming but managed to calm herself down by popping into the toilets and splashing cold water on her face. A strong black coffee and a so-called king-size Mars bar from Sian's drawer helped, too. She and Finn left the station and headed for Helen Walsh's house in Elsecar. They needed Liam's computer to find out if he had accessed the dark web as Jamie bloody Peterson had recommended.

'What will happen to Jamie? Will he face criminal charges?' Finn asked after he'd finished marvelling at the interior of Adele's Porsche.

'I don't know. He deserves to lose his job, though.'

'If Liam was so unhappy that he wanted to kill himself then was Jamie really wrong? Maybe other treatments wouldn't have worked.'

'Maybe not, but you have to try all possibilities. Besides, I think Liam would have benefited from further treatment. If he was serious about dying, why was he putting it off by saying he didn't want to die alone? It wouldn't have mattered whether he was alone or not, his misery would have been at an end. I think he was crying out for help. He even went to the one person who should have helped – and look how it ended.'

They arrived in Elsecar and walked up the path to Helen's front door. A sharp breeze was blowing. It was supposed to be spring, yet obviously nobody had informed the weather of this. Matilda was bloody freezing. She rang the bell. It wasn't answered so she knocked, loudly. Twice.

The door opened to reveal Helen Walsh wearing skinny jeans and a white knitted jumper.

'Sorry, I was in the shed. I didn't hear the door. Come on in.'

Matilda stepped in first and introduced her to Finn.

'Helen, I really am sorry to ask this, but I was wondering if we could take away Liam's computer, his laptop, tablet, mobile phone, whatever electronic devices he had.'

Helen hugged herself tightly. A look of horror appeared on her face. She was obviously trying to get on with her life, but the torment of her son's death was preying on her, and Matilda's appearance was reminding her of that dark day.

'Why?'

'There are discrepancies in the investigation into Liam's death. We need to check and double-check.'

'Does this have something to do with the sympathy card you took away with you?'

'It might have.'

'I suppose you don't want to commit to saying anything until you've run all your tests, do you? Liam's room is at the top of the stairs, second on your right. Everything you might need is in there. Take what you want,' she said, turning away from the stairs and going into the living room.

Matilda nodded for Finn to go upstairs. She followed Helen and went straight over to the fireplace.

'Helen, do you have anyone to talk to? I'm not sure it's wise to be alone at times like this.'

'The last six months have all been times like this. The pain, the knot of grief and sadness and overwhelming hurt is weighing me down from within.' She slumped onto the sofa. She looked to be in great physical discomfort. 'I lost my husband when Liam was three. I was sad. I missed him. But I had Liam to keep me going. I've got nothing left. Life is empty. Everything I do is meaningless.'

Helen didn't cry. Matilda assumed she had no more tears left. She went over to her, sat next to her on the sofa and put an arm around her shoulder.

'There is probably nothing I can tell you that you haven't heard many times before. What you're going through right now is torture. I know. I've been there. It does get easier, but it's not an overnight thing, and you cannot do this on your own. Do you have someone? A friend? A sister or brother?'

Helen shook her head.

'There must be someone.'

'I don't have anyone I'm close enough to be able to share this with.'

Something caught Matilda's eye. She looked up and saw Finn standing in the doorway. He was holding a MacBook, an iPad and an iPhone. Matilda stood up and went over to him.

'Finn, you go back to the station,' she said, fishing her car keys out of her pocket.

'You're letting me drive your car?' he asked, eyes wide and full of excitement.

'I will be examining every inch of that car. If I find so much as the tiniest hint of a scratch, I will make sure your body is so well hidden even Google won't be able to find you.'

'Wow. I promise, I'll take care of it,' he said, nervously taking the keys from her. 'How are you going to get back?'

'I'll call a taxi. I can't leave her like this.' She went to the front door, opened it, and showed Finn out.

Back in the living room, Helen was sitting on the sofa, staring somewhere off into the distance. Matilda doubted she'd noticed Finn leave.

Matilda went over to the sideboard. She poured them both two large scotches and handed a glass to Helen. Reluctantly, she took it, took a sip and pulled a face. 'I never liked spirits before Liam died. I was always a wine drinker. Someone gave me a drink after the funeral, for the shock, I was told, and it's the only thing that numbs the pain.'

Matilda didn't say anything. She knew, in cases like this, it was always best to remain silent and let the other person talk.

'Last night, I was thinking about your visit, and I wondered whether it would be better if Liam had killed himself or been murdered. There's no answer that will make any of this better, is there? He's not coming back.'

Matilda shook her head.

'I feel like I'm in purgatory. I'm not living at all. I'm just existing. I go to work, and I come home, and I can't think of a single thing I've done all day. The day Liam died, I died. Would I feel better if I had someone to blame for his death?'

Matilda didn't say anything. She hoped her presence was a comfort.

'I'm actually asking for an answer here. You're a detective. You've been around victims and their grieving families. Are they better for having someone to blame, to hate?'

Matilda thought of her husband. They had so much they planned to do with their lives when, out of the blue, he was diagnosed with an aggressive brain cancer that robbed them of a future together. Matilda was angry. She had nobody to blame. Would it have been better if there had been someone locked in prison who she knew was rotting away for the rest of their life for killing her husband?

Sian's ex-husband was locked up in prison. Was it easier to have someone to hate and channel all your negative emotions towards rather than to allow those emotions to build up and fester inside you?

'I wish I could answer you, Helen. I honestly don't know what to say. Grief is a horrible thing to go through. I don't think anyone has an understanding of it.'

'Can I ask you a favour?'

'Of course,' Matilda said, looking towards her.

'From one grieving woman to another … if you find out Liam was murdered, will you let me know who the killer is before you arrest him, so I can kill him?'

'I can't do that, Helen. You know that.'

'I'm already dead,' she said, choking on her own words. 'I don't care what happens to me. I'll kill myself straight afterwards, but I need to kill whoever did what they did to my Liam. I can't let them get away with it. And I refuse to leave this planet while they're still alive and living in some cushy prison cell.'

Matilda couldn't think of anything to say.

## Chapter Nineteen

'The point of the dark web is so you can't be traced,' DC Zofia Nowak began as she plugged Liam Walsh's laptop into her own computer. She transferred every file he had, along with a browser history. 'However, I can already see that he had a Tor browser installed, which shows he accessed the dark web. What I won't be able to see is what he did while he was on there.'

'So we won't know if he went on any of these message boards?' Finn asked.

'I'm hoping I can find something. There could be a few crumbs, or I might even find a back door I can break through. I mean, obviously I won't be able to show you any online conversation he might have had, but I could find what sites he visited. However, please don't hold your breath.'

'He's got thousands of photos and screenshots on his iPad,' Scott said as he scrolled through them.

'Anything interesting?'

'It depends on your definition of interesting. He's got aerial shots of a forest that's being cleared away. I don't even know where it is. There are some here of the melting ice in the Arctic. There's a screenshot of a graph showing the percentage increase in the world's population year on year. He seemed to have an interest in anything to do with the destruction of the planet.'

'Do you think that's why his mother was sent the card with the dinosaurs on it and the meteor coming towards them?' Finn asked. 'That was the last great extinction-level event. Liam was obviously worried about the state of the planet so maybe that card was another sign showing how clever he is that he knew Liam better than we think.'

'It's possible, I suppose,' Zofia said, not looking up from her computer.

'But you said that he doesn't care about his victims,' Scott said. 'He's looking for a way to kill someone without actually killing them. It doesn't matter who they are. If that's the case, he's not going to waste time getting to know them. By doing that, he could likely end up on our radar.'

'But there is no radar because we're not investigating. On paper, Liam's death is a suicide.'

'So if we treat this as a murder and approach it in the same way as all the other murders, we'll find him?' Scott asked.

'We might do.'

'There are too many mights, maybes, and ifs in this conversation for my liking,' Scott said. He looked back at the iPad and continued to scroll. 'Hang on a minute,' he said, his eyes widening. 'I think I might have found something.'

'Another might,' Zofia said without looking up.

Scott went back to his desk, plugged the iPad into his computer and asked Finn to close the blind and pull down the projector screen.

'As I said, Liam's iPad is full of screenshots from websites he's visited,' Scott said. 'However, I've found a series of screenshots that seems to be from a message board. Take a look at these. I'm guessing Liam is the one who posted the original message under the username "EverythingIsPointless".'

**NOHOLDSBARRED//ffL12:/_lunar_//.tor@rot.life**
**Subject:** EndOfLife. **Time:** 24hrs **Date:** 05-09-2020

**EverythingIsPointless**: *I've decided to kill myself. I've been struggling with mental health issues for as long as I can remember and it's getting worse. I can't go on like this and I just want it to end. The only thing is, death scares me, and I don't want to die on my own. Is there anyone else on here who feels like I do, who wants to die, and maybe wants to have some kind of pact? I'm 20 and from Sheffield, South Yorkshire. I can travel if you're not close.*

**JOE481992**: *If you're scared of death then maybe you're not really serious. I'm guessing you've already spoken to people but please call the Samaritans on 116 123. They will give you all the help you need.*

**Dempsie_56**: *My sister killed herself in 2012. She had a lot of issues going on and we hadn't spoken for a while. She was found in the bath by her landlord. She'd cut her wrists. Police said she'd been lying there for three days before she was found. What hurts me more is that she was alone at the end, and nobody cared to look in on her. I can't sit and watch you die, but I hope you find someone who can be with you.*

**20202020**: *You really don't want to die. If you did, you would have done it and not be on here. Please seek help. Think of your family and friends.*

**TheEndIsComing**: *If you're going to do it, live stream it. I'd fucking love to see it.*

**Tara29**: *Why not join a terrorist group or something and become a suicide bomber? No point wasting your final moments.*

**T4;up9th4[qa9**: *I have terminal cancer. I'll do it with you. I'll DM you.*

'That's excellent. I should be able to look up that web address,' Zofia said.

'Does he have screenshots of the messages he's exchanged with anyone privately?' Finn asked Scott.

'I haven't found any yet, but I'll keep looking.'

'Zofia, can you look up the username of the person who said they had terminal cancer?'

'No,' she answered straightaway. 'I'm on the message board now and there isn't a suicide chat room. The site looks like you chat in the main room then create your own separate rooms to chat in with different subjects, and people can join as and when they like. At the moment, nobody is wanting to discuss suicide. Let me have a play around. I'll see if I can grab someone's interest.'

'Thanks,' Finn said. 'Scott, keep going through the iPad, see if you can find anything else. If this was someone genuine who had terminal cancer, then why did only one person jump from the Arts Tower? Unless it's a lie and he's our killer.'

'If he is, there's no way for me to find him,' Zofia said. 'That's kind of the whole point of these sites.'

'I have no other message board screenshots,' Scott said. 'If he did chat with anyone privately, he didn't save them. I don't understand why he just saved these. If he did have a DM with someone, why not save those?'

'Who knows what was going through his mind?' Finn said. 'It's dated the fifth of September – that's three weeks before he died. If this guy who said he'd DM him is the killer, then they must have built up a connection within those three weeks. Surely someone saw Liam with someone new, or heard him talking about someone new, in that time.'

'Then this is what we need to focus on. It's all we've got right now. The three weeks between September the fifth and the twenty-fifth. We need to talk to Liam's friends, especially those he hung around with at university,' Scott said. 'Zofia, look on his social media pages and at his online activity during those periods, too. This could be our window of opportunity to find the killer.'

Zofia's phone began to ring. She answered, had a quiet conversation and quickly hung up. 'That was reception. Ruby Deighton, Natasha's best friend, wants to have a word with someone investigating her disappearance.'

'I'm just about to go and interview Natasha's parents,' Finn said.

'Fancy getting out of the office for a bit?' Scott said to Zofia.

'I've always wanted to go to the other side of the building,' she said, sarcastically.

---

Ruby Deighton was the opposite of Natasha. Where Natasha was tall and blonde, Ruby was short and dark-haired. She had her shoulder-length brown hair in a loose ponytail and wore a padded jacket over a black jumper and skinny black jeans. Scott showed her into an Interview Room where Zofia was already waiting.

Ruby took a seat. She had a nervous expression on her face. Her eyes were darting around the room, and she refused to take her coat off. She sat on the edge of the hard plastic chair and gripped her small handbag in front of her.

'Can I get you a drink or anything?' Scott asked to fill the silence.

'No.'

'Are you sure? You look cold.'

'I've been walking around outside for the best part of an hour wondering whether to come in or not.'

'You have something you want to tell us?' Zofia asked.

'I don't know,' she said. Tears filled her eyes. She looked up at the camera in the corner of the room. 'Am I being filmed?'

'No. It's not switched on.'

'I don't know if I should be here,' Ruby said. Her voice was barely above a whisper.

'Do you know anything about Natasha's disappearance?' Scott asked.

'No,' she quickly answered. 'The thing is, Natasha … she, well, she wants to be a big social media influencer. She's always posting things online that will get her the biggest number of likes or followers. She posted something last month about having to inject herself with insulin and tagged in a few diabetes charities. I think she was hoping to become an ambassador for them or something. When they didn't bite, she really kicked off. I just… I worry that someone might have contacted her through social media and… I know she's too old to be groomed by a paedophile, but she could have been trafficked.'

'Is that what you think's happened?' Zofia asked.

'I don't know.'

Scott leaned forward. 'Ruby, there's something you're not telling us, isn't there?'

'What are you talking about?'

'Look, Ruby, anything you tell us will be within the strictest confidence. You can trust us.'

Ruby's bottom lip began to wobble. Tears rolled down her cheeks and she didn't wipe them away. She quickly stood up. Her chair crashed to the floor behind her.

'I shouldn't have come here.' She ran to the door.

'Ruby, wait,' Zofia called out.

'I'm sorry. I shouldn't have come. I'm sorry.' She fumbled with the door handle, pulled the door open and ran out of the room.

Scott watched from the window of the interview room as Ruby Deighton sped out of the police station and bolted for the exit to the car park, almost colliding with a marked police car as it pulled in. He turned back to Zofia.

'What do you make of that?'

'She knows something.'

'She's frightened, too.'

## Chapter Twenty

Cara Klein was ushered into the Interview Room soon after Jamie Peterson had vacated it. By the time Christian had finished with the counsellor, he was a wreck. He'd been sent home and told not to even think about leaving Sheffield. Christian had learned more about Natasha and her feelings about her excessive use of social media. He was hoping her family could provide more information.

Cara had changed into black jeans and polo shirt. She was wearing a padded coat which she hugged around herself although the radiator was on full. Her eyes were red from constant crying. Even before Christian could ask anything, she burst into tears, and ferreted in her pocket for a packet of tissues.

'Cara, if you don't mind, we'd like to record this conversation,' DC Tom Simpson said. 'It's purely so we don't forget anything while investigating Natasha's disappearance.'

'That's fine,' she said, quietly.

'Cara, I'm guessing you know about Natasha's activities online,' Christian began.

She nodded.

'Did you speak to her about it?'

She nodded again. 'I told her to be careful what she posted. I know that there are so many people out there who take advantage of good-looking young women. She said she knew what she was doing.'

'Did you see what she was posting?'

'No. When I asked, she said they were make-up tutorials, shopping trips and fashion tips. She's really into her fashion.'

'She didn't show you any of the photos or videos?'

'No.'

'Cara, the things Natasha posted could be interpreted in different ways by whoever was watching. Yes, she talks about make-up and fashion, but she's not always fully clothed in the videos.'

'Oh my God,' Cara said, collapsing in on herself.

Christian and Tom remained silent while Cara composed herself.

'Do you and Natasha talk much?' Christian asked.

'What about?' Cara asked, looking up, wiping her eyes.

'About anything. Her college work, friends, any worries she might have.'

'Not… No. Not really. Natasha is a very confident young woman. She doesn't have any worries.'

'We've spoken to a counsellor who works at the college Natasha goes to. He's told us that she's visited him a few times and talked about her popularity on social media. She said she often has sleepless nights trying to think of new ways of keeping people interested in her. She's very anxious about people growing bored of her, disliking her new posts and unfollowing her. It sounds like she was struggling under the expectation of others. Did she ever discuss this with you?'

'No. Never.' Cara looked confused. It was obviously the first she was hearing of her daughter's worries.

'Did you ever ask her about it?'

'No. Is this what you think this is all about? Do you think someone has contacted her through social media and done something to her?'

'We don't know, Cara. It's one option we're looking at, but it's going to take time. She has thousands of followers. Is there anyone she's mentioned recently? Did a name keep cropping up in conversation that didn't use to?'

Cara thought for a moment, her brow furrowed as her eyes darted left and right. 'No. I don't think so.'

Christian looked at Tom and gave him a slight nod. They'd had a brief chat before the interview began. It was time for Tom to take the lead.

Tom cleared his throat and leaned forward on the table. 'Cara,' he began, his voice softer, more sympathetic. 'I was at your house for three days. I've seen the way you and Derek are coping with Natasha's disappearance and there is a vast difference. I've yet to see Derek show any form of emotion. Is there something we should know about? Or is there anything you'd like to share with us?'

Cara looked down. She placed a shaking hand on her forehead and took several, slow, deep breaths as she seemed to compose herself. Eventually, she gathered the strength to look up. She turned pale, ashen, as if she was about to be sick.

'Derek isn't Natasha's father,' she said. 'Derek and I met when we were both at school. We started going out but split up when he went off to university in Liverpool. I stayed in Sheffield. I met someone else. I got married and had Natasha. Angus – that was my husband – he hit me. Not just once. He broke me down. One night he said if I ever told anyone, he would kill Natasha in front of me, make me watch, then he'd kill me. I ran away that night. I went back to my mum's and … well, I was a mess.' She stopped while she wiped her eyes. 'It was a long time before I was able to think about seeing a man again. Mum told me Derek had moved back to Sheffield. I looked him up and we more or less picked up where we left off.' A hint of a smile formed on her tired face.

'Where is Angus now?' Christian asked.

'Oh, he's long since dead. He was beaten up in a brawl at a pub in Scarborough. His dad had to turn the life-support machine off. I read about it in the paper. I didn't cry. He deserved it for what he put me through.'

'Does Derek know any of this?' Tom asked.

'Yes. Derek knows everything.'

'How does he feel about Natasha? Like I said, when I was there, I was under the impression he didn't care much for her.'

'He does. He loves her,' Cara said. 'In his own way,' she added.

'What does that mean?'

Cara's bottom lip began to wobble. She struggled to maintain her hold on her emotions. She clearly wanted to speak, but the words wouldn't come.

'Cara, you can tell us anything.'

She rolled back the sleeves of her jumper. There was red bruising around her wrists.

'Last night'—she began, almost choking on her words—'I accused Derek of doing something to Natasha. I've often felt she's been in his way. He grabbed me. It was the first time I felt... I... I could see Angus in his eyes.'

'What did Derek say when you accused him?' Christian asked.

'Nothing. He said I was being hysterical.'

'Do you think he's done something with Natasha?'

She shook her head. 'I don't know. I honestly don't know. And that scares me to death.'

---

'Sorry to keep you waiting, Mr Klein,' Christian said when he and Tom entered Interview Room 3.

They had spoken at length to Cara and asked if she wanted to report her husband for assault or if she wanted them to take her to a hostel. She said no to both. She had no intention of leaving the family home, especially when Natasha could come back at any time. She promised Christian and Tom that she would call them if she felt she was in danger. There was nothing more they could do for her.

Tom went through the same introduction with Derek as he did with Cara, telling him that their conversation was being recorded merely for the purpose of helping with their inquiries.

Derek sat up straight and looked bored and impatient, his eyes dancing around the room, taking in the video camera and voice recorders, rather than looking at the detectives and paying attention to what they were saying. It was as if this whole thing was an inconvenience to him.

'Derek, we've spoken to Cara. She's told us about you not being Natasha's biological father,' Tom said. 'While I was at your home, I noticed that you and Cara had been reacting differently to Natasha's disappearance. You haven't seemed too bothered. Why is that?'

He shrugged. 'Cara's got it into her head that she's been kidnapped or trafficked. She watches far too many documentaries.'

'What do you think has happened to her?'

'She's probably just gone off somewhere. She likes to create drama, does Natasha. All this exposure she's getting online and in the newspapers, it'll all be to increase her followers on social media.'

'So you're not worried.'

'No.'

'Derek.' Christian took over. 'Natasha has been missing since Thursday afternoon. It's now Tuesday. Her mobile phone was found by the side of the road. Her social media pages haven't been accessed and her bank account hasn't been used. Don't you think that might point to something more serious than a teenager throwing a strop?'

Derek frowned as he thought. He scratched his chin and ran his fingers over his head. 'I… I suppose I haven't wanted to think about it. I mean, you don't, do you? You always think these things will happen to other people.'

'What things?'

It was a while before Derek answered. He looked uncomfortable. 'I keep… I keep picturing her, Natasha, dead, somewhere.'

'You think she's dead?'

'Well, don't you? She's nineteen years old. She goes out in next to nothing, everything on show. I've seen the things she posts online. I also know what some of these sick people think when they see a beautiful woman online. Someone's groomed her … I know it. Why aren't you out there looking for her instead of questioning me and her mother like this?' he asked, almost shouting.

Christian looked at Tom, whose expression was one of concern. Christian wasn't fooled.

'No offence, Derek, but I don't think you'll be nominated for any BAFTAs next year.'

'What?' Derek asked, his face turning red.

'We walked in here and you looked bored to tears. It was obvious you'd rather be anywhere else in the world than in a police interview room. As soon as the questions get tricky, you turn emotional. Only you did it a bit too quickly for it to be genuine and the hesitations in your speech came on too suddenly. I've been around too make fakes in my career.'

Derek pushed his chair back. He stared at Christian with a blank expression. 'Okay. You want the truth? Fine. I don't like Natasha. She's selfish. She's self-obsessed, self-absorbed, she's horrible to her mother, she flirts with every single bloke who looks at her twice then dismisses them when they come on to her. She thinks she has so much to offer the world when in reality she's just a vacuous, empty-headed, second-rate wannabe. There, are you happy?'

'Why do you hate her so much?'

'I don't hate her. I just… I don't like her. She wants everything handed to her on a plate. She wants to coast through life and be given things rather than work for them. Life isn't like that.'

'Have you told her all this?'

'She knows how I feel.'

'Does Cara know?'

'I… No. I don't think so.'

'Do you argue with Natasha?' Christian asked.

'No. You can't argue with Natasha. She's always right. Apparently. I learned a long time ago it's better to leave her to it and let her fall down in her own way.'

'Do you think that's what's happened? She's maybe attracted the attention of the wrong person, and this is her comeuppance?'

Slowly, Derek nodded. 'Yes. I think it is.'

'You don't seem bothered.'

'If Natasha is injured or something shocking has happened, I will help to pick up the pieces as long as she's learned a little bit more about what life is really like.'

'A harsh lesson,' Tom said.

'Life is harsh,' Derek said, a stern edge to his voice.

'We still don't have your alibi for when Natasha went missing on Thursday afternoon,' Tom said.

'Yes, you do. You just don't believe me. My story won't change. I was at home, on my own, in the living room, eating a sandwich and relaxing. That's my alibi.'

---

Christian and Tom returned to the HMCU feeling deflated.

'I can't believe you knew Derek was faking those tears. I was taken in.'

'When you've been a detective as long as I have and interviewed the scum I've interviewed, you start to recognise the fake emotions. Even *Midsomer Murders* wouldn't have put up with a performance like that.'

'Do you think he was telling us the truth after that?'

'I think he was. He knew he couldn't lie.'

'I can't believe he hates his own daughter, though,' Tom said, pulling out his chair and flopping into it.'

'Like he said, he doesn't hate her, he just doesn't like her. I'm sure there are members of your family you don't like.'

Tom didn't say anything. He quickly looked away. He got up, headed over to the kettle and flicked it on. 'So, where do we go from here?' he asked, without looking back.

Christian thought for a moment. 'Well, we can't rule Derek out so we keep him in our sights and continue to question him until he can provide an alibi, or he cracks. The fact he isn't her biological father adds a different spin on things, too. Even if he did like her, his feelings wouldn't be the same towards her if he was her real father.' He pulled out a chair and sat down. 'Derek said he's seen some of the things she's posted online. How much interest does he have in her posts? It's not impossible that he was attracted to her – there's no blood connection, after all. Could he have made a move, been rejected, and it got out of hand?'

'There are a good few hours missing in his alibi, from leaving work to Cara coming home,' Tom said. 'Long enough for him to hide a body.'

'Exactly. Where are the nosy neighbours when you need them?' Christian asked, more to himself.

'On the flip side,' Tom began, 'Jamie told us how obsessed she was with creating content online. What if someone contacted her, offered her something to help with gaining more followers, she's met them and … well, she's either been gang-raped and killed or she's been drugged and trafficked.'

'I'm afraid that's where my thoughts are running, too. We've no witnesses to Natasha's disappearance. Nobody has seen her anywhere. It's like she's disappeared without a trace.'

'The perfect disappearance,' Tom said.

## Chapter Twenty-One

It was dark by the time Matilda arrived at the former farmhouse she called home. There was no sign of life anywhere; even the birds in the trees were silent. She parked Adele's Porsche in the garage and went into the house. While she still had her coat on, she went to the kitchen, grabbed a bottle of wine from the fridge and poured herself a large glass.

Matilda felt drained. She had spent the whole afternoon with Helen Walsh, trying, somehow, to make her realise that life does get better after losing someone so close. Most of what she'd said had been a lie. James had been dead for six years and she still felt like bursting into tears when she looked at her wedding photographs, though that might be something to do with her dated haircut. She didn't suit a fringe.

Although she understood Helen's plea to Matilda to hand over a potential killer for her to enact her own revenge, what Matilda found more disturbing was the fact that she had given it careful consideration. She liked Helen. She was a good woman who was going through hell. She was looking for someone to blame, other than herself, for Liam's death. Would killing the person responsible make her feel any better? Matilda doubted it would, but she couldn't help but think it was a justice that needed delivering, if there was no proof of murder.

She pulled out a chair at the table and sat down. She took another long swig of wine. She was a detective. She was supposed to uphold the law. She caught the criminals, prepared the case for court, and saw them locked up. She didn't hand over killers to grieving relatives for closure. But she could perfectly understand why some people took the law into their own hands, especially when the law didn't work in their favour.

Her mobile rang, making her jump. She fished it out of her pocket and saw her sister's face filling the screen.

'Hello, Harriet, how are you?' Matilda asked.

'Knackered. Listen, I've been looking online to get Nathan a little runaround for his birthday,' she said, referring to her eldest son who had recently passed his driving test. 'You'll never guess whose car I've found for sale.'

'If it's Sebastian Stan's, I'll buy it. I don't care how much it costs.'

'Mum's.'

'What?'

'Mum's selling her Mini.'

'Are you sure?'

'Of course I'm sure. I know the number plate.'

'I didn't know she was selling her car.'

'Neither did I.'

'Have you spoken to her about it?' Matilda asked.

'No. I thought, well, you know what Mum can be like. I thought maybe you'd want to talk to her about it together.'

'We could do.'

Matilda's doorbell rang.

'Shit. Harriet, someone's at my door, can you hang on?'

'Yes, that's me. I've just arrived to come and pick you up.'

Matilda strode to the door and pulled it open to find her sister standing on the doorstep wearing a long black coat and killer heels. Her recently dyed blonde hair was being swept back by the chilly breeze.

'I've just realised, you've got your licence back, haven't you?'

'A few weeks, now,' Matilda said.

'I could have saved myself the journey.'

'You certainly could.' Matilda studied her sister. 'Have you lost weight?'

'I've joined a gym.'

'I can't think of anything worse. Let me just grab my keys and a jacket.'

Harriet entered the house and stood in the doorway. She looked around at the vast space. 'I honestly don't know how you can live all the way out here. I mean, yes, it's a beautiful house, but, well, I've seen *Scream*, I know what happens when you're alone in the middle of nowhere at night.'

'Thanks, Harriet. Why not just give GhostFace a call and tell him I'll leave a key under the mat for him?'

'Sorry.'

'Come on. We'll take your car.'

Once in Harriet's Ford Focus, they belted up and set off for Greenhill, where Penny lived, not a five-minute walk from Harriet's house.

'How are things going with you and Patrick?' Matilda asked, referring to her sister's new boyfriend, who also happened to be her boss.

'Very well, thank you,' Harriet beamed. 'We're going away in a few weeks.'

'Where to?'

'Scotland. He's got a house up there. Can you believe that? He's actually got a second house in the middle of the countryside.'

'Nice. Let me know the dates you're going up and I'll pass your details on to GhostFace.'

Harriet glanced at Matilda. 'Not a touch jealous, are we?'

'Of what? You dating an estate agent? I don't think so.'

Harriet shook her head. 'Why do people have such a negative attitude towards estate agents?'

'Because they're shysters.'

'I'm an estate agent.'

'Case in point.' Matilda grinned at her sister.

'He asks about you.'

'Does he? I've never met him.'

'The boys talk about you a lot. He almost joined the police force himself when he was about twenty.'

'Only almost?'

'Yes. He said it wasn't for him.'

There was nothing Matilda could say to that. She turned back to looking out of the side window at the darkened Sheffield landscape whizzing by as Harriet broke the speed limit. It wasn't long before they were pulling up outside Penny's cottage.

'Well, it's not been sold yet as it's still in the driveway,' Matilda said. 'Are you sure it was Mum's car?'

Harriet took out her mobile and showed Matilda a screenshot from a secondhand car website. 'It's Mum's car.'

Matilda knocked on her mother's door and stood back from the step. Penny answered the door wearing her coat. She looked shocked at seeing her daughters together.

'Are you off out?' Matilda asked.

'No. Why?'

'You've got your coat on.'

'Sodding fire's packed up again,' she said, standing back and letting Matilda and Harriet into the house.

'Bloody hell, Mum, it's freezing in here,' Matilda said, going into the living room.

'Why haven't you put the central heating on?' Harriet said.

Penny picked up the remote and turned off the game show she had been watching. 'I don't like central heating. It gives me a headache. Besides, have you seen how much energy costs these days? Greedy sods. I'm not increasing their bonuses, thank you very much.'

'So, you're going to sit here and die of hypothermia? That'll really show them,' Harriet said. 'I'm putting the heating on.' She went out into the hallway.

'What's wrong with the fire?' Matilda asked, looking at the gas fire with the fake coal frontage.

'It won't stay on. It comes on, but then it goes out. I'm wondering if there's a loose connection somewhere.'

'Have you called someone to take a look at it?'

'Not yet,' she said, sitting down and pulling her coat around her.

'Mum, what's going on?' Matilda asked, folding her arms across her chest.

'Nothing. Why?'

'It should start warming up here soon,' Harriet came back into the living room.

'Why is your car for sale?' Matilda asked.

'Who told you?'

'I saw it online. I was looking for a runaround for Nathan for his birthday.'

Penny looked down to hide her emotions from her daughters. Matilda went to sit next to her. Up close, she could see her mother's hair needed touching up at the roots and her usually manicured nails were overdue for a shape and polish.

'I didn't understand it at first,' Penny began. Her voice was quiet and shaking with tears. 'I got a letter saying the firm your dad and I have our private pensions with has gone into administration. I went to a financial adviser for some free advice, and he said that TGC were having troubles and that the pandemic had been the final straw. They've gone under.'

'Where's the letter?' Harriet asked.

'On the rack.' She nodded to the bureau in the corner of the room.

'TGC is the company you have your pension with?' Matilda asked. Penny nodded. 'Isn't there some government protection thing against pensions?'

'Usually, yes, but your dad didn't pay into it. I left all this to him. I thought… I foolishly thought I'd be the first to go.'

'Oh, Mum.' Matilda put her arm around her and pulled her close.

'The payments stopped a couple of months ago. I've only got my state pension coming in and that doesn't even cover my bills. I've got the savings your dad left and his insurance, but there's much more going out than I've got coming in.'

'That's why you're selling the car.'

'I rarely use it.'

'Mum, you're out all the time,' Matilda said. 'You go swimming, you go out for meals to see your friends.'

'Not any more I don't. I've cancelled the gym membership, and I can't afford to eat out.'

'There's nothing really wrong with the fire, is there?' Matilda asked.

'There is, actually. I just can't afford to get it fixed. I put it on and warm up this room, but then it goes out, so I usually just put my coat on until it's time to go to bed.'

Harriet had the letter from TGC in one hand and was scrolling through her phone with the other. 'According to this, they've gone under with debts of more than twenty million pounds. There's nothing about what's going to happen to the customers, because administrators are busy sorting out the recovery of assets. It says that it could be up to a year before anything is paid out to customers, and that's only likely to be the ones who took out protection insurance.'

'I can't believe Dad didn't take out any insurance,' Matilda said. 'That's not like him at all. He was always so careful with money.'

'Maybe he didn't think TGC was a risk,' Penny said, defending her late husband. 'I mean, who would have guessed a pandemic would have happened?'

'Look, Mum,' Matilda began. 'Turn the heating on. If you get a big bill, I'll sort it out. I've got all that money from the sale of the house in the bank and James was insured up to the eyeballs. I've nobody to leave it to.'

'I think Nathan and Joseph had their eye on that,' Harriet said with a sly wink.

'I wondered why they only text in the run-up to their birthdays and Christmas,' Matilda replied with a smile. 'And you can take your car off the market, too, Mum. You need that. It's your lifeline.'

Penny tried to speak but her tears took over. 'I never thought I'd be facing poverty in my old age.'

Matilda gripped her mother harder. They'd never been close, but since she was shot, they'd repaired their fractious relationship and Matilda had seen her mother as a human being rather than a battle-axe.

'Where's your purse?'

'Why?'

'Give me your bank details and I'll transfer some money across now to tide you over. Then we'll look at your bills and sort something out.'

Penny grabbed her daughter's hands and squeezed them tight. She looked her in the eye. 'I don't know what to say.'

'You're my mum. You don't have to say anything.'

'Pack a bag, Mum,' said Harriet. 'You can come and stay with me and the boys for a couple of nights until we can get your fire fixed.'

Penny lifted Harriet's hand and kissed the back of it. 'Thank you. Both of you.' She stood up and made her way out of the room.

Harriet went over to the sofa and sat beside Matilda.

'It's the first time I've looked at Mum and realised that she's old,' Harriet said.

'I heard that, you cheeky cow,' Penny called out from the stairs.

Matilda started laughing. 'Nothing wrong with her hearing.'

## Chapter Twenty-Two

Wednesday, 16 March 2021

There was no reason for Matilda Darke to attend the morning briefings of the HMCU or the CID. If there were any issues, DI Brady, or DI Drinkwater who was currently overseeing CID, would contact her. They rarely did. Matilda's role was simply to keep an eye on the budget, regulate overtime spending to a minimum, and make the tough decisions should any officer decide to share crime scene photographs over WhatsApp or take too much interest in a particular witness. Yet how could Matilda possibly know what was going on and who was doing what when she was confined to an office on the first floor with CID upstairs and HMCU downstairs? Which pen-pushing, polyester-suit-wearing, degree-waving tosspot came up with this idea?

Matilda missed the HMCU. She missed the camaraderie with her colleagues. And she missed the easy access to Sian's snack drawer. She closed the door of her small office behind her and headed down to her former unit.

'Jamie Peterson has an alibi for our time frame of Natasha Klein going missing,' DC Tom Simpson said as the morning briefing began.

Matilda's former Avengers were assembled. Coffees and teas had been made and bars of chocolate handed round by Sian, who was keen to get rid of the surplus. Matilda sat on a free chair at the top of the room while Christian took control.

'He was on a Zoom conference call with… Hang on a minute,' Tom said as he consulted his notebook. 'I'm sure I had the name of the organisation written down. Anyway, it was a really big deal. Every few months there's a meeting with counsellors and therapists who work in young mental health care at various universities around the country. They talk about what the common stressors are and try to help each other out with difficult case studies. The meeting went on for several hours. I spent a lot of time last night contacting most of the people who took part, just to make sure Jamie wasn't lying.'

'Okay. Good work, Tom,' Christian said. 'However, I really don't like the fact that he knew two people who are now either dead or missing. Also, he told Liam about the dark web and suicide message boards. He's worth keeping an eye on.'

'Do we know what's happening to Jamie at the university?' Matilda asked.

'He's been suspended while the university conducts a review,' Christian said.

'That's good.'

'Now, our registered sex offender who lives close to where Natasha went missing, Lloyd Tatlock, has an alibi.' Christian began. 'It was his day off from work as a plumber for the council. He was with a friend most of the day. They went to a betting shop and a couple of pubs. His mate backs this up and we've got CCTV from one of the betting shops and pubs that confirms it. We need to check the rest of the pubs he says he visited, but he's looking clean.'

'How did the search go of the open areas opposite East Bank Road?' Matilda asked.

'They're continuing into today. Nothing of interest has been found so far,' Christian answered.

'Zofia,' Matilda began. 'You've been looking at Natasha and Liam Walsh's social media pages. Do they follow any of the same people?'

'No. Liam wasn't active much anyway,' Zofia said. 'He hardly interacted with anyone. He posted a few articles and photos but if people commented, he didn't respond. He rarely commented on other people's posts, and he didn't follow anyone whom we could question.'

'Who did he follow?'

'People who work in conservation and animal welfare. People who work on documentaries like *Planet Earth* and *Blue Planet*. He follows people like Chris Packham, Simon Reeve, Levison Wood, and organisations such as the WWF and Greenpeace.'

'Ooh, Levison Wood,' Sian said. 'He's my kind of man.'

'I'm more of a Bear Grylls woman,' Zofia said. 'I think he's gorgeous.'

'No. I went off him when I saw that programme where he drank his own urine,' Sian said, pulling a face.

'Moving swiftly on,' Matilda said. 'I personally believe Liam Walsh was murdered, but do we have any firm evidence that backs that up?'

The room fell silent.

'We've spoken to everyone on his university course,' Scott said. 'They all said he was quiet and shy. He didn't mix. He sat apart from everyone and always had a painfully thoughtful look on his face. He wasn't approachable.'

'There's nothing more we can do, Mat,' Christian said.

'But the email and the card...'

'It's not evidence. If there were fingerprints, if we could track the sender of the email. If we had anything we could forensically follow up on, we would,' Christian said.

'We can't just leave it like this. I don't like the thought of someone taking advantage of someone who was so desperate, so unhappy, and allowing his mother to believe he took his own life,' Matilda said. She could feel the emotional intensity rising inside her. 'As parents,' Matilda looked at Christian and Sian, 'could you just leave it with so many unanswered questions?'

Sian looked down at her desk.

'As a parent, no,' Christian said. 'As a detective, we have no choice. There is nothing else we can do. We've done everything we can, and more.'

Matilda looked at the team. They all had blank expressions on their faces. The investigation had stalled before it had even got anywhere. She stood up and headed for the door.

'Where are you going?' Christian asked.

'One last push,' she said without stopping.

## Chapter Twenty-Three

It wasn't long after Matilda left the office that Sian's phone began vibrating in her pocket. She took it out, saw who was calling, and quickly walked out into the corridor, where she found a quiet space beside a broken vending machine. She swiped to answer.

'Cliff, hello,' she said in a quiet voice.

'Is everything all right?' he asked.

'Yes. I just don't want to be overheard.'

'Oh. Do you want me to send you a text? It might be full of spelling mistakes, though. I don't have the thumbs for rapid texting.'

'No. It's fine. Have you spoken to Stuart?'

'I have. He's working in the kitchens at the moment, but his time associating with other prisoners is limited. I was escorting him back to his cell yesterday when I had a chat. Now, I'm no psychologist, obviously, but I don't think he was lying when he said he had no bad feeling towards you or … what's she called again … Matilda Drake?'

'Darke. DCI Darke.'

'He's accepted why he's in here. He knows what he did was

wrong and has come to terms with his punishment, his sentence. Like I said, he's a model prisoner. He—'

'Thank you, Cliff,' Sian interrupted.

'Sian, he really would like you to visit him.'

'No,' she answered quickly.

'I...'

'Cliff, please.'

'Sian, you asked me to speak to him, and I did. He's asked me to speak to you. It's only fair that this goes both ways.'

She sighed. It would be wrong of her to end the call. 'Go on,' she said reluctantly.

'I do believe Stuart is sorry for what he's done, for the pain he's caused you and your family. He's seeing a counsellor on a regular basis, and he sees the prison chaplain, too.'

'A priest?' Sian was genuinely shocked.

'He's repenting.'

'I don't know what to say.'

'Promise me you'll give it serious consideration. He needs something to look forward to, something to hope for.'

Sian could feel the emotion rising inside her. She'd made a promise to all four of her children that she wouldn't make any decisions unless she consulted them first.

'I'll think about it,' she said and ended the call before she said something she'd later regret.

---

'I'm sorry, did I hear you correctly?' Chief Constable Benjamin Ridley loosened his tie.

'I know I have no physical evidence and it's all based on conjecture, but I think a second post mortem might reveal something missed in the first,' Matilda said.

'You want to exhume Liam Walsh's body based on a crackpot email and a weird sympathy card?'

'There's also the CCTV footage showing Liam was followed on the night he died.'

'No. You have CCTV footage showing two people walking in the same direction.'

'The screenshots on Liam's iPad show he spoke to someone on a suicide chatroom who said they had terminal cancer and would message him directly to arrange a meet.'

'And you have no evidence that conversation or meeting ever took place.'

'If Liam Walsh was pushed off the roof of the Arts Tower there could be bruising and possible defence wounds. What if Liam put up a fight? He could have skin samples or fibres under his nails. What if they arranged to meet in a pub beforehand and this other guy spiked his drink to lower his resistance to being pushed?'

Ridley sighed. 'I'm assuming the original post-mortem sent a blood sample to toxicology.'

'It did. They recorded evidence of alcohol in his system, but they only found what they were looking for. They didn't test for drugs.'

'All of which will be out of his system by now.'

'His bloodstream, yes, but not his hair. Hair follicles can store traces of drugs.' Matilda's voice was rising as she became more desperate to keep this case going.

'I'm aware of the science, Matilda. Do you know how distressing a body exhumation is for the relatives?'

'Yes, I do. But Helen Walsh wants answers. I've...' Matilda stopped herself.

'If you tell me you've already promised her, I will seriously lose my shit with you.'

'I haven't promised her an exhumation. I haven't mentioned it to anyone else. I have given Helen my word that I will explore every available avenue to find out what happened to her son.'

'And you've done that.'

'No. I haven't,' Matilda said, firmly.

'I cannot agree to an exhumation on such flimsy evidence. I'm sorry, Matilda, no. Now, I don't need to remind you that you're not an operational detective. I walk past your office many times to find you're not there. There are other cases that need attention and you're taking skilled detectives off that for your own agenda. It's not on. I'm guessing you've seen Natasha Klein on the front of all the papers this morning.'

Matilda didn't answer.

'Matilda, this is exactly what the email writer wanted: to use up resources and have us chasing our tails on a dead end. We did everything we could.'

Matilda didn't say anything. She'd refused a seat and stood by Ridley's desk. Her expression was one of resigned angst.

'I know why you're doing this,' Ridley said. 'You hate the fact that your job has changed so you're latching onto this in the hope that there's something more going on and you'll be able to return to the front line because we obviously can't do without your amazing analytical brain.'

'That's not fair,' she said, almost emotionally.

'Maybe there is a serial killer out there who's done such an amazing job he's defeated us all. But we work on evidence. Hard evidence. We cannot put a case together based on what-ifs and maybes. Look, Matilda,' Ridley said, leaning forward, interlocking his fingers, and lowering his voice. 'If this is real, then there'll be a second email. We both know that. If you hear from him again, we'll review the Liam Walsh case. For now, I'm asking you to leave it alone and stop taking detectives off an active investigation to chase after a phantom. Have I made myself clear?'

Reluctantly, Matilda nodded. She headed for the door with her head down.

'By the way, I looked up Lil Nas X,' Ridley said.

Matilda turned back.

'I was the spitting image of him when I was his age,' he said, a twinkle in his eye.

'The more I look at you, the more I think you're a dead ringer for Morgan Freeman.'

'Isn't he in his eighties?'

'Precisely.'

'That's very catty.'

'I'm feeling catty.'

Matilda left the office and closed the door firmly behind her. She wasn't looking forward to having to tell Helen her son's death would no longer be investigated.

## Chapter Twenty-Four

Danny Hanson travelled from Sheffield to London St Pancras by train on Tuesday afternoon. On the three-hour-plus journey, he went through *The Perfect Killer* on his iPad, making notes on what he wanted to know about Stuart's family that Sebastian Lister hadn't been able to discover. There were so many questions he wanted to ask Sian but knew she wouldn't let him. He could make it up. He'd been on the scene during the investigation. He knew all about Stuart's crimes and how he committed his murders, but he wanted the human angle. People would read Lister's book and understand the warped, evil mind of a killer, but what about those left behind? What about the wife and the children who were having to live with what their husband and father had done? That's what people were really interested in.

He sat back in his seat. He could feel a headache coming on, the tension rising inside him of knowing that people didn't like journalists and reporters. They saw them as vultures who preyed on the weak, and hounded celebrities. He wasn't like that at all. Yes, he was the first to admit he'd occasionally used underhand tactics to get a story, but it was always in the public's interest. Maybe sneaking into Matilda Darke's hospital room while she was in a coma was a step too far but he'd more than redeemed himself in the Magnolia House investigation. He deserved to write the story of Stuart's crimes from Sian's point of view. He'd paid his dues.

He arrived at his mother's apartment in Maida Vale after dark. She wasn't in when he knocked but the next-door neighbour came out with a message for him and a spare key.

*Sweetheart,*

*If you'd given me more notice I could have changed my plans and we could have done something. I'm away with Malcolm for the night. Help yourself to anything in the cupboards. I'll be back at lunchtime if you're still around. Mally sends his love.*

*Kisses,*

*Mum*

He thanked the kindly neighbour and let himself into his mother's apartment. Why couldn't she have sent him that information in a text? He wasn't surprised his mother was absent. She'd probably arranged to be away for the night as soon as he told her he was stopping off to see her. His parents had been divorced for more than ten years now. His father had remarried, and his mum had stayed single for a long time until Mally came on the scene two years ago. Danny took an instant dislike to him following Malcolm's opening remark that Danny should get his hair cut short if he was hoping for a future presenting BBC News. 'People trust a crewcut, Danny. They don't want Brexit explained to them by Ross Poldark.' Malcolm had muscled his way into his mother's life and taken over. Danny had no idea what he did for a living, and didn't care, but his mother was impressed and often sent Danny a selfie with her arm wrapped around the smug, fat-faced tosser, a glamorous landscape in the background.

The apartment was an open-plan affair with floor-to-ceiling windows maximising the illusion of space and giving a sprawling view of London. He looked around at the expensive furniture, all whites and creams, clean lines, minimalism. Nothing of this spoke of his mother. She loved comfort. This was all Malcolm's idea. On the positive side, there were two bottles of Veuve Clicquot in the fridge which would go very nicely with the stuffed crust pizza he'd ordered from Just Eat.

Sitting on an uncomfortable sofa, feet up on the glass coffee table, pizza box on his lap, Danny looked up Belinda Robinson on Facebook. She posted a great deal and, in Danny's opinion, most of it was mind-numbingly dull and uninteresting. Pouting selfies in the gym or in a coffee shop holding up a Frappe with her name spelled incorrectly on the plastic cup; taking part in a march in central London for a cause she probably had no interest in but felt she needed to be seen playing a part in. Danny was less than a decade older than Belinda, but he really disliked the next generation playing at caring about the future of the planet and putting the blame on people like him.

One person cropped up on Belinda's social media pages often, and was tagged in the photos, too – Rebecca Lavine. Flicking between Facebook and Instagram pages of the two, it was evident that Belinda and Rebecca were dating. He zoomed in on a polo shirt Rebecca was wearing in one picture, which revealed the logo of a pub she was working in. He smiled to himself. He would target Rebecca first, then seek out Belinda to chat with.

---

Danny woke with a hangover. He wasn't used to champagne. Thinking back, he had never had a glass of the real stuff before. He'd tasted Prosecco and hated it, but the Veuve Clicquot had woken his tastebuds and he perfectly understood why Malcolm kept two bottles in the fridge. He showered, left his wet towels on the floor of the luxurious en suite, his breakfast dishes in the sink, the empty champagne bottles and pizza box on the coffee table, and gave the whole apartment a two-fingered salute as he left. He decided against leaving his mother a proof copy of his book. She wouldn't read it. She wouldn't be interested. She never was.

It was a cool day with a stiff breeze blowing, but the sky was blue, and the sun was blazing. This did nothing for Danny's hangover and he felt around in his bag for his sunglasses. He felt sick on the Underground, and the train journey to Southampton was equally juddering. As delicious as the champagne was, he'd stick to lager in the future. His stomach could handle Heineken.

He arrived at Southampton a little after five o'clock and quickly found a café to eat something wholesome and plain to settle his stomach. Bangers and mash, onion gravy and two mugs of tea soon gave him the energy required to remove the sunglasses and formulate a plan of attack.

He took a taxi to The Stag, a student bar on the Highfield campus where Rebecca worked. It was still only early and, apart from a group of lads noisily watching a baseball match on a large screen, the pub was relatively empty, and the staff had little to do. He spotted Rebecca straightaway. She was standing by the tills chatting to two other staff members who towered over her. She was small with dark, shoulder-length curly hair. She talked animatedly, using gestures and smiling. She gave off an aura of happiness and high energy, and Danny could feel some of it leaching into him as he approached the bar, a smile on his face.

'Yes, mate,' one of the male staff members said, pulling away from his conversation.

'Could I have a word with Rebecca, please?'

'Sure. Bec, you're wanted.'

Rebecca turned to face Danny. The smile didn't leave her face.

'Can I help you?' she asked. Her accent was West Country, thick, warm and welcoming.

'Rebecca Lavine?'

'That's right.'

'My name's Danny. I'm a writer. I'm researching a book on

Stuart Mills, focusing on his family rather than his crimes. I've already spoken to Sian and I'm going around the children to get their take on everything that happened. I was wondering if you could tell me, as Belinda's girlfriend, how she's coping with it all.'

Her smile began to fade. 'I don't know. I don't know if I should talk to you.'

'It's perfectly all right. I'm not writing a hatchet job or anything. I'm not interested in the gruesome side of the crimes. That's already been covered. I'm guessing you know all about *The Perfect Killer* by Sebastian Lister.'

'Yes. Belinda didn't want me to read it, but I did. I downloaded a copy. What he did, it makes you shiver, doesn't it?' she said with a shudder.

'It certainly does. It can't have been easy for Belinda, either, what with exams and everything.'

'Belinda's strong. She doesn't let anyone get to her. She gets a bit down and sad occasionally, but that's when she's worried about her mum. She can cope with everything people say to her.'

'Do people say things to her?'

'Sometimes. Not as much as they did at first. She soon put them in their place,' she said with a grin. 'That's why I like her so much. She's got so much fight and spirit.'

'How does Belinda cope with what her father did? Does she talk about him much?'

'No. She says she wants nothing to do with him. He's dead as far as she's concerned.'

'What about her brothers? Do they have contact with him?'

'I don't know. I've only met Anthony. He seems nice. He's a bit like Belinda. I don't know the other two. I think they're more like Sian, a bit more sensitive. The youngest, what's he called?'

'Gregory.'

'Yes. I think he'd like to see his dad. Belinda said she's talked him out of it, but … well, I'm not sure if I agree with that. It's up to him, isn't it, at the end of the day? I mean, they might not like what he did, but he's still their dad.'

'So, Belinda does talk about him then?'

Two male students approached the bar. Rebecca moved further down to a quieter area. Danny followed.

'She does, sometimes,' she said, softly. 'You know when you've had a few drinks and you're just lounging talking crap.'

'What does she say?'

'She just mentions how sad she is for her mum. She thought they were so happy, that they had the best life. She can't believe how he hid a completely different side to himself from them all. She gets…' She stopped herself.

'Go on,' Danny prompted.

'No. I shouldn't.'

'I might be able to help if it's something painful.'

She seemed to think about it for a moment. 'Belinda has nightmares sometimes. She wakes up with a jolt and she'll be sweating. When I ask her what she was dreaming about it's always the same thing, that her dad has killed her mother and brothers and he's coming for her. I mean, that's what he was planning, wasn't it?'

Danny nodded, though he didn't know any of that.

'Does she see anyone, a therapist?'

'No. I've told her she should, to talk things through, but she won't hear of it. She … well, not anymore, but, at the beginning, she…' Rebecca was clearly uncomfortable and struggling with whether she should reveal any more or not. She took a breath. 'When she first started uni, she was drinking quite a lot. She did go a bit off the rails. She skipped quite a lot of lectures and was told she needed to increase her attendance if she wanted to continue on the course. I've helped. My dad's a recovering alcoholic so I can deal with it. She only drinks at weekends now and we don't have any in the flat.'

'You're looking after her?'

'I am. I really like her.'

A call came for her. 'Bec, we're starting to fill up.'

'Coming. Is there anything else?'

'No. Thanks. You've been very helpful.' He was just about to walk away when he decided to push his luck a little bit further. 'Rebecca, what does Belinda think of her father's crimes?'

'I don't know what you mean,' she said with a frown.

'What Stuart did, he always said that he got himself caught up in something and, from his point of view, there was no other way out than to commit murder. Then it spiralled. But the crime of murder – is it ever justified?'

Her mouth fell open. Even the students at the bar turned to look at Danny with a shocked expression.

'Of course it isn't,' Rebecca said.

'Does Belinda think that, too?'

'I… Well… doesn't everyone?'

Danny left her question unanswered. He turned on his heel, nodded at the students at the bar, and left with a smirk on his lips.

# Part II

DAY 15

M urder. Murder. Say it slowly. Mur-der. Mur. Der. You can put so much stress and effort into such a small word. It's like a swear word, isn't it? Fuck! Bastard! Murder!

I think we've become complacent about murder. It's everywhere you look in the guise of entertainment. Columbo, Murder, She Wrote, Cracker, Inspector Morse, Luther, Mindhunter, Dexter, Shetland, Happy Valley, Vera, Criminal Minds, they're everywhere, and they're watched by millions around the world. You get the little old dears who enjoy a Midsomer Murder or a Father Brown in the afternoons with a Mr Kipling, or the so-called intellectuals who like the foreign ones with subtitles, and the people with dull and boring lives who tune into Line of Duty week after week for their one piece of excitement. Everyone loves a crime drama. You can dress it up as a cosy crime where a country vicar spikes a cup of tea with a deadly poison because some ruffian has embezzled the church roof fund, but at the end of the day, it's a murder. Someone is dead.

Yet, when it happens in reality, when it touches our lives, we're shocked. We're horrified. 'Oh my God! Did you hear about Jean down the road? She was found dead in her living room, battered to death.' Why are these people so mortified it's happened when they probably spent the previous night watching an old Foyle's War on some obscure channel?

I don't agree with murder as a form of entertainment. It's not entertaining in the slightest. It's destructive. It ingrains itself inside you. It never leaves you. It rots away at you until you're numb. Murder is frightening. Murder is chilling. People should be in fear of murder and not spend their days wondering who the killer in the latest Netflix drama series will turn out to be.

We don't get real serial killers anymore, thanks to the advance in forensic and GPS technology and CCTV on every building. But we could still have mass murderers if they were a little bit more creative and instilled the fear back into people's lives.

Everyone before me has been caught, with a few exceptions. I don't want to get caught, but I want people to be terrified of me. I want to see *the fear. I want to see DCI Matilda Darke and her team scared out of their fucking minds.*

From: <r9q040jujy9i0@hotmail.com>
Date: Monday, 1 January 1900 at 00:00
To: Darke, Matilda <matilda.darke@southyorkshire.police.co.uk>
Subject: 2 of 5.

Hello Matilda,

I see you've been to see Liam's mother a few times. It's good to see you're taking my claims seriously, though, the fact you haven't been beating the front door down to arrest me means one of two things. Either you're not as clever as you think you are and you haven't been able to identify me, or I really have committed the perfect murder. I'm certain it's the second one. I told you the perfect murder exists.

Let me provide you with a few more details regarding Liam Walsh. I knew he suffered with depression. He was a very sad individual. I actually felt sorry for him. He absorbed far too much information about what was going on in the world. You can't do that without going mad. Unfortunately, for Liam, he went mad. He wanted to kill himself but wanted someone to do it with him. He told me he was scared of being alone at the end. I pretended I had terminal cancer and wanted to take control of my own death. He fell for it. We met a couple of times before the day we chose to 'die'. On that Friday, we had a couple of drinks for courage then went up to the roof of the Arts Tower. We sat on the edge, feet dangling over, and that's when I told him. 'Liam, I don't have cancer. I'm here to kill you.' I grabbed his collar and threw him off the roof.

So, there's my confession to you, Matilda, but until you know who I am, there's nothing you can do with it. It's not like you can come round and arrest me, is it?

I do want to help you, though, Matilda. I want you to understand the various aspects of what murder actually is. I want to cause you sleepless nights as you kick yourself trying to find me, trying to find the evidence against me. It's going to be so hard for you, Matilda, because there is no evidence. It's all conjecture, hearsay, circumstantial. If we ever did meet in a courtroom, the prosecution would tear your case apart and I would walk away Scott free.

Murder is fascinating, isn't it, Mat. Do you mind if I call you Mat? Murder is the worst crime possible. You're literally destroying lives. You're removing someone from the planet, and their friends and loved ones are going to hurt forever. But murder is also the easiest of crimes, isn't it? One push off a building, a few seconds, and that's it. Or, in the case of Josie Pettifer, one bite of a piece of salmon. So sad.

I'll be in touch again soon, Mat. You're going to love my third victim.

From Hell.

## Chapter Twenty-Five

Monday, 29 March 2021

'Everything that can be done to locate Natasha Klein has been done,' DI Christian Brady said as he began the morning briefing. 'Woodland close to where she went missing has been searched and nothing has been found. We've interviewed everyone on her courses at the college, and all her tutors. We've interviewed her father more than once; we've had his car searched and been through the entire house. Zofia, bless her, has spent the past two weeks going through her social media pages and come up with nothing. Natasha has literally vanished without trace.' He turned to look at the smiling face of Natasha on the white board looking down at him. 'It pains me to say this, but we're going to have to scale back the case. It'll be passed to the cold case review unit in due course.'

The faces of the HMCU team were ashen. They hated an unsolved case.

'Remember Ruby Deighton?' Scott began. 'She's Natasha's best mate. They do a lot together. Anyway, on Friday afternoon, I went to her home. I thought she might be more forthcoming in her own environment.'

'You've been taking tips from Finn, haven't you?' Tom asked.

'Actually, yes, I have.' He smiled. 'Unfortunately, it didn't do any good. She wouldn't even let me through the front door. The thing is, her performance this time was a lot more subdued than when she came into the station. Personally, I think she's been told to keep her mouth shut.'

'Who by?' Christian asked.

'Your guess is as good as mine.'

The doors to the HMCU burst open, making them all jump. Matilda stood in the doorway.

'I've had another email.'

It was all Matilda needed to say for them to take notice. Finn held his hand out to take the printed email from her, but she told him she'd already forwarded it to him. She handed the sheet to Sian while Finn opened his emails and projected it onto the screen Christian pulled down, covering Natasha's smiling face. Everyone read it in perfect silence. Matilda didn't need to read it again. She stood back and watched her former team digest the words that chilled her to the bone.

'It's exactly as we suspected it then,' Finn said. 'He obviously did chat to Liam on the dark web message boards, lured him into a false state of security, then pushed him off the Arts Tower.'

'Only the killer could know about posing as someone with cancer to get to him,' Matilda said.

It had been more than two weeks since they'd stopped their review of Liam Walsh's death. There really was nothing more they could do. Matilda had to admit defeat until more evidence came to light, if it ever did.

In that time, Matilda had lost count of the number of phone calls she had received from Helen Walsh asking, begging, if there was any more information, if she was any closer to identifying who had killed her son. Helen was adamant Liam had been murdered, saying there was no way someone of Matilda's stature and rank would have been following up a random email unless there was credible evidence. With every call Matilda received, Helen became more and more unstable.

Now, finally, here it was, proof, if it were needed, that Liam Walsh had been killed, and how it had been done.

'The bastard,' Christian fumed. 'He actually told him what he was doing and then just threw him off the building like he was rubbish.'

'How can anyone do that?' Sian said. 'He took advantage of him. He let him think he had someone who could be with him at the end, make it less painful for him.'

'Is anyone looking up Josie Pettifer?' Finn asked.

'I'm on it,' Zofia said.

'Give Ridley a call, Scott,' Matilda said. 'I want him to see this.'

'Poor Liam.' Sian bowed her head.

'Poor Helen,' Matilda said, almost under her breath.

'Josephine Mary Pettifer died on Wednesday the second of December last year at the age of twenty. She was found in her flat the following morning by her father, Reginald Pettifer. She died of a massive anaphylactic shock after eating a meal which had been prepared with an oil containing traces of peanut, to which Josie was extremely allergic,' Zofia read from her screen.

'What was the coroner's ruling?' Matilda asked.

'Accidental death. He recommended that more should be done in factories, when preparing products that don't include highly allergic ingredients, to stop cross-contamination.'

'How can this be murder?' Scott asked with a heavy frown.

'I'm not sure,' Matilda mused. 'Anything else?' she asked Zofia.

'There's a newspaper article from the local paper from 2018. Hang on, I'll bring it up on the screen. Erm… Finn, any chance…?'

Finn rolled his eyes, went over to Zofia's desk, and brought the article up on the projector screen.

'I've shown you how to do this.'

'I know, but I have so much important stuff in my head that there's no room for banal stuff. That's why you're here.'

'You do realise that I'm now a rank higher than you, don't you?'

'Oh bugger, I keep forgetting. Sorry. Love you to bits,' she said, blowing him a kiss.

'Really? Sexual advances in the workplace?' he mocked.

'Jesus, you can't say anything anymore, can you?'

'Adding blasphemy to sexual harassment. It's not your day, is it?' He nudged her playfully.

The article from the *Star* stated that Josie had ordered a Chinese takeaway from a restaurant in Attercliffe, told them about her allergies, yet she had still suffered an anaphylactic shock as they prepared her meal using nut oil. She successfully sued the takeaway for £20,000 and demanded more be done to make people aware of just how serious even the smallest trace of a highly allergenic ingredient could be to someone who suffered.

'Okay, like with Liam Walsh, I want the original case file,' Matilda began. 'I want the full pathology and coroner's report. I want to see photographs from the scene and any hint of this being more than a mere accident, I want to know about it. Scott, find out Josie's next of kin, get an address and we'll go and have a word and see if they received a similar sympathy card to Helen Walsh.'

'The subject is two of five,' Tom said. 'Is there anything we can do about the other three victims who might be out there?'

'Where would we even start looking? The first was ruled a suicide, this one as an accident,' Christian said. 'I've no idea how many deaths we record in Sheffield each year, but we don't have the resources to go through them all.'

'That email address doesn't exist either,' Zofia said.

'I didn't think it would,' Matilda said. She headed for the door.

'I'll let you know what Ridley says,' Christian said.

'Thanks. Tell him I'm not taking no for an answer this time. Something needs to be done about this. This is not some loser with too much time on his hands. This is a sick killer. I know it. I fucking know it.'

## Chapter Twenty-Six

Derek Klein was sitting at his desk following a terminally dull meeting. He was drained. He needed coffee, industrial strength, and maybe with a shot of whisky in it, too. His mobile started to ring. He looked at it and saw it was Cara ringing. He quickly picked it up. Cara never rang him at work. This couldn't be good news.

He swiped to answer. 'Cara…

'I've just had the police on the phone,' she said, interrupting him, her voice full of tears.

Derek swallowed hard. 'And?'

'They're scaling back the investigation. They're not looking for her anymore.'

'What? Why?'

'They said they've done all they can. There have been no sightings, no witnesses, they've got nothing from her phone, her bank account hasn't been touched.'

Derek thought for a moment. 'Well, I suppose they have done a very thorough investigation.'

'Is that all you can say?' she cried. 'They haven't done a

thorough investigation at all. If they had they would have found her.'

'Cara, I don't know what to say to you. The police obviously know what they're doing.'

'I think we should contact a private investigator.'

Derek almost laughed at the suggestion. 'Do they even exist outside of a crime novel?'

'Yes. I've been looking some up online.'

'I bet they charge the earth as well.'

'You're putting a price on your daughter's life?' Cara screamed.

'Cara, look, calm down. Let's talk about this tonight when I get home. In the meantime, don't do anything. I'll call the police and see if there is anything else that can be done.'

'I'm expected to just sit here for the rest of the day while nobody is looking for her?' she asked, barely coherent over the tears.

'Cara, you really need to try and calm down. You won't be good to anyone if you carry on like this. You'll make yourself ill.'

She was silent for what seemed like a long time as she struggled to control herself. 'Promise me. Promise me you'll call them.'

'I promise,' he said, though he had no idea what he was going to say to them. If they chose to scale back the investigation they wouldn't change their minds because he asked them to.

'Where is she, Derek?' Cara asked softly.

'I don't know, Cara. I honestly don't know.'

'She's dead, isn't she?'

'Cara…'

'Even if someone has taken her, her insulin would have run out long ago. They're not going to get her some more, are they? They'll have just killed her.'

'Cara, listen to me, please. Don't do this to yourself. Leave it with me. I'll give the police a call and we'll talk about it tonight. There'll be other things we can do. Just … trust me, okay?'

It was a while before Cara replied and Derek checked the phone to see if she hadn't already hung up.

'Okay. Okay. I'll wait. Please come home early tonight, Derek.'

'I will.'

He ended the call with his wife and sat in silence. Natasha's whereabouts were a complete mystery. It did seem as if she walked out of the gates of the college and literally vanished from existence.

Derek's mobile started to ring again. He looked at the screen, but it was blank. Then he remembered his second phone. He lifted up his briefcase and found the old, battered Samsung. His office door was closed and he knew he wouldn't be disturbed, so he answered.

'I need you to stop contacting me,' the caller said.

'What? Why?'

'I can't do this anymore.'

'Why not?'

'Natasha is missing. Or had you forgotten?'

'Of course I haven't bloody forgotten. Look, we received a call from the police. They're scaling back the search.'

'What does that mean? They've stopped looking?'

'There's no evidence that Natasha has come to any harm. They've had no witnesses, no sightings, nothing to suggest she's been injured, kidnapped, or killed. It's like I said right at the beginning, she's just walked away from things.'

'From us,' the caller said. 'She knew. Natasha knew. She was going to tell Cara.'

'But she didn't.'

'Only because she didn't get a chance.'

'Look, why don't we meet up? We'll go for a drive somewhere. There's a new Italian opened up in Bakewell. I know you love Italian.'

It was a while before the caller said anything.

'I don't think so.'

'Why not?'

Silence.

Derek was growing impatient.

'You don't think I had anything to do with Natasha going missing, do you?'

More silence.

'I don't know,' the reply eventually came. It was softly spoken, barely about a whisper. 'I don't know what to think anymore.'

'You do, don't you? You think I've done something with Natasha.'

'I have to go. I'm sorry.'

'No. Wait. I...' The call ended. He looked at the blank screen. He snapped the phone closed and dropped it into his briefcase.

On his desk was a framed photograph of Cara and Natasha. It was taken at a family wedding three years ago. Both happy and smiling at the camera, dressed to the nines.

'You bitch,' Derek spat at the picture.

## Chapter Twenty-Seven

It wasn't easy trying to track down Reginald Pettifer. Zofia had managed to find out his home address, landline, and mobile numbers, where he worked and the fact his blood type was B+, but actually pinpointing his location wasn't easy. Scott spoke to him on the phone, and he said he would be at his daughter's flat in Hillsborough. They could meet him there.

'I can feel your eyes burning into me,' Matilda said as she drove the short distance from the police station to Bradfield Road. 'You're grinning, too. Whatever it is you're wanting to say, please say it now while we're doing forty miles per hour, so I get the full impact when I throw you out of the car.'

'It's nothing.'

'Liar.'

'Donal was mentioning last night how Odell seems to be a bit chirpier lately.'

'Did he actually use the word "chirpy"?'

'No. I'm being polite.'

'Thank God for that. Well, good for Odell. It's about time someone cracked a smile.'

'You're a tad brighter too. You seem to have a bit of colour in your cheeks lately.'

'Well, I have been sitting out in the garden more of an evening.'

'Despite the fact it's spring and still bloody cold.'

Matilda turned the Porsche into the narrow road where the apartment block was. There was very little parking space, but she managed to find somewhere to squeeze into. She turned off the engine.

'This seems familiar,' she said, looking up at the building.

'Stop changing the subject.'

She sighed. 'What do you want to ask me?'

'Are you and Odell ... you know?' he said with a ridiculously wide grin.

'What?'

'You know.'

'You're a whole generation younger than I am, Scott. Your version of "you know" could be a world apart from what I think "you know" means.' She loved teasing Scott and took pleasure in seeing a film of sweat appear on his forehead while he struggled to find the right words to use.

'Well, I know you went to the David Lynch films at the Showroom, and Sian told me that you've been out to dinner a couple of times since. I was just wondering if you and he had ... you know.'

'Scott, there is only you and me in this car. If you want to be crude, I'm not going to take offence. Ask your question.'

'Have you shagged him?'

'Scott! Don't be so vulgar,' she said, removing her seatbelt and climbing out of the car.

Scott followed. 'Aren't you going to tell me?'

'No.'

'Why not?'

'Because it's called a personal life for a reason.'

'I told you about me and Donal having that weekend away in Paris.'

'Yes. And I'm still having bad dreams.'

'Really? I'm having fantastic dreams.' He smiled.

'I don't call being asked to leave France for showing your love for each other in a public place anything to brag about.'

'I always thought the French were more liberal than that. Still, excellent weekend,' he said with a cheeky grin.

Matilda looked up at the building and saw a man looking down at them from a small window. She surmised this was Reginald Pettifer. She recognised him from the photos Zofia had found online.

'Put your smile away, we're being watched.'

---

Reginald Pettifer showed them both into Josie's tiny studio apartment. Sadness seemed to emanate from him. He was tall and broad, a rugby player's build, but with more padding around his waist. He was bald and had an unkempt salt-and-pepper stubble. He wore ill-fitting jeans, trainers, and a jumper that strained over his stomach. He sat down on the two-seat sofa, taking up most of it and leaving Matilda and Scott to find a seat at the small table and two chairs that made up the dining-room part of the flat.

'I've finally got around to putting this place on the market,' Reginald said. His accent was pure gruff Sheffield, but his voice sounded tired, and he spoke slowly. 'I've been putting it off and putting it off. It's only small, but Josie loved this flat.' He looked around the small space with a wistful smile on his face, as if marvelling at it for the first time.

Matilda gave him a sympathetic smile. She could feel the hurt in every word.

'I lost my wife three years ago. Breast cancer.'

'I'm so sorry,' Matilda said.

'Josie was my rock. I fell apart. When Josie had the anaphylactic shock that put her in hospital, I thought I was going to lose her, too. After that, after everything that happened, she made a point of being very careful with what she ate, always studying the ingredients. She didn't want to leave me on my own.' He smiled, painfully. 'She knew I wouldn't be able to cope,' he choked.

'Mr Pettifer—' Matilda began.

'Reg,' he interrupted.

'Reg. As my colleague said to you on the phone, we're taking another look at your daughter's death. We've received information that, well, I'll be honest with you, we're not sure what to do about it. We'd like to talk to you about your daughter and the events leading up to her death.'

'I don't understand,' he said, looking deflated.

'I want you to trust me on this, Reg. If we can talk about Josie, about what happened, I'll keep you informed of what's going on.'

He looked at Matilda. He seemed to be studying her. Eventually, he nodded.

'Josie was … she was so old for her years. I'm pretty sure she was older than me.' He gave a snort of laughter. 'She grew up incredibly quickly after her mother died. When the life insurance came through and when she was awarded that money from the Chinese restaurant, she put it all down on this place. It only cost £52,000. I've already been quoted £60,000 by the estate agent and she only bought it last year. She was so sensible. How many twenty-year-olds buy a flat with money they've been given? When I was twenty, I would have probably spent a month in Spain getting drunk with my mates.'

'She was a credit to you and your wife,' Matilda said, telling him what he wanted to hear.

He nodded and looked happy for the first time since Matilda and Scott arrived.

'She loved property. That's what she wanted to do: buy

something, fix it up, sell it on. She always said she'd sell this place once it reached £75,000 in value and then put that straight onto a bigger property. She was working two jobs in the meantime. A call centre during the day, which she hated, and behind a bar in town in the evenings, which she loved. She loved being around people.'

'How many people knew about her allergies?' Matilda asked.

'Everyone who knew her. She made a point of telling them so that they'd know what foods she couldn't be around, or they'd take extra care if they made anything for her. She had one of those bracelets on, too, that told medical staff what she was allergic to.'

'And what was she allergic to?'

'Most nuts and seeds. Pumpkin seeds and poppy seeds were the worst and peanuts and cashews. No idea why those particular ones. There was a whole list that she carried around with her. She had it on her phone and I had a copy, too.'

'Tell me about the people she had in her life. Did she have many friends?' Matilda asked.

'Yes. She got on well with everyone she met. She said the job in the call centre was mind-numbing, but she loved the people. They were always going out together. The same in the pub, too.'

'Did she have a boyfriend?'

'She did. But I hadn't met him. She dropped the name "Ben" into the conversation a few times. I asked if he was more than a friend and she said maybe. They were taking things slow. I couldn't get in touch with him, though.'

'Why not?'

'He was in her phone as Ben, but he didn't answer when I rang him. I sent a few texts, and I told him when the funeral was, but I didn't get anything back. I… I did think they might have been more casual than Josie was making out. What is it they call it, friends with benefits?' he asked, looking at Scott for confirmation. Scott nodded. 'I'm not a prude by any means, but I didn't think my Josie was like that. I wouldn't have judged her though.'

'Do you still have Josie's mobile?'

'Yes. It's at home.'

'Could we take a look at it?'

'Of course.'

'Did any of her other friends know Ben?'

'I don't know. A few people came up to me at the funeral, and afterwards. We had a gathering at the house. Most were her colleagues and they said how much they loved her, how much they missed her...' Reg took a tissue out of his jacket pocket and wiped his eyes and nose.

'Did you ask any of them about Ben?'

'No.'

'Reg, I've looked at the forensic report and when you found Josie, she was on the floor in this flat, and the meal she'd been eating was on the table. That meal was analysed and was found to contain an oil on the salmon. Large traces of peanut oil were found on it. When you went through the flat, did you find a bottle of oil?'

'I boxed everything up. It's in my garage. I don't know what to do with any of it. My sister said I should take things slowly. Get rid of things when I want to and not be too hasty and regret throwing anything away.'

'That sounds sensible,' Scott said.

'I don't think she was referring to what Josie had for breakfast. I've got Weetabix and packets of crispbreads going soft. I just... I can't part with them,' he said, crying again.

'Would it be possible for us to come and have a look?'

'Now?'

'If you wouldn't mind.'

'No. Of course not.' A frown developed on his brow. 'Can you explain to me why you're taking an interest in this all of a sudden? It's like you're suggesting there's more to Josie's death than originally thought.'

Matilda took a breath. 'Reg, I said I wasn't going to lie to you, and I'm not. I've received two emails in the space of a few weeks.

The first mentioned a young man who we believe took his own life. The sender of the email says he killed him. We can't find definite proof of that, but I'm willing to believe him. I received a second email today saying he is responsible for your daughter's death. I need to find out if it's true or not.'

Reg's facial expression didn't change. He blinked hard a couple of times.

'But … how? I… I don't…'

'I really don't know myself at the moment, Reg.'

'Responsible for her death? That sounds like you're saying she was murdered. How would they have killed her? I mean, she died from anaphylactic shock. The coroner said so.'

'I'm not sure,' Matilda said, though she had a fair idea it centred around Josie sitting down for her final meal and whoever was in her flat with her at the time.

---

Matilda and Scott followed Reg in his Vauxhall Astra to a three-bed semi-detached house in Shirecliffe. He led them into a brightly decorated hallway and showed them the living room while he went into the kitchen to make them all a cup of tea.

The living room was decorated in neutral colours, which Matilda assumed were chosen by either his wife or his property-mad daughter. Everything was neat and tidy. Reg was obviously still following his family's instructions to keep the place well-tended to help with resale value.

He came into the living room carrying three matching mugs on a tray. Matilda was standing by the fireplace, marvelling at the array of family photographs on the mantel.

'Hard to believe that was me, looking at me now,' he said with a smile.

Matilda was looking at the wedding photograph of a very slim

Reg Pettifer with a full head of hair, beaming at the camera with his demure wife on his arm.

'Everything seemed to go wrong for me once I hit forty. It was like my body decided old age had arrived. I was bald within a year, and it didn't matter how healthily I ate, food seemed to attach itself to my waist. Help yourself to milk and sugar. I can't offer you a biscuit as I've none in the house. I need to do a shop.'

He sat down on the sofa and Matilda and Scott took a matching armchair each.

Matilda poured a splash of milk into her tea and sat back in the comfortable chair. She took a sip. A cup of tea always felt lost without something to dunk in it, but she could hardly ask Scott to pop out to the nearest Co-op for a packet of Bourbons.

'Strange question, Reg, but did you receive many sympathy cards after Josie died?'

'I had loads. The people at the call centre all signed a big one. All the neighbours round here sent me a card. I hardly speak to most of them, but they were so kind.'

'Have you kept them?'

'Yes. Something else to add to the list of things I need to sort out. Would you like to see them?'

'Yes, please.'

Reg put his tea back on the tray and hauled himself up from the sofa, left the living room and headed upstairs.

'What do you think?' Matilda asked in a hushed tone.

'Josie sounds like a very sensible young woman,' Scott said, leaning towards her and lowering his voice. 'Even more so after her mother's death. She takes care of her father, looks after him when he falls apart. She knows what she's allergic to and makes sure she stays away from it. It could have been a genuine error, but I'm thinking not. I don't think she would have made that mistake.'

'I don't either.'

'I've brought you Josie's mobile phone,' Reg said, entering the room with a large cardboard box in his hands. He handed the phone to Scott. 'I keep it charged. No idea why, and I've taken off the passcode, so you won't have problems unlocking it.'

'Thank you. We'll get it back to you,' Scott said.

'Reg, could you show Scott the boxes in the garage while I take a look at these cards?' Matilda asked.

'Sure. Follow me.'

Matilda waited until they both left before she dropped to the floor and emptied the box. She was met with a sea of white and pink cards, all bearing the same generic front – birds of peace and bunches of pastel flowers. Matilda remembered the card sent to Helen Walsh of the dinosaurs and the meteor hurtling towards them. What kind of card would the killer send to Josie's father to show how much he knew about her?

She spotted one. A white card with a drawing of a country cottage with a rainbow in the sky above it. It was more the sort of card you'd send to someone who had recently moved house.

Matilda opened it. The message inside read, 'Thinking of you'. It was signed by Roland T. Owen. In the top right-hand corner it said, '2 of 5'.

## Chapter Twenty-Eight

'So, we've got similar sympathy cards, similar emails, and two deaths that were ruled to be anything other than murder,' Matilda said. She was standing in front of the murder board in the HMCU suite. The team was looking on and CC Ridley had joined them.

'The bottle of oil that Reg Pettifer removed from his daughter's cupboard does not contain any peanut oil. The ingredients state it's pure olive oil. However, I've sent it to forensics to check it hasn't been spiked,' Scott said.

'The mobile number for Ben doesn't exist anymore,' Zofia said. 'It looks like it was a burner. I've downloaded the messages from Josie's phone and while she messages him a great deal, he rarely messaged her. When he did, it was very non-committal stuff. Things like "meet at 8" or "see you soon". Nothing to reveal anything about himself.'

'I thought as much,' Matilda said.

'What about her colleagues?' Christian began. 'You said she had two jobs. Surely she would have mentioned this Ben to one of them. Maybe they even saw him.'

'It's possible,' Matilda mused. 'Finn, you and Tom pop along to the call centre, chat to her colleagues. Ask if they knew she had a boyfriend. If so, what did she say about him? Did she ever show his photograph, or did they meet him? If not, do they know anyone who might know of him? Then go along to the pub and do the same there.

'We also need to trace Josie's last moments. Now, Josie died on Wednesday the second of December. Her father found her the following morning. What did she do on the Wednesday? Did she work? Where? What hours? What time did she arrive and leave? I know it's almost six months ago, but is there still CCTV footage of her somewhere? We need as much as we can to piece together her final hours.' Matilda spoke rapidly and with purpose.

Her mobile started to ring. She lifted it out of her pocket and saw it was Belinda, Sian's daughter, calling her. She silenced the call and stole a look at Sian, who was busy scrutinising the second email.

'Could there be a connection between the victims?' Zofia asked. 'Liam and Josie were both twenty when they died. Could they have had similar interests?'

'It's not impossible. Zofia, have a trawl through social media. See if you can find any connection, no matter how tenuous. Did they have friends in common, did they visit similar places, did they belong to any groups? Even if it's as banal as having an account in the same bank, I want to know about it.'

'I'm already on that.'

She turned to Ridley. 'He's choosing his victims somehow. We know he found Liam through the dark web; we don't know how he found Josie. I very much doubt she was using suicide message boards. However, we're going to get Josie's laptop and tablet and have a good look through.'

'What about through her allergies? I'm guessing she was regularly at the doctor's or maybe she had to keep going for tests, I don't know. Was Liam also at the doctor's often for medication for his depression?' Ridley said.

Matilda nodded, turned to Zofia and asked her to find out if Liam and Josie shared a GP.

'The key to this is finding the link between the victims. There will be one. I know it. Finn, what have you got from the email itself?'

'Well, again, he mentions mother very early on in the email. He could have said he's seen you've been to see Helen Walsh a few times, but he doesn't, he says "Liam's mother". His relationship with his mother is crucial. However, it can swing one of two ways. They'll either be incredibly close or not close at all.'

'That narrows it down,' Matilda said.

'If they're close,' Finn continued. 'The mother will be a domineering kind. If they're not, whoever is writing these emails will wish they were close.'

Matilda looked at Ridley who raised an eyebrow.

'I know it's not giving us much to work on, but I can only tell you what I can get from the subtext here. He's also very confident and sure of himself. He's really got it stuck in his head that the perfect murder exists, that he's beaten us all. Also, the fact that he's given you the name of his first victim and you still haven't been able to track him down has just fed into his ego. The longer this goes on, the longer he goes without being captured, the more his confidence will grow. That can either lead to him making a mistake or going for glory in some massive way.'

'You mean like a killing spree?' Sian asked.

'Not necessarily a spree but he'll want to do something memorable, and I think memorable to you, Matilda. He mentions your name seven times, more than in the first email, and he asks if he can call you Mat. Shortening someone's name is very personal. Do many people call you Mat?'

'I don't know. I've never thought about it.'

'I do,' Sian said.

'I don't,' Ridley said.

'I think I might have done,' Christian said.

'I call you various different things when you're out of the room,' Scott said with a grin.

'What about away from work?' Finn asked.

'I only really have my family. My mum never shortens my name. My sister does.'

'He's asked to call you Mat, yet obviously he can't get a response from you, so he calls you it anyway. I think this is someone who wants to be close to you. I think you have someone in your life who would like to be closer to you than he is now. He might have seen others call you Mat and want to be among that group.'

'You still think this is personal to Matilda?' Ridley asked.

'I did, but there's one part of the email that's led me to think otherwise. Towards the end, he says, "If we ever did meet in a court room, the prosecution would tear your case apart and I would walk away Scott free." He spells it S-C-O-T-T. The correct spelling is S-C-O-T. I don't think this is a mistake. He's taken care to make sure this email is correct.'

'He's threatening Scott?' Matilda asked.

'Hang on, don't drag me into this,' Scott said.

'I'm not suggesting it's a threat,' Finn answered quickly. 'I think he's just showing you how clever he is. He knows you have a Scott on your team. He's watching you. He's watching us all.'

'Should we be worried?' Sian asked.

'Well, I certainly am now,' Scott said.

## Chapter Twenty-Nine

DC Tom Simpson was on his way back to the HMCU from the toilets when his mobile vibrated in his pocket. He took it out and saw it was Derek Klein calling. He swiped to answer.

'Tom, it's ... it's Derek Klein here. Am I okay to call you?'

'Of course. Is there anything wrong?'

'I... Cara tells me that you're scaling back the investigation.'

Tom bit his bottom lip. He really didn't know what to say. 'I'm afraid we are, yes, but that doesn't mean we've given up on finding Natasha. I promise you. The case will be getting reviewed on a regular basis. All evidence will be looked at again and any new angles or lines of enquiries followed up. I promise, Derek, we are still committed to finding your daughter.'

'Right. I see.'

Tom waited in awkward silence to see if Derek had any more questions.

'Is there anything else I can help you with, Derek?'

'I don't know what to say to Cara,' he said, almost pleading for any help and advice.

'Just be there for her, Derek. Reassure her. Like I said, we haven't given up hope of finding her. It's just ... there really is no evidence to point us in the right direction. I wish there was more I could tell you.'

'It's all right. I know you're doing all you can. I... I really do appreciate everything you're doing.'

'You can call me any time, Derek.'

'Thank you.'

Tom was struggling for something to say. There were no more words he could use that wouldn't simply be banal platitudes. Eventually, the line went dead. Derek had ended the call. Tom released a heavy sigh of relief. He put the phone back in his pocket and headed back to the office. He suddenly felt incredibly heavy.

---

'Close the door behind you, Tom,' Matilda asked as he entered the suite.

She was standing at the end of the room. Everyone was stony-faced and silent as they waited for her to begin. Tom looked at Zofia with a questioning frown. She shrugged her shoulders. She had no idea what was going on either. He sat down.

'I need to ask you all a question,' Matilda began. She had the team's undivided attention. 'There is no doubt in my mind that whoever is writing these emails is a highly intelligent person. He's managed to kill two people, that we know of so far, without them appearing on our radar. Finn seems to think that the killer knows this team by name. I think so too. I did think that this might be about me, someone targeting me, but I'm starting to wonder if it's someone I don't know, but you might. So, I'm asking you to look into your own lives. Is there someone new among your group of friends, or someone who has started to take an interest in your work who hasn't in the past?'

Matilda looked at the worried faces staring at her. She knew each and every one of them. She felt sick at the thought of someone worming their way into their lives, taking advantage of them, manipulating them, in order to keep tabs on what the unit was getting up to. And how long had this been going on? Liam Walsh was killed in September. How long has this killer been watching them all?

'Basically, I want you to look at the people who've recently entered your lives and question their motives.'

'You want us to spy on our friends?' Zofia asked.

'If they're genuine friends, you'll soon be able to cross them off your list,' Christian said.

'I know this is a horrible thing to do, Zofia, and I wouldn't be asking you if it wasn't necessary. Do you have anyone new in your life?'

She looked at Tom. He looked down.

'Zofia,' Matilda raised her voice slightly.

'While you were talking, my mind immediately went to Wes,' she said, hesitantly.

Tom shot her a look. 'Wes? Why?' he asked.

'Who's Wes?'

'Wesley Blackstock. He's one of my mates,' Tom said. 'I'm in a biker group. We all go out riding together.'

'How long have you known this Wesley?'

'He's pretty new to the group. He moved to Rotherham from Essex at the back end of last year. He's a good bloke.'

'He came to our house a couple of months ago after they'd been out on a run to Derbyshire,' Zofia said. 'He asked if he could use the toilet. I told him where it was. I was going from the kitchen to the living room, and I swear blind he was coming out of the spare bedroom.'

'He'd been snooping?' Matilda asked.

'He probably got lost,' Tom said, making an excuse for him. 'It was his first time in the house.'

'He was really questioning me about my work,' Zofia added.

'He was interested. He was asking how she was able to be a

detective while in a wheelchair. It was genuine, normal interest,' Tom said.

'We need to run a check on him. Do you have his home address?' Matilda asked.

'You're going to start making us all paranoid,' Tom said, visibly upset. 'You're going to have us questioning everyone from good friends, neighbours, to family members. Wesley is not a killer. He's not some psychopath who delights in taunting the police. I know he isn't. You can't have us doing this. It's not fair.'

'There is someone very close to this unit who—'

'No. You're wrong,' Tom interrupted. 'Have you ever considered this bloke might be some kind of fantasist, that he could have a screw loose and either believes he's committed these crimes or wishes he had the courage to? No. You've immediately gone down the murder route yet there's no evidence.'

'Tom, calm down,' Sian instructed.

'Now you're having us question everyone in our lives. If we turn on them, we lose them as friends. They'd never trust us again. And can you blame them? We'd end up on our own, lonely, isolated, and alone like...' He stopped himself.

The whole room fell silent as the atmosphere thickened. Matilda and Tom locked eyes, neither turning away.

Matilda felt her throat constrict. She suddenly felt as if she was back in the windowless basement of the cottage where she was held captive. She couldn't breathe.

'I'm sorry,' Tom said, his voice barely above a whisper. 'I didn't mean...' He trailed off.

Matilda swallowed hard. It hurt. Her throat was dry. She turned on her heel, headed for her former office, saw it was now being used as storage and made a U-turn. She left the HMCU and headed for the stairs.

Sian jumped up and followed her.

'I think I should...' Tom said, getting up and hurrying out of the suite.

'Mat,' Sian said.

Matilda stopped mid-stride. She turned around.

'Tom didn't mean anything by that. He was just frustrated, angry, maybe. It's a frightening thought having to look at the people in your life and question their motives for being your friend. Nobody should have to do that.'

Matilda didn't move.

'Are you all right?' Sian asked.

'He's right, isn't he?' Matilda asked. 'I'm seeing murders where there's no evidence of any being committed. Maybe this is just a nutter who enjoys wasting police time.'

'We both know that's not true. He knows things about the Liam Walsh case that only a killer could know. The guy on the dark web saying he had cancer. How could he know unless it's the same person? I think we might have been allowing our emotions to get the better of us in there. Maybe we should take a step back. Let's wait until we get the results from that oil in Josie's cupboard before we move on. If it matches the oil found in her stomach contents, then it could simply have been a labelling error from the manufacturers and then it's up to her father to decide if he wants to take proceedings against them. If it isn't a match, then the only explanation is that her food was spiked in some way. Then, it's a criminal matter.'

Reluctantly, Matilda nodded. 'What Tom said…'

'He was just getting emotional. We all do when we're working on complex cases. You've done it yourself. He didn't mean anything by it.'

Matilda took a deep breath. 'I've been neglecting everything else I've got going on. I should be jumping down Christian's throat and demanding why Natasha Klein hasn't been found yet. I've been too preoccupied with this. And we all know why.'

'We do?'

'Because I'm no longer operational. The minute someone

messages me I jump on it like it's new evidence of a second man behind the grassy knoll.'

'You have received two very chilling emails. It's what any normal person would do.'

'Maybe.' She turned and headed for the exit.

'Where are you going?' Sian asked.

'I'm going to get some air.'

'Do you want me to come with you?'

'No. I want to be on my own for a bit.'

---

In the rear car park of the police station, Matilda sat behind the wheel of Adele's car. She took her mobile out of her inside pocket and was about to place it in the holder on the dashboard when she noticed a voicemail had been left by Sian's daughter, Belinda.

'Hi, Mat, it's Belinda. I'm glad it's gone to voicemail actually. I don't really want Mum to be around while I'm talking to you. Listen, something's happened and I really need to speak to you. Can you give me a call? But make sure you're on your own. I don't want Mum listening in. Thanks.'

Matilda was about to call her back when she caught someone out of the corner of her eye leaving the station. It was Tom. He was digging around in a pocket of his leather biker jacket and brought out a packet of cigarettes. He lit up. She wasn't aware he smoked.

She started the car and drove out of the car park, not making eye contact with Tom as she passed him. When she joined the traffic, she used the voice command to return Belinda's call.

'Belinda, it's Mat. Are you free to talk?'

'Hi. Yes. Just let me go to my room. Kel, if you even think about touching my food, you're not coming out with us tomorrow night.' A door was slammed closed. 'Okay. Are you on your own?'

'Yes. I'm out driving.'

'Good. Is Mum okay?'

'She's fine. What's happened?'

'Right, well, it happened a few weeks ago but I've only just got Rebecca to tell me. I knew something was bothering her as she's been a bit quiet and if there's one thing that Rebecca isn't, it's quiet.'

'Belinda, you're rambling, love. What's going on?'

'Okay. Rebecca works behind a bar not far from campus. A couple of weeks ago she had a bloke come in who was asking her all kinds of questions about me, my dad, how I was coping and everything. Guess who it was?'

'I have no idea,' Matilda said as she passed the dreaded Meadowhell on her left.

'Danny Hanson.'

'What?' Matilda cried. She had to slam on the brakes to stop her from ploughing into the car in front at a red traffic light.

'He came all the way down to Southampton to question her. He even told her that he had Mum's permission to write some kind of a book about the family. Can you believe that?'

'Bastard. Have you spoken to your mum about it?'

'No. According to Ant, she's been a bit on edge since that other book about Dad came out. Have you read it?'

'Erm, no,' Matilda lied.

'I have. It makes us sound like a right distant family, as if we don't know each other at all. Look, Mat, I'm just worried that if Danny came all the way down to Southampton just so he could fish for information, well, what if he turns up at Gregory's school or something? I don't want him getting upset or anything. Jesus, maybe I *should* have chosen a university close to home.'

'No. Belinda, you can't live your life thinking about how other people might miss you. You need to do what's best for you.' *Hark who's talking*. 'Leave Danny Hanson to me. I'll go round and have a word and, well, if that doesn't work, I'll cut off his testicles. Would you like me to send you one as a souvenir?'

'I'd put it on a chain around my neck.'

Matilda smiled. 'How are you getting on in Southampton? Uni going okay?'

'It's great. Loving every minute of it. The studying's getting on my nerves, but I've met some amazing people.'

'Good. I'm glad. Look, let me know if anything else happens with Danny Hanson or if anyone else comes sniffing around. We don't need to tell your mum unless we have to.'

'Thanks, Mat. I knew I could trust you.'

'Of course you can. Look after yourself.'

'Will do.'

The call ended and Matilda pulled over at the first opportunity, performed an illegal three-point turn and headed back towards the city centre. She needed to find Danny Hanson. She was in the right mood to tear someone's arm off and beat them to death with it.

## Chapter Thirty

Ruby Deighton was much calmer when she entered South Yorkshire Police HQ this time. She wanted to see the detectives she saw last time but couldn't remember their names so told the civilian member of staff at the front desk that one of them was tall, blond, and gorgeous and the other was dark, pretty and in a wheelchair. They both smelled good, too.

A few minutes later, Scott popped his head around the door and asked Ruby to join him in the same interview room as last time, where Zofia sat at the desk.

'Nice to see you again, Ruby,' Zofia said.

Ruby gave her a brave smile and went to sit down. Scott sat beside Zofia, who had a pad open in front of her, pen poised. They waited for her to speak.

'I'm sorry about last time,' she said. 'I've been on the phone to Natasha's mum; she told me you're scaling back the investigation.'

'At the moment, yes, we are. We've done all we can, but the case isn't closed. If we receive any fresh evidence, we will, of course, look into it. Also, we have a cold case review team who will review the case at regular intervals,' Scott said.

Ruby looked down. She was playing nervously with her fingers.

'I didn't tell you the truth when I was last here,' she said, not looking up at them. 'I held something back because … because I was ashamed.'

'Do you want to tell us now?' Zofia asked.

Ruby nodded. She took a sharp breath and blew it out. She looked up at the detectives waiting expectantly for her to speak. 'I've been having an affair with Derek, Natasha's dad, for about a year.' A tear rolled down her left cheek. She swiped it away. 'I know you probably think it's disgusting. I'm nineteen and he's almost fifty, but…'

'We're not here to judge you, Ruby,' Zofia said, reaching forward and placing a hand on Ruby's.

'Do you want me to… I mean, what do you want me to tell you now?'

'Whatever you want. Start at the beginning if you like.'

Ruby nodded. 'I go round to Natasha's often. I help her make her stupid videos. Sometimes I spend the night. She's … she's not very nice to her parents. If I spoke to mine like that, they'd ground me for a month. Anyway, I went round once, but Nat had gone out. She'd completely forgotten she'd asked me to go over, which is just like her. Anyway, Derek was there, and he made me a drink, and we got talking. Could I get a drink of water, please?'

'Sure,' Scott said. He jumped up from his seat and went out of the room. It wasn't long before he came back with a plastic cup and a jug of water.

Ruby took a healthy swig and continued her story. 'Sorry. Dry mouth. Anyway, Derek was asking about Nat's obsession with social media. He didn't understand it. To be honest, neither did I. She'd post a video and spend the rest of the day watching how many likes it got, and it had to have more than the previous video, and she'd be seriously pissed off if it didn't. It really was an obsession with her. Anyway, one thing led to another with me and Derek and … well, I don't need to give you all the details, do I?'

'No,' Zofia said.

'We didn't … you know … have sex, that first time. We just kissed. But he was lovely. He really was. He asked if he could take me out on a date. We went to a restaurant on Ecclesall. I've never been to such a posh restaurant before.' Ruby smiled at the memory and her face lit up. 'Derek was … he was just sweet; do you know what I mean? I've been out with guys my own age and they're complete tossers.

'The first time we actually slept together was at my house. I still live at home, but Mum and Dad were going to a wedding in Crewe and decided to stay over. It really was the best night of my life with Derek. He was gentle and caring. We started seeing each other regularly after that. Only, a week before Nat went missing, she found out.'

'How did she find out?' Scott asked.

'She was moaning about Derek, saying how she wanted this new camera so she could set up a studio in her bedroom and film herself from different angles at the same time and edit them together to look a bit more professional so it wouldn't just look like she was filming from a mobile. The camera she wanted was well over two grand and Derek flat out said no. Well, Nat really kicked off. She was calling Derek all the names under the sun and I just… I just lost it with her. She was being so selfish. I told her, she wouldn't have half the things she had if it wasn't for Derek giving her money and he didn't have to. She's over eighteen, she could get a decent job, and it's not like he's her real dad.'

Ruby paused while she poured herself more water and drained the plastic cup.

'I've never defended Derek before. I'd always sided with Nat, but she was being a real bitch. Anyway, she turned on me then, asking me why I was sticking up for Derek. Did I fancy him or something? I don't know, maybe my face changed or something, because she suddenly latched onto me fancying her dad. She started making fun and saying that Derek's fat, old and balding, and that just made me see red even more. I told her she didn't know him at all. I mean, she doesn't. Derek is such a kind man. He…' She stopped herself.

'What is it?' Zofia asked.

'Natasha said she was going to tell Cara. Then she stormed off. I phoned Derek and told him what had happened. He said he'd deal with it and hung up on me.'

'What happened then?'

'I didn't see Nat the next day. I was on a course placement. She posted online that she was getting a new camera. I guessed that Derek had bought her silence. When I saw Nat, she blanked me, at first, but then she started making these slight digs about sleeping with old men, that kind of thing. This was in front of our other mates, too. She never said anything, but you could see she was enjoying herself, you know, taunting me. I couldn't stand being humiliated like that, so I called Derek and… I didn't finish things with him then, but I said maybe we should stop for a while.' She paused and took another drink.

'I had a good long think about what we were doing. It wouldn't have gone anywhere, would it? I really did like him, but, well, he's married, and the age gap. It wouldn't have worked in the long term.'

'How did Derek take it?'

'He … he didn't … well, he was quite angry. He told me not to do anything I'd regret and to think about it a bit more.'

'Did you?'

'I did.'

'And?'

'And … nothing. The next day, Natasha went missing. And…'

'Go on…' Scott prompted.

'Derek doesn't have an alibi,' Ruby said quietly.

'You think Derek has done something to Natasha.'

Ruby collapsed in on herself. She couldn't hold back the tears any longer. Zofia handed her a tissue.

'I don't know what to think. I've been... I've been going over it again and again in my mind. The Derek I know doesn't match the kind of person who could ... I don't know, make someone disappear, but then I think about Natasha and how... If she really riled Derek up, maybe ... I mean, nobody knows how they're going to react in certain situations, do they?'

'Ruby, calm down,' Zofia said. 'Would you like to take a break?'

'Yes, please.'

'I'll go and get you a mug of tea,' Scott said, standing up. He went out of the room, leaving Zofia to stay with the clearly distraught teenager.

Scott went along the corridor into the HMCU suite where Christian was in his office gluing the sole back onto his shoe. He looked up when he noticed Scott in the doorway.

'My mum always said you buy cheap, you buy twice. I think she was right. I've only had these a fortnight.'

'How much did they cost?'

'Thirty-five quid in the market.'

Scott rolled his eyes. 'I spend more than that on a pair of boxers.'

'Well, that says more about you than it does about me.'

'Listen, Ruby Deighton's just come into the station. You know, Natasha Klein's best friend.'

'I know who Ruby Deighton is.'

'She's just told me and Zofia that she's been having an affair with Derek Klein for the past year; that Natasha found out and might have been blackmailing Derek over it for her silence. Ruby called the affair off because she couldn't stand Natasha's taunts and the next day, Natasha went missing.'

'And Derek doesn't have an alibi,' Christian said.

'Precisely.'

'Is Ruby giving a statement?'

'I think she will.'

'Okay. Get it filmed. I'll watch it from up here. We'll get a warrant to search the Klein house from top to bottom and impound Derek's car and bring him in for questioning under caution.'

'Tom said right from the start there was something dodgy about Derek.'

'Well, don't get excited just yet. This may not go anywhere.'

'It's a big step forward, though. I'm going to make Ruby a cup of tea, take her a bar of chocolate or something, and we'll start the statement properly, get her to reveal everything and give us the full lowdown on Natasha Klein.'

He headed for the drinks station. Christian, left to sort out his shoe, let go of the sole to see if it had stuck. Unfortunately, the leather of the shoe hadn't stuck to the rubber of the sole, but the rubber of the sole had stuck to the skin of Christian's palm.

## Chapter Thirty-One

Danny Hanson was sitting in a Caffè Nero in Meadowhall. He needed a new pair of trousers, and as Sheffield city centre was a veritable ghost town with all the good shops closing down and massive building work going on, he decided to bite the bullet and drive out to the most hated place in South Yorkshire – Meadowhell. The second he turned into the car park and saw the green dome of the shopping mall ahead, his feet started to ache at the prospect of all that walking he'd have to do from shop to shop to shop. Trousers bought (overpriced), he found a coffee shop, bought a double shot espresso (overpriced) and a tomato and mozzarella panini (overpriced), and sat in the corner.

He took his laptop out of his bag and decided to take advantage of the café's electricity by charging it up and using their free Wi-Fi. He didn't have anything specific to work on at the moment. He hadn't written an article for weeks for any newspaper and the BBC seemed to have taken against him. He'd fired off an email to an editor he knew within the news department to see if there was any freelance work in the offing, but he didn't even get a reply. When his book about Magnolia

House came out in the autumn and hit the bestseller charts, they'd be begging to interview him. If he didn't need to make his publishers happy or keep his sales up, he'd tell them to piss off.

He logged onto his emails. There was the usual subscription rubbish that he deleted without reading. No new offers of work. He was about to close the laptop when an email pinged. It was from his agent, Tiffany McNamara. The subject 'Brace Yourself' did not inspire confidence. Danny wondered whether he should open it in a public place. It wouldn't do his image any good if someone filmed him breaking down in tears and posted it all over social media.

He drained what was left of his espresso, took a sharp intake of breath, and opened the email. He almost stopped breathing on the third line. When he finished, he sat in stony silence while his brain caught up with what his eyes had just read. He took another breath and read it a second time.

A smile spread across his face as the news began to sink in and the realisation dawned that he was going to be a very rich man.

HarperCollins loved his pitch, and the first three sample chapters, for the personal account of the crimes of Stuart Mills from the point of view of the journalist who worked so closely with the police (slight exaggeration). They were offering a high six-figure deal, twenty-five per cent of which would be paid upon signing the contract. Deadline for the first draft was the end of the year, to be published in the run-up to Christmas 2022.

To say Danny wanted to jump up and scream and cheer and holler at the top of his voice was a slight understatement.

He hit reply and had to amend his short message several times because his fingers were shaking with excitement.

This was immense. This was brilliant. This was the best news ever.

Calming down, initial shock over, Danny realised he needed to get straight to work. There wasn't going to be a fast turnaround on this story. His publishers believed he had an in with the Mills family, that he was close to them, and already knew everything they'd gone through as he'd witnessed it firsthand. It wasn't a complete lie, but it also wasn't the truth. He needed to be incredibly creative here. He allowed himself a wry smile. This was where his journalistic training kicked in.

## Chapter Thirty-Two

Matilda was getting used to coming home to an empty house and all that deafening silence, but she still hated it. While she looked in the cupboards for something to turn into an edible meal, she phoned her mother.

'Hello, Matilda, how was your day?'

Matilda smiled to herself. She couldn't remember the last time her mother had asked how her day was. Since the conversation regarding Penny's finances, the last bit of tension between mother and daughter had melted away. Matilda called Penny more often for a chat and their conversations no longer had awkward silences. They found they were laughing more with each other, too.

'It was good, thanks,' she answered. 'I foiled a few terrorist plots and brought down a president for embezzling.'

'I was going to do something similar today, too, but I decided to have a day in with a Patricia Cornwell. Nathan and Joseph have asked if they can stay at mine while Harriet's in Scotland with Patrick.'

'They're old enough to be left alone, surely.'

'Well, yes, but … between you and me, I think they like having a bit of stability. Their dad was never much cop and, no offence to Harriet, but she is spending a lot of time with Patrick. I don't think the boys see her much. At least when they come to mine they get a home-cooked meal.'

'I think Harriet's just enjoying herself. It's about time she put herself first.'

'Oh, I don't blame her at all. Brian was a complete shit. But she needs to remember she's also a mother from time to time.'

Matilda's doorbell rang.

'Mum, that's the door, I'm going to have to go. I'll call you tomorrow.'

'You're not ordering takeaway for your tea again, are you?'

*That's a good idea.*

'Of course not. I've got a quiche in the oven,' she lied.

'Shop bought.'

'Of course it's bloody shop bought. Who makes their own quiche?'

'I do.'

'Of course you do. Bye, Mum.'

'Bye bye, sweetheart.'

Matilda ended the call and smiled to herself as she went to the front door. She was enjoying this new relationship with her mother.

Through the spyhole, she saw DC Tom Simpson standing on her doorstep. She frowned. He had never been to her house before. This didn't bode well.

She opened the door and saw Zofia in her wheelchair next to him. Under the bright light of the sensor above the door, Matilda took in the grave expressions on their faces.

'I want to say what a lovely surprise it is to see you, but something tells me you're not here to show me your holiday snaps.'

'Would it be possible for us to have a word?' Tom asked. His voice was low, and he could barely look Matilda in the eye.

'Of course. Come on in.' She stepped to one side as Zofia wheeled herself in and Tom followed. She pointed them in the direction of the living room.

'Oh my God, this is a gorgeous house,' Zofia marvelled as she looked around. 'A real fire. I'd love a real fire. Is it true you've got a library?'

'Yes.'

'Can I see it?'

'Sure.'

'Zof…' Tom said.

She looked at him. Her smile dropped.

Matilda instructed Tom to sit down. She took the opposite sofa. The silence grew between them all.

'For a conversation to begin, there needs to be words,' Matilda said.

'Sorry,' Tom said. He cleared his throat. He was sitting on the edge of the sofa, his legs together, his hands squashed between his knees. 'I want to apologise for what I said earlier. I didn't mean… I didn't mean to insult you.'

'You didn't.' Matilda shrugged, despite the fact that he had.

'I was wrong. My outburst was wrong. I'd not long since spoken to Natasha Klein's dad. Cara is in bits not knowing where she is, and we've got no answers to give them. I took it out on you, and I'm sorry.'

Matilda could see how much pain this was causing him. 'Tom, it's fine, honestly. We're doing a job where emotions are often running high. They're bound to spill over occasionally. I appreciate you apologising, though. Not many people say sorry for their actions. I'm very grateful.'

Tom looked at her and made eye contact. His smile was one of relief.

'Are we okay?'

'Of course we are.'

Tom looked over to Zofia. She took a short breath. It was obviously her turn to say something.

'Matilda,' she began, looking down at her hands as she twiddled her fingers. 'I was wondering if it would be possible to reduce my hours at work.'

'Reduce them? Why?'

'Me and Tom, we want to start trying for a baby. I've been to see a doctor and he said there's no reason why I shouldn't be able to conceive naturally, but I need to look after myself. Too much stress isn't going to help, and our job is stressful.'

'The selfish part of me wants to say absolutely not. You're a vital member of our team and I want you living in the office twenty-four-seven. However, there is life away from the police force, and I'm incredibly happy you've found each other. Leave it with me. I'll have a word with the chief constable. I can't see it being a problem, though.'

They both visibly relaxed.

'Oh, that's good,' Zofia said.

'Zof was scared of asking. She's been trying to find the right words for weeks,' Tom said.

'Am I that much of a monster?' Matilda asked.

'No. It's a big change though, isn't it?' Zofia asked.

'It is. But, hopefully, it's a change for the better. Your personal happiness is much more important than work. That should always come first.'

---

Matilda didn't bother making herself an evening meal. By the time Zofia and Tom had left, following a tour of her library, she wasn't in the mood to mess about cooking. She boiled the kettle, grabbed a tube of Pringles and a packet of biscuits from the cupboard, and went into the living room where she sat on the sofa with her feet up on the coffee table. A few months ago, she and Adele would have put on a Marvel film. Adele would have been making lurid comments about Captain America while Matilda drooled over the Winter Soldier. It wasn't the same on her own, and she hadn't watched a Marvel film since Adele had left.

Her mind drifted towards work, like it always did. She was consumed by this supposed killer who had been emailing her, but how credible was he? He seemed to know a great deal about Matilda, and the team. Maybe Tom was right. Maybe Matilda was just seeing a killer where really there was simply a fantasist and, at worst, a stalker. Then there was the threat of who to choose for redundancy hanging over her head. Sian, Scott or Finn. She felt sick at the thought of having to give one of them their marching orders. It wasn't fair. It was a horrible decision to try and make.

Matilda's mobile vibrated with an incoming text. She looked at the screen and saw it was from Odell. She smiled, opened it, and read a very flirtatious text, which made her smile even wider. Less than an hour ago she had told Tom and Zofia that their happiness was more important than work. She should take a leaf out of her own book. She sent back an equally flirtatious text. Ten minutes later, Matilda was taking the stairs two at a time to jump in the shower and freshen up. Odell was on his way over.

After her shower, sitting on the edge of the bed in a dressing gown, Matilda wondered whether this was such a good idea after all. She looked at the framed photograph of James on the bedside table and her heart sank. She still loved him so much that there were days when she physically ached for him. However, life had to go on whether she liked it or not. Matilda was only in her forties. Was she going to be alone, lonely and miserable for another forty or fifty years?

*'For crying out loud, Mat, do yourself a favour and get a bloody good seeing to.'*

Matilda laughed to herself. They weren't James's words in her head, surprisingly; they were Adele's. And she was right.

'I'll always love you, James,' she said to his photograph. 'But I need to move on. You understand, don't you?'

She wiped a tear away from her cheek and waited for James's reply. It didn't come. She was glad she didn't hear him. It obviously meant she was ready to finally let go.

The doorbell rang.

## Chapter Thirty-Three

Tuesday, 30 March 2021

DI Brady and the team decided to swoop on Derek Klein first thing in the morning. Christian pulled up outside the house on Park Lane in Broomhill with Finn Cotton in the front passenger seat. Behind him, Scott and Tom followed in a pool car and bringing up the rear was Crime Scene Manager Felix Lerego and his team of CSIs to tear through the house and car to find any evidence that Derek Klein had killed his daughter.

Christian climbed out of the car and shivered at the cold. It was a bright morning. The sky was blue, and a few whispers of light grey cloud floated in front of the sun. But it was chilly, with temperatures in the low single figures. He pulled a beanie hat out of his pocket and pulled it down over his head.

'Right then, let's go,' he said to his team.

They marched up the garden path and, with a gloved hand, Christian hammered loudly on the door, the noise echoing around the quiet neighbourhood.

'Curtain twitchers,' Scott said as he looked over his shoulder at the houses opposite.

Cara opened the door. She was still wearing a dressing gown and her hair was sticking up. She looked like she'd had a restless night. She blinked a few times at the brightness.

'Mrs Klein, is your husband home?'

'Of course he is. It's still early. What's going on?' Her eyes widened when she took in the four detectives on her doorstep. 'Have you found her? Have you found my Natasha?'

'No, Mrs Klein, we haven't. Could we come inside?'

'Oh. Yes. Of course. Sorry.' She stood to one side and allowed them to enter, closing the door behind them. 'What's happened? Something has happened, hasn't it?'

'We need to speak to your husband.'

'Right. Derek,' she called out. 'I think he's upstairs.'

There was movement from upstairs and then the sound of heavy footfall as Derek hurried downstairs. 'What?' He sounded annoyed. 'I was just about to go into the...' His eyes fell on Tom, whom he recognised. 'What's going on?'

'Mr Klein, I have a warrant here to search this house, including any outbuildings, and also impound your car.'

'My car? What are you talking about? What are you looking for?'

'We'd also like you to accompany us to the station where you will be interviewed, under caution, regarding the disappearance of Natasha Klein.'

'What... This is ridiculous,' he said, taking a step back. 'Surely you don't think I have anything to do with Natasha going missing.'

'Derek?' Cara asked, tears streaming down her face.

'Mrs Klein, why don't we step into the kitchen,' Tom said, putting his arm around her and leading her away from the drama.

'You can't do this,' Derek said, anger setting in. 'I have done nothing wrong.'

'Mr Klein, please, it would be helpful if you remained calm and came with us,' Christian said.

'Remained calm? Would you remain calm if police turned up on your doorstep and accused you of something you hadn't done?'

'Mr Klein, if you refuse to come with us voluntarily, we will arrest you. We can then keep you in custody for twenty-four hours and apply for further time should we require it.'

'This is wrong. I have done nothing with Natasha.'

'Go and finish getting dressed and we'll take you to the station where we can talk about this.'

Derek remained standing, looking fixedly at Christian. His expression was one of pure confusion. Eventually, he turned and headed back for the stairs.

'Go with him, Scott,' Christian said.

Tom came out of the kitchen, where he'd left Cara with a female PC making her a cup of tea.

'His acting skills have got better since the last time we saw him,' Tom said.

'Hmm. I thought that, too.'

## Chapter Thirty-Four

Matilda left her house struggling to hide her grin. It had been a long time since she'd had a night as perfect as last night. Odell left with her. She headed for her garage and Odell followed. He placed a hand on her shoulder and turned her around. He kissed her, passionately, on the lips.

'I didn't expect last night to turn out like it did,' he said.

'Hopefully it turned out better than anticipated.'

'Well, I am in the middle of researching a paper into brain rheology in the immediate minutes after death which I'm finding fascinating.'

'Oh. It sounds like gripping stuff. I'm surprised you came over then,' Matilda said, flippantly.

'We all need a break sometimes.'

'You certainly know how to make a woman feel special.'

'Sorry. I really did enjoy last night. I'm not one for small talk. I'm sure you've worked that out by now.'

'It had crossed my mind.'

'Would you like to come over to mine tonight? I can cook for us. I make a mean chilli.'

'Can I let you know? I really don't know how today is going to pan out.'

'Of course.' He kissed her again. 'I'll see you … whenever.' He turned and headed for his Tesla.

Matilda watched him drive away before going to her car.

'I can't believe I just slept with someone who drives a Tesla, for crying out loud.'

---

Matilda's first port of call was Hillsborough to see Danny Hanson. He was lucky that she was in a good mood and didn't intend to rip his testicles off with her bare hands. Though, depending on the outcome of the conversation, she could soon flip. Danny had that effect on her.

The apartment block Danny lived in had a tight security system with an intercom that had a camera above it so residents could see who was calling and choose whether to allow them in. Fortunately for Matilda, the door had been left open, so the element of surprise was on her side.

At Danny's front door, she rang the bell and deliberately stood to one side so she wouldn't be in full view of the spyhole, should he be the kind of person who vetted his visitors before deciding whether to open the door.

The door opened and Danny stood in the entrance with a blank expression on his tired face. His hair was ruffled in a just-got-out-of-bed look. He was wearing boxer shorts and a creased T-shirt with the Cookie Monster on the front.

'Matilda,' he said, surprised. 'What are you doing here?'

'I've come for a chat,' she said, hands in her pockets clenched into hidden fists. There was something about his smug face that immediately made her hackles rise.

Matilda had never been Danny Hanson's number-one fan. In

fact, she would go as far as saying she loathed the parasitic gobshite. However, over the past couple of years, her feelings towards him had softened. He'd done sterling work with the Magnolia House sexual abuse investigation, and more and more victims were coming forward to report people, thanks to his stories. She gladly shook his hand when thanking him for saving Adele and Sian's lives in January. But, at the end of the day, Danny Hanson still had the mentality of a sleazy tabloid hack who would probably sell a kidney to get a front-page lead.

'A chat? About anything in particular?'

'Are we really going to do this on your doorstep? I'm not sure if your neighbours are ready to see your gangly legs just yet.'

He looked down at himself. 'Oh. Shit. Sorry. Come on in.' He stepped to one side.

Matilda entered and looked around at the narrow hallway. Danny closed the door and led the way into the open-plan kitchen and living room.

'I'm surprised you're still living here. I thought you'd signed a six-figure deal for your book about Magnolia House.'

'You don't get it all at once, unfortunately. Coffee?'

'Please.'

'I got a chunk on signing the contract which I used to pay off a credit card and a down payment on a car. Another chunk when I handed in the final manuscript which I'm saving until I get the next chunk and hopefully that'll be a deposit on a house.'

'Seen anywhere you like?' she asked as she perused Danny's bookshelves.

'I've seen plenty I like, but none I can afford. I can't believe how expensive property is in Sheffield. There's nothing here. Shops are closing down. Pubs and nightclubs are disappearing. I could understand it if this was Manchester or Leeds where there's decent shopping but it's dead. And Meadowhall's just a nightmare.'

'The perils of city living.'

'Well, things seem to be on the up, so who knows where I'll end up. Milk and sugar?'

'Just black. Thanks. So, what are you working on at present?'

'Erm ... is that why you've come over, to see what I'm writing about?'

He handed Matilda a mug of coffee and invited her to sit down on one of the uncomfortable-looking sofas. She sat, took a sip of the instant coffee, and placed the mug on the coffee table.

'I hear you had a little trip to Southampton a couple of weeks ago,' she said.

'Ah.'

'Indeed.'

Danny seemed to think for a while. His eyes darted left and right as if he was searching for what to say, the correct words to use.

'I'm writing a book.'

'Fiction or non-fiction?'

'Non-fiction.'

'What's this one about?' she asked, sitting back and crossing her legs.

'I'm guessing you already know.'

'Do I?' She feigned surprise.

'I'm writing about the Stuart Mills case from the point of view of the reporter on the scene.'

'I see.'

'I've emailed a proposal to my agent, who has shown it to HarperCollins, who are publishing the Magnolia House book, and they're working on an offer.'

'There's already a book out about Stuart Mills,' Matilda said, her tone laced with venom.

'And there are hundreds of books about Jack the Ripper, but it doesn't stop people still writing about him.'

'What makes you think you can write something different that Sebastian Lister hasn't already covered?'

'Because I was there,' he answered, almost forcefully. 'I attended many of the crime scenes of Stuart's victims. I know the family.'

'Wrong.'

'I know *of* the family. And I'm familiar with all the investigating officers.'

'Do you honestly think we're going to sit down and be interviewed by you for a book about one of our colleagues?'

'It's not a book about Sian. I know what you're thinking: that I'm going to write some kind of a hatchet job about why Sian couldn't see she was living with a serial killer, but I'd never do that. I'm not that kind of writer. I like Sian. I've got a great deal of respect for her.'

'Really? Then why did you go all the way down to Southampton to interview Belinda?'

'I didn't speak to Belinda.'

'No. You went behind her back and got information, personal information, from her girlfriend.'

'Look, Matilda, people love true crime in this country. They're hungry for it. And we don't get many serial killers. When we do, we can't get enough of them. If I don't write this book someone else will. More people like Sebastian Lister who weren't even involved will write and make assumptions about Sian and her children. I won't do that,' he said, slapping a hand to his chest. 'I will be considerate to Sian. I'm just going to write the facts and about how I felt during the course of the investigation.'

'I do not want you approaching Sian, or any of her children, or any of their friends, about this book.'

'Matilda, I have a great of respect for you, I really do, but, no offence or anything, you can't tell me what to do.'

'I can give you a warning.'

'Would that be an official warning? Because I don't think that's possible.'

'Not an official one, no. However, if you try to talk to Sian or the children, or anyone they know, I swear to God I will make your life hell.'

Danny smiled. 'No, you won't.'

'You don't believe me?'

He shook his head. 'No. I've shadowed you for too long. I know you've done some things in your time that might not exactly be in the police rulebook, but you're not one for breaking the rules, and you wouldn't do anything to jeopardise your career. You love your work. You need your work. Without it, your life is empty. I'm sorry, but you've wasted your time in coming here. I will be writing this book and I'll be talking to whoever I want to. Whether they talk to me is entirely up to them. Not you. Not Sian. And besides, I won't need to talk to you and your colleagues. I know you all well enough to know what you'd say.'

Matilda could feel her blood boiling inside her. It was a while before she said anything.

'I want to call you names but I don't think one has been invented for you yet, and I really don't want to lower myself by swearing at you. I think I'm going to go,' she said, standing up.

'I'll show you out.' He followed her to the door. 'It was lovely to see you, though, Mat. You must come round again sometime. I'll get the Mr Kipling's in.'

Matilda turned on her heel, grabbed Danny by the throat and slammed him up against the wall. 'Listen to me, you little prick,' she hissed. Her eyes were wide and her face red with anger. She squeezed his neck hard and could feel the veins beating against her fingers. 'You write one word about Sian, about Stuart, about her children, and I don't care what happens to me, I will literally gut you. Do you understand me?'

Danny didn't react. He couldn't. He was gasping for breath, clawing at Matilda's hand with his blunt fingernails.

'I asked if you understood,' she said.
He nodded.
'Good.' She let go and he fell to the floor.
At the door, Matilda turned back. 'One more thing, your coffee tastes like shit.' She left the flat, slamming the door behind her.

## Chapter Thirty-Five

'Did I tell you who Roland T Owen was?' Zofia asked.
Matilda turned to Zofia with a frown.
'The sympathy card Josie Pettifer's father received was signed by Roland T Owen.'
'Of course it was. Go on.'
'First of all, Roland T Owen wasn't his real name. His real name was Artemus Ogletree.'
'I can see why he changed it.'
'He was found dead in a hotel room in Kansas City, Missouri in 1935. He was stabbed and beaten to death. He wasn't formally identified until a year and a half later by a woman who saw a photograph of him and recognised him as her son. He'd left Birmingham, Alabama, the year before at the age of seventeen to hitchhike to California. She later received letters from him saying he was in Egypt. The letters were sent after his death. There's a lot of mystery surrounding why he was in that hotel and the people he met in the run-up to his death, and to this day, nobody knows who killed him.'
'Interesting.'

'And we all know that "From Hell" is a reference to Jack the Ripper. You did know that, didn't you?'

Matilda raised an eyebrow. 'Yes, Zofia, I did know. Just because I was born before the internet doesn't mean I'm completely clueless about history. So, these emails to me are signed by killers who got away with their crimes, but the sympathy cards to the family are signed by people whose murders were never solved.'

'It would seem like it.'

The double doors opened, and Scott entered the suite. 'There you are. I've just been up to your office,' he said to Matilda. 'I don't know why you bothered moving out.'

'Neither do I.'

'I've got the forensics back on the oil found in Josie Pettifer's kitchen.'

'Go on,' Matilda instructed.

'The oil in her kitchen is pure olive oil. There isn't a trace of peanut oil in there at all. Also, according to the forensic report, any oil that does contain peanut oil wouldn't contain the amount found in the sample in the dish she was eating at the time. It looks like it was deliberately spiked to make her have a massive anaphylactic shock.'

'Fingerprints on the bottle?'

'Josie and her father's prints. My guess is that the killer brought it with him and took it away with him when he left.'

'And unfortunately, Reg has cleared out the whole flat since his daughter died so we can't go in with a forensic team.'

'I'm afraid not. He's a smart cookie, our guy, isn't he?'

'It would appear so,' Matilda mused.

'Where do we go from here?'

As much as Matilda hated to admit it, so far she was being beaten. 'All we can do, Scott, is wait for him to contact us again with news of his third victim.'

'We said that after the first victim,' Zofia said.

Scott shook his head. 'It's ghoulish. It's like waiting for people to die.'

'The only thing we can take from this is that they'll already be dead. We can't save them.'

'Yes, he says he's killed five, but what if he's planning others? What if he wants to be the most prolific serial killer ever? What if he's planning victims six, seven, eight right now?'

'What can we do?' Matilda asked, exasperated. 'What can we *actually* do?'

He didn't answer. He couldn't. Nobody could.

# Part III

DAY 27

Eight serial killers were given the nickname 'Angel of Death'. Five were called the 'Freeway Killer'. Three were called the 'Railroad Killer' while four were called 'Doctor Death'. I wonder what I'll be called: the Sheffield Slayer perhaps or maybe the Steel City Slaughterer. I like that one. I wonder if there'll be a book written about me. There's bound to be. Or maybe I could write my own.

I've read Mindhunter by John Douglas and Mark Olshaker so many times that I've had to buy a second copy as my first was falling apart. David Wilson has written some pretty chilling books, too, and Picking up the Pieces by Paul Britton gave me a few sleepless nights. I've read The Perfect Killer by Sebastian Lister hoping it would be as dark and blood-curdling as his first book, The Riverside Killer: The Double Life of Richard Button, but I was very disappointed. It lacked atmosphere and depth.

I'm growing impatient waiting for Matilda Darke and her supposedly crack team of experts to announce to the media they're on the hunt for a highly dangerous killer. I've given her the name of two of my victims. I've told her how I've killed them. What do I have to do to break this team?

I've obviously been too clever. I bet they're still having doubts that Liam Walsh and Josie Pettifer were murdered. Fortunately, I've planned for such an eventuality with my third victim.

Time to get your hands dirty, Matilda.

**From:** <t89u5q3w-2@outlook.com>
**Date:** Monday, 1 January 1900 at 00:00
**To:** Darke, Matilda <matilda.darke@southyorkshirepolice.co.uk>
**Subject:** 3 of 5.

Hello Mat,

What's your favourite method of murder?

The norm in this country, at present, is stabbing. I can see the attraction there. The killer and the victim have to be incredibly close for a stabbing to occur. So much emotion and electrifying tension is there. You've already got the hatred of the victim by the killer, add in the rush of seeing the life die in someone's eyes and, wow, I bet there's no other feeling like it in the world. I really must try a stabbing one of these days. I just need to find someone I hate so much. I'm getting close, though.

Another favourite in this country is beating someone to death without a weapon. I'm not sure I could do that. I'm not a physical person. I don't have the power behind me. Mentally, I'm incredibly strong. I think you have to be to commit murder. So-called experts say it's the most basic crime as it doesn't take a great deal of brain power to take another life, but I think they're wrong. The method may be easy, but the aftermath is where you need the stability, especially if you don't want to get caught, and I have no intention of getting caught.

Josie Pettifer was an easy kill. She came across as an independent, strong-willed woman who didn't need a man to survive in the world, but she soon fell for my words. It wasn't long before she was inviting me into her flat, into her bed. I resisted that. I know all about the world of forensics and trace evidence. She allowed me to cook for her, though. She trusted me that much, despite her many allergies. She showered while I cooked. She had no idea I was using pure peanut oil on her salmon. I watched her as she died. I sat back and watched as her throat closed, her face bloated, she gasped for breath, looked at me pleadingly, begged me to get her epi pen from the bathroom. I think it dawned on her what was happening just before the lights went out. Then, I sat back, finished my meal, washed up, and left. Goodnight Josie.

I want to play a game with you now, Mat. The third victim is called Audrey Wildgoose and she's waiting for you to find her. I could just tell you where she is, but where's the fun in that? To locate her, you need to look into your past. Where did it all go wrong for you, Mat? Where were you when you realised life was shit, hopeless and pointless? I'll tell you where I was when we speak. In the meantime, this is all about you.

Bye for now, Mat,

Bible John.

## Chapter Thirty-Six

Friday, 9 April 2021

Matilda knew exactly where she was supposed to look for Audrey Wildgoose. She knew exactly where she was when she knew life was shit. She printed off the email and grabbed it as she stormed out of the office.

'Zofia, find me everything you can about Audrey Wildgoose.'

'Who's she?'

'Just do it,' she said, throwing the email at her. 'Scott, Finn, come with me.' She was putting on her coat as she headed for the door. She stopped at Christian's office. He was in there with Tom. She pushed the door open. 'Christian, I've had another email. Zofia's got it. Get a forensics team on standby. Can I have Tom?'

'Erm, sure. What's going on?'

'He's making sure I find this one myself.'

'Jesus Christ! Do you want me to come with you?'

'No. Just wait for my call.'

'Where are we going?' Scott asked as they charged after Matilda as she raced down the corridor towards the car park.

'Graves fucking Park,' she called out over her shoulder.

---

In 2015, when her husband James was diagnosed with an inoperable brain tumour, Matilda Darke was leading the investigation into the kidnapping of seven-year-old Carl Meagan. His parents were wealthy restaurant owners and a ransom demand of £250,000 was made. A date was set for the exchange and Matilda was going to be the one to do it. On the day in question, Matilda's husband lost his fight and died with her by his bedside. She should have handed over the case. She should have told her superiors what had happened and that she needed to grieve. She did the opposite. She went to work believing, hoping, she could distract herself from her emotions.

Graves Park covers almost two hundred and fifty acres of land in the south of Sheffield between the districts of Norton, Woodseats, and Meadowhead and is a mixture of open areas and woodlands. There are two car parks; one is near the tennis courts, the other is near the animal farm. Even to this day, Matilda is convinced she was supposed to meet the kidnappers in the car park close to the tennis courts. They were waiting for her in the car park at the animal farm. When she realised her error, she set off on foot, running in the dark and the rain, weighed down with a quarter of a million pounds in bank notes stuffed in a holdall over her shoulder. Tears were streaming down her face, her vision blurred. She was crying for her husband, for her mistake, for Carl. When she arrived at the car park, it was empty. The smell of exhaust fumes in the air. She had failed. As she dropped to her knees, her mobile ringing, her boss asking for an update, she knew that it was over. Her career, her marriage, her life. Everything was over. Everything was pointless and hopeless.

By the time her former team joined her in the car park, Matilda was taking a bag out of the back of Adele's Porsche, slamming the boot closed, and throwing it into the back of one of the pool cars, a Vauxhall Astra in desperate need of a wash.

Matilda was driving, Scott was in the front passenger seat while Finn and Tom were in the back. Matilda handed Scott her mobile and told him to read the email out to Finn and Tom.

'He's talking about methods of murder,' Finn said. 'He's asking you what your favourite method is, but he hasn't said what his is. That makes me nervous. What condition are we going to find this Audrey Wildgoose in?'

'Any word from Zofia yet?' Matilda asked Scott.

He glanced at his own mobile. 'Not yet.'

'My theory about Josie Pettifer was right,' Finn said. 'It looks like he did bring the oil with him and took it away when he left.'

'He watched her die,' Tom said. 'He sat there with a dead body not a foot away and finished his meal. That's cold. That's fucking evil. How can you just sit there and watch someone die?'

'Only a psychopath can do that.'

'So, why is Graves Park where everything went to shit for you?' Tom asked Matilda.

Finn looked at Tom with wide eyes and shook his head. 'Later,' he mouthed.

Scott's phone rang. It was Zofia. He swiped to answer and put her on loudspeaker.

'Audrey Wildgoose is listed as a missing person. She was reported missing on the morning of Sunday the twenty-seventh of March this year.'

'Thirteen days ago,' Scott interrupted.

'She's eighty-six years old and lives in Greenhill. She was reported missing by her neighbour Sylvia Culverhouse. According to her statement, Audrey was waiting to go into a nursing home. She was diagnosed with dementia just before the pandemic hit. Sylvia, along with another neighbour, Jenny Savage, went round most days. They did her washing and shopping and looked after her. Sylvia went round on the Sunday morning and found the back door wide open. There's been no sign of her since.'

'Shit,' Matilda said, slamming her foot down on the accelerator as the traffic light ahead changed from green to amber.

'Now,' Zofia continued. 'There have been extensive searches for her in woodland around Park Bank Wood, Abbeydale Golf Club, Moorview Golf Centre, and in Greenhill Park. There's been no sign of her. It's like she's just disappeared.'

'Just like Natasha,' Tom said to himself.

'Any family?' Matilda asked.

'No. She was married but her husband died in 1998. They didn't have children.'

'Okay. Zofia, get the original missing persons report and all the statements together. Tell Christian to make sure there's a CSI team on standby.' Matilda told Scott to end the call.

She turned off Hemsworth Road without indicating, earning her a few beeps from passing motorists, and turned into the car park at Graves Park near the animal farm. It was mid-afternoon and cloudy. It had been a dull day and the temperature was in single figures. The car park was practically empty. One battered Ford Focus and a council van. She pulled up in a space and they all climbed out. The smell of manure from the nearby farm filled the air. Matilda shivered in the cold as she pulled her coat around her. She turned a full three hundred and sixty degrees, taking in the wide open space, the expanse of grass, the trees and woodland ahead.

'This bastard wants me to walk through shit, doesn't he?' She went to the back of the car, opened the boot, and took out a pair of wellingtons and a torch from her kitbag. 'We're not leaving here until we've found her.'

Matilda didn't know where to start. Graves Park seemed to stretch for miles. There were wide open spaces and pockets of dense woodland. It was also an incredibly busy park where people came to run, exercise, walk their dogs, bring their kids to the animal farm, play tennis, bowls and cricket, weather permitting, or simply to walk through from one side of Sheffield to the other. If Audrey Wildgoose was here, surely she would have been found by now.

She set off along the grass, taking long strides. The ground was sodden following recent heavy rain and Matilda's wellington boots squelched with every step, pulling her into the ground. She stopped and turned back. Scott, Finn, and Tom were still standing by her car.

'Tom, call Zofia,' Matilda called out. 'Find out what Audrey was wearing on the night she disappeared.' He nodded as he took out his mobile. 'You two, this is the part of the job where you have to get mucky.'

Scott looked down at his shoes. 'These are brand new Loakes,' he said.

'If you came closer, Scott, you would see the expression on my face telling you that I couldn't give two fucks. We've got an elderly, vulnerable woman out here who needs to be found.' She turned back and continued her trek across the unstable ground.

*Vulnerable.*

Liam Walsh was vulnerable. He suffered greatly with his mental health. Josie Pettifer was vulnerable due to her severe allergies. Now, Audrey Wildgoose. She had been recently diagnosed with dementia, making her vulnerable, too. Matilda frowned as she walked. In her head she pictured the killer as young, someone in his twenties, someone who was able to join Liam and Josie's life without standing out. They were both of a similar age, so a young man wouldn't attract attention among their peer groups. But Audrey was in her eighties. Someone new, someone young, would stand out. How the hell was he choosing his victims?

Matilda reached the end of the field, crossed the concrete pavement, and entered woodland. Trees were bare, the ground littered with soggy brown leaves. She shivered as the cold and dark enveloped her. She switched on her torch and waved it around at ground level. Nothing stood out. Small wildlife scattered once the torchlight hit them, but there was no sign of an elderly woman, no abandoned clothing or shoes. Matilda ploughed on, determined, a woman on a mission. She was not going home until Audrey was found.

'Matilda!' Scott called out.

She heard him, distantly, but didn't respond. She climbed over a fallen tree, not caring if a jagged branch snagged her coat or cut her skin. She aimed the torch behind the tree, but there was nothing there. She continued, walking further into the darkness.

'Matilda! Wait!' Scott shouted.

Matilda turned back to see Scott struggling over the rough terrain. She pointed the torch in his direction. She saw the mud spatter up to his knees and his once shiny black Loake shoes were hidden beneath wet dirt and leaves.

'Matilda, this is ridiculous. You can't see a thing.'

'And the inventor of the torch rests peacefully in his grave,' she said, shining her torch into his face.

'You could walk past her and not notice. Why don't we wait until morning when it gets light?'

'Why don't we just wait until it's summer when it's warm and dry? We could bring a picnic.'

'Matilda. Mat,' he said, stalking after her. 'First thing in the morning, we can get a search team out here, arc lights. With the bare trees, we can send a drone or a helicopter up to search. According to Zofia, Audrey was wearing a white nightie when her neighbour put her to bed on the night she went missing. That'll be easy to see from above.'

'If she's still wearing it. If she hasn't been partially buried. If the wildlife hasn't got to her. Scott, look at you, you've not been in these woods five minutes and you're filthy. Do you honestly think a white nightie is still going to be white after two weeks in this?'

She turned away from him and continued, slipping on a pile of soggy leaves.

'I've called Felix Lerego,' Scott shouted. 'He's got a team on standby. He said they can be out here first thing in the morning.'

'Then we need to find them a crime scene to search. Right now, all we've got is two hundred and fifty acres of park and woodland,' Matilda said without stopping.

'Do you want me to get you anything?'

'A team with the correct footwear would be great right now,' she shouted, her voice full of venom.

It took a while, but Scott eventually caught up with her. 'I have the right footwear. I have a pair of boots in the back of my car. If you'd said we'd be searching woodland when you charged out of the station, I would have brought them with me. Instead, I'm ruining a pair of two hundred quid shoes my boyfriend bought me for my birthday.'

Matilda looked over to Scott. 'I'm sorry,' she said, softly. She placed a hand on his shoulder. 'I'm sorry, Scott,' she repeated. 'I… I don't like this.' Her voice broke with emotion. 'There's someone out there thinking he can get away with killing people. He's picking off the vulnerable and using them in his own twisted game.' Matilda wiped away a tear with the back of her dirty hand, leaving a muddy smudge on her cheek. 'Audrey is eighty-six years old. She should be living out the rest of her life in peace and comfort. She should be in her own home right now, warm, cosy, and safe. Instead, she's out here somewhere because some fucker thought it would be fun to test his murder theory. I need to find her, Scott.'

He nodded. He scrabbled in his pocket and took out his mobile. He scrolled through the contacts and made a call.

'Christian, it's me. We're going to need as many as you can find to help us search Graves Park. Finn's at the car park close to the animal farm, he'll tell you where we are. Tell everyone to dress for the Somme and bring as much portable lighting as they can.'

When he ended the call, Matilda pulled Scott towards her and kissed him on the cheek. 'I'll buy you a new pair of Loakes. I'll even buy Donal a pair, too.'

'Why? He's not done anything. When I texted and told him where I was he sent me a selfie of him on the sofa watching *The Crown*.'

'He watches that?' she asked, pulling a face.

'And *Bridgerton*.'

'Oh, Scott, I'm so sorry. I had no idea.'

'Neither did I. If I hadn't put a deposit down on the venue, I'd call off the wedding.'

Matilda smiled. She placed her arm through Scott's, and they walked off, further into the dark woodland, using each other as support over the rough ground, Matilda lighting the path ahead with her torch.

---

It was close to midnight by the time Audrey Wildgoose was found. Matilda and Scott had been searching for almost six hours. They were chilled to the bone, filthy from head to toe, and physically and mentally shattered, yet they ploughed on.

They entered Waterfall Wood just past Graves Park Beck. Matilda raised her torch, and there she was, Audrey Wildgoose, slumped at the base of an oak tree. Matilda couldn't move. She couldn't speak. The small figure in a dirty and torn white nightie had been left to the elements. It had been a relatively cool spring so far and airborne insects were flying around her, beetles and maggots crawling over her exposed skin, eating what they could find to stay alive. The woman's features were disfigured. Her eyes had long since been ravaged by wildlife, and there was evidence of rodent damage to her fingers, toes and nose. A few fingers on her left hand had become detached, the remnants a few feet away from her. The body had gone through the bloating stage of post-mortem decay and had entered the liquefying phase. Her head was down on her chest, the skin of which had already started to slip away from the bones, giving her a deformed look. Years of living with a pathologist had told Matilda this was known as degloving. She turned to Scott who had already turned his back on the scene.

'Call Felix,' she said, softly.

Scott walked away, head down, as he fished out his mobile.

'And call Odell,' she added, louder.

Matilda stepped forward, careful not to disturb any potential evidence, though she doubted there would be any. This was a very clever killer they were dealing with and even if, by chance, a stray hair or skin sample had been left behind, the wildlife would have destroyed it as they feasted on the elderly woman.

Matilda squatted to her knees. The smell emanating from the corpse was vomit-inducing. She covered her nose and mouth with her free hand and looked closely at Audrey Wildgoose.

'I am so sorry,' she said, her voice barely above a whisper. Tears streamed down her face. 'I'll find who did this to you. I promise. I will find him. And I'll fucking annihilate him.'

---

With the CSIs in full flow and Odell overseeing the safe removal of the body, there was nothing more for Matilda to do, though she wanted to stay. She felt she owed it to Audrey to see she was well looked after, even in death. It took a lot of cajoling, but Scott eventually was able to tear her away from the scene.

'Mat, you're freezing. You're not going to do anyone any favours staying here catching pneumonia.'

She allowed herself to be led away from the woods and towards the car park. They walked in silence, Matilda with her head down, a painful expression on her face as she gave the matter deep thought, wondering where the hell this was all going, who his next victim was going to be, how much more shit she was going to have to wade though, and what kind of a sick bastard was behind all this.

'Do you want me to drive?' Scott asked once they reached her car.

She took the keys from her pocket and tossed them to her DS. She climbed into the front passenger seat, not changing out of her muddy wellington boots, and put her seatbelt on. She sat perfectly still, waiting to be taken home.

Before he got in behind the wheel, Scott fired off a quick text to Donal, telling him to turn off Netflix and to meet him at Matilda's with an overnight bag for them both. They had a spare key to Matilda's in case of emergencies and by the time Scott pulled up outside, Donal was already there. A light was on in the living room, the curtains were drawn, and, as they could feel the moment they walked into the house, a fire was burning.

By the time Matilda spoke, all three were in the lounge on the sofas, mugs of tea in hand.

'I can't get my head around any of this,' Matilda said. The room was dimly lit by a single standard lamp in the corner of the room. The flickering orange flames from the fire provided most of the light. 'Why's he doing this? What's the reasoning behind it?'

'I think you should be asking Finn that question, not me,' Scott said.

'It's cruel, isn't it?' Donal said in his soft, smooth Irish lilt. 'It's like when you see kids pull the legs off spiders or lift up flagstones and stand on the insects beneath. It's just pure cruelty.'

Matilda looked up at him. 'But what's the point?'

'There is no point. It's a power thing. He's thought of something and he's just going ahead and doing it. He's not caring about the consequences. He's doing something he knows he can get away with.'

'It's like he said in his email,' Scott began. 'If this went to court, nothing would happen. To all intents and purposes, Liam Walsh died by jumping off a building. Josie Pettifer died from an allergic reaction and Audrey Wildgoose could very well have walked out of her home and become confused. A good lawyer would get him off. We probably wouldn't even be able to pin the emails on him because there's no trace. He could easily come up to you in the street and say that he'd been sending the emails, that he'd killed them all, and we wouldn't be able to prove it.'

'And that's what's feeding him,' Matilda said.

'It's scary,' Donal said. 'We've all got something that could be used as a way to kill us, if you think about it. I mean, look at you, Scott. You go out running every morning, whatever the weather. He could follow you one morning in the rain and hit you on the head with a rock or something and make it look like you slipped on the wet road and hit your head. We'd all think it was an accident.'

'Why do I get the feeling I should be checking my insurance policies?' Scott asked.

Donal snuggled up next to him on the sofa and held his hand. 'I'm suddenly very worried about you right now.'

Scott looked over at Matilda. They made eye contact. Matilda could see the fear in his eyes. She gave him a sympathetic smile. He tried to return it, but his emotions wouldn't let him. The tears in his eyes were welling up.

'We'll stay with you tonight, Mat, and for as long as you want us to,' Donal said.

How many other colleagues would do something like this? Matilda thought. At the drop of a hat, Scott and Donal were always there for her whenever she needed them. She didn't even have to ask, and they were there. Over the last couple of years, especially since the shooting, she and Scott had developed an almost sixth sense whereby each knew how the other was feeling without a word being uttered. She couldn't lose that. She didn't want to lose that. Her mind wandered back to the policing cuts and the fact she still had to choose one of her colleagues, her friends, to be made redundant. There was no way she was going to choose Scott. If Ridley wanted to save money, he'd have to find it another way.

## Chapter Thirty-Seven

Saturday, 10 April 2021

Derek Klein was currently being held on remand at HMP Lindholme in Doncaster. Although Natasha was still listed as a missing person, the evidence against him was mounting. He had no alibi for the time she went missing. He had seemingly paid for her silence when she found out about his affair with her best friend, Ruby Deighton. During the forensic search of his car, samples of blood were found in the boot that matched Natasha's. A murder charge without a body was incredibly difficult to uphold, but it wasn't looking good for Derek. At Sheffield Crown Court, he had pleaded not guilty and a provisional trial date for next September had been set. In the meantime, he was to be held in custody while a case was being prepared by the Crown Prosecution Service.

Derek spent his days confined to his cell for as long as he was allowed. He had found himself plunged into a nightmare world that made absolutely no sense. A month ago, his life was plodding along at its usual pace. He was in a job that he didn't exactly love, but one that he was competent at and that was bringing in a decent wage. His marriage to Cara was lacking in passion and romance, but they were content in each other's company. Natasha, though she was self-centred and continually asked for money, was turning into a strong and independent young woman. The one thing in his life that set him apart from every other late-forty-something with a bald patch and a paunch was his affair with nineteen-year-old Ruby Deighton. It was wrong. He knew that. He was cheating on his wife. He was going through a mid-life crisis, it was blatantly obvious, but he was loving every minute of it. Derek had no idea what Ruby saw in him, but she constantly reassured him how much she liked him, how much she enjoyed his company and how much she loved him. Yes, she'd said love. Did nineteen-year-olds really know what love was? Maybe.

How had he gone from all that to being charged with murdering his stepdaughter and sleeping in a prison with his freedom torn from him, his life in ruins, his entire existence being scrutinised by the media, the police, lawyers, and the newspaper-reading members of the public?

'Where is she?'

He knew the question was directed at him. It was a question he'd had thrown at him more than once a day since he arrived here. He didn't look up.

'What have you done with her?'

Derek was sitting in the day room reading a newspaper. He'd just finished an article about a candlelit vigil being held in the Peace Gardens in Sheffield city centre tonight to keep Natasha's name in the news. It was being organised by Ruby. She'd given a very impassioned interview to the paper.

He was deliberately nudged by a heavyset man reeking of body odour and baked beans who sat down next to him.

'Did you rape her?' he asked.

Still, Derek didn't say anything.

'Or did you want to shag her, she turned you down and you had to silence her?'

There was a ripple of laughter among the men.

'Here, Tony, have you seen her? His Natasha? Fit as fuck, isn't she? I would.'

'Dave, you'd shag a hole in the ground.'

More laughter.

'She's well tasty, though, isn't she?' Dave said, snatching the newspaper from Derek and holding it up, showing the room the double-page feature, most of it taken up by a picture of a smiling Natasha. 'You just know she's got amazing tits under that top. Did you shag her then, Derek? I mean, we wouldn't blame you if you did.'

'And it's not incest, is it, because she's not your real daughter,' Tony said.

'Exactly. I mean, yeah, it's a grey area, but we wouldn't call you sick.'

Derek remained in stony silence. He didn't move a muscle.

'A lad I was at school with, his uncle went out with his sister. They weren't blood relatives; he'd married into the family.'

'Did he go to prison?' Dave asked.

'No. Why should he? They were both over sixteen. Plenty of rows in the family, by all accounts. Well, there would be, wouldn't there?'

'I can't see her auntie sending her anything for Christmas,' Dave laughed.

'So, come on then, Derek,' Tony said, sitting on the other side of him, squeezing him in between himself and Dave. 'You can tell us. We're not going to tell anyone. Did you fuck her? Did you kill her? Where did you bury her? Dave'll tell you where he hid his stash from that Post Office he turned over.'

'Fuck off, I won't. As long as the council don't Tarmac over it, that's my nest egg when I get out in six to eight years' time, providing I get a good jury.'

Derek tried to get up. Tony reached up, grabbed him by the shoulder, and pulled him back down into his seat.

'There's something you need to learn about surviving in here, mate. We're all exactly the same. Out there, you might be an accountant, drive a shit-hot car and live in a fancy house, but you're in here now. We all piss in the same pot. The sooner you realise that the better.'

'I didn't do anything,' Derek said, quietly, on the verge of tears.

''Course you didn't. And Tony didn't throw his wife's boyfriend over a balcony.'

'I didn't!' Tony exclaimed. 'I threw him over a bridge.'

They both laughed.

Derek managed to get up and head for the door, but Tony was too quick for him. He slammed the door so Derek couldn't get out.

'Listen to me, Mr Accountant,' Tony said, his nose almost touching Derek's. 'You're not going anywhere. You're as guilty as we are, and we're going to be spending a long time together, so we need to get on. As soon as you realise you're the same as us, the easier it'll be.'

'I'm not like you,' Derek said without thinking.

Tony exaggeratedly sucked in his breath. 'It's words like that that get your teeth punched down your throat. Dave, you want to start?'

## Chapter Thirty-Eight

Chief Constable Ridley would have a fit if he knew Matilda had called the entire HMCU to come into the station on a Saturday. The overtime budget would go through the roof with what she had planned.

It was after two o'clock that morning when she finally went to bed. She, Scott and Donal had spent hours talking, mostly about nothing. It was only when Donal started snoring that they realised he'd fallen asleep, and it was time they all went to bed. The spare bedroom was always made up for visitors, so Scott and Donal had slept in there.

Matilda woke at eight o'clock. Despite having a fitful night's sleep, she felt buoyed and full of ideas. Last night, she had been angry, sad, depressed, scared, dejected. This morning, she looked at herself in the mirror and saw the determination in her eyes. Matilda would never be defeated. She would literally fight until the death if she had to.

Once in the HMCU suite, she gave the orders.

'First priority is identifying Audrey Wildgoose. Now, she had no family, but she did have neighbours and close friends. However, due to the severity of decomposition, I wouldn't put my worst enemy through that.' She stopped as she thought. 'Actually, I'd probably put Danny Hanson through it.' This was met with a few light-hearted giggles from her team. 'I also want the post-mortem done as soon as possible. I've called Odell and he's coming in specially to do it. Audrey had support from her neighbours. They reported her missing. I want Jenny Savage and Sylvia Culverhouse brought in and interviewed. Scott and Tom, I want you to interview Jenny. Finn and Zofia, you two are interviewing Sylvia. Sian, pop along to Watery Street and observe the PM.'

'Oh God, I knew I shouldn't have had that bacon butty for breakfast,' she said.

'Christian, we'll observe the interviews.'

He nodded.

'Just to let you all know,' Christian said. 'There's a candlelit vigil tonight in the city centre. It's been four weeks since Natasha Klein disappeared, and her friends have organised a gathering in the hope of jogging people's memories. It's all over social media and we're expecting a large crowd. Uniformed officers will be there to supervise and make sure things don't get out of hand. However, we're looking for volunteers in plain clothes to join the group to see if anyone can pick up on something or someone acting suspiciously. Anyone?'

'I'll be there,' Tom answered straightaway.

'I'm going with Scott and Donal,' Finn said.

'Good. Thanks,' Christian said.

While the team set about getting ready for the interviews, Christian went over to Matilda, who was leaning on the windowsill looking out at the uninspiring view of the bins at the back of the station.

'Is everything all right?' he asked her.

'Fine. I'm just... I'm really struggling with this one, Christian. Usually, we get dead bodies and there's either a gunshot wound or a knife sticking out of them. We know how they died, and we can usually find the killer by looking through their lives. This is different. In all my years on the force, I've never come across anything like this. It requires a different approach and I'm not sure what that is.'

'If I say something, will you promise not to get mad?' he asked.

'That depends. If you tell me you're the killer, I'm going to be fuming.'

'No. It's not that. This bloke, whoever he is, he's writing to you. He's asking if he can call you Mat. Finn's said that he knows you, that he might even be in your life. Do you think it's possible you're too close to this, that maybe you should bring in a separate team?'

'I never like the idea of another team coming in. It reeks of failure.'

'It's not failure. It's asking for help. It's pooling resources. You've just said this requires a different approach. Maybe that approach is someone who is detached from us.'

'I'll give it some thought,' she said, looking Christian in the eye and seeing genuine concern in his face. 'I will. I promise.'

'I'll back you up whatever you decide. You know that.'

'Thanks. Shall we go and grab a shite coffee from the machine and watch the interviews?'

'Slight problem. The toilets above the observation room sprang a leak. We'll have to watch from here on the monitors. On the plus side, our coffee is much better.'

'True, but I'll have nothing to moan about,' Matilda said with a slight smirk.

'I'm sure you'll find something.'

'Cheeky sod.'

Coffees on the table in front of them, with several empty chocolate wrappers from Sian's drawer, notepad and pen at the ready, they watched on the projector screen as Jenny Savage was brought into the Interview Room. She walked slowly with her head down. She was wearing tight jeans, ankle boots and a puffy anorak. She sat down and Matilda could see she was crying, having been told Audrey's body had been found. Scott and Tom sat opposite and told her this wasn't a formal interview, but it was being recorded to help with their investigation. She either didn't mind or didn't listen as she didn't react.

'She looks gutted,' Matilda remarked.

Christian was looking at his phone. 'Text from Sian. They've matched DNA from a sample taken from her house when she went missing to the body found last night. It's definitely Audrey Wildgoose.'

Matilda let out a deep sigh. 'Always good to have it confirmed.'

'Jenny, I know in your original statement you told officers that you helped look after Audrey following her diagnosis of dementia,' Scott began. 'Can you give us more details of her day-to-day life?'

Jenny wiped her nose with a tattered tissue and nodded.

'Audrey had lived on School Lane for as long as anyone could remember,' she said with a haunting smile. 'I've been there twenty-odd years, and she was an established figure then. She was a lovely woman; would do anything for anyone. About … it must be five years ago, she had a fall in the back garden. I'll never forget the sound of her scream for as long as I live. She displaced her hip. She was in hospital for a couple of weeks. When she came home, she struggled with the stairs. Anyway, my husband, Philip, he's a plumber by trade. He got one of his mates to knock through the downstairs toilet into the utility that she didn't use and turned it into a downstairs bathroom for her. We turned her living room into a kind of big open-plan bedroom, and she just stayed downstairs. She was quite comfortable.

'In the January, before the pandemic hit in March, she was diagnosed with dementia.' Jenny wiped the tears from her eyes. 'She was devastated. I didn't even know she'd taken herself off to the doctor's. She's always been scared of having Alzheimer's, and she said she noticed she started forgetting where things were around the house, what day of the week it was, and the name of her husband, which really upset her. I told her not to worry. I only work part-time so I said I'd help her as much as I could. I did her washing for her and made sure her cupboards were stocked with food and she had all the toiletries she needed. When I cooked, I made an extra plate and took it round for her. Between us, that's me and Sylvia who lives on the other side, we made sure she was well looked after.'

'How was she coping with her dementia in the run-up to her disappearance?' Tom asked.

'It had gotten progressively worse. It was a slow decline. She kept asking for her Richard. That was her husband. When I went round, she'd ask me what time he was due home. It really upset me. We had a sheet made up of all the people who called round to help, with our photos and who we were, so she'd recognise us. It was always on the little table by her chair. I think that helped.'

'Was it just the three of you who helped her? Did any of the other neighbours?'

'No. We thought it best to keep it to just us three. We knew her the most. We didn't want her getting more confused. Annie, she lives opposite me, she bakes a lot and used to bring me muffins and cookies to take round to Audrey. Oh…' She stopped herself as she remembered something. 'There was Alex.'

'Who's Alex?' Scott asked.

'Well, I'm not actually sure he even existed,' she said. 'A few times I'd ask Audrey if she needed anything specific and I'd mention something like toilet rolls or something and she'd say that Alex had brought her a load round. The thing is, none of us know an Alex and there's no Alex living in the street. I thought it was someone from her past who she was suddenly remembering, an old boyfriend or childhood friend maybe. It was only in the last few weeks or so that she kept saying Alex had been to visit her and he was helping her.'

'But you never saw him?' Scott asked.

'No. Well, I didn't expect to.'

'What did she say Alex was doing?'

'She said he was bringing her bulky items. Big boxes of washing powder and loo rolls. I've only got a Smart car so I can't fit a lot of stuff in. Sylvia, her husband goes to Costco a lot, so I assumed they'd be fetching her the bigger items. When I asked her about it, she said she hadn't bought her anything as she'd looked, and she hadn't needed anything. So who'd been bringing her these big bulky items?'

'Did you ever ask Audrey about Alex?'

'I did. A couple of times. I asked her to describe him to me. During the summer of 2020 when we were social distancing, I caught Covid, so I didn't go round to see Audrey. I spoke to her on the phone and over the fence, but I arranged a delivery online. I thought it might have been the Tesco delivery man who she was getting confused with, but she couldn't seem to describe this Alex. She said he was a young man, always helpful and smiling.'

'Did you ask any of the other neighbours about Alex?' Tom asked.

'Only Sylvia and her husband. They didn't know anyone called Alex either. Sylvia said that Audrey mentioned him once or twice. She told Sylvia that Alex called at night. Again, we just thought she was confused. Do you think she was? Do you know who this Alex is?'

'We don't, I'm afraid,' Scott said.

'But you think he's real?'

'Someone was bringing her those items.'

'True. But who? Why?'

Scott didn't answer her question. He couldn't. 'Tell me about the last time you saw her.'

Jenny's eyes turned glassy with tears. She wiped them away before they had a chance to fall. 'I went round as always at seven o'clock. I made her a cup of tea and sat with her for a while. We watched *Pointless*. I helped her get ready for bed when it finished. She liked to sit up in bed and do a wordsearch until she nodded off. I made sure all the windows and doors were closed and locked, then saw myself out. The next morning, I went round. She wasn't in bed, the duvet had been thrown back, you know, as if you've just got out to pop to the toilet, and the back door was wide open.'

'And it was definitely locked when you left?' Tom asked.

'Definitely.'

'Who had a key?'

'Me and Sylvia. My Phil's got one, too.'

'Was there a key in Audrey's house?'

'Yes. It was on a hook next to the door.'

'Was the key still there?'

'Yes.'

'What did you think happened?'

'I thought she'd woken up, confused, and wandered off. You read about it all the time, don't you?' Jenny's voice broke and the tears started to flow. 'She was on a waiting list to go into a nursing home, but the pandemic was slowing everything down. She wasn't a priority either because she had me and Sylvia looking after her. I just... I think of her on her own, not knowing where she was or how to get back home, just lying down and dying. It shouldn't end like that, should it?'

Scott swallowed his emotion. He shook his head. 'No. It shouldn't.'

In Interview Room 2, Finn and Zofia were interviewing Sylvia Culverhouse. She was somewhere in her fifties with a shock of dyed blonde hair. She wore no make-up and her clothes looked as if they'd been thrown on in a hurry. Her zipped-up hoodie was creased and there was a food stain of some kind on her right thigh. Her eyes were puffy from crying. She repeated Jenny's story of looking after Audrey following her fall and increasing their care for her following the diagnosis of dementia. Zofia brought up Alex first.

'Yes, she did mention someone called Alex,' Sylvia said, suddenly becoming animated. 'Now, we don't know an Alex and when I mentioned the name to Jenny, she said she didn't know anyone by that name either. The thing is, I took Alex to be a woman, but Jenny said she immediately thought it was a man. Funny, isn't it, how certain names conjure up certain images? That's why, the next time I went to see Audrey, I sat down and asked her to describe Alex.'

'And did she?'

'Yes. She told me who he was.'

'Who was he?'

'She said he worked in the Spar in Greenhill and his father was manager there.'

'Did you ask in the Spar?' Finn asked.

'Well, I didn't, because they'd not long since had a new manager. The old one left, and he had a son. This new one's a woman, only a young lass, too young to have kids the age this Alex was supposed to be, at any rate. I assumed Audrey was confused and mixing up the managers. I should have looked into it more, shouldn't I?'

'Did Audrey say if this Alex was young?' Finn asked.

'She called him a lovely young man. But, well, she was eighty-six. Someone in their forties is going to be a young man to her, isn't he?'

'Did she say anything that could contribute to a description?

Hair colour? Eye colour? Accent? Did he remind her of anyone?'

'No. All she ever said was that he was a lovely young man with a lovely smile who was very helpful.' Sylvia looked from Finn to Zofia and back again. 'You think he killed her, don't you? You think he lured her out of the house somehow and killed her.'

'Right now, Sylvia, we don't know,' Finn said.

---

'That's exactly what I think happened,' Matilda said. She was sitting back in the chair at Sian's desk with her arms folded. 'I think he's been watching the house, working out who visits her at what times, and he's made sure he's avoided detection.'

'It certainly seems so. The question is, how the hell do we prove it?' Christian asked.

'We asked ourselves that with Liam and Josie, too.'

'And we still haven't answered it.'

'We need to work out what the connection is between all three victims. There has to be one. He's finding them somehow. I can understand someone young chancing upon Liam and Josie, but how the hell has he been able to find Audrey Wildgoose without anyone else knowing? I'll get Zofia to try and work her magic.'

'Is it true she's going part-time?' Christian asked.

'Yes, in the summer.'

'What are we going to do? Her job is full-time.'

'The chief constable has pointed out that she may have to be transferred back to CID. She said she's fine with that.'

'I wouldn't be.'

'Neither would I. But she's happy with Tom. That's the main thing.' Matilda leaned forward and took her mobile out of her back pocket. 'Oh my God!' she exclaimed.

'What is it?'

'I've had another email.'

'Already? Jesus, he's escalating.' He went round to her side and looked at the screen over her shoulder. 'There's an attachment,' he said, pointing to the paperclip icon.

'Pass me a laptop.'

Christian went into his office, grabbed his laptop and handed it to Matilda. She logged into her emails.

Matilda opened the email. There was no message, no signature, nothing in the subject box. There were five photographs as an attachment. 'Should I open them?'

'I think you should.'

They exchanged worried glances. Matilda opened the first attachment. Her mouth fell open.

'What the fuck?'

'Open the others.'

She did. 'Oh my God!' she cried.

## Chapter Thirty-Nine

Sian was a tough woman. She had been in the job for almost thirty years. There wasn't anything that could shock her anymore. She'd seen it all. She'd also been shot, had her throat cut, been hit on the head and run over, and discovered her husband was a serial killer. Surely there was nothing that would make her faint. She was wrong. As soon as she entered the autopsy suite and saw Audrey Wildgoose on the slab, her legs gave way and she collapsed to the floor.

Odell and Donal had run to her rescue, helped her up, and walked her to Odell's small office. Radiologist Claire Alexander sat with her and kept bringing her mugs of hot, sweet tea until the post-mortem was finished.

'I can't remember the last time I fainted at an autopsy,' Sian said. 'I remember fainting at my first one and then next time was because I was pregnant with Belinda, though I didn't know it at the time.'

'The first time I saw one, I actually vomited,' Claire said. She was a small woman with dark shoulder-length hair, and always seemed to be wearing scrubs that were a size too big for her. She wore a cheerful expression permanently on her face, despite the dark job she did, and was always great company. 'And it wasn't just a bit of vomit, either, it was projectile. I got it all over three other people.'

'I don't know how people like Odell do this kind of job. I mean, what makes them think they'd like to spend their careers cutting up dead people?'

'I don't think they think of it like it. It's more the search for answers. It's like you with joining the police. You joined because you want to see justice done. You want to find out why people commit the crimes they do. You've had to get inside the heads of some pretty scary people over the years, I imagine.'

'You can say that again. Maybe, deep down, we're all a bit ghoulish.'

'I remember when I was in my twenties going out with a guy who was a gynaecologist. I could never relax during sex. I always wondered what he was actually doing down there. Was it foreplay or an examination? We weren't together long. How are you feeling now?'

'Fine, thanks. Though if I have any more of your sweet tea, I'm worried I might slip into a diabetic coma.'

'I've got a bottle of vodka in my bottom drawer if you fancy a sip.'

'Better not.'

The door opened and Odell Zimmerman stepped in, having changed out of scrubs and into black trousers and a tight-fitting white shirt, open at the collar. 'Three times I've washed my hands, and I can still smell that sodding peach handwash. It's giving me a headache.'

'Better than the smell of decomposing organs, I'm guessing,' Sian said.

'I'm not so sure about that. If you catch it at the right time, the smell of a rotting pancreas can be quite pleasing to the nostrils,' he said with a cheeky grin.

'You're a ghoul, do you know that?' she said, pulling a face.

'It has been commented on a few times over the years, yes. You need a strong constitution and a strong character to be able to cut open a body, and a dark sense of humour helps you get through the day. There are some things even a pathologist shouldn't have to do, though, and that includes performing a PM on a child and a dear little old lady.' His smile dropped.

Sian nodded. 'I can understand that. I remember Adele crying her eyes out when she had to autopsy a two-year-old girl, especially when she discovered she'd been sexually abused.'

'It's a grim job.'

'Why do you do it?'

'Because every single day is different. I can't do normality or routine. So –' he clapped his hands together '– would you like me to tell you how Audrey Wildgoose died?'

'Please.'

'I'll leave you to it,' Claire said, standing up. 'Lovely to see you again, Sian. Say hello to Matilda for me.'

'Will do.'

'How are you feeling?' Odell asked Sian as he took the seat Claire had vacated.

'I'm fine. I don't know what came over me.'

'Probably seeing a woman whose face had slid off her head.'

'Probably.'

'It's called degloving. It's when…'

'I'm aware,' Sian interrupted.

'Right. You don't want all the technical lingo, do you?'

'Not unless you want me to vomit all over your nice clean shirt.'

'I'd rather you didn't. This is my spare. I'm thinking of asking for a clothing allowance. Now,' he said, as he sat back and folded his arms across his chest. 'I found no evidence of foul play with Mrs Wildgoose. As I noticed at the scene, there was evidence of red patches on her knees and elbows. What we call hide-and-die syndrome. A clear sign of hypothermia. Internally, she couldn't tell us much at all. She had a very good heart and lungs. Her organs were in excellent working order for a woman of her years. I'm afraid I couldn't do a stomach content analysis as...' He paused and looked at Sian. 'You may want to swallow hard for this next bit. It seems wildlife had eaten through her stomach and devoured what was inside.'

Sian closed her eyes and shook her head. The horror of what her body had gone through after death was too shocking to think about.

'Was there any evidence she was tied up or anything?'

'No ligature marks on the wrists or ankles. No bruising from fingermarks.'

'Would she have suffered?'

'I don't think so. Her death wouldn't have been quick, but I don't think she would have known what was happening. Given her advanced Alzheimer's, let's hope she simply lay down and closed her eyes. Everything that happened to her body came after she died. It's the decomposition of the body, the smells it gives off, that attracts the insects and the wildlife to come to the party.'

'So, if you were doing this post mortem having no prior knowledge of Audrey Wildgoose, you'd assume she'd wandered off and died of natural causes?' Sian asked.

'I can only record what the evidence tells me. Everything points to her dying from hypothermia. A natural death.'

'Despite her being lured there,' Sian added.

'How's the investigation going?' Odell asked. He took out a Granny Smith apple from his top drawer, rubbed it on his shirt and took a large bite.

'Slowly.'

'How's Matilda?'

'Difficult to tell at the moment.'

'What do you mean?' he asked, looking concerned.

'When we're dealing with a complex investigation, and they don't come more complex than this one, Matilda occasionally retreats into herself. She becomes an island and tries to do everything on her own. It doesn't help that she's suddenly found herself on her own again. Scott has moved out. Adele's gone. When she leaves work and goes home, there's nothing for her to do other than sit and wallow. Matilda with nothing to do makes for an unhappy Matilda.'

'I was thinking of going over this evening. Do you think I should?'

'Most definitely,' Sian said. 'I saw her the day after you went to the Showroom to see those weird films. She had… I don't know … there was a brightness about her. She obviously likes you. Will you do me a favour?'

'Go on.'

'Make her smile. She hasn't had much to smile about lately. She needs someone good in her life, someone away from the police station.'

'I haven't known Matilda long, obviously. This is the first major investigation I've seen her involved in. Is she always like this on a case?'

'Only when they get personal.'

'I like her, Sian. I really do.'

'Then tell her. She needs something good to cling on to right now. Normally, it's a big box of Maltesers.'

'They're not as big as they used to be.'

'Tell me about it. I can eat one box in a single sitting.' Sian stood up. 'I should be getting back. Look, Odell, if you really like Matilda, make your feelings known. She's in a place right now where she could do with some comfort.'

He nodded. Sian left the office, closing the door behind her.

Odell made a mental note to check his fridge when he got home, see what wine he had left. Matilda was obviously in need of being pampered and wanted. He'd like to be wanted. He'd like Matilda to want him, to turn to him when she needed someone. He could definitely be that person. He was that person.

## Chapter Forty

When Sian's husband Stuart was unmasked as a serial killer of street workers, she decided her role within South Yorkshire Police was untenable and resigned. She was eventually talked into returning but in the interim she set up a dog-walking business called Donnie Barko (her kids chose the name). When she went back to being a detective, her eldest son, Anthony, picked up the lead as something to do when he finished university and while he looked for a job in an unstable post-Covid world. He'd kept the business going and even added to the number of clients. He could often be found in one of the many parks in Sheffield with a number of dogs scurrying around his ankles.

In a layby on Abbey Lane, which cut through Ecclesall Woods, the black Donnie Barko van with the yellow cartoon dog on the side was parked up and the sound of distant barking could be heard from deep within the thicket of trees.

Danny Hanson was driving along Abbey Lane, head full of ideas, when he recognised the van recently pimped by Anthony, slammed on the brakes, reversed, and parked just behind it. He climbed out and buttoned up his coat. He looked down at his feet. Chelsea boots and a muddy woodland floor didn't go together, but he headed for the sound of barking and could eventually see Anthony, and one of his brothers, in a gap between the trees.

'Anthony!' Danny called out.

Anthony turned at the sound of his name being shouted. The look on his face was one of ruddy happiness as he played with the dogs and enjoyed the outdoors. As soon as he saw the journalist, his face changed.

'What the f…?'

'Wait!' Danny held out his hands in surrender. 'I know you're angry. I can see that. Let me explain.'

A couple of the dogs came running up to Danny. Not a fan of animals, he looked concerned and tried to back away. A Labrador jumped up at him, leaving muddy paw-prints on his black jeans and designer jacket.

'Oh, for God's sake!' he exclaimed.

'You want to watch Edwin, there. He takes a liking to someone, and he'll be humping your leg until Christmas.'

'Will you call him off?' Danny asked as he was pinned to a tree by the slobbering Labrador.

'I could, but this is fun, and, as you know, I haven't had much to smile about lately.'

The Labrador started to lick Danny's face.

'Oh shit, no,' Danny cried.

'You're either wearing Calvin Klein Eau de Wet Dog or you've recently eaten meat and he can smell it on you.'

'I've just been to McDonald's.'

'That'll be it, then. He loves a Big Mac does Edwin.'

'Look, Anthony, please, call him off,' Danny begged.

Anthony whistled. The dog turned, saw Anthony had taken a snack out of his pocket, and raced over to snatch it from him.

Danny looked down at himself. He was filthy and there was a tear in one of his jacket pockets where Edwin's paw had grabbed the flap.

'Oh no, he's torn your lovely jacket,' Anthony mocked. He

took out another treat and tossed it to Edwin. 'What are you doing here, Hanson? Or are you taking up dog-walking, too?'

'No. Look, I was going to call round tonight to see your mum, but I saw your van, so I thought I'd stop by. I… I've decided I'm not going to write that book about your dad.'

'Don't tell me you've suddenly developed a conscience.'

'I took a step back and had a think,' he said. 'I was turning into the type of journalist I always said I'd never become. I never set out to ruin people's lives. I've seen it done by other writers and promised myself I'd never become that guy. It turns out it's a fine line between being a serious reporter and being a hack. I'm sorry,' he said, looking from Anthony to his younger brother, Daniel. 'To you both. To your mum, to Belinda and … sorry, I can't remember your other brother's name.'

'Gregory,' Daniel answered, nonplussed.

'Yes. I'm sorry. I really am.'

Anthony glared at him. He handed his brother a few leads he was holding and walked slowly to Danny, who backed away slightly, fearing a thump in the mouth.

'To be honest, Danny, I don't give a fuck what you write. But you've upset my mum, my sister, and my brothers.'

'I know. I'm sorry. I never meant to. I have a great deal of respect for your mum, and I will be apologising to her, too. Look, can we make amends?' he asked, holding out his hand for Anthony to shake.

Anthony looked down at the proffered hand. He seemed to be mulling over whether to shake or to simply walk away. Eventually, and reluctantly, he shook his hand.

'Thank you, Anthony. That means a lot.'

'You owe our Daniel an apology, too,' Anthony said.

'Of course.' The journalist turned and held out his hand. 'I really am sorry for upsetting you too, Daniel, and your family.'

Daniel didn't move.

'Shake his hand, Dan, then he can leave us alone.'

Daniel stepped forward, gave the reporter's hand a limp, quick shake, then walked away.

'Thank you,' Danny Hanson said.

'I'm going to round up the others,' Daniel said before heading off into the woods, taking the dogs with him.

'He's struggling with all the attention,' Anthony said. 'I've grown out of all that social media shite, but Daniel takes it all to heart. His friends are reading that book by Sebastian Lister and talking about it online. It's not much fun having your family life torn apart and analysed like that. Nobody wants their life turning into a hashtag.'

'I can imagine.'

'No. You can't.'

'No. I don't suppose I can. I suppose you feel a lot of responsibility, too, trying to protect your family.'

'Somebody's got to.'

'It can't be easy.'

Anthony didn't reply. He put a lead on a stray dog and set off after his brother.

'How are things going for you, anyway?' Danny asked, running after him to catch him up. 'You've finished university now, I'm guessing.'

'Yes.'

'How's the job market for—'

Anthony stopped and turned around. 'What are you doing?' he interrupted.

'Sorry?'

'Why all the questions?'

'I'm ... I'm trying to be pleasant.'

'Well, don't. It's creepy. And it doesn't suit you. Look, I've shaken your hand – now leave us alone.' He headed off, taking large strides, to reach his brother.

Danny remained still and watched them until they disappeared into the thicket of trees. He wasn't sure if he'd won them over or they'd seen through his lies. He'd try again another time and he'd make a heartfelt apology to Sian at some point, too. He'd been practising in the mirror all morning to appear sincere. The truth was, he needed the family on his side so he could find out how they were really coping with the aftermath of Stuart's crimes. That's what his readers would want to know. That's what his editor at HarperCollins said should be at the heart of his book. So much so, they were willing to gamble a high six-figure sum on the depth of his research.

'Fuck,' he said to himself as he turned and headed back to his car. This was going to be harder than he first thought.

## Chapter Forty-One

There were five photographs sent to Matilda by email. She'd printed them all off and laid them on the table at the top of the HMCU suite. The whole team were gathered around looking at them. None of them knew what to say.

The photographs showed Matilda, Scott, Finn, and Tom as they searched various areas of Graves Park last night looking for Audrey Wildgoose. The last photo showed Scott leading Matilda back to the car to take her home once the elderly woman had been found. The expression on both their faces was one of pure horror.

'Did anyone have a feeling they were being watched?' Scott asked.

'No,' Finn said.

'We were too busy trying to work out where she might be. It never entered my head to think someone might be watching,' Tom added.

'I remember seeing a crowd of people gathered when we were going back to the car,' Scott said. 'There were plenty of marked police cars around then with flashing lights, so it drew out the nosy neighbours. I don't remember seeing anyone with a camera.'

'I saw a couple of people with their phones held up,' Finn said.

'Can you remember what they looked like?' Christian asked.

'No. I mean, everyone has their phone held up nowadays when something's going on. People film things all the time. I didn't take any notice.'

'How bloody far away was he?' Matilda asked. She was studying the photographs in turn, picking them up and analysing every detail. 'Zofia.' Matilda turned around to look at Zofia, who was sat at her desk. 'Isn't there something imbedded in photographs so that you can tell where they were taken?'

'Yes, there is. Not in this case, unfortunately.'

'Why not?'

'My best guess is that he took the photos either using his phone or a normal camera and, rather than send the originals, took screenshots and sent them. There's no information attached to these photos at all.'

'Sneaky bastard,' Christian said.

'He's really covering all his bases, isn't he?' Finn asked.

'Is there any CCTV around Graves Park?' Christian asked.

'No,' Zofia answered. 'I've checked. If we'd been at the other entrance close to Meadowhead and the big Morrisons, maybe, but not around the animal farm.'

'We're no closer, are we?' Matilda asked, agitated. 'We've got three victims. We've got a killer stalking the team, watching our every move, bloody photographing us, yet we know nothing about him. Not one single person has seen him. How is that possible?'

Tom's phone began to ring. He went over to his desk to answer it.

'I know it's frustrating, but this guy is clearly an attention seeker,' Finn said. 'The worst thing we can do is give in to him and let him think he's getting to us.'

'But he is getting to us,' Matilda said, almost snapping.

'I know. But we can't let him see that. He's obviously keeping tabs on us, so we have to show that we're getting on with our usual work and not letting him and his cruel game get the better of us.'

'He's right,' Christian agreed.

'Matilda, that was the front desk. Helen Walsh is here. She's asking for you,' Tom said.

'Shit. That's all I need. Give me a few minutes.' She turned back to Finn. 'I see your point, Finn, but how do we show him we're not allowing him to dictate our agenda?'

'By getting on with the rest of our work. The vigil for Natasha Klein is tonight. There's going to be a great deal of coverage from the press and on social media. If we all go along, we'll be showing him that he's not hampering us, which is what he's trying to do.'

Matilda thought for a long moment. 'You're right. Okay. Everyone, put your thermals on, we're having a night out.'

---

Matilda went down the corridor to reception and found Helen Walsh sitting on the edge of one of the hard plastic chairs. Her left leg was jiggling, and she was chewing on her thumbnail. As soon as she saw Matilda, she jumped up out of her seat.

'Have you any news? You said you'd be in touch. You said you'd let me know what was going on and you haven't. I haven't heard a thing from you. You promised me,' she said, her words falling over each other.

Helen was without make-up, her hair pulled back into a loose ponytail with strands falling around her face. She looked tired, drained, and clearly wasn't looking after herself.

Matilda opened her mouth to speak but saw she was being watched by two uniformed officers at the front desk.

'Come with me,' she said, holding Helen by the elbow and leading her through to the corridor. She managed to find a spare room, pushed the door open, and let Helen go in first.

'You promised me you'd keep in touch,' Helen said on the verge of tears.

'I know I did and I'm sorry. I truly am. Have a seat,' Matilda said.

Reluctantly, Helen pulled out a chair and sat down. She sniffed hard.

'I was slowly coming to terms with Liam having killed himself. It's not easy. He was my only child. I… I only ever wanted one. I knew… I…' She was struggling to speak through the emotion. 'Then you turned up,' she said, looking up at Matilda with tears in her eyes. 'You just waltzed in and said Liam had been murdered. I don't know how but it somehow made it better knowing that he hadn't taken his own life. But you said you'd keep me informed. You said you'd let me know what was happening and you haven't. Do you have any idea what I'm going through?' Helen practically collapsed. She sank forward, her head in her lap.

Matilda went over to her and placed an arm around her shoulder.

'Helen, I'm so sorry I haven't been in touch. This investigation … it's…' She struggled to find the words. 'It's not simple. We're uncovering more victims, but we don't know who's behind it.'

'More victims?' Helen asked, looking up. 'You mean, like a serial killer? My boy was killed by a serial killer?'

'I can't go into the mechanics of it at the moment, Helen. I wish I could tell you more, I really do, but the truth is, I don't know what's going on.'

'But … you're supposed to be in charge of this prestigious unit. I've read about you online. You're one of the best detectives in the force. How can you not know what's going on?' Her face was reddening with anger.

'Don't believe everything you read on the news, Helen. It's all puffed up to make it sound more exciting than it is.'

'Exciting?' Helen asked, pulling a disgusted face.

'Sorry. Wrong word. But you know what the press is like. They blow things up out of proportion. Look, Helen.' Matilda dragged a chair towards her and sat down. 'I'm really sorry I can't give you the answer you're looking for. I have no evidence that Liam was murdered, but I truly believe someone was behind his death. I just need time to find him.'

'Is it linked to this Natasha Klein who's gone missing? She's roughly the same age as Liam. Is it connected?'

'No, Helen, it's not.'

'This is killing me. You don't know what it's like. I can't... I can't grieve for him until I know if he was murdered or took his own life. I know it sounds strange, but ... it's different. It feels... I'm in agony here, Matilda. I need you to find the truth about what happened.'

Matilda could feel the rage, the grief, the frustration, emanating from her. She was torturing herself and unable to move on with her life while there was still a massive question mark hanging over the last few days of her son's life. Nothing would bring him back, but knowing the truth would help her deal with his loss all the more.

There was nothing Matilda could say to help Helen. She had promised her she would find the killer, something she shouldn't have done. Any other promises would sound empty, but she had to tell her something.

'Helen, look at me. Does the name Alex mean anything to you?' She was thinking of the young man who had helped Audrey Wildgoose with her shopping.

Helen thought for a moment before shaking her head. 'No.'

'Liam never mentioned a friend or an acquaintance called Alex?'

'No.'

'When he used to go for a night out, did he ever tell you who he was meeting?'

'No. More often than not he went on his own. He never said

where he was going because he didn't know himself. He just liked to go out walking. He said it helped to clear his head.'

Matilda nodded. It wasn't what she wanted to hear, but it seemed to be the norm for this investigation. Every question she hoped would lead the team down a particular path always ended up at a brick wall.

'I know my promises aren't going to mean anything to you, Helen, but I'll keep in touch. Even if I don't have anything new to tell you, I'll call you on a regular basis. I am doing everything I can to find out what happened to Liam.'

They made eye contact. Helen's eyes darted left and right as she looked deep inside Matilda. She must have spotted something as her face softened. She believed Matilda's words.

'I'm sorry,' she said, quietly.

'You've nothing to apologise for.'

'He was my whole world. I'm lost without him.'

'I know. I'll get someone to run you home.'

'It's okay. I've got my car outside.'

'Are you all right to drive?'

Helen stood up. She wiped her eyes. 'I'm fine.' She smiled through the pain. 'I have to be, don't I?'

## Chapter Forty-Two

Natasha Klein had been missing for exactly twenty-nine days and her whereabouts were still unknown. Since she left the Olive Grove campus on that fateful Thursday afternoon, there hadn't been a single sighting of her. Despite Derek's arrest for her murder, there was still hope among her peer group that she was alive and well somewhere. Maybe she wasn't coping with college life as well as she projected and had decided to spend some time away. Maybe she'll turn up in another couple of weeks and create a series of vlogs about her disappearance. But there were others at the college who suspected something darker had happened to Natasha; that, when she was eventually found, she wouldn't be found alive; that her stepfather had murdered her. Either way, it was hoped that a candlelit vigil, streamed on as many social media platforms as possible, would help find her whereabouts and bring the whole drama to a conclusion – for her mother's sake, at least.

Throughout the day, people had been gathering at the Peace Gardens in Sheffield city centre. Ruby Deighton took charge. Hastily prepared banners had been hung from trees and an art student from the nearby university had drawn an uncanny likeness of Natasha on the ground, more than six feet long. The hope was that it wouldn't rain this evening and tea-light candles would be placed around the drawing.

By early evening, darkness had fallen, and the park was already packed with students, friends, family members, well-wishers, and anyone who had seen the vigil mentioned across social media or on local radio. Reporters from the *Star*, BBC Radio Sheffield, *Look North,* and *Calendar* were there to cover the event. Uniformed officers stood on the perimeter to make sure there was no trouble among the crowds.

A platform had been erected at the water feature with a microphone so that people could speak, plead for Natasha to come home, and ask anyone who saw her that Thursday or had seen her since to come forward with information.

There was nowhere for Matilda to park close by, so she parked around the back of the City Hall. She had picked Sian up on the way and they bumped into Christian, who had pulled up behind them. They made their way to the park on foot. It was a chilly evening, and the temperature was falling by the hour. They hadn't expected such a mass turnout.

'Wow,' Sian marvelled.

'The hashtag Find Natasha is trending on Twitter,' Christian said as he zipped up his coat and pulled a beanie hat out of his pocket. 'Apparently, Jessica Ennis-Hill is coming down and someone from One Direction has retweeted.'

'I had no idea it was going to be so crowded,' Matilda said.

Since her kidnapping, it wasn't only confined spaces she was afraid of, but huge swarms of people, too. She found it overwhelming to be surrounded by people, all of them talking at the same time. It was a cacophony as each voice screamed for her attention, and she couldn't focus. She could feel the prickle of a panic attack crawl up her back. She was getting hot. She took a deep breath and tried to remember the breathing exercises Doctor Who had given her.

'Are you all right?' Sian asked.

'Yes. Fine,' she lied. 'I think I made a mistake wearing these thermals. They're warmer than I thought.'

Sian linked her arm through Matilda's. 'Just squeeze my hand. You'll be fine,' she whispered.

'Thank you,' Matilda mouthed.

They had no intention of joining the throng. It was all about keeping their eyes open and fixed firmly on the crowd.

'This is bonkers,' Scott said as he, Donal and Finn approached them. 'I didn't think there would be this kind of turnout.'

'I was just thinking,' Finn began, 'how many people here actually know Natasha, and how many are jumping on the bandwagon so they can give themselves a pat on the back for doing a good deed?'

'Bloody hell, Finn, that's a bit cynical,' Christian said.

'It's true, though. People don't do things out of the goodness of their heart. It's all about making themselves feel better. If Natasha is found safe and well, they'll sit there feeling all smug, saying they helped find her.'

'I'm beginning to think that psychology degree wasn't such a good idea. It's turned you against the human race,' Christian said.

'You don't need a degree to do that to you,' Matilda commented. 'Just join the police force. Look, I suggest we split up, but stay on the edge of the crowd.'

'What are we actually looking for?' Scott asked.

Matilda thought for a moment. 'You'll know when you see it.'

'Is that your clever way of saying you've no idea what we're looking for?' he asked.

'Got it in one.'

---

'My name is Ruby Deighton. I've known Natasha since we were both nine years old.' Ruby was standing on the platform with two other women, one either side of her, all wrapped up against the elements, all with serious expressions on their faces. 'We've grown up together. We've laughed together. We've cried together. She's always been there when I've needed someone to talk to, when things haven't gone how I've hoped they would. Natasha is a strong person. She's a good person. She's always been independent and known what to do during the dark times. I'm here tonight to ask each and every one of you to think back to Thursday the eleventh of March. Natasha was last seen at half-past three leaving the Olive Grove campus. Where did she go? What happened to her? Somebody must have seen something. We need your help. Natasha needs your help. It's heartening to see so many police officers attending this rally. Please, if you have any information, speak to one of them, speak to us, speak to me. We need Natasha to come home.'

'She's got all the makings of a future politician with a speech like that,' Matilda said to Sian.

'She spoke very well, though. Clear and concise. Passionate and from the heart.'

'Do we know who she is?'

Sian nodded. 'That's Ruby Deighton, who was having an affair with Natasha's father.'

Matilda pulled a sour face. 'I wonder what she saw in him.'

'Maybe she has father issues.'

'Would you ever go out with someone a lot younger than you?' Matilda asked.

'Shall I let you in on a secret?'

'Oh God, do I really want to hear this?'

'Felix Lerego asked me for a drink earlier this year.'

'What? He's a child.'

'He's in his thirties.'

'Early thirties. That's about twenty years' age difference.'

'Fifteen, actually, you cheeky cow,' Sian said, nudging Matilda in the ribs.

'What did you say?'

'I said no, obviously.'

'Why? He's not bad looking.'

'After Stuart went to prison and the divorce came through, I went through this patch of thinking, *That's it, I'm not going to have another man in my life.* I mean, who's going to want to go out with the ex-wife of a serial killer? I did actually get quite down about it. Anyway, when Felix asked me out, it put a smile on my face, gave me a bit of a boost of confidence.'

'Yet you still said no.'

'I don't need a man in my life. That's what I realised. I don't give a toss if I never go out with a man again. Who needs men? All they do is fart in bed, leave towels on the bathroom floor, and forget your birthday. No, this time is my time.'

Matilda linked arms with Sian and squeezed her hard. 'Good for you.'

---

Ruby looked down from the small stage at a friend who had been filming her throughout her speech.

'Did you get all that?' she asked her.

Her friend nodded. 'I've uploaded it to TikTok. That should get your followers soaring.'

'I've gained so many new followers on Instagram since I posted that I'm Natasha's cousin,' Charlotte said, who was on the stage next to Ruby. 'I've now got more followers than Nat. She'll hate that,' she said with a slight smile. 'Shall we take a selfie?'

'Better not,' Ruby said. 'That fit bloke over there with the camera pointing at us is from *Look North*.'

---

Matilda looked around the crowd. So many had their phones held aloft. The majority were focused on Ruby on the stage, but plenty were scanning the crowd, recording the sheer mass of people who had gathered.

'Are we filming this, too?' Matilda asked.

'Yes. Uniformed officers have got their bodycams on as well,' Sian said.

'What about Natasha's mother? Is she here?'

'Tom called her earlier. She's not coping too well, by all accounts. It's understandable if she's decided to stay away.'

'Matilda, I didn't expect to see you here.'

Matilda turned at the sound of her name. She knew the voice instantly. Danny Hanson came towards her through the crowd, looking smug. He wore a thick winter coat, gloves and scarf, and a beanie hat pulled low, resting on his eyebrows.

'Why wouldn't I be?'

'It seems to be Christian who's been leading this investigation.'

'I am aware of every single major investigation taking place in South Yorkshire Police's jurisdiction, Danny. I…' She stopped herself. *Why am I justifying myself to this prick?*

'Sian, I was hoping to see you,' Danny said. 'I was going to call round tomorrow—'

'Come anywhere near my front door and I'll slap an injunction on you,' Sian interrupted.

'No. It's nothing like that. I wanted to apologise. I saw your Anthony and Daniel this afternoon.'

'I know. They said,' she said, icily.

'Look, Sian, I'm sorry. There's nothing else I can say. I lost my head for a moment. I really am sorry. I think…' He looked down. 'I think I was a little jealous of Sebastian Lister beating me to writing the book. I shouldn't have reacted the way I did and I'm sorry. I hope you can forgive me.'

Sian looked at Matilda with a cynical frown. Matilda shrugged.

'You're forgiven,' Sian said, though they seemed a painful two words to utter.

'Friends?' he asked, holding out his hand for her to shake.

'I wouldn't go that far.'

'Quit while you're ahead, Danny,' Matilda said.

He nodded and gave one of his famous sickly smiles he usually reserved for his social media posts.

'Well, I'll leave you to it. I hope this works in helping you find Natasha,' he said, walking away.

'Parasite,' Sian said.

'He saved your life earlier this year.'

'Yes. And he's not letting me forget it.'

'Playing devil's avocado for a moment,' Matilda said, linking her arm through Sian's and giving her a playful squeeze. 'Would it be so bad to sit down with Danny and put your side of the story to him?'

'What? Are you serious?' she asked, incredulously.

'I'm almost halfway through Sebastian's book, Sian. You're really not coming across well in it at all. You're a detective sergeant on a prestigious team in the police force, yet Sebastian is painting you as a dowdy housewife who has no idea what's going on in the real world.'

'Is he?'

'In nearly every mention you're at home making the tea while Stuart's out killing. You're oblivious to what's going on around you.'

'I *was* oblivious!' she protested.

'Yes, to Stuart's crimes. Sebastian's making out you can't see past your own front door. I'm not asking you to sit down with Piers Morgan and give an in-depth interview, nor do I expect you to write your own kiss-and-tell book, but maybe think about setting the record straight. Do you really want people thinking badly of you unnecessarily?'

'Why should I care what other people think?'

'Because you're in a job where you meet other people on a daily basis.'

After a long pause, Sian said. 'I'll think about it.'

Matilda squeezed her tighter.

'I only said I'll think about it. But I'm not talking to Danny Hanson. I'm not talking to Sebastian Lister, and I'm certainly not talking to Piers Morgan.'

'You're holding out for a *Panorama* special, aren't you?' Matilda joked.

'I was going to see if *Hello!* would like to photograph me draped over my new sofa in my gracious drawing room,' she said, an attempt at levity.

---

'My name is Charlotte Tate,' the next young woman on the podium said. She was tall and very slim with long brown hair tied back into a ponytail. She wore a thin, flowing black coat and knee-high black boots. 'I'm Natasha's cousin.'

'Do we know about her?' Matilda asked Sian.

'Yes. She gave a statement over the phone. She lives in Birmingham. According to her Facebook post, she's come up especially for the vigil.'

'Another one of Finn's publicity seekers, do we think?' Matilda smirked.

Charlotte continued. 'There are photographs of Natasha all around you. You know what she looks like. We've all been posting pictures of Natasha all over social media. She's young. She's pretty. She has no shortage of admirers in reality and online. Yet she's putting herself and her career first. However, there are some men out there who won't take no for an answer. What kind of a world are we living in where an attractive woman can't walk the streets on her own in the middle of the day without being accosted by men? The man who did this to Natasha was known to her and is awaiting trial, and I hope he gets life. But locking away one man won't stop others from targeting women based on how they look.'

'Oh dear,' Sian said. 'Why do I get the feeling she's going to stir up trouble?'

'When will men realise that we're not living in the nineteenth century anymore, that women are not the inferior species they think we are? You can't claim us for yourselves. Until men get this into their heads, there should be a curfew…'

The crowd erupted. There were a few cheers, but most were taunts.

'Bloody hell,' Matilda said.

A young man jumped up onto the platform, knocking Charlotte out of the way. He held his phone aloft.

'Have you seen the stuff Natasha posted on TikTok?' he shouted into the microphone. 'Every video, she's got her tits on show. She's pouting. She's asking for it.'

'Oh my God,' Sian said.

Uniformed officers rushed to the stage to grab the young man, who was clearly under the influence of alcohol.

Charlotte was still shouting, despite not having the microphone, desperate for her voice to be heard.

'This is exactly what I'm talking about,' she screamed. 'Natasha is a beautiful young woman. Why shouldn't she post photos and videos without men thinking it's an invitation for her to be kidnapped or attacked?'

All hell broke loose. Women were cheering on Charlotte's side. Men were heckling. Several were scrambling to get to the front, to grab the microphone, to have their say.

Matilda watched as people were shoved to the ground in the scuffle. She turned and saw Christian on the phone. Scott and Donal were among the crowd, trying to break up the fighting before a full-scale riot developed. It was a wall of noise that Matilda struggled to cope with. She took a step backwards and she was knocked out of the way by people rushing towards the front. She lost Sian. She turned quickly, trying to find a way out of the throng of people rushing forwards. She felt her head grow heavy and quickly closed her eyes, trying to block out the sounds. It wasn't working. Where was David Tennant's sodding train now?

'Sian!' she called out, but her voice was barely a whisper among the shouts and screams of the crowd.

Matilda felt people knocking her in all directions as she scrambled to be free, to get some air into her lungs. She was panicking. She couldn't breathe. She fell to the ground, hitting the cold pavement hard. She felt herself being lifted.

'It's all right. I've got you.'

'Christian?' she asked, still with her eyes closed.

'No. It's Jamie. Jamie Peterson.'

Matilda opened her eyes. She saw Liam Walsh's counsellor from the university in front of her. He was wearing a thick parka with a fake-fur-trimmed hood and a Sheffield United bobble hat.

'Are you all right?' he asked. He had his arms around her and was guiding her away from the crowd.

'I… I just… I lost my bearings.'

'It's all gone a bit manic, hasn't it?' He sat her down on one of the benches opposite Costa. She wished it was still open. She could do with a triple espresso right now. 'Put a group of young people together with emotions running high and look at what happens.'

Matilda turned back to see the crowd. Police were struggling to bring it under control.

'Here, let me,' Jamie said. He held a tissue to Matilda's forehead.

'Am I bleeding?'

'Just a graze.'

She took the tissue from him and looked at it. There was a small amount of blood on it, nothing to worry about. She placed it back on her head. She looked at him with a worried expression. 'What are you doing here?'

'I've come to pay my respects. No, that's the wrong thing to say, really, isn't it? I've come to show my support,' he said. 'I only met with Natasha a couple of times, but I found her to be a very intelligent and forthright young woman.'

Jamie sat down on the bench next to Matilda. She didn't say anything and allowed Jamie to fill in the silence.

'Natasha is very sociable. Her popularity on social media was growing. She was struggling under the weight of all the expectation from strangers to provide more and better content online.'

'What did you say to her?'

'I told her what I tell everyone else: leave social media. You don't owe these people anything. You don't have to continually post photographs and videos of yourself. What actually is the point in having millions of followers online? I can understand it if you're a singer or an actor, possibly even an author, but a student at college doing media studies? It's not necessary. It's empty validation. Look into yourself and see what's important.'

'Did she take your comments on board?'

'She was posting less, yes.'

'She told you she was posting less?'

'I…'

'Matilda, there you are,' Sian interrupted, a little out of breath. 'What's happened to you?'

'Oh, nothing, just a scratch.'

'I lost you. I was looking everywhere.'

'I'd better be going. I'm pleased you're all right. You'll let me know if there's anything I can do, won't you?' Jamie asked, standing up. He smiled at Matilda and nodded at Sian before turning and heading in the direction of the Moor.

'Isn't that the counsellor, what's-his-name?' Sian asked.

'Jamie Peterson. Liam Walsh's counsellor. He spoke with Natasha Klein, too.'

'What was he saying?'

'I'm not sure.' She thought for a moment. 'Sian, make a note to check where Josie Pettifer went to college and university and find out if she had any contact with Jamie Peterson.'

'Okay. Shall we go?'

'I think we should stay.'

'I'm pretty sure Christian and the uniformed officers have everything under control. What to hear something funny? I heard Donal trying to arrest someone.'

Matilda laughed. 'Really?'

'Yes. Scott shouted at him and reminded him who he was.'

'Oh dear. I'd hate to be a fly on the wall in their house tonight.'

'Come on, let's go and get a drink.'

'That's the most sensible thing you've said in weeks,' Matilda said, standing up.

'Does that bang on the head hurt?'

'No. It just stings.'

'Pity.'

---

Sian drove Matilda's car back to her house rather than Matilda's farmhouse. Despite Matilda saying she was fine, Sian said she shouldn't be alone following a bang on the head. She unlocked the front door to find every light on in every room downstairs and the volume on the television in the living room screamingly loud. Daniel and Gregory were still up and watching a horror film.

'You can turn that tripe off,' Sian said as she entered the room. 'And any chance of you turning a light off when you leave a room? This isn't Blackpool, you know.'

'What happened to you?' Gregory asked Matilda as he got up from the floor and grabbed the remote to turn down the television.

'I fell,' she said as she shook her coat off and sat on an armchair.

'I'll make us a mug of tea,' said Sian. 'Have you two eaten?'

'We had a McDonalds,' Gregory said.

Sian looked at Daniel. 'There are leftovers in the fridge. It only needed heating up.'

'We fancied a burger.'

'Full of grease and salt. What's the point of me cooking if it's going to go to waste?' Sian shook her head and went into the kitchen.

'How was the vigil?' Daniel asked Matilda, sitting on the sofa, crossing his legs.

'It started off fine and quickly descended into a mob.'

'I thought you only had a vigil if you were trying to find what happened to someone,' Gregory asked. 'Mum said Natasha's father killed her.'

'That's what the evidence is telling us.'

'I read on Facebook that you found a pool of blood in the boot of her dad's car,' Gregory said with ghoulish relish.

'It was a speck of blood, smaller than a pinhead,' Matilda corrected him.

'But if he didn't kill her, how did her blood get into his boot?'

'No idea,' Matild admitted. 'I suppose we'll have to wait for the court case to find out.'

'So, this vigil, was it to try and find out what happened to her so her dad can get life?' Gregory asked.

'It was to help find her body and bring her home so her mother can say goodbye to her properly.'

'Isn't her dad telling you?'

'No.'

Sian came back into the living room carrying two mugs of tea on a tray with the biscuit barrel.

'Mum, I had a call from Marc after you left,' Gregory said, all talk of dead bodies, blood and vigils suddenly forgotten. 'His dad has said he can get us to see Lando Norris next month. Can I go?' His face shining with wide-eyed excitement.

Sian frowned. 'Where's Lando Norris? I've never heard of it.'

Daniel stifled a laugh. Gregory blushed.

'Oh dear, Sian, even I've heard of Lando Norris,' Matilda said.

'It's a person?'

'Yes. He's a Formula One driver.'

'Oh. I thought it was a place.' She nudged Daniel to take his feet off the sofa and sat beside him.

'God, Mum, you're so old.'

'You shouldn't say that, Gregory, if you want me to let you go.'

'Can I, then?'

'Let me speak to Marc's dad about it first.'

'As long as you don't tell me you thought Lando Norris was a place. I'll never live it down.'

'I promise I won't embarrass you.'

'Thanks, Mum,' he said. 'I'm going upstairs to play F1. Night,' he said, running out of the room.

'I'm going to grab a snack,' Daniel said, getting up from the sofa and going into the kitchen.

'I feel so old,' Sian said.

'You are old.'

'I'm a year older than you.'

'Fourteen months, actually.' Matilda winked. 'Forget about it. We all make little slips from time to time. Many times I've been out with my mum and she's looked in her handbag for her mobile and pulled out the remote control for the television.'

Sian smiled. 'I've done that, too. How is Penny these days?'

'She's doing okay. I told you about that business with the pensions, didn't I?'

'Yes. Is it getting sorted?'

'It's going to drag on. At least I've got her to start spending a bit of money on herself again. And she's finally turned the heating on.'

'Bless her.'

'I've told her to turn it on and not worry about the bill. I'll pay it. You know what mothers are like. She's not really a fan of central heating anyway.'

'Has she got the fire fixed?'

'Not yet. The bloke's having to send off for a part. I've told her to just buy a new one but she's of the generation who'll try their best to get something repaired.'

'We live in the throwaway society,' Sian said.

'You sounded just like my mum then. Are you sure it's only fourteen months you're older than me by and not fourteen years?'

Daniel came back into the living room with a doorstep sandwich on his plate. 'I'm taking this upstairs to finish off the movie.'

'Don't drop any crumbs.'

'Yes, Gran,' he said, looking at Matilda and winking.

Sian turned to Matilda. 'You're all against me.'

'It's because you're such an easy target.'

'Do you want to stay the night? The spare room is made up.'

'I'd love to. I'm so comfortable here now,' she said, snuggling into the cosy armchair.

'I think we should Irish these drinks up then, don't you?' Sian stood up and went over to the sideboard. 'And perhaps you can give me the Technicolor details of what Odell's like in bed?'

Matilda smiled. A boozy night with a good friend was just what she needed right now. She suddenly felt guilty. Odell had left her a voicemail earlier asking if he could come over tonight and she hadn't replied.

Sian sat down. 'Right then. First of all, let's have some measurements…'

## Chapter Forty-Three

Sunday, 11 April 2021

Matilda returned home at ten o'clock in the morning, having consumed two extremely (non-Irish) strong coffees to help sober herself up. She drove well under the speeding limit and managed to arrive home in one piece and without scratching Adele's car. It had been a long time since she'd stayed up so late drinking. It had been an enjoyable night, though.

She spent the morning on her own. After a meagre lunch of a crisp sandwich, she sat at her dining-room table, laptop open, the three printed emails from the killer in front of her, along with the photographs of her and her team at Graves Park while they were hunting for Audrey Wildgoose.

She read through the emails again. She wished Finn was with her so they could bounce ideas off each other, though it would be unfair to drag him out on a Sunday when he had a wife and a social life to occupy him. She thought, again, of the threat of redundancy hanging over the heads of the three detective sergeants in the HMCU. She had spent a pleasant evening with

Sian, and now she felt like a Judas for not telling her what was happening. She needed Adele back.

Matilda shook her head to get rid of the excessive thoughts. She needed to concentrate on this investigation. This really was a game to the killer. He was enjoying himself, taunting Matilda by showing how clever he was. She looked at the photographs closely, studied them, something niggling away in her brain. She grabbed her mobile and called Christian.

'Not interrupting anything, am I?' she asked when she heard chatting and laughter in the background.

'Not in the slightest. The kids are teasing the dog and he's playing along with them. It's a shame neither of them is showing signs of being a child genius so I could pack them off to university ten years early.'

'If only we still had child labour; they'd be down a coal mine right now.'

'Ah, yes, the good old days,' Christian said with a snigger. 'I missed you last night. What time did you get in? Sian told me you were knocked over in the rush.'

'Just a graze. Listen, Christian, I've been looking at the photos the killer sent me of us all at Graves Park, wondering why the hell I didn't notice I was being photographed.'

'Simple, you weren't looking for anyone.'

'I know, but I've had a thought. This killer, he's clever, isn't he? He really is committing the perfect murders. Now, how do you take photos like the ones he's taking without being noticed?'

Christian thought for a moment. 'I've no idea,' he eventually said.

'You make sure you fit in.'

'You think he was disguised as a tree?' he asked, sounding flippant.

'Nothing quite so elaborate. Who was at Graves Park in an official capacity to take photographs?'

'The CSIs.'

'Precisely.'

'You think the killer is a CSI?'

'This killer knows far too much about forensics and how to avoid detection. Who better than someone qualified in that role?'

'Jesus! I hadn't thought of that.'

'Me neither. Until now.'

'I'll give Felix Lerego a call first thing—'

'No,' Matilda interrupted. 'Truth be told, Christian, we haven't actually known Felix that long. Bring him into the station tomorrow morning, ask him who was at the park when we were, and we'll look into their backgrounds. We need to keep this between ourselves until we're certain.'

'Understood.'

'Sorry to call you on a Sunday. I'll let you get back to the madhouse.'

'I think I'd rather talk about serial killers for another hour or so.'

Matilda smiled. 'See you tomorrow.'

She ended the call and returned to looking at the photographs. Thinking back, as Scott led her to the car after finding Audrey's body, she would have seen someone pointing a camera at her. Yes, she had just been viewing a rotting corpse so her mind was on other things, but even if she hadn't seen a photographer, Scott would have. But would he have taken any notice if this person was wearing a crime scene oversuit? Possibly not.

---

Matilda lost track of time. She was concentrating on the emails, analysing every word, every sentence, every comma. When the doorbell rang, she almost jumped out of her chair. She stood up and had to stop herself from swaying. She noticed the empty wine bottle on the table in front of her. She didn't even remember opening it, let alone drinking it.

She opened the front door to find Odell Zimmerman on the doorstep. He looked comfortable in black jeans and a reefer coat over a thick jumper. The smile on his face and the relaxed attitude oozing from him made Matilda want to snuggle up to him, bury her head on his chest, and fall asleep.

'Odell! What are you doing here?'

'It's Sunday. The day of rest. I thought I'd come and make sure you were resting,' he said with a wide smile.

'Ah.'

'You're working.'

'I am.'

'When my father became ill, he spent a lot of time in bed. In the weeks before he died, he was going over his life, looking back, the way you do. His last words to me were, "Odell, I should have spent more time working," then he died.'

'Really?'

'No, of course not. Mat, nobody will think badly of you if you take a few hours off. I've come here to turn your Sunday into a Funday.'

'I should slam the door in your face for a pun like that.'

'And I wouldn't blame you. Can I come in?'

'Yes.' She stepped to one side, let him enter, and closed the door behind him. When she turned, he had taken off his coat, kicked off his shoes, and was going into her living room.

'I hope you've got Netflix.'

'Erm, yes, why?'

'I thought we could watch a shit film together and snuggle up on the sofa, maybe forget it's on,' he said with a sly wink.

Matilda felt herself relax, though that may have been the effects of the bottle of wine she'd just downed.

'I like the sound of that.'

Matilda had fallen asleep on Odell within fifteen minutes of *NYC: Tornado Terror*, a made-for-TV movie from 2008. She woke as the credits started to roll.

'That was possibly one of the worst films I've ever seen,' Odell said. 'And I've seen *They Saved Hitler's Brain*.'

'That's a real film?' Matilda asked, sitting up and rubbing her eyes.

'Yes. From 1968. It averages two-point-four out of ten on IMDb.'

'You know a lot about films.'

'I'm a complete nerd when it comes to films, you should know.'

'I'm a big film fan, too.'

'Yes. I was having a look at your Blu-ray collection while you were snoring.'

'I was snoring?'

'At one point I looked out of the window to see if they'd started fracking in your driveway.'

'Oh my God!' she said, embarrassed.

'I'm joking. It wasn't that loud.'

She slapped him playfully on the arm, stood up, and stretched. 'I'm sorry I fell asleep. I'm a bad host. Can I get you a glass of wine or something?'

'I'd actually prefer a coffee, if you don't mind.'

'Sure.' As she left the living room, she looked through the linking door into the dining room where her notes were and where the empty bottle of wine was. She wondered if Odell asked for a coffee simply so she wouldn't drink any more. Was she drinking more? *Does it matter? You don't smoke or do drugs. Everyone's entitled to a vice.*

Matilda returned with a pot of coffee on a tray along with a full box of Tunnock's Tea Cakes. She placed it on the coffee table and joined Odell back on the Chesterfield sofa.

'I'm really sorry for falling asleep on you like that,' she

apologised again.

'I should make you sit through the film again as punishment, but I think it would be more punishment for me to have to watch it a second time,' he said, pouring milk into his coffee.

'I haven't been sleeping much lately. I seem to be finding it hard to switch off.'

'Work?'

'I don't know,' she said. This was her regular response to any question she didn't feel comfortable in answering. She always knew the answer but preferred to keep it to herself rather than face more questions, more intense questions.

'I think you do.'

Matilda looked at him. Although his deep-set eyes were smiling, he had a serious look on his face. He seemed genuinely concerned for Matilda.

She felt her mouth go dry. She reached for her coffee and took a sip. The caffeine seemed to hit hard. She took another drink.

'I've been struggling since Adele left,' she said, turning away from his gaze. 'I can see why she did. When you're attacked and left for dead by someone you're supposed to be able to trust, it's perfectly understandable to want to make a massive change in your life. She needed to get away from Sheffield, from … everything that had happened. A complete break. I just… I wish she…'

'You wish she'd have given you time to get used to the idea of her leaving before she actually left.'

'She did sort of spring it on me. When I came home in January and found she'd kicked Simon Browes between the legs and was sitting on him until I arrived, I couldn't have been prouder of her. Less than a week later she's packing her bags.'

'Maybe she thought you'd try and talk her out of it.'

'Maybe.'

'Matilda, there's only so much one person can take before they explode. Adele leaving like that was her way of making sure she doesn't explode. She needs time to come to terms with everything that happened.'

Matilda nodded. She wasn't so sure about that. 'I... Adele was the one I relied upon the most. I suppose, in hindsight, I shouldn't have done. I thought she would always be there whenever life became too difficult. She's been with me through my darkest days for well over twenty years. To go from that to never seeing her again is…'

'Never seeing her again? What makes you think that?'

Matilda didn't reply.

'Have you even spoken to her since she left?'

Again, Matilda didn't answer. She looked down and played with her fingers.

'You haven't, have you?'

'She's texted. She's sent emails. I…'

'You're angry.'

'I'm jealous.' She looked up at Odell with tears in her eyes.

'Jealous?'

'That she was able to break away and I haven't.'

'You could have gone with her.'

Matilda snorted. 'She's a member of Doctors Without Borders. She's currently in Sierra Leone travelling to remote villages that don't have access to healthcare. The country has the third highest maternal mortality rate in the world. Ebola, cholera, yellow fever, and meningitis are endemic. What could I do there?'

'Wow. You certainly know a lot about Sierra Leone. Good luck in your audition for *Mastermind*,' he said, sarcastically. 'Haven't you chatted via Skype or anything since she's been away?'

'Internet is intermittent.'

'And the truth?'

She looked up at him again. He seemed to be able to look inside her and spot her lies. She couldn't answer him.

'You feel abandoned,' he said.

'I do. I know I shouldn't. But I do.'

'She's putting herself, and her needs, first. There's nothing wrong with that,' Odell said.

'I know.'

'But you feel let down.'

'Why can't there be a charity called Police Without Borders?'

Odell laughed. 'Would you join?'

'Like a shot.'

'I'd miss you if you left.'

'Would you?' She looked at him.

'Yes. I know we haven't known each other long, but I like to think we've connected. You make me smile. You make standing over a rotting corpse in woodland that little bit more fun.'

She smiled at him. 'Thank you. That means a lot, you big weirdo.'

He reached over, grabbed her hand, and held it firmly in both of his. 'I know you've been through a great deal of trauma over the years, Mat, and your defence shields are up, I can see that. But there are some people who'd like to get to know you more, who'd like to help and support you, if you'd let them.'

'You?'

'If you'd let me.'

She looked into his eyes and could feel the warmth radiating from him, though that could be the wine. She felt safe with Odell. She felt comforted, calm, relaxed, and bordering on happy in his presence.

'I'll let you,' she said, not quite hesitantly.

'Good.' He leaned forward, gently raised her head with a smooth finger beneath her chin, and kissed her tentatively on the lips. He pulled away. 'You okay?'

She couldn't speak, so nodded.

He leaned forward and kissed her again, harder. His arms wrapped around her, and he pulled her towards him. Matilda allowed herself to be led. This was what she wanted. It was what she needed. She was sure of it.

## Chapter Forty-Four

Monday, 12 April 2021

Odell tried to get out of bed without waking Matilda, but putting on your trousers in the darkness in an unfamiliar room is not an easy task. Banging a knee against a bedpost, falling onto the floor and shouting 'fuck' would wake anyone up.

'You'd see better if you turned on a light,' Matilda said, sitting up and doing just that.

'I was trying not to wake you.'

'How's that working out?' she asked, squinting in the light.

'Sorry.'

'Are you running out on me? Am I going to turn up at the mortuary and be told that you handed in your notice by text and you're currently on a plane bound for New Zealand?'

'That was the plan, but I seem to have been rumbled. Shall I change it to Tuvalu?'

Matilda threw a pillow at him. 'What time is it?'

'Just after six.'

'What the hell are you doing up at this time?'

'I've got a meeting in Coventry at nine.'

'Oh. At least that's closer than Tuvalu.'

Odell finished putting on his trousers. He went over to Matilda and sat on the edge of the bed. 'I had a great time last night.'

'So did I.'

'That wasn't my plan, by the way, to come over here and … you know, but I'm pleased we did.'

'Me too.' She smiled coyly.

He leaned forward and kissed her. He pulled back with a sour expression.

'Morning breath?' she asked.

'Yes. It's never like this in Hollywood films, is it?'

'No. Jennifer Lopez always wakes up looking perfect with neat hair and full make-up, and in reality you're heading for Coventry and I'm bursting for a pee.'

'I'll call you later,' he said, kissing her on the forehead.

Matilda remained in bed while Odell finished dressing and left. She waited until the front door closed, then threw back the duvet and ran into the bathroom. It was while sitting on the toilet that she realised she'd spent the whole night in complete darkness for the first time since her kidnapping. She hadn't had a bad dream. She hadn't woken up with a scream and sweating. She'd slept through the night in the arms of a man she had genuine feelings for. It didn't matter what she did, she could not remove the grin from her face.

---

Two hours later, Matilda was in the kitchen making breakfast. She'd showered, dressed for work, and was drinking her second coffee while waiting for the toast to pop up when she heard the sound of an incoming Zoom call from her laptop, which was still plugged in in the dining room.

She went in, coffee in hand, and looked to see who was calling.

'My God!' she said to herself.

Sierra Leone was one hour behind the UK, making it 7:03 where Adele was calling from. Matilda pulled out a chair, sat down, and accepted the call.

Adele's face filled the screen. It was clear that a change of country was doing her the world of good. She had let her hair grow to below her shoulders, her skin had caught the sun, and she looked healthy. Matilda couldn't remember the last time she had seen Adele smile so broadly. She looked happy. It had been less than two months since she'd left but the change was immense.

'Adele,' Matilda said, barely above a whisper, taking in the transformation of her best friend.

'Matilda, it's good to see you,' she said. 'How are you?'

The picture wasn't great quality and Adele kept freezing due to the intermittent internet connection.

'I'm good,' Matilda said automatically. She was still trying to take in how well Adele looked.

'Well, that's a big fat lie if ever I heard one.'

'How's life in Sierra Leone?'

'I honestly don't know where to begin. It's a whole other world from Sheffield.'

'Keeping busy?'

'I never stop. I've lost almost a stone since I got here. I can fit a whole hand down my jeans. It's just a shame it's my hand,' she said with a laugh.

Matilda gave a genuine laugh in return. 'You've caught the sun, I see.'

'I had the piss taken out of me from the second I landed about how pale I was. You should see my white bits. Even at forty degrees, Ariel wouldn't get anything whiter than my arse.'

Matilda found herself relaxing. It was good to be in Adele's company once again, even if they were four thousand miles apart.

'I'm sorry I haven't been in touch. I've no excuse.'

Adele's smile finally slipped. 'I understand. I really do. I did sort of spring it upon you that I was leaving. I can see why you were so upset.'

'I was being selfish.'

'No. You weren't.'

'I was. I couldn't see that you needed to get away. You needed a break. I just…' She couldn't finish her sentence.

'You should get away too, Mat. You're looking tired.'

'I actually slept better last night than I have done all year.'

'Maybe you've turned a corner. At last.'

'I think I might have,' Matilda said, thinking of Odell.

'Oh my God, you had sex, didn't you?'

'What? What makes you say that?'

'Come on, Mat, I know that look. You got lucky last night, didn't you?'

'I don't think people say that anymore.'

'Stop prevaricating. Let's have some details. Do I know him?'

Matilda pulled a face, almost cringed, as she told her.

'Odell! As in my replacement, Odell Zimmerman?' Adele asked.

'That's the one.'

'You lucky sod. He's gorgeous.'

'I'm aware.'

'So, is it serious or were you just fooling around?'

'I… I don't know,' she said wistfully.

'Last night wasn't the first time, was it?'

'No.'

'Well,' Adele said, stretching the word out. 'I'm glad. Finally. Mat, it's good to see some colour in your cheeks.'

'You just said I was looking tired.'

'Well, yes, but now I can see you're actually shagged out,' she laughed.

'It's been a while.'

'Of course it has. Mat,' Adele said, leaning closer to the camera and dropping her voice, 'you need to be careful with Odell.'

'Why?'

'He's not one for staying in one place for long. He only took the job in Sheffield because he knows I'm on temporary leave. If I do end up staying out here, he won't take the job permanently there.'

'You're planning on staying?' Matilda's smile dropped.

'I haven't decided anything yet, Mat. I'm just saying, there may come a time when you have to make a serious decision – either break up with Odell, or, if your feelings for him are strong, you may have to leave your job, and Sheffield, to be with him.'

'Oh,' Matilda said.

'That might not necessarily be a bad thing, though, Mat. Just then, when you were smiling, you looked… I don't know, you looked happier than I've seen you since before James died. Maybe you'd benefit from leaving Sheffield.'

'I can't,' she said.

'That's an excuse.'

'There's a killer…'

'There always is,' Adele interrupted.

'This one's different. He's not simply killing his victims. A young man suffering with depression wanted to kill himself but didn't want to do it on his own. He found someone online, thought he'd entered into a suicide pact, only for this other guy to push him off a building. Then this guy lured an elderly woman with Alzheimer's into the woods and left her there to die from exposure.'

'That's awful. But how do you know all this?'

'He's writing to me, Adele. He's emailing me, bragging about his crimes.'

'Jesus Christ.'

'I don't know who he is. I have no witnesses, no evidence, no forensics, nothing.' She wiped away a tear. 'Judging by what he's saying in his emails, we suspect the killer knows me and that I know him.'

'Has the chief constable got you going through your address book?'

Matilda tried to smile, but it wouldn't come. 'The number of people I know could fit on a Post-it and there'd still be room for a shopping list.'

The two friends were silent for a long moment.

'Mat, why don't you take a step back? I can see how this is affecting you. I bet you're not sleeping or eating properly. You need a break. Go and visit the Meagans in the Lake District.'

'I can't,' she choked.

'Why not?'

'I need to see this through.'

'No. You don't. You need to be selfish and put yourself first, for once. Matilda, let me give you some advice. Now, this may sound harsh, but I'm only saying this because I love you and it's in your best interests. You need to leave the police force. You need to get out of Sheffield. I'm looking at you right now and, despite the odd smile when you talk about Odell, all I see is pain. If you tell me you're enjoying your work, I'll call you a liar. You're killing yourself.'

Matilda couldn't speak. She didn't know what to say, anyway, but she was worried that if she opened her mouth, a torrent of emotion would pour out. She looked away from the laptop.

She looked back at the screen. Adele was glaring at her. A few seconds passed before Matilda realised Adele wasn't blinking.

'Adele? Adele?' Matilda asked.

Suddenly, Adele disappeared. The connection was lost. In almost every email Adele sent her she mentioned the poor internet service.

Was Adele right? Was Matilda killing herself slowly from within? She didn't think so, and there were a few sparks of lightness in the distance. She knew Odell wasn't the settling down type, and she didn't really want to marry again, but there could be something that could trigger a hint of happiness in her life.

'Fuck!' she said, releasing some built-up frustration.

## Chapter Forty-Five

Matilda parked in her usual space in the rear car park and trotted to the entrance.

'Morning, Matilda. I've got some post here if you fancy taking it, save my legs trekking all the way up to the HMCU,' said Rose, a civilian member of staff who had been at the station for as long as anyone could remember.

'Sure,' Matilda said, taking the pile from her. 'Hang on, trekking all the way up to the HMCU? It's on the ground floor.'

'Well, you're holding it now, you may as well take it.'

'You're a cheeky sod, Rose.' Matilda smiled at her.

'I'm winding down. I retire in July.'

'I never thought I'd see the day. What are you going to do?'

Rose walked up to Matilda and lowered her voice. 'Five numbers on the lottery. Me and Alan are off to France. The house is already on the market. Keep it to yourself,' she said, tapping the side of her nose.

Matilda leaned forward and gave her a hug. 'I'm so pleased for you, Rose.'

'I've never been able to get the shooting here out of my mind. I said to Alan, when the time comes to retire, I'm not just going to sit back and wait for death, I'm going to enjoy myself. Life's too short.'

'It certainly is, Rose. Make sure you send me a postcard.'

Matilda turned and headed for her office. Life was far too short. South Yorkshire Police had lost some bloody good officers in the shooting in 2019. Matilda had lost some good friends. DC Rory Fleming was only in his twenties, had just got engaged, and he and his fiancée were gunned down. If Odell did say he was leaving Sheffield, she would seriously consider going with him, providing he wanted her to, obviously.

Matilda entered the suite, rifling through the post. There were a few junk letters and police federation circulars, and a thick padded envelope for Matilda which felt like it contained a book. She threw it down on a table.

'Any response from the vigil?' she asked, looking up at the whiteboards.

'Yes. Five arrests and twelve people sent to hospital for minor injuries,' Scott said.

'Ah. I meant, any leads?'

'None whatsoever.'

Christian came out of his office and hissed loudly at Matilda to get her attention. He beckoned her inside. She looked over her shoulder, smiled at Sian, and went in.

'I've been on the phone to Felix Lerego,' he said, whispering as he closed a venetian blind.

'Have you ever considered undercover work?' Matilda asked.

'No. Why?' He frowned.

'Because you'd be terrible at it. Everyone out there now knows you and I are talking about something secret. You could have just handed me a Post-it and said you had a message for me.'

'I hadn't thought of that. Anyway, I've spoken to Felix. I've asked him to come in for the morning briefing. I'm going to mention the photos to him and ask for a list of who was there so we can question them to see if they spotted anyone. Do it in a roundabout way.'

'Good idea. Now, I'm going to pop to my office. Should I leave by the door or tunnel under the floorboards?'

'Sarcasm really doesn't become you, Mat.'

Matilda left his office, picked up the padded envelope where she'd thrown it, and headed for the door. Sian called to her before she could leave.

'Sign this.' She handed her a card. 'It's Zofia's birthday on Friday. I'm going to buy her a bottle of that expensive perfume she likes, so you need to hand over a tenner, or more seeing as you're on more money than the rest of us. The kettle's on a go-slow so I've ordered a new one. It's coming tomorrow. I've emailed you the invoice.

'Now, for something work-related,' Sian continued. 'I had a call first thing this morning from Jenny Savage, the neighbour of Audrey Wildgoose. On Saturday morning, she woke up to find a card had been put through her letterbox overnight. She opened it and it was a sympathy card. All it said inside was 'Thinking of you' and it was signed by Annie Bella Wright. Jenny doesn't know anyone of that name, so she googled it. The only Annie Bella Wright she could find was a woman from Little Stretton in Leicestershire who was murdered on the fifth of July, 1919. Her death was never solved.'

Matilda, in the process of opening the padded envelope, stopped. 'Anything else in the card?'

'I asked Jenny that. In the top right-hand corner, it said '3 of 5'. She's bringing it in.'

'Bloody hell.'

'It was also hand-delivered, whereas the others weren't. I told her to put it in a freezer bag or something. You never know.'

'What was the picture on the front of the card?'

'An elderly couple sitting on a park bench. I was thinking

maybe it represented Audrey Wildgoose and her husband. Maybe it shows them in happier times, or maybe reunited in heaven.'

'You big softie.'

Sian leaned forward and lowered her voice. 'I don't mind telling you this, Mat, but this case is really creeping me out, especially after you received those photographs. I can't help but feel like we're being watched.'

'I know the feeling.' Matilda looked over Sian's shoulder to make sure nobody was close and listening. 'Felix Lerego's coming in. I spoke to Christian yesterday. We're wondering if the reason we didn't notice anyone taking photos of us at Graves Park was because whoever it was should have been taking photos anyway. You know, a CSI?'

'Oh God.'

'I know.'

'Sian, reception on the phone,' Finn called out. 'Jenny Savage is here to see you.'

'Thanks, Finn.'

'Are you staying for the briefing, Mat?' Finn asked. 'Zofia's been doing some digging and she thinks she might have found something.'

'Sure.' She threw the half-opened padded envelope onto a spare desk and went over to the tea station to start a round of drinks.

'I wouldn't flick the kettle on if I were you,' Finn said. 'It doesn't switch off. Steam fills this place in no time.'

'Never mind. I've had two coffees already this morning. Any more and I'll be bouncing off the walls.'

Scott rose from his desk, went over to Sian's, and helped himself to a Snickers. He threw a small packet of Maltesers to Matilda.

'Is everything all right with you this morning?' he asked.

'Fine. Why?'

'You look different,' Scott said.

'Do I?'

'Yes. You look… I don't know … sort of … different.'

'I'm using a new shampoo. It adds body, apparently,' she quickly said, trying to deflect attention from herself. 'Zofia, Finn said you've found something.'

'You said about the killer being young to be able to mix with Liam Walsh and Josie Pettifer, but then we've got Audrey Wildgoose, who is in her eighties, so how was he able to be in her life without raising suspicion?' Zofia said. 'So I looked online and not long after the Covid pandemic began in March 2020, Audrey contacted the *Star* and they printed a feature. She'd recently been diagnosed with dementia, but she was still well enough to know what was going on around her. The feature is all about how her neighbours were helping her, looking after her, a good news story. Josie Pettifer was also in the local paper when she sued a Chinese takeaway for not clearly marking the ingredients on their menus, and I've found a story about Liam Walsh being arrested while protesting about the council chopping down healthy trees. All three victims have been in the local newspaper at some point.'

'Of course,' Matilda said. 'Liam's mother has the cutting in a frame on her living-room wall.'

'The killer could be trawling the local newspaper to find his victims,' Zofia said.

'But we know he found Liam Walsh via a suicide chat room on the dark web,' Finn said.

'Yes, but what if his main source of resource is the local paper? How else could he have found Josie Pettifer and Audrey Wildgoose?' Zofia said. 'The only thing those two have in common, as far as I've been able to find out, is that they were both in the local paper. Josie mentions her severe allergies and Audrey talks about being newly diagnosed with Alzheimer's.'

'She's right,' Matilda said. 'It's possible that after killing Liam Walsh, the killer turned his attention to the local newspaper to find further victims.'

'I do have one more theory,' Zofia said.

'Go on,' Matilda prompted.

'We're working on the basis that whoever is behind these killings is someone known to you, Matilda, or to the team in general. Who do we know who has a background in newspapers, particularly the local newspaper?'

The penny dropped. 'Danny Hanson,' Matilda said.

## Chapter Forty-Six

Felix Lerego was used to working in the cold. When he wasn't attending a crime scene in the open air, he was in his office above a warehouse on the aptly named Letsby Avenue whose windows didn't close fully, and the single radiator was for ornamental purposes only – it wasn't connected to anything. He was shown into Christian's warm office and sat down, unbuttoning his coat and pulling off his scarf.

'We have a delicate situation,' Christian began, leaning forward and knitting his fingers together.

'That's a very serious start to a conversation.'

'The other night at Graves Park, when Audrey Wildgoose was found, members of our team were photographed. The photographs were emailed to Matilda by a person claiming to have killed Mrs Wildgoose.'

Felix's eyes widened. 'Bloody hell.'

'The thing is, we don't know who the killer is or who took the photos. Matilda and I have questioned the team and none of them saw anyone wielding a camera. So we're having to widen our search and think about who else was there. That's what led us to members of your team, many of whom used a camera in their duties.'

The penny dropped. Felix's mouth fell open.

'You think the killer is a member of my team?'

'We really hope not, but, as you're aware, we need to check and double-check these things. Can you give us a list of all the people who were at Graves Park? We'll need to question them and find out their whereabouts on the nights of the crimes in question.'

Felix sat back in his chair. He whipped off his beanie hat revealing his recently shaven head, which he scratched. He remained silent.

'What are you thinking?' Christian asked.

'None of my team are killers, Christian,' he said, confidently.

'I can understand you wanting to protect them, Felix.'

'No. This isn't about me protecting them. Trust me, I wouldn't. If any of them do anything they shouldn't, they're out. We had one bloke, Shaun Hackett, sharing crime scene photos on WhatsApp earlier this year. He was straight out. I'm sorry, Christian, but you're looking in the wrong place here.'

'I need to check all bases. It's purely for elimination purposes.'

'Then let me ask you,' Felix began, sitting back and folding his arms against his chest. 'Have you checked your own team? Have you looked into the backgrounds of all the uniformed officers who were at Graves Park? What about civilian staff here? What about your own chief constable? If we're suspects, so are they.'

The silence between the two was palpable.

'It's so easy to suspect people who aren't right next to you, isn't it?' Felix added. 'If you're looking at one branch of investigation, you need to look at the whole tree. Fine, interview my team, but interview your own first.'

Felix stood up and left the room. He had given Christian a great deal to think about.

The plan was for uniformed officers to go to Danny Hanson's flat and bring him back to South Yorkshire Police HQ to be formally questioned. In case he resisted, Matilda had asked the officers to turn on their body cameras so she could watch the journalist get tasered. Unfortunately, Danny wasn't at home and an elderly neighbour told officers he'd said he was off to Wakefield for the day on a research trip.

Matilda waited in the HMCU suite impatiently, wondering where to go next. There was no doubt in her mind that Danny Hanson was a reptile, but he wasn't a killer. It didn't alter the fact that several fingers seemed to be pointing at him. He either really was hiding a dark persona in his background, or he was being set up.

'He didn't look happy,' Sian said as Felix Lerego stormed out of the suite.

Matilda didn't say anything. She hadn't noticed.

'Matilda,' Sian said, louder.

'Huh?' She looked up.

'You look deep in thought,' Sian said.

'I am.'

'Care to share them?'

'If I could understand them, I would.' She stood up and made her way towards the door. Maybe some fresh air would help. Her eyes fell on the padded envelope she'd tossed on the table. She grabbed it, pulled off the tab and opened it. Inside was a hardback book: *The Perfect Killer* by Sebastian Lister. Why had someone sent her this in the post? She opened the front cover. There was a message on the title page, written in red, written in blood: 'Where Lucy Dauman was found'.

In the background, Matilda could hear the sound of voices she recognised. Sian and Christian were chatting. Scott said something and Zofia laughed. A phone rang. Someone was tapping away loudly on a keyboard, probably Finn, who was very heavy-handed. Matilda turned on her heels and walked slowly, almost in a daze, into the suite, the book held open.

Christian looked at her. 'What's that?'

'It came to me in the post this morning,' she said. 'Don't touch it!' she snapped as Christian reached for it.

'Sian, get some gloves,' Christian said. He leaned forward to read the message. 'Is that blood?'

'I think so.' Matilda's voice was shaking.

'"Where Lucy Dauman was found." What does that mean?'

Matilda shook her head.

'Who's Lucy Dauman?' Tom leaned over to Scott and asked.

'She was the pathological technician to Adele Kean. She was killed by Simon Browes when she unwittingly stumbled across what he was doing.'

Sian, wearing latex gloves, approached, handed a pair to Christian, and held open a large evidence bag. Before they could put it inside, Finn held up his mobile phone and took a photo of the message. Carefully, Sian and Christian took the book from Matilda and placed it in the bag.

Sian took off her gloves, placed her arm around Matilda's shoulders, and sat her down on a chair. 'Are you all right?' she asked.

Finn plugged his phone into his laptop and brought the photo he'd taken of the message up on the projector screen.

'Does that look like blood to you?' Finn asked.

'Is it possible to actually write a message in blood outside of a Hollywood film?' Scott asked.

'I suppose it depends on what you use to write it with. It's thinner than a fingermark, that's for sure,' Finn said, zooming in on the individual letters.

'Lucy Dauman was found at Wigtwizzle, wasn't she?' Sian asked. 'It was where Simon Browes had his makeshift body farm. Why does he want us to go there? Do you think there's another body we haven't found?'

'Or maybe there's a new one for us,' Scott added.

'I've sent the book off to forensics,' Christian said, coming back into the suite. 'I've asked the chief constable to come down, too.'

'I don't understand,' Scott said. 'We know who killed Lucy. Simon Browes admitted it.'

'Maybe he's not saying he killed Lucy,' Finn suggested. 'Maybe's he's just… I don't know,' he trailed off. 'He's all about the perfect murder. Maybe he thinks Lucy's was the perfect murder.'

'But it wasn't because she was found. Simon was arrested and he's in prison,' Scott said. 'The only way her murder was perfect was if Simon wasn't the killer, but he is because he admitted to it.' Scott was clearly getting frustrated. 'I don't like this. Who the fuck does he think he is, playing around with us like this?'

'Calm down, Scott,' Christian said. 'I think the best thing we can do is get a crime scene team on standby and go out to Wigtwizzle and see if there is anything there for us to investigate.' He looked at Matilda for confirmation.

She nodded, then stood up.

'I think you should stay here, Mat,' Sian said.

'No. He's sent that book to me. He wants me to go there.'

'Then we're all going.'

## Chapter Forty-Seven

Scott drove with Matilda in the front passenger seat next to him and Sian and Finn in the back. Christian and Tom followed in the car behind.

'I can cope with murderers,' Matilda said, shattering the silence. They'd been quiet since they all got into the car. Now they'd left the city and were in open countryside, there was little to distract them. 'I can get my head around all manner of killers and why they do what they do, but this, playing games, it's beyond sick. This is not a fucking game,' she seethed.

'People who do this kind of thing,' Finn began, his voice quiet, 'taunt the police or their victims or even the victims' families, it's all about power and control. It's about having the upper hand. But when you look at the person who is doing all this, they can fall into two categories. They've either got some kind of brain trauma, some chemical imbalance, or they've witnessed some kind of trauma, or suffered an abuse, that's seriously messed them up.'

'So we're looking for a complete psycho?' Scott asked. 'That's comforting.'

'No. We're looking for a human being who is suffering,' Finn corrected.

'Suffering? Suff… How the fuck can he be suffering?' Scott almost exploded. 'He pushed Liam Walsh from a tall building. He spiked Josie Pettifer's food. He somehow led Audrey Wildgoose, a frail, vulnerable old woman, to the middle of the woods and left her to die. How is he suffering?'

'Calm down, Scott,' Sian said, reaching forward and placing a comforting hand on his shoulder. 'And ease off the accelerator. It would be nice to get there in one piece.'

'Sorry,' he said, slowing down.

'What kind of trauma are we talking about here?' Matilda asked Finn, turning around in her seat. 'If this man has suffered something catastrophic, maybe we can find him through that. A big, life-changing event is bound to have made the news.'

'Not necessarily,' Finn said. 'What might be life-changing for him might not be life-changing to others. He could have come home from work one day and found his wife in bed with his best friend. Maybe he's had all his hopes of getting straight-As in his A Levels and failed the lot. To us, they're not life-changing, but to him, they're massive.'

'Oh,' she said, turning back to look out of the window.

'What were you thinking of?' Sian asked.

'Strangely, I was trying to think of what might have happened to Danny Hanson to turn him into such a killer.'

'You can't think Danny Hanson is behind all this, surely.'

*Who would have thought your husband would turn out to be a killer?*

---

Wigtwizzle is a hamlet north-west of Sheffield and on the very edge of the Peak District National Park. Earlier this year, the body of Lucy Dauman, technical assistant to Home Office Pathologist, Dr Adele Kean, was found when bones were discovered in the surrounding area. Lucy had been missing since December 2019, weeks before her wedding. She had inadvertently stumbled across pathologist Simon Browes killing sex workers and the homeless and burying them at varying depths in the woodland at Wigtwizzle to study their rate of decomposition. It had been Adele who had found Lucy's rotting corpse, which led to a chain of events in which Simon threatened Adele's life while he was on the run from police.

In the spring and summer, Wigtwizzle was a stunning place to visit. It was peaceful, calm, and relaxing. There were beautiful walks among the trees, in the thick woodland and over fields and the view stretched as far as the eye could see. On a windy spring day, in the cold, the damp, and the dark, Wigtwizzle was not the first place you'd think of visiting for a day out. The bare trees with their twisted, gnarled branches reaching into the grey sky, swaying slowly in the breeze, were menacing and haunting. The ground, slippery and uneven with a carpet of decaying leaves, squelched underfoot. In the air, a disturbing smell of dying nature added to the sense of foreboding that wrapped itself around Matilda Darke as she stood at the edge of the woods and looked deep into the blackness.

The one saving grace was that she wasn't alone. She was surrounded by her trusted team. Sian was by her side, their arms linked together. They would go in here as one.

'It doesn't seem like two minutes since we were standing at this exact spot with Adele and Felix,' Sian said.

'We had no idea what horror was waiting for us,' Christian added.

'They say history has a way of repeating itself. I always thought that was a load of old shite. Now I'm not so sure,' Sian said.

Deep in the woods was a makeshift hut with a raised floor. Simon had stumbled across it while he was burying his bodies. It was beneath the floor that he hid Lucy's body. She was found still wearing the clothes she was last seen alive in. Neither Sian nor

Christian knew if the shed had been removed by police or the local council. Both had tried to forget about the darkness that lay within these woods.

Christian led the way. Everyone was dressed in sensible clothing and shoes and was careful where they trod. They strode over fallen branches and held onto trunks to keep their balance in the sodden areas. The deeper they went into the woods, the darker it became. Despite the trees being bare, sunlight was struggling to break through the thick grey clouds, and visibility was falling.

A chilly breeze was blowing. Occasionally, it picked up, and the icy fingers of air caused them to shudder. Branches clacked together and echoed in the silence.

'I think it's coming up on the right, isn't it?' Sian asked. She was third in line behind Christian and Matilda.

'I think so. I don't remember coming this far in though,' Christian called back.

'I remember slipping and falling on my arse a couple of times. I had a bruise on my bum the size of an apple for weeks,' Sian said.

'Bramley or Braeburn?' Scott asked.

'I might have known you'd ask something like that,' she said, turning around.

He winked at her.

Up ahead, Christian stopped. 'It's still here,' he said.

They joined him and looked at the rotting wood of the poorly constructed shed. There was no door, but they couldn't see inside because of the darkness. Matilda reached out and grabbed Sian's hand.

'I've got a really bad feeling about this,' Sian said.

'Did anyone think to bring a torch?' Christian asked.

'I've got one,' Finn said. He reached into his pocket and handed it to the DI.

Christian flicked it on, pointed it at the entrance, and stepped forward. Everyone else stayed back.

He jumped and cried out. The others screamed as something shot out of the shed.

'It's all right. It's only a rat.'

'*Only* a rat!' Sian cried.

'That was a bloody big rat,' Tom said.

'My mum's Yorkshire Terrier's smaller than that,' Finn added.

'I don't think there's anything in here,' Christian called out from inside.

Scott turned on the torch on his phone, held it up, and headed for the shed. Slowly, Finn and Tom followed.

'He's right. It's empty. Just like it was when we were last here,' Scott said.

Matilda remained where she was. She looked around her at the barren woodland.

'I wonder if he's watching us again,' she said quietly. 'I wonder if he's taking our photograph and I'll get another email.'

'Are you worried?' Sian asked.

'I'm worried about what he's going to do next. I'm worried about how this is all going to end. It's unpredictable.'

Matilda headed for the shed, but Sian reached out and held her back.

'Wait,' she said. 'Lucy wasn't found inside the shed. She was found beneath it. We had to go down the small embankment around the back and look underneath.'

Matilda pulled her phone out, turned on the torch, and wielded it aloft. 'Let's go.'

At the side of the shed, there was a steep drop. Matilda reached out, held onto a tree, and quickly trotted down it. She slipped the last couple of feet but managed to stay upright.

She held out her hand and Sian ran down and grabbed hold of her.

'You okay?' Matilda asked.

Sian nodded. 'You?'

'I think so.'

Together, holding onto each other, they made their way around the back of the shed. Beneath the floor, there was a recess between the shed and the woodland. It was dark, hidden. Matilda pointed her phone towards it and the space lit up. They both stared in silence as they tried to make out what they were seeing. It wasn't possible. Surely.

Sitting with her back against the far wall of the shed, legs outstretched, tied at the ankles, arms on her lap, tied at the wrists, and a gag over her mouth, sat the decomposed remains of Natasha Klein.

## Chapter Forty-Eight

It was rare for Chief Constable Benjamin Ridley to attend a crime scene. His role was mostly behind a desk and despite being proud of achieving so much in his career, after being abandoned as a baby and flitting from one foster home to another, he missed the thrill and unpredictability of an active crime scene. He climbed out of his car, slammed the door closed behind him, put on his cap, and headed with a spring in his step for where Matilda was sitting in the unmarked Astra. He tapped on the driver's side window. She hadn't seen him pull up in front of her.

Matilda opened the window. 'Sir?' She seemed confused to see him here and had a quick look around her to make sure she was still at Wigtwizzle and hadn't made the journey back to the police station without being aware of it.

'I want to ask what the hell is going on but that makes me sound like I'm clueless about day-to-day life among my officers. However, what the hell is going on here, Matilda?'

'I wish I knew.'

'Can I get in? It's a tad brass monkeys out here.'

'Sorry. Sure.'

Matilda closed the window and unlocked the front passenger

door. As Ridley climbed in, she looked out at the confused activity in the woods. Christian had taken charge and was currently directing a suited-up Felix Lerego and his team where to head.

'I had a call on my way over here,' Ridley said, making himself comfortable on the heated seat. 'I had a word with Zofia before I left the station. She told me about the book you received in the post. The message inside was written with blood and it's a match for Natasha Klein.' Matilda didn't react. She simply stared straight ahead out of the windscreen. 'There's a bookmark on chapter seven. It's a black leather bookmark that comes to a point at the bottom. It says Monsel Head on it. Do you think that's a message about his next victim?'

Matilda snapped her head around to look at him. 'Monsel Head?'

'Yes. I've looked it up. It's a place—'

'I know where it is. It's in Derbyshire. I go walking there often. It's a beautiful place. I use a bookmark bought from the gift shop there ages ago.'

Ridley stared at her.

'What?'

'I was about to ask if you saw the bookmark, given that your fingerprints are all over it.'

'It's my bookmark,' Matilda said, her voice full of emotion. She thought for a long moment. 'I'm reading that book at the moment. Oh my God. Is it my book?'

Matilda didn't wait for an answer. She started the engine, put the car into gear, and slammed her foot down on the accelerator.

'Where are we going?' Ridley asked, fumbling for the seatbelt to secure himself in place.

'To see if the fucker has broken into my house and stolen my book.'

Neither of them spoke as they made the journey from Wigtwizzle to Ringinglow. Matilda drove at speed, ignoring traffic lights when they began to change colour and not stopping at stop signs, which earned her more than a blast from the horn of an irate driver. Ridley heard the four-letter insults. Matilda's head was full of more pressing matters.

She turned off Ringinglow Road, down the narrow lane, bare tree branches clacking against her car as she swung it round to the left. She slammed her foot on the brake and came to a stop close to her front door. She whipped her seatbelt off and jumped out of the car, rummaging in her coat pocket for her front door keys. Ridley was behind her, and they entered the cold house together. Matilda turned off the alarm with the fob on her keyring, swiping it over the sensor.

They stood still in the vast hallway listening intently for any sound that something wasn't quite right. Matilda headed for the living room, pushed open the door and looked down at the coffee table. *The Perfect Killer* by Sebastian Lister was gone.

'It was there,' she said. 'On the coffee table. It's been there since I bought it on the day it was published.'

'Could you have taken it to bed with you to read?'

'It's not really bedtime reading. I'm more skim-reading it, really. I'm worried about how Sian and her kids are represented. The point is, that book has been on that table and hasn't moved.'

'Did you see it last night?'

'I… I don't know. I was late home. I didn't come in here. I was in the kitchen until it was time to go to bed.'

'Are you sure you didn't take it into the kitchen to read while you were having your tea?'

'I wouldn't have done that.'

Ridley ignored her and headed for the kitchen. Matilda couldn't take her eyes from the empty coffee table.

*Someone has been in here.*

'It's not there,' Ridley said, coming back.

'I told you.'

'Mat, who's been in your house recently?'

She went over to the sofa and sat down on the edge. She took a deep breath. 'My mother. Sian. Scott. Donal. You. Odell.'

'Could one of them haven't taken it?'

'And then written a message in Natasha Klein's blood?' she asked, incredulously. 'My mother can't even spatchcock a chicken without heaving.'

Ridley sat on the opposite sofa. He leaned forward. 'Who has a key to your house?'

'My mum. My sister. Scott. Sian. Adele, though I think she left her set here.'

'Do you want to go and check, make sure they haven't been stolen?'

She nodded.

'I'm going to get a forensic team out here to dust the room for prints. Do you have CCTV?'

'No. I was going to have it installed when I was being stalked last Christmas. I was kidnapped before I got to do anything about it and it didn't seem necessary after that. I thought... I thought everything was fine. Stupid, right?'

'Not stupid. This is your home. You should feel safe here. You shouldn't have to turn it into a fortress.'

'Shouldn't. But probably should.' She gave him a weak smile and left the room, heading for the stairs to go check Adele's keys were still there.

---

Matilda hadn't been in Adele's bedroom since she left. When she opened the door, there was a fusty smell. She should probably come in to open a window from time to time, let in the fresh air. It was the second largest bedroom in the house and had a king-size bed in the middle, a wing chair by the window and an en suite leading off from the fitted wardrobes. It was spacious, bright, and clean, exactly how Adele had left it. Matilda sat on the edge of the bed and opened the top drawer of the bedside table. The set of keys was still there, sitting on top of a Hilary Mantel paperback.

Matilda sighed. She wasn't sure if she should be glad they hadn't been stolen. What did it mean?

*It means someone with a key came into your home while you weren't here and stole the book.*

Matilda closed the drawer and picked up the framed photograph of Adele with her son Chris. They were both smiling for the camera, sitting in the back garden of her old house. She felt a wave of emotion pass over her. Chris was a credit to his mother. A young man with his whole life ahead of him. He was working hard as a teacher when he was gunned down trying to save his pupils in 2019. Adele took the death of her only son hard. She struggled to come to terms with it. She thought she'd found someone in Simon Browes who could show her life was still worth living – until he turned out to be a psychopathic killer. Was it any wonder Adele had left? If she'd stayed… It wasn't worth thinking about.

A tear fell on the glass. Matilda wiped it away. She hadn't realised she'd been crying.

There was a tap on the bedroom door. She looked up and saw Ridley standing in the entrance.

'I was calling.'

'Sorry. I was miles away.' She looked back at the photo. 'I wish I was miles away.'

Ridley came over to the bed and sat beside her. 'Have you heard from Adele?'

'Yes. We had a chat via Zoom the other day. Internet is patchy over there.'

'How's she getting on?'

'She's loving it. She's… she looked so much brighter, healthier. She looks happy.'

'There's a forensic team on the way,' he said.

'Thank you.'

'I'm not sure you should stay here tonight. Do you have anyone you can go to?'

She nodded. 'I'll go to my mum's.' *I've no intention of being hounded out of my own home.*

'The only advice I can give you, Mat, is to change your locks, maybe think about getting that CCTV installed. Limit who you give a key to.'

She nodded. 'Thanks.'

'Do you want me to bring in an outside team?'

She looked at him. He wasn't the first person to suggest that. 'Why?' It was a silly question. She knew why.

'Someone is targeting you. Someone is targeting your team. It might be better if someone from the outside, with no connection whatsoever, took over.'

'No,' Matilda replied firmly. 'We're the best people to find this fucker. Besides, bringing in a new team isn't going to stop him from emailing me and phoning me. I'd say he'd do it all the more. No. We stay as we are,' she said, determined.

The doorbell rang.

'That'll probably be the forensic team. Felix said he was sending someone straight over. I'll go.'

Ridley left the bedroom, leaving Matilda behind on the bed, the picture of Adele and Chris in her hands. She looked down at it and found herself smiling through the tears at a happier time. Chris was gone. Adele had gone. Maybe she should go, too.

## Chapter Forty-Nine

'Where's Matilda?' Odell Zimmerman asked, jumping out of his car almost before it came to a stop at the edge of the woodland at Wigtwizzle. His face was a map of concern.

'She's gone home,' Sian told him.

'How is she?'

'I'm not sure.'

'Is it true someone has broken into her house?'

Sian looked across the bonnet of the car at a sheepish Donal Youngblood.

'Scott told me,' Donal said. 'They're going out. He has a right to know.'

'To be honest, Odell, we don't know what's happened. The chief constable is with her now.'

'Right,' he said. He took a deep breath and calmed himself. Slightly. He turned to Donal. 'Get the things out of the back. We'll suit up and head for the scene.'

Sian saw Donal look up and smile. That brilliant, sickly, wide-eyed smile could only be for one person. She turned round and saw Scott heading towards them. She reached up and slapped him around the ear.

'What was that for?'

'You told Donal about the book?'

'He's practically my husband.'

'And he's told Odell.'

'Who is his boss and Matilda's unofficial boyfriend. So?'

She grabbed Scott by the elbow and pulled him away from the car.

'Simon Browes. Steve Harrison. Stuart. Do those names mean anything to you?' she asked through gritted teeth.

'We seem to have a high proportion of killers in Sheffield whose names begin with the letter S.'

She ignored him. 'They were all people we trusted. They were people we took into our confidence, and they abused that trust. What we discover about anything in the line of our work should stay within our team, and our team alone.'

Scott frowned. 'So, I shouldn't talk to my fiancé, tell him how my day's been?'

'By all means tell him, just leave out sensitive information.'

'Seriously? What kind of a relationship am I going to have if I lead two completely different lives?'

'You just need to be careful who you talk to.'

'No. I'm getting married to Donal. I love him. I trust him. I tell him everything. He's not a killer, Sian.'

'I said exactly the same thing about Stuart.'

'So, by your reckoning, everyone's partner here is a killer? Should Zofia not talk to Tom? Should Finn not talk to Stephanie? I've met Christian's wife. Should I be shunning her, too.'

'Now you're just being silly.'

'No. *You're* being paranoid. If you're going to look at people you work with, people who are your friends, and see them as being potential killers, then you should think about looking for another job, Sian. I'm sorry. I love you to bits, you know I do, but you're going to do yourself some serious mental health damage if you don't relax a bit.'

He walked away before Sian could say anything. She remained at the edge of the road, a blank look on her face, taking in everything Scott had said. He was right. She couldn't look at people she knew, worked with, trusted, and wonder what darkness was lurking beneath the surface. Yet as this case progressed, the evidence was there that this particular killer was someone they all knew very well.

---

Suited up in blue plastic onesies, Odell and Donal made their way over the rough terrain of Wigtwizzle and joined crime scene manager Felix Lerego and his team at the makeshift shed where arc lights had been erected and a white forensic tent positioned precariously over Natasha Klein's body, protecting her from the elements. She had been missing since the eleventh of March. Had she been here all that time, any trace evidence might already have been lost due to strong winds, rain, and wildlife, but the site needed preserving, just in case.

Under the stark lighting, it was easier to make out the scene of utter horror before them. Odell had seen more than his fair share over his life and career, but Donal was still relatively new to the world of pathology. He balked at the sight of a former human being slowly decomposing. It was difficult to picture the blonde, beautiful young woman who had been gracing the front pages of newspapers over the last couple of weeks.

Within days of Natasha dying, flies would have picked up the scent of rotting flesh and descended, laying their eggs in any orifice they could access as well as the folds of skin in her neck as gravity caused her head to droop forward. The breaking down of membranes, the release of bodily fluids, urine, and faeces, would have added to the pungent smell, which would have drifted on the breeze and summoned local wildlife. Foxes and rats were rife in this area. They were omnivores, and opportunistic.

Odell studied the scene. He could tell, simply by looking, that Natasha had been dead for several weeks, that she had died in this spot. Hundreds of dead flies and pupae surrounded her. What hadn't been covered by clothing, and where wildlife hadn't been able to access, had been devoured or pulled off and taken away to be eaten. Her fingers were missing on both hands. The radius and ulna of her left arm were dangling out of the sleeve of her coat, suggesting animals had tried to pull it free from her body. They hadn't succeeded but had managed to eat as much of the flesh as they could get at, leaving her bones behind. Natasha's nose was missing, as were chunks of flesh from her face. What was left was black, leathery, and desiccated.

'We've found what we believe are phalanges a few feet away,' Felix said, breaking the heavy silence. 'They've been bagged and are ready for you to take back to the mortuary.'

'Thank you,' Odell said.

He stepped forward and squatted. He looked at Natasha's face, what was left of it. He looked down at the ground surrounding her.

'There's no blood.'

'No,' Felix said.

'I can't see any holes on her clothing to suggest a stab wound or a gun shot.' He lifted her head carefully with the tips of his gloved fingers. 'No evidence of strangulation either, but that's not going to be easy to tell just by looking, due to discolouration. Have you taken enough photographs, Felix?'

'Yes. We're all done.'

'I think we're best getting her back to the mortuary, running her through the 3D scanner and seeing what shows up.'

Natasha's body was fragile. She was held together by the clothing she was wearing and what was left of her skin. A sheet was laid out on the ground as close as they could get it to her and she was carefully lifted by Odell and Donal onto it, then wrapped up and placed in a body bag, before being sealed and put into the back of a private ambulance to be taken to the mortuary.

Felix stood back and watched as the slow process was done with painstaking precision. When they carried the body up the slight incline to the road, Felix looked into the makeshift hut and what had been left behind. His team needed to give the shed another sweep in case there was more evidence they'd been unable to find before.

Beneath the mulch of decaying leaves, Felix found a small purse. He opened it and looked inside. There was a National Union of Students card showing Natasha's smiling photo, along with a library card from The Sheffield College in her name and a provisional driving licence. Behind that was a business card. Felix had heard of the person, and knew it was someone Matilda Darke would be more than interested in.

'How's it going?'

Felix jumped, turned, and saw DS Sian Robinson standing in the entrance to the hut.

'I think you should see this,' he said. He went towards her. 'I think this is Natasha's purse. It could have fallen out of her pocket when she was brought in here. I've just found it. There's a business card inside it belonging to Danny Hanson.'

## Chapter Fifty

Matilda refused Ridley's offer to drive her to Greenhill to her mother's house. She had no intention of leaving her home, but she didn't want to be there while forensic officers were dusting her living room for foreign fingerprints. Ridley said he would stay, lock up when they'd finished, and post the keys through the letterbox. Matilda had no choice but to trust him.

On her way over to her mother's, Matilda called and asked if she was home. Penny told her she was round at Harriet's.

Matilda pulled up outside the detached house on Westwick Road and walked up the short garden path. Her legs felt like they were made of lead and her head was heavy with dark thoughts. She knocked on the door and it was quickly answered by her sister.

'You look like shit,' Harriet said, her smile dropping when she saw Matilda.

'I feel like shit.'

'Has something happened?'

Matilda nodded.

Harriet reached for her and practically hauled her into the house. She slammed the door behind them and took Matilda into the living room, where Penny was with Nathan and Joseph, Harriet's sons. They looked the picture of a happy family, sitting in front of a roaring fake fire, soft lighting, comfortable sofas, and the smell of baking in the air.

'What's happened?' Penny asked, jumping up from the sofa when she saw Matilda's pale face.

Matilda sat on the sofa next to her nephews. 'Someone's broken into my house.'

'Oh my God!' Penny gasped, hands slapping against her chest. 'Did they take much?'

Matilda shook her head. 'It wasn't a burglary, and they didn't actually break in.'

'Mat, you're not making a lot of sense,' Harriet said, sitting on the arm of the sofa next to her. 'Joseph, go and get your auntie a drink. Do you want a cup of tea or something strong?'

Before Matilda could open her mouth, Penny chimed in. 'She'll want a cup of tea. It's good for shock. Put a couple of sugars in it, Joseph.'

'Tea's good for shock?' he asked with a frown. 'I think people caught up in terrorist attacks would appreciate something a bit stronger than a mug of tea,' he said, leaving the living room.

Matilda told them about someone potentially having a key to her house, entering without setting off the alarm, and stealing the book from her coffee table.

Penny grabbed her handbag and looked inside. 'I've still got my key.'

'Nathan, where are my keys?' Harriet asked.

He shrugged. 'Probably on the hook on the dresser in the kitchen.'

'Can you look?'

'Can't I stay and listen?'

'No, you can't.'

'I'm not a child anymore.'

'Nathan, just go and check my keys are still there, for crying out loud,' Harriet said, her voice raised.

Reluctantly, Nathan stood up and padded into the kitchen.

'I don't think they'll ever stop being belligerent teenagers.'

'What does your boss say?' Penny asked.

'He's told me to increase my security.'

'Is that it? Bloody hell, Matilda, you're going to be the death of me with this job of yours. I thought once you'd stopped being an operational detective we wouldn't have any more of this.'

Matilda looked at her sister and rolled her eyes. Harriet squeezed her shoulders as a show of support.

'It's not Mat's fault,' Harriet said. 'There are some people in the world who are just … complete nutjobs.'

Joseph came back into the room with a mug of tea. He handed it to Matilda. 'I've put three sugars in. No idea why,' he said, slumping back down on the sofa. 'Nate says your keys are still on the hook,' he said to his mother.

'Do you want to stay here tonight?' Harriet asked.

'I was going to see if one of you wanted to stay at mine with me. I'm going to order some CCTV, add a few more locks.'

'I'll come,' Penny said, standing up again.

'We could all go,' Joseph said. 'I love your house.' He smiled at Matilda.

'And leave this house empty? I don't think so,' Harriet said. 'Mat, come with me into the kitchen for a minute.'

Harriet practically lifted her sister from the sofa and led her into the kitchen where Nathan was scrabbling in the biscuit barrel.

'We're having tea in less than an hour.'

'I'm going out with Lisa in a bit.'

'His new girlfriend,' Harriet whispered to Matilda.

'She's not my girlfriend,' he protested, blushing slightly.

'Sorry. She's a friend who's a girl. Look, give me and your auntie a few minutes.'

'Bloody hell! Go into the kitchen, go back into the living room.

I thought we lived in a democracy, and we could go anywhere we wanted.'

'My house is a cruel dictatorship. Out.'

'Heil Hitler,' he saluted before stomping out.

Harriet pushed the door closed behind him and waited a while before she spoke.

'Mat, I know they're just films, but I've seen *Red Dragon* and *Seven*. I've seen where psycho killers go after the detective's family. You had that stalker woman last year and now this. Are we safe?'

Matilda leaned against the kitchen worktop. She was looking in the open biscuit barrel Nathan had left behind.

'Of course you're safe.'

'You don't sound one hundred per cent confident.'

'I've no reason to suspect anyone is in any danger. This killer … he's just trying to show off how clever he is.'

'If he was able to break into your house without you knowing it, he's very clever. That also makes him dangerous. Look, Mat, maybe Mum's right. Maybe you should think about packing this all in, or maybe going for a promotion where you have a desk job.'

'My new job is mostly deskbound. This killer obviously didn't get the memo,' she said with a twisted smile.

'How can you make jokes?'

'It's a defence mechanism.'

'So, you are scared?'

Matilda didn't say anything. She went back to looking in the biscuit barrel and took out a plain digestive.

'You are. Aren't you?'

Matilda looked up. She had tears in her eyes. 'I'm not scared. I'm angry.'

'What are you going to do?'

*I have no fucking idea.*

Fortunately, Matilda's phone started ringing so she avoided

having to lie to her sister. She pulled her iPhone out of her pocket. It was Sian calling.

'I need to take this,' she said, leaving the room. 'Hi, Sian, how's it going?' Matilda asked, heading into the hallway.

'Felix found Natasha's purse when they moved her body. It looked like it had fallen out of her pocket or something. He was going through it, and he found a business card with Danny Hanson's name on it.'

'Danny Hanson? Why…? Hang on… I…' She was trying to process what was happening.

'I've tried calling him and there's no answer. Should I go round to his flat?'

'What?' Matilda asked, suddenly aware she wasn't fully concentrating on what Sian was saying. 'Oh. No. I called by this morning, and he wasn't there. A neighbour told me he'd gone to…' She stopped herself. The penny suddenly dropped, and she didn't like where it had fallen. 'Sian, I'll call you back.'

'What is it?'

'Just … give me a few minutes.'

Matilda ended the call and scrolled through her contacts.

Not long after the shooting in January 2019, when Steve Harrison's involvement was discovered, Matilda was worried that Steve would somehow launch another attack. He seemed to have a fixation on her, and she was petrified he'd try something on a larger scale, and more people would die. She began calling a member of staff she became friendly with at Wakefield Prison to keep a long-distance eye on Steve and what he was up to. She hadn't called for a while – she hadn't needed to – but discovering Danny Hanson was visiting Wakefield this morning could only mean one thing.

Grey Saunders was a Chief Officer on the Supermax wing at Wakefield Prison where Steve Harrison was living. It was also the wing in which Stuart Mills was currently residing. If Danny Hanson was visiting Wakefield today, Matilda could only assume it was to pay a visit to Stuart. The simple explanation was that he was visiting friends, but Matilda doubted a parasitic leech like Hanson would have many friends, and surely the good people of Wakefield had better taste.

Grey answered the phone on the third ring. 'Hello, Matilda, long time no chat. How are things with you?'

'Fine thanks, Grey,' she lied. It sounded genuine as she was so used to lying when people asked how she was.

'Good-oh. Now, what can I do for you?'

'Erm, well, actually, I was wondering if you could check to see if Stuart Mills has had any visitors lately.'

'I don't need to check. I know the answer already. Stuart hasn't had any visitors for a very long time, until today. You must be psychotic.'

'The word is psychic, but I'll let that one pass. Just this once,' Matilda said. She took a breath. 'Who visited him?'

'That bloke who used to be on the telly. Danny Hanson. Said he's writing a book about him. Jumping on the bandwagon, I see.'

Matilda squeezed her eyes shut. *The bastard lied to me. Why am I not surprised?*

'You know what these journalists are like, Grey, they can't have an original thought.'

'That's true. Look, I'm going to have to go, my shift ends in half an hour.'

'Okay. Look after yourself.'

'You too.'

Matilda ended the call. She chewed her bottom lip, chomping down hard until she could taste blood. Danny had told her he wasn't writing a book about Stuart Mills yet he had visited him in prison today. She could get her head around the fact he'd lied to her. He was a journalist, lying was in his DNA, but that didn't answer the question of what his business card was doing in Natasha Klein's purse, unless…

'Unless Danny Hanson is the fucking killer,' Matilda said out loud. She immediately shook the thought away. Danny Hanson was a lot of things: he was a scummy journalist, he was a liar, he was vain, he was self-centred, he was egotistical, he was a complete and utter knobhead, but he wasn't a killer. She was sure of it.

*Are you?*

*Am I?*

*Yes. I am.*

*I think.*

'Everything all right?'

Matilda jumped, turned around and saw her mother standing in the doorway.

'Yes. Fine.'

'You should never lie to your mother. So, am I coming over to your house for a few days in order to act as bait in case your mystery intruder comes back?'

'That's not how I'd put it. I need to get some decent security put in. It would help if there was someone I could trust there to let them in the house and have a look around.'

'I'll go and pack a few essentials. Maybe on the way over, you can tell me the truth about what actually is going on in your life at the moment,' she said, sternly. 'I'll go and get my coat.' She disappeared back into the living room.

Matilda was about to make another call when her phone burst into life, making her jump. Christian was calling. She swiped to answer.

'Sian told me about Danny Hanson. We've run his registration number through the PNC and we've picked him up on the M1. He's just this minute passing junction thirty-four. It looks like he's heading for home. Do you want me to bring him in?'

*Shit.*

Matilda wanted to interview Danny herself. Actually, what she wanted to do was grab Danny by the throat and squeeze the life out of him. She looked at the clock on the wall. It was getting late, and what evidence did they really have that Danny was linked to this investigation? Did he have time to research a book and think up such elaborate murders when he spent so long on his hair?

'We'll wait until tomorrow,' Matilda said.

'Tom's telling Natasha's mum right now that we've found a body. The public's going to learn about it soon enough. If Danny is behind this and finds out what's happened, he could do a runner.'

'He won't. As far as he knows, we don't know it's him. All he'll do is send me another email. Look, put eyes on him. Have an unmarked car parked outside his flat and we'll pick him up first thing in the morning.'

'The chief constable is going to love you with all that overtime.'

'Christian, when it comes to counting the pennies, I couldn't give a tiny rat's arse.' She ended the call.

Matilda went to the living room and stood in the doorway. Penny, Harriet, Nathan, and Joseph were chatting. They were her family. They were all she had left. She made a decision right there. She would see this case to a conclusion then she would reconsider her future. She would take a leaf out of Adele's book and put herself first rather than her work, and if that meant giving up the job, so be it. There were more important things in life.

## Chapter Fifty-One

Tom and Sian were sitting on the sofa in the living room of Cara Klein's home in Broomhill. Cara was sitting in an armchair wearing jeans and a creased jumper. She had grown much thinner since the last time Tom had been here. Her cheeks were sunken, and her eyes were drooping and tired. The entire house was silent, the atmosphere heavy. A little over a month ago this was a normal family home. Now, only Cara stalked its rooms, alone, in a house far too big for one person.

'Cara,' Tom began, 'we were called out to woods in Wigtwizzle earlier this morning. We found a body and I'm afraid we've matched the DNA to Natasha's. I really am so sorry.'

Cara stared at Tom. Her blank expression didn't change. Eventually, a single tear rolled down her cheek. Slowly, she began to nod. She tried to speak. She opened her mouth a few times, but nothing came out.

Eventually she managed to say, 'I suppose I should be thankful that at least she's been found. I can bring her home. What ... what happened? What did he do to her?'

'We don't know yet,' Tom said. 'There needs to be a post-mortem.'

'Can I see her?'

Tom and Sian exchanged a glance.

'Cara, we've matched DNA we took from Natasha's hairbrush. There's no denying that it's her. It's up to you, of course, but I wouldn't recommend you viewing the body. It's always best to remember people as they were when they were alive.'

'Are you saying she's been disfigured? Jesus Christ! What did that bastard do to her?' she seethed, her emotions taking over.

'No,' Tom quickly answered. 'But she has been outdoors for over a month. Decomposition is not a pretty sight.'

Sian leaned forward. 'Cara, as one mother to another, I really don't think you should view the body. Natasha was a beautiful young woman. You need to remember her as she was in life, not how she is in death. It won't help you at all.'

'Perhaps you're right. I just... I keep thinking of the last thing I said to her, when she left for college that morning, and I can't remember. It was just a normal day. If I'd known it was going to be the last time I saw her alive I'd have said something more profound, but it was just a regular morning. I don't even remember saying goodbye to her.'

'Maybe that's how it should be,' Tom said. 'Everything was normal, and you and Natasha didn't need to say anything profound because you were close. You knew what you wanted to say to each other without actually saying it.'

Cara smiled at Tom through the tears. 'I like that. Thank you.'

'Cara,' Sian said, changing her tone. 'Does your family know Danny Hanson?'

She looked at her and frowned. 'The name sounds familiar.'

'He's a journalist. He used to read the news occasionally on the BBC.'

'Oh, yes, I know who you mean. No, we don't know him. Why?'

'Natasha had his business card in her purse. We were just wondering if there was a connection between them.'

'She had his card? Why would she be talking to a journalist?'

'We don't know.'

'Natasha wanted to work in the media. Maybe she contacted him for advice on how to get started,' Cara guessed.

'It's possible.'

'Why are you asking, though? You know who killed her. I know he hasn't confessed, but you've charged Derek with Natasha's murder.'

'I know. It's just a loose end we're trying to tie up.'

'Oh. I see.'

'Cara, is there anyone you'd like us to ring, someone who can sit with you tonight?' Tom asked.

'No. I… I actually think I'd like to be on my own,' she said. She looked over at Tom, but her gaze didn't quite land on him. It was as if she was looking somewhere off into the distance.

'Are you sure?'

'Yes,' she replied, a small smile appearing on her lips. 'Yes. I'll be fine. It's strange. I actually feel a bit lighter, knowing that I can bring her home.'

'You have my number,' Tom said. 'If you need to call me or ask me anything, please, get in touch at any time.'

'I will. Thank you. You're a lovely young man.'

Tom gave her a warm smile.

---

Outside, in the cold and dark, Tom and Sian made their way back to the pool car parked down the road.

'I've got the strangest feeling that Cara might end up doing herself in,' Tom said.

'It's a shame she doesn't have any family. What about neighbours?' Sian asked, looking around her at the houses with their curtains closed.

'It's weird. I've worked on missing persons cases before and neighbours have always popped round to see how people are doing, even if they're just being nosy, but when I was here just after Natasha had gone missing, they didn't have a single knock on the door.'

'Poor woman. I don't think I'd want to be on my own tonight.'

'Me neither.' Tom pointed the fob at the car and unlocked it. He opened the door and lowered himself in behind the wheel. 'What's going to happen to Derek?'

'Ridley's contacted his solicitor and told him of developments. He could be released pending further inquiries. We'll need to know his alibis for the dates of the other murders.'

'Is it true he's been beaten up?'

'I'm afraid so.'

'Jesus,' he said, clicking his seatbelt into place. 'What did we do wrong?'

'We didn't do anything wrong. We followed procedure. He had no alibi. He was having an affair with his daughter's best friend. She found out and was planning to confront him about it then went missing. We even found Natasha's blood in his car. Everything pointed to Derek.'

'And all Derek said about that was that it came from a towel when Natasha had a nosebleed a few months back.'

'Which could possibly be true, but we've nobody to corroborate that.'

Tom didn't say anything.

'Are you planning to start the car or are we staying here all night?'

'Oh. Yes. Sorry.' He started the engine but didn't set off.

'Tom? Are you all right?'

He turned to her. 'Their marriage is over, isn't it? Derek and Cara's. If the charges against him are dropped and he's allowed to return home, there's no future for them, is there?'

'I wouldn't have thought so.'

'We've ruined their marriage.'

'No. Derek did that when he had an affair. Bloody men. They can't be trusted.'

'I hope you're not including me in that statement.'

She turned and looked at him. Her eyes narrowed. 'No. I'm pretty sure you're one of the good ones.'

'Only pretty sure?'

'Until you return those Chunky KitKats to my drawer, yes.'

Tom let out a genuine laugh, put the car into gear, and pulled away from the edge of the road. He looked back at Cara's house through the rearview mirror and saw the living room light go out. Sadness fell over him once again.

## Chapter Fifty-Two

Tuesday, 13 April 2021

Matilda pulled into her parking space and dragged herself into the station. She was shattered. She had hardly slept, as she and Penny had spent the majority of the night on the sofas scrolling through the internet to find a reputable company to come to the house and give an estimate for CCTV cameras. Penny questioned whether a panic button could be installed in Matilda's bedroom and then asked if one of the bedrooms could be turned into a panic room. That's when Matilda decided it was time to go to bed. Yes, she wanted extra security, but she did not want her own personal high-security prison.

As Matilda approached the HMCU, Sian caught up with her from the other end of the corridor.

'Good morning. You look knackered.'

'I think I spent more time talking to my mother last night than I've done in the whole of my life.'

'She lives on her own. She probably doesn't talk to many people.'

'She certainly made up for it last night. I can still hear her voice ringing in my ears.'

They walked into the suite, where everyone else was at their desks.

'Derek's being released from prison today,' Finn said.

'That's quick.'

'He has a good lawyer.'

'He must do. Christian,' Matilda called to the DI in his office, 'was Danny's flat watched all night?'

'Yes. He arrived back home about seven and he's still there, as far as I'm aware.'

'Okay. We need to bring him in for questioning. Obviously, I'd love to go out there, cuff him and beat him up in the back of a police van, but that's not going to look good on the front pages. Are the officers still outside his flat? Can I use your computer?'

'Sure. And, yes, two PCs in plain clothes are outside Danny's flat.'

'Get them to bring him in. Have him sweat in an interview room for an hour, then I want you and Finn to lay into him. We'll work on a strategy while he's in there panicking.'

'Anything new?' he asked, nodding at the computer.

'No. Eerily quiet. Do we have any news on how Natasha Klein died?'

'PM is taking place now. Scott's over at Watery Street.'

'We need to keep an eye on Natasha's family. If this is following the pattern of the others, they'll be receiving a cryptic sympathy card very soon. Tom needs to go back out there.'

'I don't understand this, though. How did he find Natasha? Why hide her away to die such a slow death like that? The others could have seemed natural, or suicide in the case of Liam Walsh, but this is out-and-out murder. She was tied up and gagged, for goodness' sake. What's he playing at?'

Matilda frowned and shook her head as she thought. 'Finn!' she called out.

Finn sighed. 'I've been thinking the same thing myself. The

only thing I can come up with is that he's upping his game. When you put together the crimes of a serial killer, you see how they've mutated, evolved, over time. What this guy is doing here is using someone's illness against them. In the case of Liam Walsh, he was severely depressed. Josie Pettifer had severe allergies, Audrey Wildgoose had dementia, and Natasha Klein had diabetes. He turned that to his advantage. Now, either researching new victims is a long and arduous process and he simply doesn't have time for it, or he daren't risk getting caught in playing the long game. Don't forget, Josie was incredibly careful about her food. She must have really trusted this killer to allow him to cook for her. All that takes planning and time. I think he's seen how much he's got away with, and it's excited him. So he's gone to the next level.'

'Which is?' Christian asked.

'Taking people at random. Natasha had been missing for five weeks. I wouldn't be surprised if the PM doesn't reveal she's been dead for most of that time. He probably spent five weeks just to get Josie Pettifer to invite him round to her flat.'

'So he's growing impatient?' Christian said.

'Not impatient as such,' Finn said with a heavy frown on his brow. 'He's finding new ways of killing people without getting his hands dirty, without us finding any evidence. He's worked out how to choose a victim without immersing himself in their life. The victims mean nothing to him. It's about killing and getting away with it.'

'So, Danny Hanson's card found in her purse?' Matilda asked.

'Danny Hanson isn't the killer,' Finn said confidently.

'How can you be so sure?'

'If Danny killed someone, he'd leave his DNA all over the scene. He'd panic. He doesn't have the brain power to come up with all of this.'

'Who does?'

'Someone with a great deal of time on their hands. Someone who is capable of giving this a lot of thought and who can sit on the sidelines and watch without being noticed. Danny would give himself away.'

'But that doesn't change the fact his card was in Natasha Klein's purse,' Christian said.

'Nor does it change the fact that he lied when he said he wasn't writing a book about Sian's husband, when he clearly is,' Matilda added.

Finn remained silent. He looked down at the floor and nibbled on his bottom lip.

'Are you wanting to say something, Finn, but worried about offending us?' Matilda asked.

'Danny's card left in Natasha's purse. The fact that three of the victims appeared in the local newspaper and that Danny Hanson used to work on the local paper. Everything is pointing to Danny being the killer. I think the killer is setting him up.'

'Why?' Matilda asked.

'Maybe he has a grievance with Danny,' Christian suggested. 'Though I expect that puts him on a very long list.'

'Or maybe the killer knows Matilda has a grievance with Danny,' Finn said. 'If Matilda thought Danny was the killer, because the scant evidence pointed that way, she'd concentrate all her efforts on finding out the truth, leaving the real killer to continue without detection.'

Matilda leaned back in her seat and folded her arms. She was silent for a long moment while she thought. She could feel the beginning of a headache at the back of her head. But then, chatting with Finn always left her like that.

'Okay, this is what we're going to do. We interview Danny. We find out if he knew Natasha Klein, tell him his card was found in her purse. We find out his alibi for the dates we roughly know the previous victims were killed and go from there. In the meantime...' She stopped. She couldn't continue.

'In the meantime, what?' Christian asked.

'In the meantime, we're still at square one and bloody clueless.'

## Chapter Fifty-Three

The Medico-Legal Centre in Sheffield was one of the leading centres in the country for digital post-mortems. The body, in this case Natasha Klein, still sealed in the black body bag, was placed on a flatbed scanner, similar to an MRI scanning machine. The body was scanned in a spiral, like a slinky moving around the body from top to toe. The closeness of the spirals was set to the smallest possible setting, 0.6mm, to get as much detail from the body as possible.

The computer was operated by radiographer Claire Alexander, who was sitting behind a bank of three large monitors. It wasn't long before the image of Natasha's body was brought up on screen and she was able to manipulate it, turn the body upside down and sideways, look at it from every angle, without physically touching it and potentially destroying any trace evidence. She changed the image from photographic to x-ray. She was looking for bullet entry wounds or knife wounds. There were none. Natasha's death was not caused by bullet or blade.

Odell Zimmerman would have to perform a full invasive post-mortem to establish cause of death.

By the time Natasha's body was wheeled into the PM suite,

everyone was scrubbed up and ready for the procedure to start. A uniformed officer was in the exhibits room which ran alongside, to note any relevant information or take anything that might be found in, or on, the body.

Scott was hoping there would have been nobody free so he could have taken on that role. Unfortunately, he'd been told to scrub up and he stood at the back of the room, dreading the Y-incision and the stench of decomposition and death stinging his nostrils. He looked over at his soon-to-be husband, Donal, and could only see his eyes, which seemed to be permanently smiling. Donal winked at him. He couldn't bring himself to wink back. It was nice for them to meet during the day, but most couples would meet for a chat over a meal deal from Boots, not over the rotting corpse of a nineteen-year-old.

Natasha was taken out of the body bag and gently transferred to a gurney, where she was then carefully cut out of her clothes, which were bagged and handed to the PC in the exhibits room.

'There's certainly evidence of the hide-and-die syndrome,' Odell said as he studied Natasha's fingers.

'What's that?' Scott asked.

'When she was found beneath the shed, she was at the very back of the recess. Now, I know she was tied up, so movement would have been difficult, but as hypothermia sets in, it can lead to some mental aberration. It's not unusual for someone who is hypothermic to completely rend their clothes.'

'But surely when you're cold, you want layers, not to strip off.'

'True, but the mind is a very complicated instrument. Affected by cold, delirium sets in, and the mind starts to play tricks. It's strange, yet fascinating.'

'I always associate hypothermia with, like, the Antarctic or somewhere freezing,' Scott said.

'All manner of things need to be taken into account,' Odell said. 'Wind speed and direction, falling temperatures. Then we need to look at the individual themselves. Were they suffering from any illnesses or diseases that could be affected by outside conditions? It wouldn't hurt to look at the weather map over the last few weeks at Wigtwizzle. The same could be said for Graves Park for Audrey Wildgoose's death, too.'

Something clicked in Scott's mind. 'I'm sorry?'

'I said it wouldn't hurt for you to check out the weather for—'

'No,' Scott interrupted. 'Wigtwizzle and Graves Park.'

'What about it?'

'The Arts Tower.'

'Sorry?' Odell asked.

'Scott, what's going on?' Donal asked.

'I have to go,' Scott said, charging for the door.

'Scott?' Donal called out.

'I'll call you later,' he said over his shoulder.

Once in the corridor, he pulled off his mask and hood and tore at the scrubs. He fumbled in his pocket for his mobile and scrolled through the contacts to get to Matilda's number.

'Mat, please tell me you're sitting down,' he said in place of a greeting.

'Oh God. What's happened?'

'Are you on your own?'

'No. Christian and Sian are with me.'

'Can you put me on speakerphone, please?'

There was a shuffling noise from the other end. 'Okay, you're on speakerphone and we're all gathered. What's going on?'

'I've just been in the post-mortem suite with Odell and he believes Natasha died from hypothermia. He mentioned getting a weather report for Wigtwizzle over the last couple of weeks just to see what conditions were like. He then said I should do the same for Audrey Wildgoose and Graves Park.' He paused, waiting for a reaction.

'Okay. Is that it?' Matilda asked. 'I thought you were going to reveal something huge.'

'I haven't finished.'

'Then why did you stop?'

'Dramatic licence,' Sian said. There was a smile in her voice.

'I wanted to make sure you were keeping up, when you're done being sarky.'

'Sorry. Go on,' Matilda prompted.

'As soon as Odell said Wigtwizzle and Graves Park something fell into place, and I immediately thought of Liam Walsh throwing himself off the top of the Arts Tower.'

'Right. Can you stop with the silences, Scott?'

'Haven't you worked it out yet?' Scott almost shouted.

'Worked what out?'

'What do Wigtwizzle, Graves Park, and the Arts Tower all have in common?'

'I've no idea,' Matilda called out.

'I have,' Christian said. 'Lucy Dauman was found at Wigtwizzle. Carl Meagan went missing from Graves Park. Laurence Dodds jumped from the Arts Tower. They're the scenes of some of our biggest crimes in the past few years.'

'Precisely,' Scott said. 'Thank you, Christian.'

'What about Josie Pettifer?' Sian asked.

'Well, I hadn't actually worked that one out yet,' Scott said.

Matilda gasped. 'Oh my God!'

'What is it?'

'Bradfield Road. Where Josie lived. It's where Faith Easter lived. It's just come to me,' Matilda said. 'I don't know why I didn't think of it before. Why didn't I realise?'

'It's all right, Mat, none of us got it either,' Christian said.

'Scott, can you get back here as soon as possible?' Matilda asked.

'I'm on my way,' he said, ending the call.

Matilda pulled out the chair at Scott's desk and sat down. She had a painful, pensive looked etched on her face.

'Well?' Christian asked.

'It's a theory.'

'The best we've had so far.'

'If that's the case, we're looking at people who have known us, or the cases we've worked on, for the past eleven years since this team was first created.'

'Or just someone who knows his way around Google,' Christian said. 'Let's face it, Mat, in recent years, you've had Danny Hanson following you like a faithful puppy itching to report on your cases, and he's succeeding in making you front-page news. It wouldn't take much for someone to become obsessed with you.'

'Why are you making this all about me suddenly?'

'Faith Easter died in the line of duty. You tried to save her but couldn't. Carl Meagan. Well, that case almost destroyed you. Lucy Dauman was the technical assistant to Adele, your best friend. Laurence Dodds jumped from the Arts Tower after a standoff with you. The killer is emailing you. The killer broke into your house, stole a book you were reading, and posted it to you with a message inside written in blood.'

'Christian, go and interview Danny Hanson,' Matilda said. Her voice was low and calm, but she quickly sat on her hands to hide the fact they were shaking. 'Tear him apart. Break him until we get the truth out of him.'

He saw the seriousness, the fear, and the horror in her eyes. He didn't say anything. He nodded, turned on his heel, and left the room.

No longer having an office of her own in this suite, Matilda went into Christian's. Before her kidnapping, she would have closed the door and pulled the blinds, but that wasn't happening now. Even just facing the wall and with a slight breeze on her back from an open window in the suite, she could feel the grip of claustrophobia. She took a deep breath. She closed her eyes and pictured David Tennant's sodding train coming into the station. It didn't stop. It continued going, into the tunnel, and out of sight. She opened her eyes. Her breathing was still laboured. The weight of the investigation, the realisation that four people had lost their lives because of her, was pushing her down. She felt sick. She couldn't breathe. She wanted to open her mouth and scream, but that would be highly inappropriate.

There was a tap on the door. She looked up and saw Finn on the other side of the glass.

'No offence, Finn, but if you've come up with any more of your theories, I'd rather not hear them right now. I'm loving your insight, but you're actually scaring me to death.'

'Oh,' he said, looking crestfallen. 'No. It's... Chief Constable Ridley wants a word. He's on the phone for you.'

'Oh. Thanks,' she said, picking up Christian's phone.

'Matilda, have you heard of a Detective Chief Inspector John Campbell?'

'Yes. He's based in Manchester. He's the son of retired DI Pat Campbell. She's a very good friend of mine.'

'He'll be coming over to head up the investigation. We need a fresh pair of eyes on this.'

'I really don't think that's necessary, sir,' she said. Matilda always called him 'sir' when she wanted to get on the right side of him.

'And I do. You have no suspects, not even a person of interest, yet you have four victims, and we've both been at this game long enough to know the death toll will rise. DCI Campbell will be coming over next Monday. If you can't solve this thing by the end of this week, he'll be taking over.'

'If you say so.'

'I do say so.'

Matilda put the phone down. She looked around the room for something to pick up and lob through a window, then realised this wasn't her office. Seething, her hands clasped into fists, she needed to release the pent-up anger she was feeling. She wanted to kick, to scream, to shout.

'You can swear if you want,' Sian called out.

She turned and looked at her good friend through the window.

'I can see you're dying to do something.'

'Can I say the c-word?'

'Just this once.'

Matilda took a deep breath and screamed, 'Christmas!'

Everyone left in the suite burst into laughter. It helped to lighten the mood.

## Chapter Fifty-Four

By the time DI Christian Brady and DS Finn Cotton opened the door to Interview Room 1, Danny Hanson had been waiting for just under an hour. The look on his face told them more than words ever could. He had a sheen of sweat on his forehead and upper lip, his brow was heavy with worry, and he seemed to be on the verge of tears. His left leg beneath the table was jiggling and the plastic cup of water he'd been given as a courtesy was now empty and had been torn to shredded splinters.

'Mr Hanson, sorry to have kept you,' Christian said with a faux smile. He was holding a thick cardboard file which he slapped down on the table. He pulled out a chair and sat down. Finn closed the door to the Interview Room and joined DI Brady at the table. They both looked at Danny in silence.

'Where's Matilda?' Danny asked.

'She's in a meeting,' Christian lied.

'She's behind there, isn't she?' he said, pointing to the large mirror on the side wall. It was a one-way mirror, behind which was an observation room, but it was currently out of use due to a leak in the toilets above.

'Nope. Now, Mr Hanson, just to let you know that you are not under arrest, and you haven't been charged with any crime. However, this interview is being recorded purely in the interests of our investigation. I assume you have no problem with that.'

'No. No, I don't,' he said, looking into the corner of the room at the camera glaring at him.

'Now, Danny, do you know why you've been brought here?' Christian said, opening the file and bringing out a few sheets of paper.

'No. And I'm not happy about it,' he said, sternly. 'Two of your PCs practically dragged me out of my flat in front of my neighbours.'

'Would you like to submit a complaint at the way you were treated?' Christian asked.

Danny looked at Finn, then back at Christian. 'No. I wouldn't. It's fine,' he said, his voice returning to normal. 'I would like to know what's going on, though. You're treating me like a suspect.'

'You're not a suspect,' Finn said. 'You are a person of interest, however. Do you know this woman?' he asked, placing a glossy print of Natasha Klein in front of him.

'Of course I do. Natasha Klein. Her face is all over the papers. I should think everyone in the country knows her.'

'Had you heard of Natasha Klein before she went missing?' Finn asked.

'Of course not.'

'Why of course?'

'I just meant… I meant that I hadn't heard of her. Why should I have?'

'For the benefit of the recording, I am showing Mr Hanson item DZ121,' Finn said, taking an evidence bag out of the folder with Danny's creased business card inside and pushing it across the table to him. 'Do you recognise this?'

'Yes. It's my card.'

'Who would have one?'

'I give them to people who I'm working with, when I'm

working on a story, for them to contact me. Interviewees. Why?' he asked, looking up, suddenly worried.

'This card was found inside Natasha Klein's purse. Her purse was found on her person when she was discovered dead yesterday.'

Danny's eyes widened in surprise before a look of confusion spread across his face. 'I don't understand.'

'That's a shame because we were hoping you could fill in a few blanks,' Christian said. 'Why would Natasha Klein have your business card, Danny?'

'I don't know.'

'She was studying media studies and psychology at The Sheffield College. She was hoping to work in TV. You work in TV. You both live in Sheffield. I'm guessing it wouldn't be unusual for a media student to contact someone already working in the media to ask for advice, tips, maybe even some work experience.'

'She didn't contact me.'

'She was very ambitious, by all accounts,' Finn added. 'Very prolific on social media, too. TikTok, Instagram, Twitter. She posted a great deal of content. She had plenty of followers, too. Even more than you, and you're already on TV.'

'She didn't contact me,' Danny repeated, his voice lower, fear edging in.

'She's very attractive, don't you think?' Christian asked, tapping the photograph.

It was a while before Danny answered. He looked to the two detectives, as if wondering what his reply would reveal. 'Yes. Yes, she is.'

'Beautiful smile.'

'I … yes. I suppose so.'

'We've all heard stories about people looking to others for help and encouragement in their chosen field only for those in a position of power to abuse that power for their own gains.'

'A position of power? What power?' Danny asked, clearly

exasperated. 'I don't have any power. I'm not even on TV anymore. I'm a writer. I'm a journalist.'

'You've written a book,' Christian said. 'According to early reviews released by your publisher, it's sensitively written in elegant prose. They're hoping for some major awards to come your way. I'm sure you're already aware of this.'

'It's just industry jargon. They big these things up to increase sales.'

'And inflate an author's ego,' Christian said.

'What?'

'Being told how wonderful you are is bound to sink in at some point, if you hear it often enough. If people are calling you a, what was it?' He opened the file again and pulled out a single sheet of paper. 'A new literary talent in investigative writing,' he said, reading from the printout. 'You must be very proud.'

'I am. That book took a great deal of research to put together.'

'People are saying wonderful things about you. It's not surprising if the next generation want advice on how to launch their own careers.'

'I... I do get people messaging me on social media. I... I don't reply to them all. I...'

'Did Natasha Klein message you?' Finn asked.

'No. She didn't,' he said, firmly. 'I would have remembered.'

'Why would you have remembered her over the others?'

'I... I just meant that I would have remembered what with her going missing.'

'Where were you on the afternoon of Thursday, March the eleventh?'

'I was at home.'

'All day?'

'From around lunchtime onwards.'

'On your own?'

'Yes.'

'You weren't working?'

'No. I... Look, that Thursday was the day *The Perfect Killer* by Sebastian Lister was published. I was pissed off that he'd got to write the story when I felt I should have written it. I wanted to see what kind of a job he'd done with it. I went out mid-morning and bought a copy from Waterstones in Orchard Square. I went back to my flat and started reading.'

'You spent all day reading?'

'Yes. I was surprised by how good it was, actually. I was gripped.'

'So, you've no alibi for the time Natasha Klein went missing?' Finn asked.

'I don't need an alibi because I haven't done anything. I've never met her before in my life.'

'Can you tell us where you were on the evening of Friday, September the twenty-fifth last year?'

'No,' he said. 'That was ... seven months ago. How am I supposed to remember that?'

'Wednesday, December the second last year?'

'What? No. I don't... Look, what's all this about? What are those dates?'

'Do you recognise this man?' Finn asked, showing Danny a photograph of Liam Walsh.

'No.'

'This woman?' he asked, taking a photo of Josie Pettifer and placing it over the one of Liam Walsh.

'No.'

'And how about this one?' Finn showed him a photo of Audrey Wildgoose.

'No. I don't know any of those people. Who are they?'

'Danny, you're really not helping yourself here,' Christian said. 'We have four people who died in suspicious circumstances, all of whom featured in the Sheffield *Star* over the past couple of years, a newspaper you used to work for. One victim in particular had your card in her purse. You can see how this looks.'

'I didn't give Natasha Klein my card. I never saw her before. I don't know how she got it,' he said, almost shouting in frustration.

'We would like to look at your computers and tablets. You don't have to hand them over to us, obviously, but we can apply for a warrant to have these items seized.'

'A warrant?' He ran his hands through his hair. They came away wet. 'But I haven't done anything wrong.'

'Then you'll allow us to look at your computers.'

'What are you looking for?'

'Evidence of any involvement by you in the deaths of these four people.'

'I don't know any of them. Why would I have killed them?'

'You know,' Christian said, leaning forward, 'for a journalist who has worked on a lot of murder investigations, you ask some pretty stupid questions.'

---

Eventually, Danny Hanson was allowed to leave the station. He wasn't charged with anything, and he promised to be at home later in the day when a detective would come round to look at his laptop and tablet.

He pulled open the door and stepped out into the cool April air. The blast felt like a slap in the face after more than two hours in a stuffy interview room. He buttoned up his coat, fished a beanie hat out of the pocket and pulled it down over his curly hair. He was almost at the gates when he heard his name being called. He turned around and saw Matilda Darke heading towards him.

'Did you see any of that?' he asked, pointing towards the building.

'Any of what?'

'That travesty in there. I've just spent three hours being

interviewed by Christian and, what's his name, Finn. They think I've killed four people. Me. Can you believe that?'

'They follow the evidence, Danny. You know how we work,' she said.

'The evidence was planted.'

'Are you accusing any of my team of planting evidence?'

'No. I'm not. I'm saying someone planted my business card on a murder victim and now your team thinks I'm guilty.'

'Who would want to do something like that?'

'I don't... I don't know.'

Matilda looked Danny up and down. She smiled at him. 'It's always satisfying when bad things happen to bad people.'

'Bad people? What have I done?'

'Are you seriously asking that question?'

'Yes. I am.'

'Okay. Let's start with you going to Southampton to interview Belinda's girlfriend to get information about Belinda behind her back. Let's move on to you denying you're writing a book about Stuart Mills, even apologising to Anthony, Daniel, and Sian, yet you went to Wakefield Prison yesterday and spent an hour with Stuart. Care to add anything?'

A smirk appeared on Danny's face. 'I'm a writer, Mat. I'm an investigative reporter. It's what I do.'

'You lie to people.'

'I'm researching a story. A story that I have been commissioned to write. If people refuse to sit down with me and let me interview them then I'll find the information another way.'

'By lying, by deceiving, by hurting people.'

'It'll get me a story.'

'You're destroying people's lives,' she said, stepping closer to Danny. They were almost nose to nose.

'It's an amazing story, Mat. A detective, married for over a quarter of a century, comes home from work every night and tells her husband how her day has been and he's storing it all up here,' he said, tapping the side of his head. 'When he starts killing, he has the mind of a detective. He knows what to do to evade capture. And it works. He kills without appearing on your radar and the fallout … wow, the fallout is just perfection. It would make a great movie.'

Matilda was seething. Her hands were plunged deep into her pockets to keep warm, but they were squeezed tightly into fists. She was seconds away from punching him in the face.

'The story has been told. Sebastian Lister has written about it. We don't need another book.'

'We've had this conversation before, Mat. How many books are there about Jack the Ripper? How many books have been written about the Zodiac killer? People love this shit.'

'You're a parasite, Danny. You go ahead with this, and you will be banned from this station. You'll not be invited to any press conferences. I will make sure you're blacklisted.'

'Matilda, I'm getting six figures for this book. My book about Magnolia House that comes out in the autumn has already been sold abroad and is getting translated into eight different languages. So far. You've given me so much over the years, I can write several books about you alone. Ben Hales. Carl Meagan. Steve Harrison, and we all know what really happened on the roof of the Arts Tower with Laurence Dodds. I can almost hear the money landing in my account.' He winked at her. 'See you later, Mat.'

He turned and walked away. There was a spring in his step and his head was held high. A marked difference to how he had felt leaving the station just a few minutes earlier.

---

Matilda watched as he walked away. She could feel her blood boiling in her veins. Her eyes widened. Danny had mentioned Jack the Ripper and the Zodiac killer. The sender of the emails had signed them using their signatures. Why had Danny Hanson chosen those two killers in his examples unless he was involved in all this?

She shook her head, mostly in frustration. Danny was many things. Every swear word invented could be used as an adjective to describe him, but she had never thought he could be a murderer. It didn't fit. Then again, the killer wasn't physically murdering his victims. He was manipulating them, and Danny was proving he was very good at that. Could Danny Hanson really be a murderer?

## Chapter Fifty-Five

'I can't see it,' Scott said. 'Danny Hanson isn't a killer. I could find him standing over a dead body with a knife in his bloodied hand and I still wouldn't think him capable of doing it. He's just too… I don't know.'

Matilda, Christian, Finn, and Scott were sitting in the open-plan office of the HMCU. Everyone else had gone home for the day. They were still no closer to discovering who had killed Natasha Klein and the others, and their only suspect so far was a reporter who neither of them could imagine coming up with such clever ways to kill his victims.

'Everything's pointing to Danny, though,' Matilda said. She was sitting at Sian's desk. She had a mug of tea in hand and was rummaging through the jam-packed snack drawer looking for something she fancied. The Maltesers had already gone. She selected a Topic.

'He doesn't have an alibi for any of the killings,' Christian said. 'Forensics are going through his laptop. Fingers crossed they can find something, maybe even a trace that he sent the emails to you, Mat.'

'He could have a second laptop he's hidden away somewhere,'

Matilda said. 'He's an intelligent bloke, there's no denying that, but is he a criminal mastermind?'

'He could be right when he said someone is fitting him up,' Finn said. 'Maybe the card was planted in Natasha's purse.'

'I thought we said the link to all the victims was this unit, and me,' Matilda said. 'The Arts Tower, Wigtwizzle, Hillsborough, Graves Park. One minute we say it's all pointing to me, the next we're saying Danny is being fitted up. Surely both can't be right.' She slumped back in the seat in frustration. 'Maybe Ridley's right. Maybe it is a good idea he's bringing in a fresh pair of eyes to look at the case.'

'I feel like we're in touching distance of solving this,' Finn said. He broke off another finger of KitKat and nibbled at it. 'It's like I've got all the pieces in front of me, but I can't work out how they go together. This bloke has got a fixation on you, Matilda. He's emailing you. He's stolen a book from your house. On the other hand, we've got Danny Hanson being lined up as a killer. Yet I think it's safe to say we all know it's not him. So, what links Matilda Darke and Danny Hanson? If we can answer that question, I feel we'll be closer to finding the killer.'

'What links the two of them is all the investigations Danny has reported on,' Scott said. 'Outside of work, there is no connection.'

'He hounded you about Carl Meagan's disappearance,' Christian began, counting the cases on his fingers. 'He was there at Starling House. He was all over us when the Mercers were killed in Dore. The Magnolia House investigation. Steve Harrison. The shooting. Stuart Mills. He's always been there in the background.'

'So has someone else,' Finn said. 'There is somebody out there who feels Matilda Darke and Danny Hanson are to blame for something that has either happened to them or to someone they care for. Maybe we've arrested someone and they're currently in prison and they've left behind a relative whose life has gone downhill since it happened and blames the lead detective and whoever reported on the incident.'

'Makes sense,' Scott said.

'I keep going back to Magnolia House,' Matilda said. 'Danny was heavily involved in that, and we used him, too, to get more victims of abuse to come forward. He's even got the book coming out in the autumn.'

'The killer could be trying to discredit Danny. Set him up for murder so either this book gets pulped before it hits the shelves, or it will be seen as a load of bollocks because there's a suspicion of murder hanging over the author's head.'

'There have been plenty of arrests following the sex abuse scandal,' Christian said. 'The fallout is still being felt. That newsreader from *Look North* in the 80s killed himself a few weeks back in his prison cell.'

'I read about that,' Scott said. 'Did you hear how he did it?' He pulled a face and shuddered. 'It must have been a slow death.'

'That radio DJ was stabbed to death in prison, too,' Finn said. 'He didn't have anything to do with Magnolia House, but his accusers came forward following the story breaking.'

'And don't forget that Liberal Democrat councillor who is still protesting his innocence. His wife and kids are standing by him. There was something about it in the *Daily Mail* last week,' Scott said.

'I didn't have you down as a *Daily Mail* reader,' Christian said.

'I don't think I've ever read a newspaper a day in my life. I saw it online.'

'I think we should focus on the Magnolia House case. That's been our biggest investigation for a long while,' Matilda said. 'It's also been the one that Danny Hanson has got the most out of. He wrote all those features for the *Guardian*, and he's got a book coming out.'

'Do we warn Danny that someone is out to potentially ruin his career?' Scott asked.

It didn't take long for Matilda to reach a decision on that one. 'No. He's plotting to ruin Sian and her children's lives with a book about Stuart. Let him suffer for a bit longer.'

'Are we discounting him as a suspect?'

'Not completely. I don't think he's a killer,' Matilda said. 'But until we have firm evidence to the contrary, he's the only suspect we've got. Right then, everyone go home. Tomorrow, we get the files out of storage regarding Magnolia House. We look at everyone who came onto our radar as an abuser and then look into their family and next of kin.'

'It sounds like it's going to be a long day,' Finn said.

'Can I go part-time like Zofia, too?' Scott asked.

'Absolutely not,' Matilda replied. 'Pull a stunt like that and I'll have you marshalling Sheffield Wednesday home matches.'

Scott and Finn left the suite, leaving Matilda and Christian behind.

'Are you all right?' Christian asked.

'I feel like that's all you've been asking me lately.'

'I'm worried about you.'

'I know you are, thank you,' she said. 'I'm actually fine. I know that's my stock answer, but I am. If I've got something to focus on and the right people around me, then I really am fine.'

'Good to know. Listen, Mat, have you given any more thought to who you're going to recommend for redundancy?'

Matilda sighed. 'I've tried not to think about it, but it keeps popping to the front of my mind. This case isn't helping, either. They're all working flat out to try and help me. How can I turn around and say thanks for your help, now piss off? Have you thought about it much?'

'Plenty.'

'And?'

'I can't choose between them. I feel sick every time I do.'

'Maybe we should make a list of their good and bad points like Ross did with Rachel in *Friends*,' Matilda suggested.

'I don't think you can make someone redundant for having chubby ankles,' Christian said. He placed his arm around her shoulder and pulled her into a tight embrace. 'I promise I'll give it more serious thought. I'll see you in the morning.' He grabbed his coat from the back of a chair and left the suite. Matilda remained the last woman standing. The room was lit only by a few spotlights in the ceiling. Most had burned out and nobody knew who to ask to replace them. She surveyed the empty room and looked at the untidy desks. Sian, Scott, Finn, Christian, Tom and Zofia – yes, she definitely had the right people around her.

She headed for the door, flicked off the lights, and left. Everything might be falling apart in the outside world, but in this office, with this team, they were unstoppable.

## Chapter Fifty-Six

Derek Klein knocked on the door of his home on Park Lane. He'd been released from the remand centre pending further enquiries, but DC Tom Simpson told him it was likely all the charges against him would be dropped in the coming days. Tom had offered him a lift home, which he accepted. As he walked up the path, he felt for his door keys in his pocket, but something told him he should knock rather than simply walk in.

Cara opened the door. Behind her, a yellow glow from the light in the hallway lit her up and caused Derek to squint. Her mouth dropped open when she saw her husband and the fading bruises on his face.

'Derek,' she said, softly.

'Hello, Cara,' he said.

Neither of them knew what to say next. They stood, barely six feet apart, but it felt like a chasm. They'd been married for close to twenty years, but they were suddenly like strangers.

'I've been released,' he said, stating the obvious.

'So I see.'

'I didn't do it, Cara. I didn't kill Natasha.'

'I know. Tom phoned and told me.'

'How … how are you feeling?'

'How do you think I'm feeling, Derek? I'm numb. My daughter is dead. My husband…' She paused as the anger rose inside her. 'My husband was sleeping with a nineteen-year-old girl, for crying out loud.'

'I didn't mean—'

'Don't,' she interrupted. 'Please, don't say anything. I don't want to hear anything about you not wanting to hurt me, that you didn't set out to have an affair. Don't be a cliché, Derek. At the end of the day, you cheated on me with someone young enough to be your daughter and I find that disgusting,' she said, looking sick.

'I'm sorry.'

'You're not. You're only sorry because you were caught. If you were genuinely sorry you wouldn't have allowed it to happen in the first place.'

A gust of wind caused him to shiver. 'Can I come in?'

'Why?'

'It's my home too.'

'You gave up the right to call this your home when you cheated on this family.'

'Where will I go?'

'That's not my problem anymore,' she said, starting to close the door.

Derek slapped a hand on the door to keep it open. 'Cara, please. It's late. I'm cold. I'm tired. Please. Let me come in.'

She studied him. 'I have nothing to say to you,' she said, slamming the door in his face.

Derek remained on the doorstep. He turned his back on his house and looked out at the darkened street. He knew nobody on this road. There was nobody he could call upon to give him a bed for the night, or even a sofa to crash on until the morning.

'What the hell am I going to do?' he asked himself.

## Chapter Fifty-Seven

'Will somebody get that? I'm on the phone.'

Matilda continued to wait on the doorstep of Sian's home in Whirlow. She'd rung the bell and heard Sian shout out an order from somewhere deep in the house. Nobody came to the door. She rang again. Twice.

'For crying out loud. Daniel. Gregory. The door.'

Eventually, the door was opened by Greg, wearing a Sheffield United football shirt and black tracksuit bottoms.

'Matilda,' he said with a smile. He stood back to let her in. 'Mum didn't say you were coming over.'

'An unexpected visit,' she said, looking at him with hooded eyes. She still expected Greg to be a small child. In the past couple of years, he'd gone through a growth spurt and was almost as tall as she was.

'Mum's upstairs. I think she's talking to Auntie Ruth on the phone. I'm in the living room playing F1. Do you want to watch?'

*I cannot think of anything worse.*

'Love to,' she lied and followed him into the lounge.

Greg had paused his game to answer the door. He dropped onto the cushion on the floor, picked up the control and re-started the game, which, to Matilda, was a cacophony of noise. The television was far too loud, and Greg was sitting far too close to the screen.

Daniel came into the living room with a bowl of cereal in his hand and slumped onto the armchair. He was dressed in skinny jeans and an oversized hooded sweater with the hood up, for some reason.

'Turn the bloody noise down, you prick,' he said.

'Hello, Dan,' Matilda said, trying to sound breezy.

He looked up and nodded to her, chewing on his Crunchy Nut Cornflakes.

'So … how's the studying going?' she asked either or both of them after a long and awkward silence.

Gregory held up his hand and put his thumb down.

'Oh. Dan? Your mum tells me you're going back to college.'

He shrugged. 'Might as well.'

'Good for you. Looking forward to it?'

He shrugged.

*Talking to young people is hard.*

'Dan, where's Anthony tonight?'

He shrugged again.

'Greg, do you know where Anthony is tonight?'

'With Lisa.'

Matilda waited for him to elaborate. He didn't.

'Who's Lisa?'

'Girlfriend.'

'Okay. Where does she live?'

'Rotherham.'

'Right. This is a really fun conversation, isn't it?' She smiled at Dan before rolling her eyes. 'Can you do me a favour?'

Daniel looked at her and stopped chewing. His face was blank but there was a worried look in his eyes as if she was going to offer him a fiver to wash her car.

'You need to say something, Dan, in order for this conversation to move forward.'

He swallowed. 'I'm waiting for you to tell me what the favour is before I agree to it.'

'Wow. You're really expecting the worst, aren't you?'

'You're not disappointed if you expect the worst.'

'Not exactly thinking positive, is it?'

'What's there to be positive about? Have you seen the news lately? Everything's shit,' he said.

Matilda held in a sigh. She didn't envy the next generation. They had the world at their fingertips and the world was a huge place to try to understand. No wonder so many of them were suffering with anxiety issues.

'Okay, well, before we all start crying, do you think you can set up a group Zoom chat so I can talk to you all? Anthony and Belinda included.'

He looked at Matilda with a heavy frown. 'Why? Something happened?'

'Not yet. Can you get everyone around the table? I'll go and have a word with your mum.'

'Am I in trouble?' Daniel asked.

'Have you done anything to get you into trouble?'

'No.'

'Then you're not. Just get everyone assembled and leave it to me, okay?'

'Suppose.'

'Thanks for your cooperation,' she said, standing up and leaving the room. The noise from the television grew louder as she left.

Sian was just coming down the stairs as Matilda entered the hallway blowing out her cheeks with exhaustion.

'Mat, this is a lovely surprise. I didn't expect you,' she said, hidden behind an overflowing laundry basket. 'I was just on the phone to Ruth.'

'How is she?' Matilda asked.

Ruth was Stuart's sister, making her Sian's sister-in-law. She had a breakdown after Stuart's crimes were exposed and spent time in hospital. Following her discharge, she left Sheffield for good and escaped to Scotland, where she changed her name and opened a bed and breakfast, mostly for hikers and ramblers on holiday.

'Fine. She's settled into her new home in Inverness. Well, it's not quite Inverness but it's the closest city. She sounds a lot happier.'

'I'm glad,' Matilda said, following Sian into the utility room. 'Sian, I need to have a word with you.'

'Okay,' she said as she began separating colours from whites.

'I need to have a word with all of you, actually. I've asked Daniel to set up a Zoom call so I can talk to Anthony and Belinda at the same time.'

Sian stopped what she was doing and looked at Matilda with concern. 'What's happened?'

'It's about Danny Hanson.'

The life seemed to drain from Sian as she slumped over the laundry basket. 'What's that bastard done now?'

'Come into the dining room. I'll explain everything.'

Sian took a deep breath to compose herself. Matilda knew she was putting on a brave face to remain strong for the four children. She was protecting them from the horrors of the fallout from Stuart's crimes and the seemingly never-ending barrage from journalists and writers, but who was protecting Sian?

In the dining room, a laptop was open showing Anthony and Belinda on screen. Anthony was unshaven and, like his brother, was wearing a hoodie with the hood up indoors. Belinda was all smiles and seemed to be ready for a night out with her hair up and panda eyes.

Sian sat in the middle of Daniel and Gregory to one side of the laptop while Matilda sat centre stage so everyone could see her.

'Have you called us all together to name the murderer, Miss Marple?' Anthony asked.

'I have indeed, Anthony. And if you look out of the window behind you, you'll see a police car waiting.'

Curiosity got the better of him and he turned around to look out of the window, which made everyone laugh.

'I need to talk to you all, well, warn you all really, about Danny Hanson. I know he said that he was no longer writing the book about your father, but I saw him earlier today and he admitted that he's still working on it. In fact, he was at Wakefield Prison yesterday and spent an hour with your dad.'

'Bastard!' Anthony seethed.

'I tried to tell him that he would be upsetting a lot of people. I even threatened to cut him off from receiving the station's press releases, but it didn't work. He's been offered a sizeable advance for the book, and he intends to see it through.'

'The little shit. After everything we've been through,' Sian said.

'Do we have to talk to him?' Gregory asked.

'Definitely not,' Sian said, putting her arm around her son.

'I can't stop any of you talking to him, obviously. But when he said he wasn't writing the book, I think he was using that to get on good terms with you, and then he'd ask you about your dad in a friendly way when he was really fishing for information.'

'He's not our dad,' Daniel said, barely audibly.

'Did he say what kind of book he'd be writing?' Belinda asked.

'It's going to be from his point of view. He was a reporter at the time of the killings so he's writing it from the investigative angle. However, he wants to go one better than Sebastian Lister. The only way he can do that, I can see, is if he puts more personal information into it about all of you, about how you reacted and coped with the fallout. The only way he can do that is if he talks to you.'

'Or he makes it up,' Anthony said.

'If he does that, you can sue him.'

'We're never going to be free of this, are we?' Belinda asked, a catch in her throat.

'Belinda, I wish there was something I could do to stop him writing it.'

'Can't we get an injunction against him to stop him writing about us?' Anthony asked.

'I wouldn't have thought so. He's writing it based on his experiences as a reporter.'

'He's a prick,' Anthony said.

'I've used stronger words to describe him,' Matilda said. 'I just wanted you all to know what's happened so you can be forewarned. We know Danny is not averse to using underhand tactics. We saw that when he went to Southampton to speak to Rebecca about you, Belinda. Just be on your guard if anyone starts asking you personal questions about your dad. Not just Danny. He could pay one of your friends, or anyone, to get information out of you.'

'Thanks. I think,' Belinda said.

'Yes. Thanks, Mat. I really appreciate it,' Anthony added.

---

'Am I a bad mother?' Sian asked.

The Zoom call was over. Daniel had gone to his room and Greg had retreated to the living room. The sound of roaring cars on a Formula One track resounded off the walls. In the kitchen, Sian and Matilda were sitting having a strong coffee.

'What? No. How can you even say that?'

'I can't protect my kids from all that's happening.'

'Okay. For a start, they're no longer kids. Anthony's in his mid-twenties and Belinda isn't far behind…'

'It doesn't matter how old they are, Mat, they're my children and I'll always worry about them.'

'I know. I'm sorry.'

'No. I'm sorry. I should be thanking you. Do you think I should contact Danny Hanson, agree to do an interview with him on the proviso he leaves the kids alone?'

'I don't know about that,' Matilda said, looking worried. 'Only you can make that decision.'

'What would you do if you were me?'

Matilda thought for a while. She had no idea what she would do in Sian's position. 'Personally, I'd like to take a very sharp knife and go all horror film on Danny Hanson, but as a civilised woman I'm not going to lower myself.'

'A strongly worded letter to a national newspaper?' Sian said, a twinkle of mirth in her eyes.

'Perhaps a petition.'

'A picket line.'

'We could tut loudly and roll our eyes.'

Sian let out a laugh. She rummaged in the biscuit barrel and took out a custard cream. 'Why isn't life easy anymore? When did everything get so serious and complicated?'

'I think it goes back to when Marathons became Snickers,' Matilda said.

They both gave a genuine, hearty laugh. Sadly, it didn't last long. It never did. Not anymore.

---

'How do you cope in this house on your own?' Penny asked Matilda. They were sitting at Matilda's kitchen table while the casserole Penny had made was warming up in the oven. 'I sneezed earlier, and it echoed. This place is far too big for one person.'

Matilda topped up her wine glass. 'It's never felt big until recently. When Adele left, I noticed the space more,' she said, looking around her at the vast kitchen. 'I really don't need all these rooms, do I?'

'Nope. Your hallway is bigger than my bathroom. Do you mind if I go home tomorrow? I like my little cottage. Besides, the first security firm can't come until Friday so I can just pop back for that.'

Matilda smiled. 'Of course not. Have you heard anything more about your pension?'

'No. I did have a lovely chat with the woman at the receivers this morning. She was very sympathetic, but nothing new to report.'

'Promise me you won't worry about bills or anything like that. I'll help you.'

Penny smiled, but her lips wobbled as she tried to stave off the tears. 'You shouldn't be helping me. I'm your mother.'

'We're family. It doesn't matter what order we come in. We help each other.'

Penny stood up and went over to the oven. She bent down to look through the glass. 'I think another ten minutes, and this should be done.' She retook her seat, reached across the table, and took Matilda's hand in hers. 'Thank you.'

'What for?'

'Looking out for me.'

'You're my mum,' she said with a shrug.

'I'm not good at the whole business side of things. I always let your dad take care of the money and the bills. This thing with the pensions, it's too much for me. It goes over my head.' There was a catch in Penny's throat. She was struggling to hold onto her emotion.

'I think they make it complicated so we don't ask too many questions.'

Penny squeezed Matilda's hand harder. 'I don't know what I'd do without you, Mat.'

Matilda put her glass down and put her other hand around her mother's. 'Promise me you'll tell me everything. I can help, but I need to know.'

Penny nodded. 'I promise. Shall we have a bottle of wine with this?'

'Sounds good to me.'

Penny stood up and went to the fridge. On the way, she paused, bent down, and wrapped her arms around Matilda, hugging her tight.

'Your father would be so proud of you,' she said quietly.

Now it was Matilda's turn to swallow her emotion.

'I'm proud of you, too,' Penny added.

The floodgates opened and Matilda started to cry. She couldn't understand why her mother was proud of her when, to herself, she was a complete and total mess.

# Part IV

DAY 38

*I'm feeling frustrated. This isn't moving fast enough for me. I do want people to know who I am. I want people to be scared of me. I want the entire world to know my name. I want people to be living in fear. I want roadblocks. I want to see people walking around in groups so they're not alone. I want to see parks empty and parents holding their children's hands for dear life. I want people to start looking at their colleagues differently, wondering if it's them who's stalking the people of Sheffield and mercilessly killing them. I want friends to fall out. I want families torn apart. I want my legacy to be felt by everyone for decades to come.*

*I used to think it was just the fact I was killing people and getting away with it that was more important, but now I've realised it isn't. I need people to know my name. When that happens, it might well be game over, but it's what's left behind that counts. The fallout will be epic.*

*But I'm not there yet. If I was arrested tomorrow, all my legacy would be is Liam, Josie, Audrey, and Natasha. A good lawyer could easily get me off those deaths. Number five is equally banal. This really is too easy.*

From: <89yw470y@aol.com>
Date: Monday, 1 January 1900 at 00:00
To: Darke, Matilda
<matilda.darke@southyorkshirepolice.co.uk>
Subject: 4 of 5.

Hello Mat,

Let's talk about murder.

I feel like the word murder conjures up images of a perpetrator following someone down a poorly lit street and stabbing them or breaking into their home and chasing the victim around the house horror movie style. Yet, there are so many different kinds of murder, aren't there? We talk of euthanasia and assisted suicide as putting an end to someone's suffering. Friendly fire is an accidental death in a war zone. Then you have all those fancy names like matricide and siblicide and senicide. It's all murder, just dressed up. Why all these labels?

Have you worked it all out yet?

I've been watching you, Mat. I've seen you up close and personal as you're struggling with this investigation. It is a struggle for you, isn't it? You can't quite reach out and put a finger on what's going on. You're so close, trust me. You're incredibly close, but you're not quite there yet.

Liam Walsh, Josie Pettifer, Audrey Wildgoose, Natasha Klein. Ignore them. They don't mean anything. It's not about them. It's never been about them. Look deeper.

I bet you're wondering how long this is going to go on for. I told you in my first email that I'd killed five people and there are only four names listed above. Is there a body out there somewhere waiting for you to find them or do you have a closed case that needs reopening? I'll let you in on a little secret. Number five is still very much alive and well. You can save them. You can stop their death from happening. You just have to find me first.

The clock is ticking, Mat. Tick tock. Tick tock.

Bye for now,

The Alphabet Killer

## Chapter Fifty-Eight

Wednesday, 21 April 2021

'I really don't like this,' Sian said, reading her copy of the email.

Matilda had printed out several copies and handed them round. She stood at the top of the room and watched their faces as they all read it. Each member of her team was looking more concerned, the deeper into the message they went.

'He's watching you,' Sian said, looking up. 'Is he watching you all the time or just at work? Is he following you when you go home? Matilda, this is frightening.'

'Where's John Campbell?'

'He's in with Ridley.'

'I feel like he's choosing his words very carefully,' Finn began. 'In the first paragraph, when he talks about the different kinds of murders there are, he mentions matricide, siblicide, and senicide. Why those three? There are so many others he could have chosen: genocide, regicide, parricide. Why these?'

'I know matricide is the killing of the mother,' Scott said. 'I'm guessing siblicide is named after the killing of a sibling, but what's senicide?'

'It's the killing of an elderly person. Sometimes called geronticide,' Finn answered. 'He's mentioned that he's killed five people, although now we know he hasn't killed his fifth yet. But say if we don't catch him and he gets around to killing his number five, what then? Is he just going to go away? I don't think so. I think this "matricide, siblicide and senicide" is a hint: either who victim number five is or who he's going to go for afterwards.'

'You think he's going to kill his mother, a sibling, or an elderly person?' Scott asked.

'We know he's got a slight obsession with his mother as he mentioned "mother" unnecessarily in the first two emails. I think he'd really like to kill his mother.'

'But we can't save her if we don't know who he is,' Tom said.

'No trace on the email,' Zofia said, almost nonchalantly. Nobody expected there to be. 'I've also googled the Alphabet Killer and he was a murderer in New York in the early 1970s. They called him that because his three victims all had names beginning with the same letter. There were a few persons of interest, but he was never caught.'

'He's telling us to ignore the victims and look deeper,' Finn said. 'I think he's actually telling us something there. Look deeper. Look deeper into what?'

'Into the cases we've worked on, perhaps?' Sian guessed.

'Maybe look deeper into ourselves,' Zofia suggested.

'What does that mean?' Tom asked.

'I don't know. It's just – ever since we looked into Felix Lerego and his team, I've been thinking that maybe this is someone we know. It could be a uniformed officer, someone from CID...' She trailed off.

'Felix suggested that to me,' Christian said. 'I've been looking into people's backgrounds lately; I'm not finding anything. A huge part of me is relieved by that.'

There was a knock on the door. Matilda looked up and

beckoned the civilian staff member to come in. She held up a few letters and handed them to Matilda before leaving.

'This email reads slightly differently from the others,' Finn said. 'He's told us that his fifth victim is still alive, that we've a chance to save them. It could be possible that he wants us to catch him. Maybe he's not enjoying what he's turning into.'

'Unless it's just part of his sick game,' Sian added. 'He's keeping an eye on us, so he knows how close or far we are from knowing who he is. What's to stop him, when we discover who he is, from suddenly striking his final blow with victim number five?'

'It does all seem like he's got it perfectly planned out,' Finn said. 'I think...' He stopped when he saw Matilda's face. 'What is it?'

'I've received a sympathy card.'

'What?'

Everyone jumped up out of their seats. Scott grabbed a pair of latex gloves and an evidence bag from his desk. He struggled to put the gloves on in the rush.

'What's the picture of?' Zofia asked.

'It's of all of us.' Matilda held up the card and showed them the front. It was the team when they were in Graves Park, searching for Audrey Wildgoose.

'What does the message say?' John asked.

Matilda swallowed hard. 'It says, "Thinking of you. It's important to be around family at a time like this."'

'What does that mean?' Tom asked.

'I don't know.'

Scott took the card from Matilda and placed it in the evidence bag.

'We need to get this tested.'

'Hang on,' Christian said, getting his phone out of his pocket. 'Let me take a photo of the front and message first.'

'"It's important to be around family at a time like this,"' Scott said. 'Are we the family you're supposed to be around, or should you be around your actual family?'

'I really don't know,' Matilda said, falling into a nearby chair.

Sian ran over to her and put a comforting arm around her.

'Someone I know is going to die, aren't they?' Matilda asked.

'We don't know that,' Christian said.

'Then why send me the card?'

'Because he's a sick fucker who's enjoying watching you suffer,' Scott said. 'If he sees you panicking, he's won.'

'He's right,' Sian said. 'This is a game to him. It's a sick game. We just need to find him.'

'How can we find him when we don't know who the fuck he is? Christian, get Danny Hanson back in here. Question him. Tear him apart. Ask him about his mother.'

'Mat, you don't believe it's Danny Hanson any more than I do,' Sian said.

Matilda shrugged herself out of Sian's hold, jumped up and went over to the window. 'I can't just sit here and do nothing. We have to be proactive. Why haven't we got anything? This has been going on for more than a month. We've got four victims and not one shred of evidence, not one suspect.'

'Mat, we're going through every case this unit has investigated,' Christian said. 'We've got people interviewing relatives of suspects and victims from Magnolia House. That's a bloody big list. It's going to take time.'

'Then we need to work faster,' Matilda said, almost shouting. 'He's sent me this card as a threat. He's going to kill someone I know and make it look like an accidental death.'

'Matilda…' Christian began.

'No,' she said. She grabbed her coat from the back of the chair and headed for the door.

'Where are you going?' Sian asked.

'I don't know. I'm not sitting around here waiting for my

phone to ring to be informed someone I know has died. I'm ending this.'

'How?'

Matilda didn't answer. She slammed the door behind her and charged down the corridor towards the car park.

## Chapter Fifty-Nine

'Hello. You're through to Penny Doyle. I'm either on another call or I've misplaced my mobile. Leave me a message and if I find it, I'll give you a call back. Bye.'

Matilda smiled at the message. 'Hi, Mum. I'm going to come round later. There's something I need to discuss with you. In the meantime, I don't want you to worry or anything, but … don't do anything … don't answer the door to anyone you don't know. Actually, don't answer the door at all unless it's me. I know this sounds weird, but, please, trust me on this. I'll see you later.'

Matilda ended the call and shook her head, knowing full well her mother would be panicking and reaching for the wine the moment she heard that message. She selected her sister's number and called.

'Hi. This is Harriet Doyle. I'm not available to take your call at the moment. Leave a short message and your number and I'll call you back as soon as I can. Bye for now.'

She sounded very breezy in her message.

'Harriet, it's me. Listen, where are you? Mum said you were coming back from Scotland today, but I really need to speak to you and it's quite urgent. Can you give me a ring the second you get this message? Also, it might be better if you're on your own when you ring me. I'll try you again later. Bye.'

Matilda ended the call. *Why is nobody answering their bloody phones?*

She threw her mobile onto the front passenger seat, started the Porsche, drove out of the car park and headed for Watery Street.

It didn't take long to drive from South Yorkshire Police HQ to the Medico-Legal Centre but all the way there Matilda had a dark sense of foreboding. Something was going to happen. She could feel it. The killer was obviously watching her. Was he watching her right now? Was he following her? She looked in the rearview mirror. There was a silver Audi behind her, practically up her bumper, but that was typical of an Audi driver in her opinion. She couldn't make out the car behind that. Surely the killer wouldn't make themselves so obvious that Matilda could spot them following her.

At the traffic lights, the Audi indicated left and put his foot down the moment the lights turned to amber.

'Prick,' she muttered to herself.

---

It was quiet in the mortuary suite without the loud Irish brogue of Donal Youngblood resounding off the walls.

'He's off this afternoon,' Odell said when Matilda enquired about him. 'He's got his final exams coming up, so he's taking a few hours off here and there to revise.'

'How's he getting on? Will he pass?'

'Absolutely. He knows his stuff. Adele taught him well.'

'She's an excellent teacher,' Matilda said.

She was hovering, looking about her at the sterile environment, the clean stainless steel gurneys, the shining instruments glinting beneath the harsh strip lighting.

'How … how's it going here? Keeping busy?'

Odell looked at her, his brow furrowed.

'You've come all this way to see if I'm busy?'

'Erm … no. I…' She released a heavy sigh.

'Has something happened?'

'Yes. No. I…'

'You're in one of your decisive moods, I see.'

The double doors opened, and two technical assistants came into the suite carrying boxes from a delivery.

'Come in here.' Odell took her by the elbow and led her into his office. He closed the door behind them.

Matilda took a deep breath. This room was smaller than her own office. She suddenly felt penned in. She sat down on the only seat while Odell perched on the desk and folded his arms across his chest.

'Whoever is doing all this, sending me emails saying he's committed the perfect murder, he's been sending mock-sympathy cards to relatives of the victims.'

'That's sick.'

'I know. This morning, in the post, I received a card, too.'

'You received a sympathy card?'

She nodded.

'But you haven't lost anyone.'

'I know. I think he's stepping up his game. I think this time the sympathy card has come first, to prepare, to warn me, that he's going to kill someone I know, someone close to me.'

'Jesus. Is there anything you can do?'

She shook her head. She felt on the verge of tears.

'We don't have a clue who he is. We've no evidence. No witnesses. Nothing. We're blind. And…' She stopped as the tears came.

Odell jumped up, grabbed Matilda, and pulled her to her feet. He wrapped his arms around her and squeezed her tight, her head on his chest.

'This is a game to him. It's a sick fucking game and he's going to kill someone I love. I know he is.'

'Can't the police offer your family any kind of protection?'

She pulled away, grabbed a tissue from the box on the desk, and wiped her eyes. 'It's not just my family. Christian, Sian, Scott, Finn, Tom, Zofia, they're all very important to me. Then there's Christian's family and his two young kids. There's Sian's four. There's Donal. There's … you.' She looked up at him and quickly looked away.

'Me?'

'I'd be lying if I said I didn't have deep feelings for you, Odell.'

'Matilda—'

She interrupted him. 'When James died, I thought that was it for me. He was the love of my life. I hurt very badly when he died. I swore I wouldn't put myself through that again. I did see someone else for a while, but that was just a casual thing. When I met you … it was different. I had the same feelings as when I first met James. It was electric. I know we've only known each other for a few weeks, but my feelings for you have grown.' She swallowed hard. Her mouth was dry. 'I'm not saying this very well, am I?'

Odell took a single step towards her. He raised her head to face him. They made eye contact. He was smiling at her. He didn't say anything. He didn't need to. He leaned down and kissed her softly on the lips.

When they pulled apart, Matilda sat back down. It felt as if her legs were about to give way. She felt warm and comforted, yet there was an icy fear gripping her. She couldn't lose anyone else. She couldn't lose Odell. It would be better to break things off with him right here, right now, before it developed any further, to save them both agony later on.

But something kept her in her seat. She genuinely felt safe here, in Odell's company. She didn't want to go anywhere.

Odell crouched, took Matilda's hands in his, and squeezed

them tight. 'I know things are very difficult right now. I know this case is a nightmare, but you're not on your own. You have your team around you to share the burden with. And you've got me.'

She looked up and into his eyes. 'Have I?'

'If you want me, you've got me,' he said and smiled at her.

Matilda found herself smiling back. 'I do want you,' she said. She could feel tears rolling down her face.

'That's good. I want you, too.'

'I want to be happy.'

'You deserve to be happy. Bloody hell, after everything you've been through over the past few years, you deserve a lifetime of happiness.'

'I don't think I can remember what it's like to be happy. Everything hurts.'

'Let me show you.'

'I'd like that.'

## Chapter Sixty

Matilda left the Medico-Legal Centre with a smile on her face and a spring in her step. She and Odell had sat and chatted about how they were going to tackle this crisis together. Matilda shouldn't be living on her own right now, especially if there was a killer following her. She needed protection. Odell was going to come round straight after work, and he'd stay with her for as long as she wanted him. They didn't have to share a bed, he told her, he could move into a spare room, and in the meantime, they could really get to know each other and see if they had a future together.

As Matilda headed for her car, she wished she'd said she wanted him to share her room. On the other hand, would Odell want to sleep in a bedroom that had three framed photographs of James glaring at him? Maybe she should put them in a drawer.

James would be proud of her for moving on, for finding someone else, but she couldn't help feeling that she was forgetting him. What would happen if she and Odell went away on holiday and she forgot James's birthday, or the anniversary of his death? She would never forgive herself.

She slipped into the Porsche and slammed the door behind her.

So many thoughts were racing around her mind. She needed to concentrate on the killer, not whether she and Odell should share a bed.

Her mobile rang and made her jump. She pulled it out of her pocket and looked at the display, hoping it was her mother, or Harriet, calling her back. She swiped to answer.

'I'm so sorry for your loss,' said a robotic voice.

Matilda's heart sank. She looked around to see if there was someone watching her from somewhere. There was nobody.

'Who is this?'

'It must be so difficult for you, right now, just as everything seems to be going well for you.'

She looked at the display. There was no number displayed. 'No caller ID.'

'What are you talking about?'

'It's sad the way something so big, a death in the family, could have been avoided by doing something so simple.'

'Who are you?' she asked. She was trying to keep calm, but she could hear the blood gushing through her brain. She was talking to a murderer. She put the phone on speaker and went into her text messages, firing a quick one off to Zofia with shaking fingers: *The killer has called me. I'm talking to him. Trace my phone and see if you can locate him.*

'Do you really expect me to give you my name?'

Matilda took a few shallow breaths. She was struggling to remain calm. 'Do I know you?'

'Oh yes. You know me.'

She squeezed her eyes tightly closed. A tear rolled down her cheek.

'Why are you doing this?'

'Because you made me. You made me look at myself and question everything that's gone before me. This is all your doing. You killed me, Matilda.'

Matilda tried to speak, but she didn't know what to say.

Anything she did say could make this so much worse than it already was.

'Tell me your name.'

'I don't want to do that.'

'Why not?'

'You destroyed me. So I'm going to destroy you.'

'What do you want me to do? What do you want me to say that will stop all this?'

'There is nothing you can do or say. It's too late.'

'No, it's not.'

'It is.'

'I don't know what you mean,' Matilda said.

'Oh, Mat, it's strange, isn't it, how the little things we put off tend to have the biggest consequences.'

Matilda frowned. 'What are you talking about?'

'If only you'd arranged to have your mother's fire fixed before now.'

Matilda's mouth fell open. She froze. She tried to speak, but she couldn't find the words.

'What have you done?' she eventually asked.

The line went dead.

'Hello. Hello! Fuck!' she screamed.

She started the engine and reversed out of the parking space. Once she was on the road, she slammed her foot down on the accelerator and tried to steer with one hand while working her phone with the other. She scrolled through her contacts for Christian's number. It took a while before he answered.

'Shit! Get out of the fucking way!' she screamed at a pedestrian on a zebra crossing.

'Matilda!' Christian asked, concerned.

'Christian, I've just had a call from the killer. He knows about my mother's fire not working,' she said. She wiped the tears from her eyes. 'He told me he was sorry for my loss and if only I'd arranged to have my mother's fire repaired sooner, she'd be fine.

He's done something to my mum, Christian.' She was barely audible through the tears.

'Jesus. Where are you?'

'Where do you think I am? I'm going to my mum's house.'

'I'll get a unit to go there now. Matilda, whatever happens, don't go in there. If it is a crime scene, you could damage any evidence.'

'There won't be any evidence. He doesn't leave any behind.'

'Matilda, do not go into your mother's house. Do you understand me?'

She ended the call and was scrolling through her contacts when it started ringing. Harriet's face flashed up on the screen.

'Harriet!' Matilda called out.

'Mat, what's going on? Your message sounded weird. Everything all right?'

'No. Not it's not all right. Where are you?'

'I'm on Woodseats right now. I'm headed for Mum's house. Why?'

'Shit. Harriet, don't go into Mum's house. Wait for me to get there.'

'What are you talking about?'

'I think… I think something might have happened. I need you to trust me on this. Promise me you won't go into Mum's house,' Matilda screamed down the phone as she drove straight through a red light.

'Mat, you're scaring me. Why shouldn't I go into Mum's house? Nathan and Joseph are in there.'

'What?' Matilda turned away from the windscreen. She had to slam on the brakes when she saw a car stop ahead. She banged her fist against the horn. 'Move out of the fucking way. Harriet, what do you mean, Nathan and Joseph are there?'

'They were staying with Mum while me and Patrick were in Scotland.' Panic was rising in Harriet's voice. 'What's happened, Mat?'

'Jesus,' Matilda said under her breath. 'Harriet, I'm about ten minutes away. Promise me you won't go in that house.'

'What am I going to find in there?'

'Harriet, please, I'll explain when I get there.'

'Matilda, has something happened to my boys?' she cried.

'I don't know, Harriet. Look, I need to get off the phone. I'm going to end up crashing here. Do not go into Mum's house. Promise me, Harriet.'

Harriet didn't say anything. All Matilda could hear through the phone was the sound of her younger sister struggling to breathe through the tears.

'Harriet!'

The phone went dead.

'Shit!' Matilda screamed.

Harriet was on Woodseats. With little traffic, she would be at her mother's house in less than five minutes. Matilda was still on Ecclesall Road South, battling with traffic that wouldn't move out of the way for her. She saw the turn-off for Abbey Lane and took it without slowing down or indicating. Behind her, several cars beeped, but she paid no attention. She concentrated on the road ahead and what could possibly be waiting for her at Greenhill.

---

Harriet, driving a silver Ford Focus, struggled up the steep incline of Bocking Lane in the wrong gear. The gears crunched as she tried to find the right one. She could barely see through the tears blurring her vision. Her hands were shaking, and the steering wheel was slipping through her fingers. She should pull over. She should wait for her sister to call her back and tell her everything was fine, but she couldn't. She needed to know what was happening. She needed to know her mother, her sons, were okay.

'Shit, shit, shit,' she muttered to herself as she put the car into the correct gear and slowly began making her way up the hill.

'Call Mum,' Harriet called out to the voice command on her phone. Nothing happened. 'For fuck's sake,' she said under her breath. 'Call Mum,' she screamed. Still nothing happened. She grabbed the phone and scrolled through the contacts, but her fingers were shaking, and she could barely hold on.

'Hello. You're through to Penny Doyle. I'm either on another call…' Harriet ended the call as the voicemail kicked in.

She scrolled down to Nathan's number, but in her panic she dropped her phone.

'Oh, no. Oh, Jesus fucking Christ!' she cried.

Harriet had put her own happiness first. For the first time in her life, she had put her own needs before those of her children. She'd found someone she could develop some kind of a future with. She had strong feelings for Patrick. She hadn't felt like this before, not in all the years she'd been married to that cheating shit of a husband, Brian. Now the boys were in their late teens, independent, and able to care for themselves, Harriet thought it was time she concentrated on herself. The boys would soon move out, once they went to university, and then she would be left alone. She hated being on her own and Patrick was offering her a chance of happiness. She'd grabbed it with both hands and now she was being punished for it.

At Greenhill roundabout, Harriet didn't slow down. She spun round it at speed, passed the library and onto Hemper Lane, a long road that would lead her to her mother's cottage close to the golf centre.

On the straight road, she allowed herself to take her eye off the road for one moment as she bent down to pick up her mobile. She cleared her throat and calmly asked Siri to call Matilda.

'Harriet. Where are you?' Matilda asked, answering before the end of the first ring.

'I'm just getting to Mum's house now,' she said, slowing the car down. 'Where are you?'

'I'm on Twentywell Lane. I'm literally minutes away, Harriet.'

'Mat, the curtains are closed,' Harriet said with a shaking voice as she pulled up outside their mother's cottage.

'Shit,' Matilda muttered.

Harriet turned off the engine and climbed out of the car. Slowly, she walked down the short path to the front door. She reached into her coat pocket for the bunch of keys. A noise of squealing tyres caused her to stop and turn as Matilda's Porsche came to a screaming halt in front of her own car.

'Harriet!' Matilda screamed as she jumped out of the car and ran towards her sister.

Harriet's face was white with horror. Tears were streaming down her face.

'What the hell is going on?' she asked, her words strangled by emotion.

'I don't know. Give me the key. I'll go inside. You wait here.' Matilda reached out and took the keys from her.

'I'm coming with you.'

'Harriet, I'm a detective. I have to go in first.'

'My mum and my children are in there. There is no way I'm staying out here.'

'Okay, but keep back and don't touch anything until we know what's happening. Understood?'

Harriet nodded.

Matilda unlocked the front door, pushed down the handle, and slowly opened it. The hallway was dark and cold. She stepped inside.

'Mum,' she called out. She waited but there was no answer. No sounds were coming from any of the rooms.

There were three doors leading off from the hallway, all of them ajar. Harriet pushed past Matilda and went straight into the living room.

'Joseph? Nate?'

Matilda followed Harriet into the living room. It was in

darkness. The curtains were drawn at both windows. Her eyes fell on the fireplace.

Matilda moved towards the kitchen. She pushed the door open. That too was in darkness. As was the small dining room.

'Mum?' she called out again.

'Where are they?' Harriet cried, coming out into the hall.

'I'll go upstairs and look. You wait here.'

'No way.'

'Jesus, Harriet.'

Matilda tentatively took the stairs one at a time. She could feel her sister's hot breath on the back of her neck. The further up the stairs they went, the darker it became. The small landing had three doors leading to the two bedrooms and a bathroom.

Penny's room was straight ahead. She pushed open the door and saw her mother in bed, the duvet pulled up around her.

'Mum,' Matilda said, putting her hands on her mother and gently shaking her. There was no movement.

The fire. The gas fire. Carbon monoxide poisoning. It had to be.

Matilda went over to the window, pulled back the curtains and threw open the windows.

'Joseph? Nathan? Wake up. Please. Please.' Harriet was screaming, pleading, from the next room.

Matilda turned back to look at her mother in the beam of spring light that was streaming through the window. She looked so peaceful, head on the pillow, eyes closed.

Matilda walked out of the room slowly, in a state of shock, and went into the room next door where Harriet was on her knees between two single beds. She was sobbing, screaming their names, begging them to wake up.

Matilda went over to the window. She pulled open the curtains and pushed the windows open as wide as they would go.

She turned back to look at her sister, grief-stricken on the floor, struggling to cope with the loss of her two children.

Outside, a car pulled up and someone called Matilda's name.

She went to the top of the stairs and looked down to see Christian, Sian and Scott coming into the house.

'What's going on?' Christian called out.

Matilda slowly made her way down the stairs.

'He's killed them,' she said. Her voice was flat. Empty. 'He's killed my family.'

She continued walking, out into the street. Scott put his arm on her shoulder, but she didn't react.

The cool April air hit her in the face. It had started to rain, a fine rain. She walked down the short front path to Adele's car and leaned against it.

The flashing blue lights from an ambulance caught her attention. She looked up and saw it stop behind Harriet's Ford Focus. Two paramedics jumped out and ran over to the cottage. She should tell them they didn't need to hurry, but she couldn't open her mouth.

Matilda felt numb. Around her she could sense activity as a police investigation got underway and an ambulance crew battled to save the lives of her family, but her legs felt like they were made of steel. She couldn't move. She could feel the rain on her face and the cold breeze whistling around her, but nothing registered. Her body was there, but her mind wasn't.

Then she heard a voice inside the house. 'We've got a live one here!'

## Chapter Sixty-One

The killer watched from a distance as Matilda's family were brought out of Penny Doyle's house. He saw Harriet being sedated and taken away to hospital, a red blanket wrapped around her. Matilda climbed inside the ambulance with her for support.

In the aftermath, Matilda's team set to work. A forensic team arrived and went into the cottage in their white suits to dust for prints and find any trace evidence, not that they would. By the time they finished, it was dark. There was nothing more anyone could do tonight. The detectives, their faces sullen, returned to their vehicles, and headed for home.

He should be going home, too. He hadn't eaten since lunchtime, and he was getting hungry.

Home wasn't too far away. He could walk it from here, and the cool, fresh air would help to clear his mind.

He'd been walking for more than half an hour, keeping off the footpaths and making his way through Hutcliffe Wood, when he took out his phone, made sure the voice changer software was still engaged, then made a call.

'Danny Hanson,' the journalist answered.

'Do you want to interview a killer?'

There was a long moment of silence.

'I'm sorry? Who is this?'

'Your good friend, Matilda Darke, has been hunting for a killer who leaves no forensic evidence behind. There are no witnesses. There is no sign whatsoever that a murder has taken place. Talk to Matilda. She knows what's happening. She knows who I am.'

'You're the killer?'

'I am. And I'd like to give you an exclusive interview.'

'Why me?'

'I can go elsewhere if you're not interested.'

'No. I am interested. I am,' he said, quickly, desperation in his voice. 'Can you tell me who your victims are? I'd like to do my research before we meet.'

'I'll send you an email with everything you need.'

'Great. Erm, thank you,' Danny said, hesitantly.

'I'll give you a time and a place to meet. I will be watching you, Danny. If you bring the police with you, the interview will not go ahead.'

'I won't. You have my word. It'll just be you and me.'

'Good. I'll be in touch.'

The killer ended the call and let out a deep breath. This was stressful. It wasn't easy being a killer. He couldn't say he was enjoying it as much as he expected to, but he was getting there. Maybe it was because he wasn't a hands-on killer. Maybe if he kicked things up a notch and really got to grips with what it actually meant to be a murderer he would feel differently.

---

The killer reached his front door. It was completely dark now and the fine rain had soaked him through. He was also bloody freezing. He stepped into the warm house and felt the glow of a happy home envelop him. He took off his shoes and coat and inhaled the smells coming from the kitchen. If he wasn't mistaken, it was shepherd's pie. That was one of his favourite meals, pure comfort eating.

He walked into the kitchen to find his mother sitting at the table, her head in her hands. She looked as if she'd been crying. His older brother was at the cooker, spooning out the vegetables onto four plates.

'What's happened?' he asked.

'Mum's had a bad day at work. I'll tell you later. Go and tell Gregory this is about ready.'

'Okay.' He popped his head into the living room where his younger brother was playing Formula One on the PlayStation. 'Tea's ready.'

'Just coming.'

Daniel went back into the kitchen. Anthony had put the full plates on the table. It was indeed shepherd's pie. A huge helping with lots of veg. Gregory rushed past him and sat down at the table. Daniel pulled out a chair and sat next to his mother. He looked at Sian, took in the red eyes and the tearstains on her face.

'Are you all right?' he asked.

She gave him a painful smile. 'I'm fine. Just a bad day at work. You're in late. Where've you been?'

'I've just been out walking,' he said.

Sian reached over and placed a hand on top of his. 'It's not like you to go walking without being forced. Everything all right?'

He looked his mother in the eye. 'Everything is absolutely fine,' he said with a smile.

**From:** <gqw47890t5hw@outlook.com>
**Date:** Monday, 1 January 1900 at 00:00
**To:** Darke, Matilda <matilda.darke@southyorkshire.police.co.uk>
**Subject:** 5 of 5.

Hello Mat,

    I've committed the perfect murders.
    That's me done.
    It's been an absolute pleasure.

Goodbye,
    The Steel City Slaughterer

**To be continued in**
*First One to Die...*

## Acknowledgments

As I mentioned in the dedication to this book, writing is scary, especially when you want to try something different or take a new direction with a story. I've planned this, and future books in the Matilda Darke series with the help of my editor Jennie Rothwell and she has been incredibly supportive and offered great advice. A special mention to Bonnie Macleod who has worked hard alongside Jennie to kick this book into shape. To everyone at One More Chapter and HarperCollins, thank you so much for allowing me to continue this series.

My agent, Jamie Cowen at The Ampersand Agency is a fantastic sounding board for when times get dark(e). I can't thank him enough for his support – so I won't. Ha.

Philip Lumb, Mr Tidd, Simon Browes, Andy Barrett – I owe you all so much for the help and information you give me when it comes to making my fiction as authentic as possible. I'm sure there are many factual errors in this book, and they are all my fault and purely for the purposes of storytelling. Please do not blame the eminent experts.

Going back to the scary aspect of writing, it helps to have people in your corner to keep you sane (or as close to sane as possible). Thank you to my mum who always champions my work, Chris, Kevin, Jonas, and Chris. You all keep me going in your own weird ways, and I thank you for it.

To all the bloggers and reviewers and bookshop sellers who like my work and spread the word, a massive thank you.

Lastly, however you read my books, whether it's with a good old paperback, via an ereader or listen to the audio, thank you. I wouldn't have made it to book twelve without you.

**ONE MORE CHAPTER**

The author and One More Chapter would like to thank everyone who contributed to the publication of this story…

**Analytics**
Abigail Fryer
Maria Osa

**Audio**
Fionnuala Barrett
Ciara Briggs

**Contracts**
Sasha Duszynska Lewis

**Design**
Lucy Bennett
Fiona Greenway
Liane Payne
Dean Russell

**Digital Sales**
Hannah Lismore
Emily Scorer

**Editorial**
Kate Elton
Arsalan Isa
Charlotte Ledger
Bonnie Macleod
Jennie Rothwell
Tony Russell
Caroline Scott-Bowden

**Harper360**
Emily Gerbner
Jean Marie Kelly
emma sullivan
Sophia Walker

**International Sales**
Peter Borcsok
Bethan Moore

**Marketing & Publicity**
Chloe Cummings
Emma Petfield

**Operations**
Melissa Okusanya
Hannah Stamp

**Production**
Emily Chan
Denis Manson
Simon Moore
Francesca Tuzzeo

**Rights**
Rachel McCarron
Hany Sheikh Mohamed
Zoe Shine

**The HarperCollins Distribution Team**

**The HarperCollins Finance & Royalties Team**

**The HarperCollins Legal Team**

**The HarperCollins Technology Team**

**Trade Marketing**
Ben Hurd

**UK Sales**
Laura Carpenter
Isabel Coburn
Jay Cochrane
Sabina Lewis
Holly Martin
Erin White
Harriet Williams
Leah Woods

**And every other essential link in the chain from delivery drivers to booksellers to librarians and beyond!**

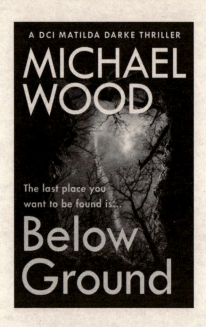

### A MISSING DETECTIVE
DCI Matilda Darke has been kidnapped and her nemesis, Steve Harrison appears to be behind it. He's currently residing in Wakefield Prison, so how could he possibly be responsible?

### A SERIAL KILLER WITH A VENGEANCE
As Matilda's team race to find her, they're alerted to a body found in an abandoned car on the outskirts of Sheffield. With forensics scouring the woodland for clues, the last thing they expect is for the body count to rise.

### A RACE AGAINST TIME
If Matilda's team don't find her soon, they might not find her at all…

**Available in paperback, eBook and audio now.**

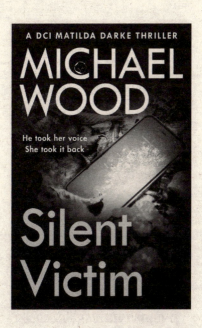

### A CENSURED DETECTIVE WITH NO LEADS
DCI Matilda Darke and her team have been restricted under special measures after a series of calamitous scandals nearly brought down the South Yorkshire police force.

### A BRUTAL ATTACK WITH NO WITNESSES
Now Matilda is on the trail of another murderer, an expert in avoiding detection with no obvious motive but one obvious method.

### A DEPRAVED KILLER WHO LEAVES NO TRACES
When his latest victim survives the attack despite her vocal cords being severed, Matilda is more convinced than ever of the guilt of her key suspect. If only she had a way to prove it…

**Available in paperback, eBook and audio now.**

**ONE MORE CHAPTER**

One More Chapter is an award-winning global division of HarperCollins.

Subscribe to our newsletter to get our latest eBook deals and stay up to date with all our new releases!

signup.harpercollins.co.uk/
join/signup-omc

Meet the team at
www.onemorechapter.com

Follow us!
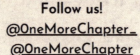
  @OneMoreChapter_
  @OneMoreChapter
  @onemorechapterhc

Do you write unputdownable fiction?
We love to hear from new voices.
Find out how to submit your novel at
www.onemorechapter.com/submissions